The
Perfect
Letter

The
Perfect
Letter

 A NOVEL

Chris Harrison

DEY ST.
AN IMPRINT OF WILLIAM MORROW PUBLISHERS

A hardcover edition of this book was published in 2015 by Dey Street Books, an
imprint of William Morrow Publishers.

FIRST DEY STREET BOOKS PAPERBACK EDITION PUBLISHED 2016.

Designed by Lorie Pagnozzi

Library of Congress Cataloging-in-Publication Data has been applied for.

ISBN 978-0-06-230523-7

16 17 18 19 20   OV/RRD   10 9 8 7 6 5 4 3 2 1

TO MY KIDS, JOSHUA AND TAYLOR, YOU WILL ALWAYS BE THE GREATEST LOVE STORY I EVER WRITE.

The
Perfect
Letter

One

Leigh Merrill had grown up surrounded by men. She'd known men who were kind, men who were good at their work, and men who were generous, but rarely had she met one who was all of the above the way Joseph Middlebury was. As editorial director, he'd taken an interest in her from her earliest days at Jenks & Hall Publishers, listening to her ideas and encouraging her to discover new authors, and she'd thrived there, moving up from a lowly editorial assistant to senior editor in only six years. When at last she'd gotten her own office and he'd finally decided it wouldn't be inappropriate any longer to ask her to coffee, she felt both grateful for all his support and flattered that he'd singled her out to be with him in this new, more intimate way. Why not? she'd thought at the time. It might be fun.

She'd never dated someone like Joseph, a man who'd grown up in

Manhattan, gone to expensive boarding schools, dined with presidents and celebrities. For two years they'd been happy together, in both love and business. They lived in apartments around the corner from each other, enjoyed Thai food and going to concerts, doing the *Times* crossword over lox and bagels on Sunday mornings. Their friends said they seemed like the perfect match.

Yet when Joseph stood up at the launch party for Leigh's latest book, tapped the side of his wineglass with his butter knife, and announced that he had something important to say, a very special question he needed to ask, she felt her whole body go stiff. He wouldn't, she thought. Not now. Not here, in front of everyone.

She'd started to suspect he might have something planned when the launch party for *The Perfect Letter* had been announced. For some reason he'd been especially attentive to all the details, choosing the venue, the food, the guest list, fussing over organic versus free-range, raw milk versus pasteurized. All for a book that wasn't even his.

So now the launch party for a high-profile novel was taking place at an impossibly romantic restaurant, in an outdoor garden lit with paper lanterns, hung with purple wisteria and mounds of vanilla orchids, over tables piled with Italian cheeses and *garganelli nero* in a chili and tarragon sauce. Violin music played in the background. The tables were covered with empty wine and martini glasses, and the guests were already a little drunk, so that everyone was falling into chairs, draping their arms around each other affectionately. The author of *The Perfect Letter,* Richard Millikin—so famous and so reclusive that this book, his first in thirty years, was already near the top of the bestseller list its first week—was not present, so in a sense it had become Leigh's party, her colleagues coming up to congratulate her with a mixture of envy and pride on the biggest publishing coup this side of J. D. Salinger. Even Randall Jenks—one of the founders of the publishing house and Leigh's biggest fan—had come for the celebration, though Randall was famous for claiming he detested gatherings of more than four people. Still he kept plying Leigh with martinis, telling her in his posh London accent to enjoy her success, that she'd earned it, that a book of this magnitude would make the house a fortune both in sales and literary heft. "I still don't know how you talked Millikin into it," he said. "I had it on good authority he'd never publish again. *His* authority."

"I learned from the best," said Leigh, holding up her glass in Randall's direction.

"That you did. And I should warn you, I am susceptible to flattery." He patted her arm. "I have great plans for you, young lady. Keep up the good work."

Leigh had to smile. No one had called her "young lady" since her grandfather had died. She hadn't realized how much she'd missed it.

It was fitting for her to remember her grandfather now. In the morning she was going home to Texas for the first time in almost ten years. She hadn't been back since her grandfather had died, since she had come home from Harvard her freshman year to bury the man who'd been practically the only family she had left. After the service she'd gone back to Boston and had her aunt Becky mail her things to her in six cardboard boxes, and in all the years since, she'd found excuses not to go back—too much school, too much work, too many other obligations. That is, until the organizers of the Austin Writers' Conference invited her to come as the featured guest speaker, all expenses paid. All Leigh had to do was give the opening remarks and attend a couple of days of pitch meetings. Her friend Chloe, an Austin nightclub singer whom Leigh hadn't seen in more than a year, practically begged her to accept. It would be suspicious not to go, and Leigh Merrill had become quite good, over the years, at diverting people's suspicions.

Still, when Joseph stood up at the head of the table and started tapping on his wineglass with the butter knife, catching her eye, she felt a momentary surge of panic. For months he'd been trying to get her to move in with him, but she'd always refused. She liked her privacy, her own space, she always said. Joseph shouldn't take it personally. She always got the sense that her answers never satisfied him. He was used to success, to commanding a room, to handling prickly authors and argumentative editors and tightfisted marketing execs and getting them to work together. He was used to asking a question and getting the answer he wanted.

Now he smiled out at them all—his tie perfectly straight, his thick dark hair perfectly combed—with the confidence of a man about to embark on his greatest triumph.

"Congratulations to the entire team who put together *The Perfect Letter*, debuting at number three on the *New York Times* bestseller list," he said, pausing while his colleagues answered with a round of applause. "Most especially I'd like to congratulate Leigh, who spent two years on the phone with Richard Millikin convincing him to let her publish the book. She won't like me telling this story, but once she even drove me up to the frigid coast of Maine for the weekend to tell him all the reasons why she was the woman for the job. Of course, she didn't tell me that's what we were doing. I thought it was going to be a romantic weekend for two. I should have known better. Leigh is nothing if not dedicated to her work." Laughter. "Well, Millikin believed in her enough to let her take on the book. And now the entire literary world will believe in her." Smiles and nods all around, with a "here, here!" from Randall.

"So now I think it's time for me to show her how much I believe in her, too," he said, pulling the box out of his coat pocket, the box she realized, sickeningly, he'd hidden there earlier in the day with this moment in mind. Her legs felt numb. She was sure if she tried to stand, she'd topple over.

She froze as Joseph came closer, standing over the place where she sat, and opened the box to reveal a single diamond glittering under the soft lights of the restaurant. "You're my equal in every way. I can't think of anyone I'd rather spend my life with, as a partner in every sense of the word. I know if I don't snap you up now, someone else will. Marry me, Leigh. Make me the happiest man in the world."

The room was utterly silent. In the background the waiters came and went, taking away the plates of food and empty wineglasses, eyeing the scene in front of them with mortification and amusement. The lamps flickered in the background; somewhere outside, a siren blared. Leigh couldn't believe this was happening. She felt her hands grip the sides of the table, saw her friends and colleagues perched eagerly in their chairs, waiting for her answer, their faces beaming. Joseph was kind; he was generous; he was successful. He loved her. They were great together—everyone said so. She owed him her career, her entire future.

But marriage, commitment. Was she really ready for that yet? She was aware of the eyes of every person in the room watching her, waiting. It occurred to her that either answer, in this case, might be the wrong one. She said the only thing she could: "Can we talk about this at home?" she asked. "In private?"

Immediately Joseph put his hand, and the ring, back in his pocket, and she watched the dawning shame and embarrassment creep up over his face, growing slowly red from the collar up. "All right, Leigh. If that's what you want." Out of the corner of her eye she could see the confusion on Randall's face, and she wanted to shut her eyes and will herself away, far away, where she wouldn't be the cause of hurting these two wonderful men, these two men who loved her and believed in her and who'd given her a life when she thought she'd had none.

There was only the room, the silence, the slow clearing of throats and murmurs of discomfort. Over Joseph's left shoulder, in a cluster of wisteria, a moth flew into the lantern, caught its wings on the flame, and lit itself on fire.

On the cab ride north Joseph was nearly silent while Leigh kept up a steady stream of chatter about the fall list, about people at work, about authors she was struggling with, gossip from the London Book Fair, the first week's sales figures for *The Perfect Letter*—anything to avoid talking about what had happened back at the restaurant, the way the party had started to break up after Joseph's disastrous proposal, people filtering out of the restaurant in groups of twos and threes, giving Leigh another (more muted) round of congratulations and shooting Joseph sympathetic looks as they departed.

Finally Leigh had collected her purse and checked around the restaurant one last time for anything forgotten, anything left behind, and only then did she look Joseph in the eyes, once, quickly, and then away. His brown eyes, usually so lively whenever they looked at her, were muddy with sorrow. She'd wounded him deeply, this man she cared about. He'd been sure, so sure, of getting the answer he wanted.

When the cab pulled up to the front of her building, she opened the door, then turned back to Joseph. "Are you coming up?" she asked.

He sat perfectly still, looking out the window. He turned toward her a little but would not meet her eyes again. "Do you still want me to?"

"You know I do. I said so before. I think . . ." But she didn't know what to think. She touched the sleeve of his jacket, feeling the warmth coming from inside. "Just come up. Nothing's changed. I promise."

"I don't know," he said, taking a deep breath and letting it out slowly. "Maybe I should leave you alone tonight. Maybe we should have some time apart, to think."

"No," she said, fear suddenly seizing at her heart. "That's not what I want. Please. I said I wanted to talk at home, and I meant it. Please come in. Please talk to me."

Finally he looked up. The hurt in his eyes was clear. "All right." He paid the cabdriver and followed her into the building.

They got in the elevator to ride up to Leigh's eighth-floor apartment, a modern one-bedroom in a high-rise filled with light and glossy surfaces—polished chrome, granite, glass—the kind of city apartment she used to dream about long ago as a kid in Texas. It was a haven for her, an oasis of calm in the middle of the city. And it was entirely hers—she didn't have to share it with anyone.

Upstairs she put her purse near the door, hung up her coat, put her keys in the dish on the table by the front door. During the cab ride home she'd been trying to think of what to say, how to say it, how to keep intact what she and Joseph had, what she valued in him and didn't want to throw away. *I love things the way they are, Joseph,* or *Let's not rush into anything,* or *You know how much I care about you.* She looked at his face in the light of her front hallway, his soft dark eyes shadowed underneath, and she knew she'd hurt him, though she hadn't meant to. She had not agreed to marry him, publicly, in front of all their friends.

Finally he asked, "Is it me? Is there something about me that you can't, you just—?"

Turning, she caught him on the mouth, her lips moving over his still ones. He was stiff; he wouldn't let himself touch her. He was resisting. He didn't want to reconcile, didn't want to let himself feel better. She pulled him toward her, but he held himself away. He was wallowing in his suffering, and that made her angry all of a sudden—what did he know about suffering? Because his girlfriend had not accepted his marriage proposal? Did he always have to get his way? Did he have to have the whole world and Leigh Merrill, too?

Joseph cleared his throat and avoided Leigh's gaze, clearly embarrassed by the emotions he could no longer keep hidden, and then she felt awful for having been angry with him. She pulled him closer, and he relaxed into her, his naturally thin, wiry frame pressing into hers. He was tall—a good six-foot-five, built like a basketball player, lanky and strong as a steel wire. She enjoyed the feel of his smooth, cool hands on her shoulders, in the small of her back, pulling her tightly to him.

Gently he stripped off her sweater. He reached his hand toward her breast and stopped. "Are you sure?" he asked. "Are you sure you want to?"

For a moment she panted in frustration. Why had he stopped? Of course she wanted him—she had initiated it, hadn't she? She took a breath and said, "Don't stop now, for God's sake."

He led her by the hand to the bedroom, where they got undressed and slid under the covers, Leigh's cool white sheets. He moved toward her, his hands and mouth moving expertly over her body, her skin tightening under his hands, her back arching to meet him. He was a practiced, considerate, skilled lover, and two years together had taught him how to please her. Yet she lay looking at the ceiling, at the reflection of the lamplight against the white paint, thinking there was something mechanical about the way he was touching her just at that moment, something maybe too familiar—first a, then b, then c, a pattern that had repeated itself for two years.

Maybe it was time to shake things up a bit.

He was positioning himself over her, raising her hips to meet his, when impulsively she sat up, pushing him off her by the shoulders, and then—a mischievous grin coming over her face—pushed him back down on the bed. She reached into her nightstand, took out a silk scarf, wrapped it around his wrists, and tied him to the bed with it. The surprise on his face was palpable. "Wait," he said. "What are you doing? Leigh—"

She teased her mouth over his chest, around his belly button, downward, downward. She could feel her own excitement building. *I should have done this a long time ago,* she thought, but Joseph was saying, "Stop, stop, Leigh, wait, *stop!*"

He was sitting up, undoing the knot in the scarf. Frowning. She sat back, prepared to ask him what was wrong, what she'd done, but she could already sense his confusion and knew that the wall had gone back up between them.

"I'm sorry," she said. "I thought it would be fun. That is, I thought we could try something different."

"I didn't know you wanted to try anything different. I thought you were happy with our sex life the way it's always been." He was frowning.

"I am. I mean, it's always good—"

"It's *good*? That's a ringing endorsement."

"I mean satisfying. It's always been satisfying. But what's wrong with something new?"

"I wish you'd talked with me about it first, that's all."

She sat back on the bed and covered her breasts with the sheet. "I thought it would be nice to, you know, be spontaneous."

"I don't mind spontaneous, but I wish you'd let me know what you're thinking."

Leigh stifled a laugh. She didn't think he'd enjoy her pointing out the contradiction of what he'd just said.

"So you don't like me taking charge?" she asked. "Turning the tables a bit?"

"I don't know. I never thought about it before. I was maybe a little taken off guard."

"Can we forget about it?" Leigh said. "Come here. Let's just do what you were wanting to do."

"Maybe not tonight," he said, standing up and pulling his clothes on. "I'm tired. I think I should go."

She felt the irritation rise to her throat again. This was what he always did when he was upset or uncomfortable: he'd disengage, detach. Whenever Leigh wanted to talk about something that made him uncomfortable, he'd simply disappear. And that was the one thing she couldn't bear. *If you love me,* she wanted to say, *you'd stay.*

"Don't leave, Joseph. Please. We said we were going to talk."

He sat on the bed with his back to her and put on his socks, his shoes. "I think it's best we both get our heads on straight, don't you?" he said, not waiting for an answer.

No, she was thinking. *No, I don't want to get my head on straight. No, I don't think it's best.* But she knew him well enough now to know he was done talking about it, and that any further attempts on her part would be met with silence.

He came over and kissed the top of her hair tenderly, and Leigh tried to think of something that would get him to stay. There was nothing—her mind was a black hole.

"You get some sleep," he said, and then he was gone.

The next morning, despite her protestations that he should stay in bed, that her flight was at an ungodly hour—really, I can take a cab, it's okay—Joseph got up early to drive her to the airport. It was something he liked to do whenever she traveled for work: picking up coffee for the two of them, chatting in the car in the early-morning sun, kissing each other good-bye at the curb like an old married couple. She thought it reassured him, somehow—that it convinced him she'd always come back.

He met her at the door, helped her carry her bags downstairs, then drove east over the Queensboro Bridge following a delivery truck with a bad muffler, the rising sun in their eyes, the noise drowning out any possibility of conversation.

After the fiasco at the launch party and the second one in the bed-room, Leigh had been up all night, trying to think of something to say. But then the truck with the bad muffler moved over a lane, and the air cleared a little. Joseph was the first to speak. "I hope you know, my offer still stands," he was saying. "About getting married, I mean. If what you really need is more time, take it. I'm not in a rush. It's just . . . I always thought maybe you didn't want to move in together because we weren't married. That maybe you were old-fashioned that way, and if I proposed, you'd know I was serious about you."

She reached over and took his hand, rubbing her palm against his, soft and cool. "I know you're serious," she said. "And I'm thinking about it. Really. I'm not saying no." She took a breath. "Maybe I need some time to think it over. You know, clear my head. It's a big decision, Joseph—I don't want to rush into anything. That wouldn't be fair to either of us."

"Maybe." He went silent, concentrating on the early-morning traf-fic. She watched him put his hands back on the steering wheel—ten and two—but they weren't strangling it, not exactly. By the time they pulled up to the curb at LaGuardia, he seemed to have lightened some-what. Perhaps he finally believed her when she said she was thinking about it, she just needed a bit more time.

He put the car in park, turning to her while the traffic around them surged, the business travelers and families with small children, the security forces eyeing everyone with suspicion. "I'm going to miss you," he said. "A week suddenly feels like a long time."

"I'll miss you, too. I'll see you a week from tomorrow." She was seized with a sudden fear that when she came back, he might not be here. That, too, was something she was afraid of. "You're still going to pick me up?"

"Yes, of course I'm picking you up." He said it like it hurt him that she would even think otherwise. Then he got out and walked around to the trunk to help her with her bags. He was so much taller than she was, naturally thin and elegant looking in a very New York, masculine kind of way. Bits of pollen stuck to his lashes and his close-cropped dark hair, the soft gray wool of the expensive sweater she'd bought him at Christmas. "Take this week to think. Maybe go see some old friends, let your hair down, figure some things out. Maybe it will do us both some good."

"I will." Leigh kissed his smooth cheek, wrapped her arms around his neck, and said, "Thank you."

"I love you," he said.

"I love you, too," she whispered, and meant it. She knew he'd never hurt her; she knew he'd always look out for her. She knew he would always be the same kind, careful, considerate man he was. She knew he could give her the one thing she'd always wanted: a family of her own. She pictured Christmases in Vermont, summers at the beach. Joseph in swim trunks, swinging a six-year-old daughter up on his high shoulders. She knew that, with him, she would never be afraid.

"Stay out of trouble," he said. He brushed her hands with his fingers, then walked back around the car and got in.

When he pulled away, she blew out a deep breath and picked up her bags. Maybe going home for a week would really do her some good. Give her time to sort out how she really felt about Joseph, New York. Her future, all of it. She could say good-bye to Texas, to her past, once and for all.

When they were first dating, first learning about each other's history, Joseph had somehow gotten the impression that Leigh's family was a broken, dysfunctional thing with some kind of dark secret at the center of it. There had to be a reason she hadn't gone back to Texas all those years. She'd tried to tell him nothing could be further from the truth, that she'd had a happy childhood, more or less. Sure, her mother had died when Leigh was ten, leaving her to be raised by her grandfather, but what girl wouldn't love to live on her grandfather's horse ranch, learning to ride, to race, reading in the hayloft on cool afternoons? Her grandfather had been good to her, spoiled her even. She'd been crazy about the old man, and though certainly she'd missed her mother, she had nothing to complain about, not really.

Her grandfather had been a true Texan, one who believed in hard work and self-determination. The fact that Eugene Merrill also happened to be the biggest Thoroughbred breeder this side of Kentucky just meant that anything Leigh had wanted, she got: a car when she was sixteen, yearly trips to the Kentucky Derby, even her own foal, a white colt named Blizzard, for her tenth birthday. It was privilege, just a different kind of privilege from the citified version Joseph had grown up with. Not better or worse. Different.

Joseph knew all this, but still he had a thing for introducing Leigh to his friends and family as an orphan, one of the few habits of his that really irritated her, because when other people learned about the Thoroughbreds, the ranch, the colt, they always felt lied to, even tricked. Even Joseph's family had, for a while, been under the impression that Leigh had been passed from home to home like a human carpetbag, and when she had to disabuse them of that notion she was met with nothing less than shock. "Who gets a horse for their birthday?" said Joseph's sister, Bennett, one Sunday during Leigh's getting-to-know-you period with Joseph's family when the two of them were having brunch alone. "It sounds like such a cliché. Like Caroline Kennedy on the White House lawn."

Leigh had taken a sip of her mimosa and given her boyfriend's sister a crooked smile. "It wasn't like that. Blizzard was one more head on a farm with three or four dozen horses. I think my grandfather figured if he pretended one of them belonged to me, I'd show some interest in learning the business."

"Did you?"

"For a little while maybe, but I guess I'm more of a bookworm at heart. Instead of training Blizzard, I spent all my afternoons reading Marguerite Henry novels. My grandfather was less than thrilled."

Bennett laughed. "Still, I always thought you were one of those Dickens characters. You know, 'Please, miss, may I have some more?' And here you were some high-class belle the whole time. You probably even had a coming-out."

Leigh actually laughed that time. "Not exactly. My grandfather wasn't the debutante sort. More the mucking-stalls sort."

Bennett, an aristocratic-looking brunette who was as outgoing as her brother was reserved, gave a toss of her hair and attacked her Cobb salad. "So did all the horses race?"

"No. Some were breeding stock. That's where the real money is— breeding. My grandfather was the best breeder on the Colorado. He did pretty well for himself, enough to buy four hundred acres in Texas Hill Country, outside of Austin. A big white house with a columned front porch. You know, the whole Southern-charm thing."

Bennett was shaking her head. "That was *not* the impression Joseph gave us at Christmas. He said you grew up on a farm in Texas, but he made it sound like a two-room shack surrounded by cactus and rattlesnakes. Scratching your way out of the desert and pulling yourself up by your bootstraps to get into Harvard, all grit and determination."

Leigh grimaced. It was the kind of remark that would have made her grandfather furious if he'd been alive to hear it. He had little patience for what he used to call "Eastern piffle" about Texas in general and horsemen in particular. "It would make a better story, maybe, if we were poor. But my granddad was the biggest breeder of Thoroughbreds in the country at one time. One of his top horses sold for fifteen million."

"Fifteen million *dollars*? For a single horse?"

"A stallion, yes. His stud fee was half a million a pop. Two of his foals won the Derby, and another took the Preakness."

Bennett nearly dropped her drink. "Joseph certainly never told us *that*. Clearly he has the wrong idea about your family history."

Leigh cut herself a bite of eggs Benedict. "I've told him all this before, but I think he likes the reactions he gets when he lets people think I lived in deprivation. I think he finds it all terribly exotic."

"It's the way we grew up," said Bennett. "Our mother thought any-place that wasn't Manhattan must be a third-world backwater. Don't take it personally."

"I don't. Since in all other ways your brother is a perfect gentle-man, I have to assume this is a minor character flaw. I can live with it. I've known men with worse, believe me."

"So," said Bennett, "you've never been back to Texas, in all this time?"

"My grandfather died my freshman year of college, and though he left me some money, he willed the property and the horse busi-ness to my uncle and his family, who moved into the place not long after the funeral to keep things running. I always got along with my uncle Sonny and aunt Becky and my cousins, but I never wanted to be an imposition, show up like I thought I owned the place. I send Christmas cards and call on birthdays, that kind of thing, but with my grandfather gone, it was always easier to stay in Boston over the school breaks. I wasn't dying to go back anyway."

"And you have your life here," said Bennett. "Your friends, your career."

Leigh grinned. "That, too. You can take the girl out of New York, but . . ."

Bennett held up her glass for a toast. "Well," she said, "I'm glad to find out my *Oliver Twist* assumptions were all wrong. I hated to think of you begging for gruel and walking barefoot through the snow."

"There's no snow in Texas," Leigh said.

"In my imagination there was." Bennett smiled. "It did make for a good story, though, didn't it?"

"Please, miss, may I have some more?" Leigh said, and she held out her champagne flute for the waitress to fill.

It wasn't until the flight attendant woke her twenty minutes outside of Austin, asking Leigh to return her seat back and tray table to their full upright positions, that she started to feel the first real stirrings of dread. Outside the window she could see the gray waters of Lake Austin tucked between the dark green hills of East Texas, the rough shape of the city center, the golden dome of the capitol glinting in the sunlight. Austin had gone through something of a renaissance in the years she'd been away, and now it was the cultural capital of the Southwest, epicenter of a thriving music, art, and lit scene. The People's Republic of Austin, some called it. She hadn't laid eyes on the place since that miserable day in February when she'd taken the late flight back to Boston after burying her grandfather. Ten years. She'd always assumed she'd come back sooner than this. Funny how time got away from you. Time . . . and guilt.

Leigh wouldn't let herself think about that—not yet. She was Scarlett O'Hara, back at Tara. She'd think about it all tomorrow.

By the time the plane pulled up to the gate and she was able to turn on her phone, she had four text messages from her best friend, Chloe Barrett. THE SECURITY GUYS AT THE AIRPORT ARE HOTTT!!! wrote her friend, and afterward WHEN ARE YOU GETTING HERE? I'M RUNNING OUT OF LIQUOR, followed by WHAT, COULDN'T SPRING FOR WI-FI ON YOUR SALARY? and finally I'M YOUR BAGGAGE. COME CLAIM ME. CAROUSEL 4.

This last made Leigh snort out loud, so that the passengers all standing around her waiting for the plane door to open stopped to stare at her—at the young woman in the designer-label jeans and bag, her long, dark hair cascading in perfect waves to her shoulders— who'd made such an inelegant sound. No matter how long it had been since they'd seen each other, Leigh and Chloe always managed to pick up right where they'd left off. Like high school all over again. More than anything or anyone else, it was Chloe whom Leigh had come to see. Her friend had been begging for years for her to come home, but there was always something holding her back. An exam to take. An internship to complete. A book to launch. When the invitation came from the Austin Writers' Conference a few months ago, Chloe told Leigh she'd officially run out of excuses to stay away, that she'd better get her butt on a plane and come home, for once.

Leigh stepped off the plane into immediate Texas heat; she could feel it radiating off the jetway, which she tottered up in heels that suddenly seemed too high, too citified, too painful. By the time she got down to Carousel Four in baggage claim, her feet were killing her. Only pride was keeping her from reaching down and pulling off her shoes.

In baggage claim Leigh didn't see Chloe anywhere, not at first. There was a church youth group gathered around Carousel Two in matching neon-yellow T-shirts proclaiming DISNEY OR BUST, several sets of beaming elderly grandparents holding stuffed animals or toy trucks, a few scrawny musicians in knit caps and long beards carrying heavy instrument cases, and a couple of middle-aged women hugging and smearing each other's lipstick. But no Chloe. Leigh sighed.

She was about to text WHERE ARE YOU? when at last she caught a glimpse of jagged-cut pink hair and bright red cowboy boots under a short flowered dress of the kind favored by cute hippie girls from Brooklyn to Portland. Only Chloe could pull off such a look so effortlessly, though—she'd have been as much at home singing the blues onstage at a hipster bar in Williamsburg as in East Austin.

Out of the corner of her eye Chloe spotted Leigh, turned her back
on the disappointed security guard she'd been chatting up, and immediately they were both eighteen again, squealing and throwing
their arms around each other and making a spectacle of themselves.
All around them, the passengers stopped to watch them embrace, the
Texas hippie chick and the cool New York brunette.

"Holy shit, look at you!" Chloe drawled, dragging it out like *ho-
leeeee-sheee-it*. She stood back to admire Leigh's outfit. "Miss Fancy
Pants. I almost didn't recognize you. You've gone uptown, baby!"

Leigh shook her head and laughed. "I look like a hog raised on concrete. I'd recognize those boots from fifteen miles away, though. And
the hair! I like the pink. It suits you. Kind of cheery, really."

"Yeah, well, I guess it was time for me to outgrow my Goth stage."

"It had to happen sooner or later."

"Damn, you look good enough to eat. Look at those heels," Chloe
said. "I can't believe you can walk in those things."

"Well, walking might be an overstatement," Leigh said, bending
down to slip them off at last. She carried them loosely on two fingers,
standing on the linoleum in her bare feet. "Oh my God, I've been
dying to do that since Fifty-seventh Street."

"Now, *that* looks like the Leigh Merrill I remember. Barefoot at the
airport. You should have left those torture devices at home."

"Agreed. I don't know what I was thinking," she said. "I'm starv-
ing. There's no good Tex-Mex in New York. I'm thinking I want the
biggest, greasiest burrito in town. You know a good place?"

Chloe grinned and said, "Don't I always?"

They headed for a sawdust-and-roses bar not far from downtown that
swirled with music, a touch of country, a touch of blues, a woman's low
voice singing sweetly about heartbreak, enough twang in her voice

to remind Leigh that she was really in Texas again, a moment both welcome and surreal. Austin had changed more than she'd thought: the downtown was nearly unrecognizable to her, crammed with shiny new high-rises that nearly crowded out the old tower at One Congress Parkway. New Vietnamese and Thai places had sprung up in East Austin, and the old Town Lake had been renamed Ladybird Lake, but it still looked the same, crammed with kayakers and dogs chasing Frisbees onshore. They crossed the Congress Avenue Bridge, a favorite landmark from their high-school days, in Chloe's rusting old Ford, and Leigh craned her neck to see if she could get a glimpse of the famous colony of bats that lived beneath the bridge. Nothing. It was early for bats—too sunny, too bright.

It was too early for lunch as well, so the two of them had the restaurant nearly to themselves. They ordered drinks—a beer for Chloe, a margarita on the rocks for Leigh—not caring about the hour. They chatted about Chloe's band, a few old friends, Leigh's job. The waitress was putting down the fattest carne asada burrito Leigh had ever seen when Chloe asked, "So how's Joseph lately?"

Leigh was midbite, her mouth so filled with steak she couldn't answer right away. She chewed slowly, buying herself time. "He's fine. His mother's been in and out of the hospital, but he's holding up. Excited about the new summer books. He's got some big meeting today with Randall about the future of the company. I expect he'll be getting a promotion."

"That's nice, but you know I wasn't asking about his career. Or his mother."

In the background the waitress was singing along with the music, an old Robert Earl Keen song called "Feelin' Good Again," and Leigh watched her, chewing for a moment and swallowing. "He asked me to marry him yesterday."

Chloe nearly dropped her fork. "He did *what*?"

"At the launch party last night. In front of everyone, even Randall."

"What did you say?"

"I said I'd have to think about it. I couldn't answer him right there."

Chloe rubbed a hand over her eyes and said, "And are you thinking about it? I mean, for real?"

"Sure. I mean, why wouldn't I?" said Leigh. The grains of salt on the rim of her drink looked like little shards of glass, like they'd cut her if she tried to take a drink. "He's probably the best thing that ever happened to me. Certainly the most stable."

"But you said you weren't serious about him. That it was just a fling."

"That was two years ago! Things change. I mean, would I be crazy to marry him? Of course not. He's successful. He loves me and treats me well. I could do a lot worse, that's for sure."

"'*I could do worse*'? Did you seriously just say that?"

"Don't look at me like that. We've been together awhile now. We see each other every day. He means a lot to me, Chloe. I owe him my whole career, my whole life in New York."

Chloe waved the waitress over for another beer. "I'm going to need more alcohol for this conversation. I can't believe what I'm hearing. Leigh Merrill is *settling*."

"Chloe, I love him."

Chloe fixed her with a level look. "Do you really?"

"I do. He's a good man. He's maybe the best man I've ever known. That isn't settling."

"I know you," Chloe said. "You're trying to talk yourself into it. Because if you were that certain, you would have said yes right away and meant it."

Leigh sighed. There was no point arguing with Chloe. *Something*, after all, was holding her back. Just what, though, she wasn't sure.

Chloe took a sip of her beer and said, "Is he okay and all, you coming home for a week?"

"Why wouldn't he be?"

"I've seen the way he looks at you," Chloe said. She squeezed a lime into her beer and then stuffed it down into the neck of the bottle. "I've seen him holding your chair out, offering you his arm."

"So he's a gentleman," Leigh said. "I like that about him."

"He treats you like a kid. Like you're made of glass or something."

"He's not as uptight as you think."

Chloe grinned.

"Really. He thought it was a great idea, me coming to the conference. Drove me to the airport, even."

"Sure, sure, he's always been supportive of your career."

"Chloe, don't start."

"I don't think I ever told you what he said to me at dinner the last time I came to visit you. It was at that restaurant you like, the one with the glass Buddhas. You had gone to the bathroom, and he leaned over and whispered to me, real softlike, 'Was Leigh's grandfather a good man? Was he . . . *gentle* with Leigh?'" Chloe broke into a crazy laugh. "I almost died. Could you imagine anyone thinking Gene Merrill was some kind of child abuser?"

Leigh put down her fork. "Jesus. What did you say?"

"I told him Gene used to whip you with a willow switch. Said he made you cut it yourself and bring it to him whenever you'd done something bad. Said he did it over your clothes, so you wouldn't have any incriminating marks."

"Chloe!"

Her friend grinned. "Kidding! I told him he was being an elitist New York prick, and that not everyone in Texas beats their children."

"Chloe! You didn't!"

"No, I didn't either. But I thought about it." That was Chloe's way: she had to make at least one joke, and sometimes two, before she could get around to being serious. "I said your granddad was the most gracious old gentleman I ever met, and you adored him. What do you think I said?" She took a sip of her beer. "I know Joseph's just looking out for you."

"Yes, he is. He is just looking out for me." She picked up her fork again and cut herself another bite. "He thinks there's a reason I haven't been home in ten years. Some kind of secret I've been keeping from him."

Chloe rubbed a hand over her hair, a gesture she made whenever she was trying to be tactful, but it always gave her away. The bell over the door rang, and a couple of hipster boys in low-slung jeans came in, bringing the heat with them. Chloe said, "Isn't there?"

"No," said Leigh. "I mean, it's not a secret."

"So you told him what happened with Jake?"

Leigh swallowed hard, took a sip of her margarita, and said, "I haven't lied to him. Everyone knows what happened. It was in all the papers, on the news. If Joseph wants to look me up, anything from my past, it's all there for him to find out. I'm not hiding anything. He maybe hasn't asked the right questions yet."

"And denial is a river in Egypt."

Leigh took another gulp of her drink, then licked a bit of salt from her lips, which suddenly felt too dry, too tight. "Really, I'm sick of thinking about it all, Chloe. It was all such a long time ago anyway. I've moved on, like Jake said we should. I'd rather forget it."

Chloe pointed at Leigh with her beer bottle and said, "Well, you better get ready to remember, babe, because there's something you need to know."

Leigh took another bite. "What's that?"

"Jake's back in town."

Two

Leigh must have told the story dozens of times to the police, the lawyers, the jury, the press, her grandfather, her friends. A man had died: Dale Tucker, one of the horse trainers who worked on her grandfather's farm. It happened in the barn late one night when she and Jake had gone out to check on a sick horse. They met after dark and slipped into the barn quietly. They left the lights off. Later they would tell the police they didn't want to alarm Leigh's grandfather or the gelding, a skittish creature under the best of circumstances, while they checked to see if he was still favoring his injured leg.

After midnight, after it became clear the gelding was doing all right under the circumstances, they heard a sound in one of the stalls farther down the barn, a sound of shuffling footsteps and a stall door sliding open. In the dark they couldn't see him clearly, but they knew someone was sneaking out with a horse on a lead. The man was a horse thief, they thought—had to be. No one should have been there at that hour. Jake went to get her grandfather's .357 revolver, the one Gene always kept locked up in the tack room. They warned the intruder to stay where he was, that they were going to call the police. Instead the man lunged for Jake and tried to wrestle the gun away from him. Jake shot once and missed. The intruder had Jake down on the ground, his hands around his throat. Jake didn't hesitate: he fired her grandfather's revolver one more time, hitting the intruder full in the chest, killing him instantly.

By the time they realized it was one of the horse trainers, by the time they realized the man was unarmed, it was too late. A misunderstanding, everyone said. Could have happened to anyone.

But still a man was dead, and still someone would have to pay. At the trial Jake had pleaded self-defense, but his lawyer had not been able to convince the jury. Jake had been sentenced to ten years all told. A lifetime, it felt like then, and still did, sometimes. Jake had told her to forget about him, to go to Harvard and move on with her life. And in most ways, she had.

Except that wasn't the real story, not even close. She'd tried to tell the real story once, but no one had believed her. Not the prosecutors or the police. Not her grandfather or even Chloe. She'd tried to tell the truth, and instead everyone had believed the lie.

It was an understatement when she told Chloe she was sick of thinking about it. For a decade she'd been replaying the events of that night in her head over and over late at night, on the subway, at work, wondering *what if*? What if we hadn't gone to the barn? What if there had been no gun? What would have happened then?

So much had been spoiled by that one night—her family, her friendships. Everything she used to plan for, everything she used to think she wanted. It was all changed, all damaged by that single rash act, the pulling of a trigger, and even now, sitting in the bar with Chloe, she could close her eyes and hear the shot, hear the gurgling noise the man made as he died, his lungs filling up with blood. She could see the shock in his face, the shock of knowing he was dying. She'd been hearing the noise in her head all these years.

Now Chloe was saying Jake's sentence was up. He'd served all of his ten years, no time off for good behavior. It was the talk of the town, apparently—people around Burnside couldn't believe he was out, that he'd come back to the scene of the crime. That he dared to show his face in town.

Jake was out, he'd been released. And he hadn't let her know.

Now Leigh realized she was holding her breath. She let it out slowly, looking for the exits, mapping a route for escape. But there wasn't one, not this time. She'd come back of her own accord, and now she was going to have to deal with the problem instead of running away.

She said, "How do you know he's back?"

"He knocked over a liquor store. How do you think?" Chloe polished off the last of her beer and set the bottle back on the table. "I saw him. He was eating supper at Dot's one night when I drove by. He was sitting in the window, drinking a beer, eating some chili, regular as you please."

Leigh was starting to feel a little sick. She could picture the spot, in a little wooden A-frame building near the highway, picture Jake as he was in high school, tanned and dark-haired, lean as a greyhound, picture herself sitting across from him drinking a root-beer float. The part of her that was still eighteen wanted to weep. "When?"

"About three days ago. Went home to Burnside to see my ma, and there he was, big as life. His hair's shorter and he looked a little bigger, like he's put on twenty pounds of muscle, but it was the same Jake, all right."

Leigh resisted the urge to order a shot of tequila and asked, "Was he alone?"

Chloe smirked. "Do you think he's been out meeting girls? The man's been in prison."

"For ten years. That's right." She had a picture of him in her mind: the faded brown Stetson he'd always worn, wrapped with a rattlesnake band, the tattoo of a bat on the back on his left triceps, barely visible under the sleeve of a clean white T-shirt. A girl—someone young and pretty, someone local—sitting across from him.

"Ten years is a long time."

Some of Chloe's pink hair fell into her eyes, and she pushed it back with one rough motion. "I didn't see him with anyone, but that doesn't mean there isn't anyone. Seriously, he's been in prison since he was twenty. He's trying to get back on his feet. Girls are probably the last thing on his mind."

"Or the first."

"Jesus, what's with you? Are you mad that he didn't call to tell you he was getting out or something? I thought you'd be happy."

"I am. I am happy."

Chloe cut her eyes at Leigh sideways, like she was judging a horse show. Leigh knew that look. "No, you're not. You're pissed off."

"I'm not. He shouldn't have been in prison in the first place. It was all a big mistake. A misunderstanding."

"A man died, Leigh."

"Yes, a man who should have known better than to sneak around my grandfather's barn in the middle of the night. Don't tell me you feel sorry for Dale Tucker now."

"I don't. But I don't think he deserved to die either."

Leigh sighed. "Me neither. But it was a mistake. Just a stupid accident." She rubbed her temples; she was starting to get a headache. In a few minutes it would be full-blown, and she'd be ill, unable to see straight. She didn't know if she was angrier at Jake for not telling her he was getting out or at Chloe for waiting until Leigh was actually in

Texas before springing the news on her. But it was too late—she was stuck, committed to the conference and the trip. She couldn't leave without embarrassing herself and causing a scandal. And if there was one thing Leigh Merrill was good at, it was avoiding a scandal. It was her greatest talent.

The music changed over to James Taylor, singing "How Sweet It Is (to Be Loved by You)," and Leigh nearly groaned. *Not now.* She sat back in her chair and stared down at the half-eaten food on the table. "I always figured that when it was time for Jake to get out, I'd be the first person he called. I never thought he'd just show up back in town without a word to me."

"You think he's going to be angry about Joseph? Is that it?"

"No. I mean—maybe. But there's more to it than that."

"You're thinking he blames you. That if you hadn't gone to the barn that night, none of it would have happened."

"Something like that," she said.

Chloe was watching her carefully. "Have you really been beating yourself up over it all this time? Leigh, you're not the one who went to get the gun. You're not the one who pulled the trigger."

Leigh pushed away the rest of her food. Suddenly she was a kid again, scared of everything, on the verge of losing control. She was standing at the edge of her grandfather's grave, watching the old man's coffin lowering into the ground—her only real family, her last tie to home—and feeling like she might pitch forward and follow him down and down, into the darkness. Like every tie she'd ever felt to the world had been cut, leaving her alone and drifting on a wide black sea. She hated that feeling. It had taken her years of running to get away from it, but here it was again, cold and smothering as a wet blanket. She shivered.

"All those years, and Jake would never agree to let me visit him in prison," Leigh said. "I wanted to, you know. I wrote to him a bunch of times when he first went away, but he never answered my letters. He couldn't bear to see me."

"He didn't want *you* to see *him,* you mean. He didn't want you to think of him as a criminal. He wanted you to remember him the way he was before any of it happened."

"He never answered me. Not even once, Chloe. I wrote him for four years straight, and he never answered me—not a letter, not a postcard, nothing. What was I supposed to think about that?"

"That Jake's always been a stubborn ass. Not much more to it than that, really."

Leigh felt tears starting in her eyes, the shame she'd always felt over what happened threatening to overwhelm her. "He hates me. I'm sure of it."

Chloe reached across the table and squeezed Leigh's hand. "None of it was your fault, Leigh. Jake knows that. End of story."

Except it wasn't the end of the story. The truth was something Jake said they should keep, always, between the two of them. Even Leigh's grandfather had never known the whole of what had happened that night in the barn. So many times Leigh had wanted to blurt out the truth to Chloe, to her friends in New York, even to Joseph. But she couldn't. She was too ashamed. How could she admit the truth to them now, after all this time?

The silence stretched out between them, long and thin and airless. Chloe was looking her full in the face now, all joking aside, and Leigh squirmed under the full weight of her best friend's gaze, her total and completely serious attention. "There's something you're not telling me, isn't there?" Chloe asked. She sat back in her chair and blew out a long, low breath. "Well, let's hear it, then."

Leigh flagged down the waitress and ordered them both a couple of fingers of bourbon on the rocks.

"Damn," Chloe said moments later, watching the waitress put down their drinks. "That bad, huh?"

"Yes," Leigh said. She gulped the bourbon as fast as she could. It burned pleasantly going down, spreading through her throat and into her belly, but it couldn't get rid of the cold pit of fear that lived at the bottom of her. That always lived at the bottom of her. "I can't right now. I have to get ready for my talk tomorrow. I still have some notes to jot down. Maybe soon. But not today, Chloe, okay?"

Chloe looked at Leigh sideways, as if she'd never seen her friend before, as if she were seeing everything new. "All right," she said, rubbing her hand over her hair again, the tactful gesture, "but only because I love you. Otherwise I'd strangle it out of you right now."

"I know. Can you drop me off at the conference? All I can manage right now is a hot bath. I just need to be alone for a little while. A little rest. We can go out again later, have a real night out if you want one."

"Of course I want one," Chloe said. "But this discussion isn't over."

"I would be surprised if it were."

The Austin Writers' Conference was located on a vineyard just outside the city limits, a stunning old Texas estate in the Hill Country dotted with tiny stone guest cottages, a dining pavilion, and an enormous stone-and-timber mansion that would serve for the next week as the conference center. As the guest of honor, Leigh had a little cottage to herself on a hillside with the view of the valley below, the miles of green vineyards and rolling hills. A cozy place with a single room dominated by a large canopy bed, a fieldstone fireplace, and a river-stone bathroom, it was too large for Leigh, but she'd nearly cried at the beauty of the view, at her first taste of home in a decade. The hills were purple with bluebonnets, and as she'd stood at the window watching the sunset turn pink and gold, she couldn't remember why on earth she'd ever thought to leave.

Now, standing under the running water of the shower, Leigh kept her eyes closed and focused on those lovely childhood memories, breathing in and out as her skin burned red and nearly raw. The trepidation she'd felt for the past month—ever since she committed to the conference, to coming home to Texas—had exploded into full-bore anxiety. If she stayed in the shower as long as possible—if she didn't turn off the water and dry off—she wouldn't have to deal with any of the emotions waiting for her on the other side of the shower curtain, any of the dread, the longing, the loneliness. The guilt.

Jake was back. Jake had been released from prison, and he hadn't told her he was coming home. It was clear now that he really didn't want to see her. It had all changed between them, even though she'd promised, she'd sworn to him, that it wouldn't. *I'll wait for you,* she'd said that day in court, when the guards were getting ready to take him away. *It will all be like it was before. I swear.*

Don't wait. Move on with your life, Leigh, he'd whispered to her. *Forget about me. I'm no good for you.*

She hadn't meant to move on. She'd tried to wait. She'd tried to forgive him when he didn't write to her, because God knows he had reasons to be angry. But ten years was a long time to be on your own, in strange cities, far from home, and Leigh was only human, after all.

They would both have changed. He might not even recognize her now—they could pass each other on the street, maybe, and never even know it. She'd been foolish to think they could pick up where they left off after he got out, as if nothing had happened. Ten years did a lot of damage to a person. And what Jake had suffered in prison, Leigh couldn't imagine. Prison was nothing you could dismiss with a wave of your hand. Whatever Jake did or didn't feel toward her, whatever he blamed her for, he had every right to be angry.

The water turned lukewarm, then cool, then cold, but Leigh stayed under the tap until she started to shiver, sliding down the wall to the floor of the tub. She couldn't get up. She couldn't do it, not after everything. She wanted to go back to New York so badly she could taste it in her mouth—the air full of exhaust and damp, the smell of Chinese food and hot-dog vendors. New York was her hideout, her haven, her fortress of solitude. And she couldn't get to it for a whole week. Maybe she'd made a terrible mistake not accepting Joseph's proposal. She should have said, *Yes, of course I'll marry you, Joseph, of course I love you, I want to make a life with you.* That's what any sane person would have done.

Maybe it wasn't too late.

It was the ringing phone that finally got her to her feet. Somewhere in her hotel room, her cell phone was ringing. She wrapped a towel around herself and sprinted from the shower soaking wet, but she couldn't find the damn thing. She looked in the bedside table, the closet, her purse, before she finally found it lying underneath the bed, buzzing angrily. She picked it up and looked at the caller. It was Joseph.

"There you are," he said. "I was starting to think you'd run away with the circus."

Leigh sat on the bed, her hair dripping onto the phone, onto the bedspread. "Not yet. You're not that lucky."

She was making a puddle on the floor, but it was so good to hear his voice, so good to hear something safe and normal. Even across time zones, she could hear the murmur of voices in the background, the clink of scotch glasses, the voice of the little waiter at the old-fashioned steakhouse next door to Jenks & Hall Publishing. "Are you at Keens?" she asked.

"How could you know that over the phone?"

She smiled. "Tell Randall I said hello."

Joseph relayed her message to his dinner companion. As if from underwater, Leigh could hear the voice of her boss answering back, could barely make out her friend and mentor saying, "Tell Leigh to hurry up and come home already. All your moping is making me bored, Joseph, honestly."

Leigh smiled. "I miss you, too, Randy," she said. She didn't tell him she *was* home. To Randall Jenks, one of the most brilliant minds in publishing, anything west of Manhattan might as well have been the moon. The thought of his protégée, Leigh, growing up on the Colorado, swimming naked in Lake Lyndon Johnson, riding horses on hot afternoons, would have filled him with horror. All he knew was that Leigh had graduated from Harvard, and that was enough for him.

It was business she turned to for comfort now. "Are you talking about the fall list?" she asked. Another voice at the table: deeper, a rich baritone with a musical Scottish lilt. "Is that Marty?" Martin Hall was Randall's partner. The two of them had forged the most prestigious boutique publishing house in New York once upon a time, but Marty had been in ill health recently. He rarely came to the office anymore, much less went out for lunch. She felt a sudden cold fear spread through her belly. Were they selling the business? Shutting everything down now because of Marty's cancer? There'd been some talk about it around the office, but nothing she'd taken seriously, not until now. "What's going on?" she asked, nearly breathless. "Joseph, I can hear Marty there. What's happening?"

"We were halfway into our salads when they sprang it on me."

"Please tell me you're talking about a promotion."

"Better. Leigh, they want to make me a full partner. Name above the door and everything."

A partner. Well, there was probably no better person in New York than Joseph Middlebury to turn to if the old guard was looking to make a change. He had a terrific track record, even when the market was bad. Also he had his own money, family money, to invest in the company. It made sense that they'd make him a partner, a man who'd overseen the company's transition to e-books, who'd pioneered bookclub chats all over the country, who'd seen what Internet sales had to offer before anyone else. Randall and Marty weren't going to shut down the company, they were going to step back and let the next generation take over. "That's amazing. I'm so proud of you. Jenks, Hall, and Middlebury. I like the way that sounds."

"That's not all, Leigh. We're talking about giving you your own imprint."

"What?"

"Leigh Merrill Books. For real."

She sat unsteadily on the bed, feeling a strange floating sensation, as if she were being picked up and carried on a huge wave, higher and higher, cresting above her head, the dark blue water below. Her own imprint, at twenty-nine years old. It was more than she ever dared to imagine. "That's—I don't even know what to say. Thank you."

"I told him you'd be thrilled. It shows a real commitment to you, Leigh. To keeping you at the company." She could almost hear what he wasn't saying: *And to keep you near me.*

"I am. I'm thrilled. I'm a bit flabbergasted, too. I mean, that's a lot of pressure. I was figuring in ten years, maybe . . ."

"It's a great opportunity, Leigh. Your own imprint. You can shape the whole literary discussion in this country."

"I know."

"Develop your own list, your own authors. It's every editor's dream."

"Yes," she said, switching the phone to her other hand, "I know. I'm very happy."

"You don't sound happy."

Breathe. Just breathe.

"I am," she said, keeping her voice even. "It's just unexpected." She was keeping a lid on her fear, but barely. "I am. I'm thrilled, like I said," she told him, "but I just got out of the shower. A bunch of people from the conference are going out for a drink tonight, and I said I'd meet up with them—"

"Sure, okay," he said. "I need to go, too. Lots to talk about."

"But call me later, okay?" she said. "I want to hear everything Randall says."

"Tell Chloe I said hi."

"I will," she said. "I know you're going to make a great publisher. He's had his eye on you for a long time."

"I won't let him down."

"I know you won't."

"Don't have too much fun."

"It's Texas," she said. "They put fun in the water here. Like fluoride."

"That's what I'm afraid of."

"Don't worry," she said, feeling a tic of irritation. "I know how to handle myself."

She was about to hang up the phone when he said, "I miss you. New York isn't the same without you here."

Her momentary irritation melted away—here he was again, the man who fit her like a pair of comfortable shoes, the one who seemed so sane, so safe. This was the man who'd taken her to hear her first symphony at Lincoln Center, who'd surprised her with a picnic in Central Park on her last birthday, who'd taken her to his family's house in the Hamptons every weekend in the summer, who rubbed her neck at the end of a long day, who knew how she took her coffee, who listened to her ideas and took them seriously. He was a partner, in every sense of the word. He was everything she'd always said she wanted.

For a minute she could picture herself marrying him—the gorgeous wedding they'd have, the long white dress she'd wear, the church full of their friends, the celebrity guests, the reception at the Waldorf, the honeymoon in the Seychelle Islands, the pied-à-terre they'd buy on the Upper West Side, the country house in Westchester. She could see them picking out china patterns, squabbling gently over the furniture for the living room. For a minute she pictured herself saying her wedding vows to him: *I, Leigh, take you, Joseph, until death do us part.* How happy it would make him if she would say yes. It made her feel warm all over to think of herself giving so much happiness to someone she cared about so much. *Yes* didn't seem so difficult all of a sudden. Maybe she *could* marry him. Maybe it was exactly what she should do.

"I miss you, too," she said. "I'm sorry about last night. I'll make it up to you when I get home, I promise."

"Really?"

"Yes. I think I was scared. Maybe I needed to let go of some old ghosts. But we'll talk more later, okay?"

"I like the sound of that."

Three

A t eight the next morning Leigh dragged herself out of bed
to grab a quick shower, pour three cups of strong black
coffee down her throat, and dress in her New York best to
give the opening address to the conference. Chloe had kept her out
in the city the night before, going from bar to bar to check out bands
she wanted to see, bands made up of friends she had made in her
years as a hot young nightclub singer in Austin's music scene. Leigh
told her friend about her promotion, about getting her own imprint,
and they'd gone out to celebrate, but at an after-party with some
friends of Chloe's, Leigh had sat on the couch drinking shot after
shot of tequila, trying to forget about Jake, to forget that Jake was out
of prison and still had not called her, had not wanted to get in touch
with her. The world had gone fuzzy and dim, the voices around her
thick as syrup, and though Leigh knew it was stupid, it was reckless

to drink so much, she hadn't cared at all at the moment. She only wanted to forget.

In the middle of the swirl of color and noise and booze, there'd been something else, someone who caught her attention. At the last show of the night, in a red-leather half-moon booth listening to a rockabilly band, she'd noticed someone staring at her from the bar, a man in his late forties or fifties with a long graying ponytail and small, predatory eyes. She'd caught his glance for a minute, then looked away, quickly, but apparently not quickly enough. A minute later he'd come over with a couple of beers, holding one out to Leigh, who politely declined. "No, thanks," she'd said. "I think I've had enough."

"One more won't kill you," he said. He was shorter than she'd imagined at first, broad-shouldered, covered with tattoos. She could see the edge of a snake's tail climbing up his neck.

"I don't take drinks from strangers, sorry."

"We don't have to be strangers," he said. "I know you. I know all about you, Leigh Merrill."

She squinted at him, about to offer a sarcastic retort, when Chloe, sensing danger, grabbed her by the arm and said she had something important to tell her in the bathroom, giving the ponytailed man an evil look as she pulled Leigh out the door and into her car. "What was that all about?" she asked.

Leigh said, "Oh, you know. Local stalker." And they both had a laugh about it.

Leigh didn't remember exactly what time Chloe had dropped her off back at her room, but the sunrise had just begun to peek over the horizon when she fell into bed, the alarm going off long before she was ready for it. She dragged herself into the shower and woke up a little under the heat and pressure of the spray.

Now, looking at the bags under her eyes while she put on her mascara, while she smeared on her best lipstick, Leigh decided that she'd been naive to think coming home would be so easy. This trip had already been an emotional whipsaw, and it was only her second day back.

The light dress she'd packed so carefully for this morning's talk was white silk, above the knee, very cool and light in the Texas heat, but standing in front of the mirror with her sunglasses on her head and her coffee in her hand, she decided it was too bridal, that it looked like she was having a quickie wedding at the courthouse, something furtive and embarrassing. Chloe would certainly have hated it, made fun of her for packing it. It was too late, though—there was nothing else she'd brought that was dressy enough for a formal speech. She decided she'd just have to suffer through.

Now, as Leigh wobbled down the hillside in her ridiculous white dress and impractical black stiletto heels, she was sure she was going to break an ankle. The path was gravel and a little bit steep, and her ankles wobbled with each step. How had she been so stupid? She was as bad as any city girl. First chance she got, she was going into town and buying a decent pair of cowboy boots. She'd thrown out her old pair years ago, when it started to look like she was never coming back. That, she decided now, was clearly a mistake.

She was late already. The conferencegoers had been assembled for hours, eating breakfast together, having coffee in the dining pavilion outside the main house, where there were picnic tables arranged around a firepit. In the front hall of the main house Leigh stopped a man with a badge to ask where she could find the ballroom. He pointed her to a tall set of curving staircases that led up to a large open room hung with tapestries and two enormous deer-antler chandeliers. A stone fireplace stood at one end, cold now in the May heat.

Maybe two or three hundred people were in the room already, lined up on either side of an aisle leading to a stage where a podium and microphone were already set up, flanked by a couple of chairs. She could feel a general murmur make its way through the crowd, many of whom turned back to look at her—the star of the show, at least for this morning—and again she felt the white dress was a terrible mistake. Somewhere, she was sure, a hidden organist was about to start playing "Here Comes the Bride." Or maybe she just had weddings on the brain after her conversation with Joseph yesterday. She hung back a little, wishing she could disappear.

Then there was someone at her elbow, greeting her with a friendly hello and asking if her trip was pleasant, if her room was nice, if all was in order. This was Saundra Craig, the director of the conference, a tiny woman with long gray hair pinned up in a loose bun and a floral skirt that brushed the floor like a feather duster. She had the fussy, motherly, businesslike manner of hippie women who'd come of age during the 1960s and 70s, the kind of manner Leigh imagined her mother might have had, if she'd lived to be as old as Saundra.

She handed Leigh a bottle of water. "We're so thrilled to have you here," she said. "Don't you look nice, though? So smart to wear white in this weather."

"Thank you," said Leigh. She was about to say how glad she was to be invited when the screech of someone turning on the microphone hit her so hard she nearly passed out.

Saundra signaled for someone to turn down the mic, and the noise died. When Leigh could open her eyes again, the room settled back into a familiar shape—the deer-antler chandelier overhead, a table of coffee and tea service in the back, trays of danishes and bagels and cut fruit to fortify the early-morning crowd. The guests were already taking their seats, still looking behind them toward the place where the guest of honor was awaiting her turn onstage. Clearly it was a mistake to have gone out with Chloe last night—she should have stayed in and watched reality TV. She took another drink of coffee, willing the caffeine to her brain. People from all over the country had come to hear her talk that morning. The least she could do was try to look awake.

"Can I get you anything else?" Saundra asked. "A couple of aspirin maybe?"

"I'll be all right, thanks," said Leigh, taking a gulp of water. "I went out for Tex-Mex yesterday with a friend, and I'm feeling a little green. Must have had some bad beef."

"Of course, sweetheart," Saundra said, patting Leigh's arm. "But let me get you a couple of aspirin anyway." She came back in a minute with two pills and a Bloody Mary.

Leigh nearly hugged the woman. "You're a magician," she said, tossing back the aspirin with a gulp of tomato juice and vodka. "I owe you my life."

"This is a writers' conference, honey," she said. "You're not the first speaker to turn up with a hangover."

In a minute she started to feel better. While Saundra went onstage to say her welcome remarks, Leigh sipped the Bloody Mary, trying to be careful of her white dress. Then she grabbed a bagel and nibbled on it a bit, looking out at the faces in the room. The attendees were all shapes and sizes: some were young college students on summer break; some were high-school teachers or advertising executives looking to reconnect with their passion; a good deal of them were obviously retired folks working on their memoirs or finally getting around to that first novel. There were a lot more Stetsons in the crowd than there would have been in New York, more blue jeans and boots, but no matter what people were wearing, they had all come to pursue a long-deferred dream of writing a book. She'd been to enough writers' conferences by now that the types were familiar even if the faces changed.

Leigh found herself searching the crowd, wondering which of them might have a truly great book in them, the talent it took to break out. There was always one, in her experience; sometimes, there might be two. But always at least one. If she could find that one, she might have the next Richard Millikin on her hands—and the first title for Leigh Merrill Books. Her stomach did another flip.

In a minute Saundra started introducing Leigh: graduate of Harvard, youngest editor at the prestigious publishing company Jenks & Hall, editor of the hugely sought-after novel *The Perfect Letter*, a *New York Times* bestseller already being optioned for a Hollywood movie starring Meryl Streep and George Clooney. As Leigh stood to enthusiastic applause, she felt a surge of adrenaline clear her head.

She smiled out at the room, took a breath, and began. *You got this.*

"So it sounds like a number of you have already read and, I hope, enjoyed *The Perfect Letter*," she said. "Perhaps some of you have even read about the provenance of the novel, how Richard Millikin had worked on the manuscript in fits and starts for thirty years, how he started other things but came back to this story time and again. Something about the story touched him completely, he told me later. All those letters that Marian writes to her lost love, letters she never sent—Richard Millikin told me he'd stay up all night sometimes, writing them. The passion in them moved him so much. But he didn't know if he could publish the story, didn't know if he could let it go. He threw the manuscript away four times, he said, but each time his wife rescued it from the trash and threatened to send it to his agent herself if he wouldn't. When I heard that through the New York rumor mill, I knew it was the book for me, and even though it took me two years of phone calls and e-mails to his agent and trips to Maine to convince him to let me see it, he finally did. I thank God every day his wife had enough sense not to let him destroy what's probably the best book of a long and storied career." More applause.

"But we've all had those moments, haven't we? Moments when we begin to doubt our gifts, when our dedication to our work starts to falter. No matter how successful, how famous, a writer always doubts his latest project. That's why the world needs editors, of course." She brought out the manila folder that held her morning's presentation and opened it: pages of neat type crisscrossed with her scrawled notes and edits. Even when it was her own writing, Leigh couldn't help editing and reediting it. She was always searching for the right word, the right phrase.

"That's why I'm here today, to talk to you about *The Perfect Letter,* about how to write a perfect letter of your own. Because that's what a book is: a letter from a writer to a reader. It's connection. Something that reaches across the divides of time and space and brings us closer together."

"The perfect letter," she began, "starts with truth. With nakedness." A smattering of embarrassed laughter. "Now, I don't mean physical nakedness. I mean emotional nakedness. The kind of writing that bares the soul." A sigh went up through the crowd. "How many of you used to regularly write letters, actual paper letters, to friends and family?" A number of hands went up around the room, mostly the older crowd. This is what Leigh had been counting on. "And how many of you have written or received a personal letter in the past year?" Across the room, only five or six hands went up—again the older crowd.

Leigh nodded in acknowledgment. "Letters used to be our main form of communication and connection. In the days before the telephone, a letter might be your only tie to a friend or loved one who lived far away, and most people devoted many hours of their days to letter writing. A day without a letter was very boring indeed. Today it would be like a day without Internet access. Horrors, right?" Another round of laughter. "But a good letter was a work of art. The best letters had the special tone and inflection of the person writing them. The unique way of speaking that belonged only to that special person, so that when you received that letter, it was like the loved one was there, in the room with you. The letter writer had to rely on the written word to convey affection, alarm, dismay, fear, love, and even anger. To take black words on a white page and make them come alive. It was truly an art form—an art form we've lost.

"People used to share letters, pass the best ones around to friends and family to read and admire, like books. Jane Austen was said to have written three thousand letters in her lifetime, most to her sister. Three thousand. Now I'm lucky to get a letter summoning me to jury duty." More polite laughter. "The art of the letter is the art of finding your voice, of revealing the most hidden parts of yourself to another person, of bridging distance and time and even death to tell something that's so important the person receiving it simply *has to read it*.

"By now you know the story of *The Perfect Letter,* how the narrator, Marian, composes a series of love letters to her lover, Bernard, over a lifetime. How she's married to a man she doesn't love, how Bernard is a newspaper reporter jumping from war zone to war zone, in agony that they can never be together for more than a few hours or a few days. The passion in those letters is what drove me to publish the story. Marian's voice comes across in every word, every inflection. Her pain. Her heartbreak.

"Now, you might be thinking to yourself that's all well and good—Richard Millikin is a Pulitzer Prize winner, a genius—but it's a genius we can all find within ourselves, if we look hard enough." Murmurs of pleasure at the thought.

Leigh continued: "My mother taught me at an early age that a letter, well composed, is worth more than any phone call, more than any blurb or blog post. A thank-you card in the mail. A note to an elderly relative or a faraway loved one. The time and energy it takes to write a letter is never a wasted thing. It is perhaps the most personal gift the writer can give another person: insight into the writer's mind and heart. Something to be read again and again. To be savored, ingested. Like good food and wine, a perfect letter isn't something you gobble and forget. It's a taste you get hungry for, start to crave."

Leigh took a sip of her Bloody Mary and continued. "Some of the earliest novels were disguised as letters. It was called the epistolary form, and it was used for some of the greatest narratives in literature: *Pamela. Les Liaisons dangereuses. Wuthering Heights.* Even *Frankenstein* was written as a series of letters, and wouldn't the world be a poorer place without *that* book?

"But now people speak in sound bites. Everything is glib, manufactured. Everything is over in a hurry. A hundred and forty characters and get out. But none of that makes for a good novel, does it?" She could see their heads shaking no; she had them.

"Even now, in the twenty-first century, we yearn for connection with other people. For experiences we haven't had. For a sense of delight and inspiration. For those human emotions—fear and love, anger and awe—and to taste them again and again like good meals we've eaten, like memories.

"If you've read *The Perfect Letter,* you know how well Richard Millikin created just those feelings in his readers. Connection. Awe. Delight. It's not something that can be rushed through. It's not something you can divulge in a status update. It takes time, and patience. The author took thirty years to create those feelings, and I can tell you without a doubt that none of that effort was wasted."

Leigh took another gulp of her Bloody Mary. "I read hundreds of books a year. No—scratch that. Thousands. Thousands of books by aspiring writers, aspiring artists just like you. My office is piled with them, piled literally *to the ceiling.*" Noises of dismay and surprise now; aspiring writers were always surprised by the behemoth called the slush pile. "Most of the authors who come to me, quite frankly, spend a lot of time chasing the latest trend, whatever genre is fashionable that month, and most of them, quite frankly, don't succeed for that very reason. The author has tried to give me something they *think* I want, instead of writing with their own voice, their own heart and soul.

"What I look for when I sit down with a manuscript from a new author," Leigh said, in the closing moments of the talk, when the room was hushed and drawing in its breath, "is a return to the intimate narrative. The revelation. The confession. In a word, the letter. Stories like *Wuthering Heights,* in which the characters tell you everything about their secret selves—the good, the bad, and the ugly. Confession, my friends, is good for literature, and good for the soul. And nothing less than the soul should be on the page. In every word. Every letter. The perfect letter.

"Thank you."

Applause. The crowd was getting to its feet, conference goers clapping extravagantly, and Leigh was glad she'd made it through, glad no one could tell how tired she was, how ill she felt, ill at ease and heartsick. She'd done it—she'd made it through the speech. Now all she had to do was get through the rest of the week.

Saundra was at her elbow, saying, "That was lovely. They were riveted; thank you so much," and the crowd was surging toward her, with questions, with comments, with eager, smiling faces shining with hope, with questions, with praise. She smiled at all of them, took a breath. Congratulations, they were saying, that was inspiring.

But she didn't feel inspiring. She felt crowded and overwhelmed. She wanted to go home, to New York. She had a new imprint to set up, a marriage proposal. She wanted to be done with strangers, to go home to her apartment, to her work. Joseph would still be there, waiting for her. *Of course I'll marry you. Of course I love you.* All she had to do was say the words.

One of the audience members who approached her was a man of maybe sixty, in a crisp white shirt and dark blue jeans, so fresh Leigh would nearly have sworn they were ironed. He had a tanned, taut face with an amused look on it, his dark hair, gray at the temples, cropped so closely and so clean, and his bearing so straight and so polite, that she knew immediately he was military, probably the Marines, probably a lifer. "Miss Merrill," he said, holding out his hand for her to shake, "thank you so much for that speech. I suspect it was just the kick in the pants many of us needed."

"You're welcome. Mister . . . ?"

"James Stephens. Call me Jim, please. I have an appointment with you tomorrow about my book."

"Ah, yes," she said. Her docket of pitch meetings was so full she hadn't even attempted to learn the names of all the writers she was meeting with—it was easier to put names to faces once she'd met them in person. She looked at Jim now with what she usually felt when talking to new writers: cautious optimism. "I'll look forward to hearing about your project."

Jim's face turned mischievous. "I'll bet you say that to all the writers you meet. Tell the truth, how often do you fall in love with a book at one of these conferences?"

Leigh laughed. So he'd been around the block a few times. "Not as often as I'd like," she said. "But that doesn't mean yours can't be one of them. I hope it will."

"Aha, you're being encouraging now. I'll bet that's another thing you say to all the writers you meet."

She leaned in and spoke in a conspiratorial whisper. "Only the good-looking ones."

"And flattery, too. I'll have to keep my eye on you."

He stuck out his hand again for her to shake, his whole body going ramrod straight once more. *That military training never really goes away, does it?* Leigh thought, and then reached out to take his hand, which was warm and firm in her own. "Nice to meet you, Miss Merrill," he said.

"Leigh," she told him. He gave a little nod and melted back into the crowd. At least she had something to look forward to tomorrow—a half-hour pitch meeting with someone she actually liked.

She was sipping her Bloody Mary and nodding while someone else asked her a question when out of the corner of her eye she glimpsed the figure of a man heading toward the door, a man in a faded brown Stetson with a rattlesnake band and a plain white T-shirt, his arms brown from the sun. She caught only a glimpse of his face under the brim of his hat, the dark blue eyes and the long straight nose, the tattoo of a bat—or was it a bird?—on the back of one arm. He was a little broader than she remembered, more filled out, and his hair was cut shorter, too, no longer curling along his shirt collar but shorn close to his head. It couldn't be him, though. She was imagining things—conjuring him up out of thin air. Jake didn't want to see her. He was still angry with her. He would have called to tell her he was getting out of prison. He wouldn't just show up at her talk. Would he?

For a moment she wavered on her feet, the room growing dim and then lightening again. Saundra caught her by the elbow. "Are you all right?" she asked, and Leigh had to say she was fine, she was tired, that's all, only a little bit. "You're not pregnant, are you?" Saundra asked in a conspiratorial whisper.

Leigh nearly fell over again. What a question! "God, I hope not," she said.

She jumped down from the stage and ran toward the door, trying to catch him—spilling red Bloody Mary on her white dress, of course—but she couldn't think about that now, she had to get to Jake before he left. As they saw her coming toward them the crowd surged in around her once more, people wanting to speak with her, ask her more questions. There were bodies in front of her, so many bodies she could barely move. A hundred people stood between herself and the door, a hundred people admiring and hopeful, and in a minute he'd become just another in the sea of faces, a sea tearing them apart once more. She stood in the doorway picking at her tomato-stained dress, but she couldn't see Jake anywhere. He was gone.

She woke up that afternoon from a sleep so deep that for a moment she forgot where she was. The light in her room was the sunshine of midday, all sharp lines and angles, and in the big, soft white bed piled with pillows Leigh had dreamed she was back in college, back in the dorms where she'd spent so much time alone. Some kind of dream of running across Harvard Commons, running from someone she couldn't see but who clearly wanted to do her harm. She'd been screaming a name at the top of her voice, but she couldn't remember which name it had been.

When her phone alarm went off, she sat up, fumbling for the off switch, and looked around the room in confusion. Eventually it all came back to her—Texas, the conference. She should have something real to eat. Two bites of bagel and a few sips of Bloody Mary hadn't been enough to calm her stomach, or to ease the panic she'd felt when she thought she'd seen Jake in the crowd. It was a mistake. A mirage, that's all, caused by too much tequila and too little sleep. If he'd been there, he wouldn't have left without talking to her, saying hello, something. There'd be no point.

She stood up and went to the window, standing behind the gauzy white curtain in her bra and underwear, looking at the view of the valley outside her window. She was less than fifteen miles away from Burnside, the small town where she and Chloe and Jake had spent so much time together during high school—where they'd gone to football games and dances and bonfires, sneaking beers on Saturday nights, watching the fireworks over the river on the Fourth of July—but it felt like a million. Thomas Wolfe was right: you can't go home again. Because when you get there, the home you thought you knew is gone.

She got dressed—a little more sensibly this time; the white dress was ruined—and went down the hill to the dining pavilion to grab a salad, sitting by herself at a picnic table and reading the paper while she ate. It felt good to have a few minutes to herself, a few minutes to think. No one bothered her; no one interrupted. Still, on her way back to her cottage she found herself looking around for a familiar face under a Stetson, the tattoo of a bat on the back of an arm, but it was no use. He'd left, or else he'd never been there in the first place.

As she opened the door to her room after lunch, she saw that housekeeping had been there: the bed was made, the towels stacked, the sink wiped. And there were two bundles of papers sitting on the dresser, tied neatly with twine. Someone must have delivered them while she had been out for lunch—slipped in with the maid, probably. She bent over, her fingers fumbling at the bundle. Letters. Someone's idea of a joke, after her talk that morning, surely.

But when she turned them over she saw it was her own handwriting on the envelopes. Her own words. Someone had given her a bundle of her own letters.

Not someone. Jake.

Here was the stationery she'd used all those years ago, here was the green pen she still favored, her own elaborate, looping handwriting. These were her letters to him—all of them from the look of it, maybe one a week for the first three years he was in prison, then gradually tapering off as she'd grown more and more frustrated that he never answered.

On top was the first letter she'd written Jake after he'd been arrested, when he was still in the Burnside County Jail awaiting trial. Farther down in the stack were the letters she'd sent after he was convicted and sent to federal prison in Huntsville to serve his sentence. The letters were all here, all kept in the order in which she'd sent them, some of them soft and yellowed with age now, some stained and smeared with fingerprints or fold marks. She'd thought she would never see them again, never again read what she'd written to Jake while they were apart. She'd always figured he must have thrown them away, or that maybe he'd never opened them in the first place. Clearly they'd been opened, and read—often. Clearly she'd been wrong.

Her heart squeezed. If he'd read her letters, then why hadn't he ever written her back?

Four years she went without a word from him. Jake had never written back to her, never called, never came out to see her when she tried to visit. So when she was about to graduate from Harvard and move down to New York, she decided to stop writing him altogether. He didn't care about her anymore, she was certain about that. She needed a clean break, a fresh start. She needed to move on. Wasn't that what he'd told her, the last time they'd spoken, the last day of the trial when the jury foreman had read the verdict, that awful, awful verdict? He'd leaned over to speak to her, just her, in the crowded courtroom while the bailiffs were preparing to take him away. She'd leaned forward in her seat to hear him, and his mouth had moved against her ear. *Forget about me. I'm no good for you. Move on with your life, Leigh,* he'd said. And she had. He couldn't fault her for taking his advice.

She opened the last letter, though she still remembered very well what it said. *Dear Jake,* it read,

> I've tried not to be so angry with you, but it isn't easy. I didn't expect when you said I should move on with my life that it meant you would cut off all contact with me, that you would refuse to give me a single word from you, no sense of how you're doing, what you're doing, if you're coping well, or badly, or at all. If you still think about me, if you still care. I'm writing into silence here—it's like broadcasting letters into empty space, waiting for some echo to come back to me. It's cold, and blank, and alone. I've given up everything except school and these letters. I

promised you I'd wait for you, and for nearly four years I've kept
that promise, shutting myself up, shutting out the world, waiting
for the day you'd get out. I have hardly any friends here, hardly
any life. I don't do anything except go to class and write to you. I
don't have any family anymore either, no one but Chloe. I think
I've been afraid to make new friends, to let anyone else into my
heart, because it's still full of you.

I'm starting to think it would have been better if we'd never
met at all.

I know you must be angry with me, that you must blame me
for what happened, but I don't understand why you won't answer
my letters. Are you trying to torture me? To make me suffer?

If you are, it's working. I'm serving a sentence, too. Maybe
it's the wrong kind of sentence—maybe you don't think it's fair,
and it's not—but I can't change that now. I can't change the fact
that you weren't the one who really killed Dale Tucker, and I can't
change the fact that you decided to tell everyone you were, and
that the jury decided to believe you. We both have to live with the
decisions we've made.

All I wanted was a letter. A note. Something. I don't think I
can keep doing this, writing and writing every week without a
word from you. Any word would do. Even "good-bye."

If you won't say it, then I will. Good-bye, Jake. I'm finally
moving on, like you said I should.

She remembered writing that, how angry she'd been, how hurt.
She had written it to a man who was in prison, convicted—*wrongly*
convicted—of killing another person. A man who had sacrificed his
future for hers. And not a day had gone by that she hadn't wondered if
she hadn't made a terrible mistake. But she couldn't take it back. She
didn't know how.

She set the letter down. There was a second bundle of envelopes, too—clean white envelopes, sealed, never opened. Each one was addressed to her in the same cramped, uneven handwriting, the same black pen, but there was no postage, no return address. They'd never been mailed. Tied around the bundle was a note in the same handwriting. It read,

I kept these for the time we would meet again. I thought maybe they would explain why I did the things I did. I thought maybe it wouldn't be too late.

Now I think it would be wrong for me to intrude on your new life. No hard feelings.

You did everything you set out to do. You really made it, kid, and I'm so proud of you. It was all worth it. I swear.

You once asked me for one word, even if it was good-bye. Now you have it. The word is "love." I'll always love you.

—J.

She slid down the wall with the letter in her hands, shaking so much she could hardly breathe, her eyes blurring with tears. The light in the cottage seemed to dim. *I'll always love you,* he'd written. But it was too late. He was too late. He'd been too proud, taken too long. She'd made a new life for herself. He couldn't undo everything she'd spent the last ten years building. *Some mistakes can't be unmade, Jake, no matter how hard you try. The dead can't rise again, can they? The sentence can't be commuted after it's served. And we both served that sentence, no matter how hard you tried to protect me, Jake. We both got locked away all those years ago.*

She had left Texas behind, but it hadn't left her. It was here, now, in this room, in her hands, and she knew immediately she would have to find him. She would have to find Jake and close the door on the past once and for all. She didn't have a choice.

Dear Leigh,

Three days I've been here, three days of fear and violence. Three
days of despair. I lie on a mattress of stones, waiting for sleep
that never comes.

I saw you today, even though you didn't know it. I saw you in
your blue dress, the one with the white polka dots, the one like
a shower of meteors streaking across the sky. Your hair was tied
up in a ponytail. The sun was shining on it, all that long dark
hair. I wanted to reach up, pull the rubber band out, and let it
fall through my hands like water. Bury my face in it and breathe
deeply. Drown in it. I thought if I could touch you one more time, if
I could feel your hands on me again just once, I could go back into
the prison and stay behind bars the rest of my life. I would face the
death penalty, if it meant I could touch you once more before I go.

I didn't know the last time I kissed you would be the last time.

It was from the window in my cell I saw you. You parked
your granddaddy's white truck in the visitors' lot. You came up
the walk to the front door of the jail wearing your red lipstick,
clutching your mama's little white purse. A vision of how you'd
look at forty, fifty—still beautiful, still brilliant and burning as
a deep blue night. I wanted to freeze that picture, bring you to a
standstill. I want to remember you like that.

The guards came to tell me I had a visitor. I told them to send
you away. I said I wouldn't come out for anyone but Jesus.

I stood at the window and watched you come out again. You
were crying. You put your head in your hands, and my heart
broke, because I knew I had done the one thing I swore I would
never do: I had made you cry.

I don't dare let you see me here. I don't dare speak to you

behind a glass window. If I see you, I know my resolve will break, and that's the one thing I can't let happen. My only comfort is knowing that I am sparing you everything I see around me. How can I look at you through a glass, lie to you, tell you I'm fine?

I don't sleep. I don't eat. Down the hall from me there's a crazy man screaming about bugs crawling on him. My clothes are filthy. I haven't had a shower or slept or eaten a decent meal. My cellmate is a car thief who punched a cop. He snores all night. I can't tell him to roll over—he's already said if I talk to him he'll stab me in my sleep. Violence in him like a sickness.

I asked one of the guards if he could move me to a different cell, and he laughed. You think this is a hotel? the guard said. You think you can switch rooms if you don't like the bed or the view?

No, sir, I said.

Take my advice, kid, he said. Pick the biggest guy here and beat the shit out of him one day where everyone can see. The others will think you're crazy and leave you alone.

That's all the protection I have here. What I can earn through violence.

I'm not complaining, not really. I deserve this terror. I deserve this darkness, after what I did. I deceived you, and I allowed myself to be deceived. I won't let myself be a curse on your life anymore. When I think of you safe and whole, getting ready to head off to Harvard, I know I'm doing the right thing. I can atone for both of us.

I already know I won't send this letter to you. I already know it will upset you. I don't want you to think about doing something foolish. You can't save me. Only I can do that.

I hope you can forgive me for today. For everything.

Love,

—J.

Four

Wolf's Head Farms, the Thoroughbred ranch owned by Leigh's grandfather, sat outside the little town of Burnside, Texas, a river town a few miles west of Austin in Texas Hill Country—spring-fed, sunwarmed, green and rolling as England. Better horse country, too, her granddad always said. It was the clear springs, Gene used to say, that made Texas Thoroughbreds grow up to be such fast runners, the fastest anywhere, and though Leigh always suspected it was an old man's sentimental attachment to the land that kept him there more than any magic springs, she never dared contradict him. Her grandfather loved Texas—loved its harshness, loved its beauty. The prickly irascible nature of the place suited him, suited his sharp mind and quick temper and taciturn disposition, his soft old heart, and she'd known, even as a very young child, that he would never leave it.

She'd grown up on the farm protected by her granddad's money and his deep love for his impulsive, restless, book-loving granddaughter. Her mother, Abby, had grown up there, too, the younger of Gene Merrill's two kids—"stubborn as a two-dollar mule," her grandfather always said, which was ironic coming from a man as stubborn as he was—but despite that one shared quality, they had little in common. Gene was old-fashioned, as strict and controlling as Abby was idealistic and adventurous. Abby's mother, Leigh's grandmother, had died of a sudden heart attack when Abby was in high school, and her absence became an ache in her daughter like a missing tooth, and afterward father and daughter never saw eye to eye on much. When Abby graduated high school she ran away to New York to live with a bunch of musicians in a cold-water squat on the Lower East Side against her father's explicit orders. It was the seventies, after all. Gene was a horseman, an outdoorsman, a self-made businessman and Texan—he didn't have much patience with punks or hippies and was suspicious of anything as unconventional as a squat. He was deeply disappointed when Abby came home pregnant and unmarried after five years. She'd broken his heart, he said. Still, he took his daughter back into his home, and after Leigh was born he doted on her as much as if she'd been his own child.

Everything between them would have been all right after that, except that Abby wouldn't name Leigh's father. The secret was a splinter that burrowed itself between Gene and his only daughter, a constant source of irritation. Leigh suspected her grandfather would have taken a shotgun to her daddy if he'd been able to find him, so Abby kept him a secret, so secret that not even Leigh knew his name or where to find him. It was possible that Abby hadn't really known herself who he was, but that didn't stop Leigh from dreaming about him, from imagining Abby as a young girl in the big city, a punk girl with black hair and big black boots and a leather jacket living a whirlwind romance with a mysterious stranger. It didn't stop Leigh from dreaming that she, too, might run away from home one day, run to New York and have her own adventure there, meet someone mysterious, wriggle out from under her grandfather's strict control.

Life was quiet at Wolf's Head—too quiet, for Leigh—and over time New York started to feel like a beacon, calling to her from her bedroom in Texas with its pink canopy, its parade of stuffed animals. At the Burnside library she'd take out all the books on New York: its politics, its complicated geography, its history. She'd cut pictures of Manhattan skyscrapers and brownstones out of magazines and hang them on the walls of her room, pore over real-estate listings to choose fantasy apartments and neighborhoods, watch Woody Allen and Nora Ephron movies and dress like the characters. And she had the perfect career in mind for a girl addicted to romance novels, one that was guaranteed to lead her to Manhattan one day—editor. All she had to do was get terrific grades, go to a top-notch school, and learn everything there was to know about books.

Her mother seemed to love the idea. She'd look at the pictures of Manhattan on Leigh's walls and the movies about Brooklyn on the TV and say, *We'll go there together one day, Leela. I'll show you all the places I lived. I'll introduce you to the people I knew. You'll be happy there. I know I was.* And Leigh would lie with her head in her mother's lap and smell the hay, the bluebonnets growing in the fields, and she'd think: *Someday I'll have a different life than this. More exciting. More adventurous.*

Leigh loved remembering her mother that way, with hay in her hair and promises on her lips, because Abby Merrill had died of breast cancer when Leigh was ten. Afterward most of Leigh's memories of her mother were of her mother's illness—Abby losing her hair, Abby sleeping all day, skeletal and hollow-voiced when she kissed Leigh good-bye. What was left of Abby were a few impressions: her mother's laugh, her mother's strong hands brushing her hair. Her mother's kindness. Leigh mourned her and mourned the dream they'd shared. In many ways, moving back east had been as much about reconnecting with that image of her mother as it had been about Leigh's own career ambitions.

As the years went on, the pain of losing her mother lessened a little bit at a time, helped along by distance and the constant needs of the farm. There were always new foals in the spring, and lambs, and her grandfather's ornery peacock, Peabody, as playmates and projects. Her grandfather insisted Leigh help with the chores—he believed chores built character, and it didn't matter if it was for boys or girls—so from the time she was old enough to hold a pitchfork, Leigh helped muck stalls and mend fences and mow grass. Gene took her all over the country to watch his horses race, Kentucky and New York and Florida and California, Leigh cheering her grandfather's swift horses. At home there were books to read and schoolwork to finish, secret places to explore, and chores, chores, chores—horses to breed, horses to break, always the horses, which managed to be both business commodities and expensive pets. Only the best trainers, the best feed and tack for her grandfather's Thoroughbreds, who were the best sires and dams in the world.

It was for this reason that her grandfather hired, when Leigh was sixteen, a couple of famous Thoroughbred trainers named Ben Rhodes and Dale Tucker, who were well known for turning even marginal horses into champions, and champions into stars. They arrived at the ranch in Burnside one summer with Jake in tow. Jake was seventeen, resentful as hell about leaving his friends and his old girlfriend back in Kentucky, which he seemed to think was paradise on earth. Real Thoroughbred men lived in Kentucky, Jake had complained, not Texas. Texas might as well be the ends of the earth.

Leigh remembered the day they arrived, a dusty Sunday afternoon in August, the kind of day that stretched out sweltering and indolent, the kind of day she usually spent at Wolf Rock, a little pool at the back of her grandfather's property fed by a clear underground spring. Above the lip of the pool stood a large limestone boulder that the wind and water had molded, over the centuries, into the shape of a wolf's head—hence the name of the farm. The water there was always cool and clean, and in the long afternoon hours of the summer, she'd strip off her clothes and soak naked in the water, her skin turning brown in the sun, the air hot and still. Animals came from all over for a drink, and Leigh would hold herself as silent as possible whenever a deer or a coyote (even, once, a small black bear) came stealthily out of the bushes. They always ignored her; she was just another animal to them, not small enough to eat, not big enough to be a threat. The horses would come, too, sometimes rolling in the cool mud at the edge of the spring, scratching their behinds against a tree trunk. When the sun started to go down, Leigh would get dressed and wander home in time for supper, her grandfather admonishing her to take a bathing suit at least. "It isn't seemly, Leela," he'd say. "It isn't ladylike. What will you do if someone sees you? You're nearly a woman now. I don't want you to get into trouble."

"Sure, Pop," she'd say, and then do as she pleased anyway. Like mother, like daughter.

The afternoon Jake arrived she'd promised her grandfather some help with a three-month-old colt that had taken ill. It had been born in May and walked just hours after birth, the way it was supposed to, but a few weeks later it had sickened, lost its glossy bay coat, and refused to stand. For weeks she and her grandfather had tended it, rubbing lotion on its dry skin, trying to encourage it to get to its feet. They'd had vets by the dozens to see it, but nothing had helped.

Finally her grandfather had made the decision to put it down. Leigh was heartbroken—the colt had the best possible pedigree, out of her grandfather's best mare and stud—but the poor thing was suffering, and it was time for its suffering to end. She had been there to see the vet give it the injection, stroking its head as it closed its eyes for the last time. Afterward she'd gone for her swim, but her heart wasn't in it. She'd managed only a quick dip, but the afternoon was already spoiled, so she'd turned and come straight home.

The truck, a big, new red Chevy with Kentucky plates, was waiting by the tire swing in the circle driveway in front of the main house when she came around the bend. She'd forgotten about the new trainers her grandfather had hired, but there was Ben Rhodes, stretching his back after the long drive, looking the place over admiringly—the long, low stables, clean and cool and shaded from the sun by deep porches; the breeding shed and equipment barns; not one but two freshly painted white cottages for the trainers and the farmhands; the brick big house with its two long, low wings fronted by an impressive columned porch, a deep blue swimming pool in back; the rows of live oaks leading up to the house; and surrounding it all, four hundred acres of the best Texas pastureland, dotted by stands of bur oaks and cedars all fed by the best clear underground springs for hundreds of miles around.

"Whoo, there's a lot of money here," Ben had said under his breath. He had dark hair shot with silver, wide shoulders stretching a red T-shirt, crinkly, friendly eyes. He gave her a little wave. "Hey, darlin'," he'd said, "I thought I was coming to Gene Merrill's place, not a mer-maid cove."

Leigh had been self-conscious all of a sudden about her damp T-shirt sticking to her skin, her dripping hair, the fact that she wasn't wearing a bra. She folded her arms over her chest.

When Ben's training partner, Dale Tucker, had come around the other side of the truck, a little too close to her, Leigh took two steps back. He was a short man, shorter than Ben by at least a head, and looked Leigh up and down like a man used to judging the value of horseflesh. "My God," he said. "We'll have to keep an eye on this one,

Ben. She looks like trouble. *Rich* trouble." Then he'd winked. Leigh was taken aback—she wasn't used to grown men speaking to her that way. Most of the grown men she'd known wouldn't have dared.

It was then that the rear door of the cab opened and a boy stepped out. She definitely did not remember her grandfather telling her the new trainer was bringing his son, and a teenage son to boot. She was sure she'd remember that part. He was tall—taller than she was, which was considerable—and his thin, wiry frame was tanned, probably from hours and hours helping his father in the barn before and after school. He had a thick shock of dark, wavy hair that curled over his ears, and dark blue eyes like his father. He looked around with a bored, almost angry expression, and she remembered being irritated immediately that he'd think anything or anyone here needed his approval. His father noticed her watching them and elbowed Jake in the ribs as if to say, *Check that out.*

Jake looked at his feet and muttered something to his father she couldn't hear. He kicked at the ground, raising the dust, and wrinkled his nose. He was looking over her grandfather's gorgeous spread the way he might have looked at a rattlesnake near his boot, something to be wary of and avoid. Leigh heard him say something to his father, some plea for them to pack up and turn around. "Not on your life," Ben said to his son. "Gift horses, son. This place is going to be the making of us, I guarantee it."

"If what you mean is making us into hicks, then I believe you," Jake had said, low but not low enough that she couldn't hear.

Leigh was immediately angry. Of course she knew a father's career meant nothing to a boy who'd been uprooted from his friends and familiar life, but Wolf's Head was everything in the world to her, and she'd decided, in that moment, to hate him. How could he not see that he'd entered paradise? she had thought. How could he not be grateful to be here? *Who does he think he is, anyway?*

He looked over at her and shaded his eyes, grimacing, giving her a glimpse of his braces, flashing silver in the hot sun. So much for his mysterious good looks. She was relieved, actually, to see he wasn't perfect. "You better watch those things, metal mouth," she called to him. "You're gonna sunburn your gums if you aren't careful."

Jake had looked surprised at first, then settled into a look of practiced, unruffled calm—a look Leigh would grow to know well in the months and years to come. He looked her up and down—her wet hair, her damp clothes, fresh sunburn across her lightly freckled nose, and streaks of light in her dark hair. She was suddenly aware of how tall she was, how skinny and young she felt. "Look at this, a talking horse," he said, almost to himself. "I didn't know they had those in Texas, Pop. Why didn't you tell me?"

Cute *and* sharp. Too bad he was awful. "Better than a talking ass," she said, and tossing her hair, she'd turned back to go into the house, leaving a trail of wet footprints behind her. She figured they would be enemies from then on, avoiding each other in the barn, at the pond, at school. *Fine,* she thought, *if that's the way he wants it, fine by me.*

She went into the house to work on her homework at the kitchen table, but the words swam in front of her eyes, and the algebra equations, which normally she was so good at, turned into Chinese. She'd had no idea that a boy was coming to live at the farm, and it had thrown her. She was going to have to stop swimming naked at Wolf Rock or even the swimming pool. She was going to have to start acting like a lady, like her granddaddy said, and all for the sake of a boy she didn't even *like*.

She was in the middle of planning a scheme that would get them to leave—something about putting scorpions in Jake's bed, or his boots—when there'd been a ring at the doorbell. She'd opened it to find Jake standing there looking sheepish. "My father said I need to apologize," he said, leaning against the doorbell and making it ring once more by accident. He jumped and stood up straight. "He says I shouldn't get off on the wrong foot the first day with you folks. So."

"So."

"That's it, then. See you around," Jake said, and started to leave.

Before he could go, Leigh called back to him, "You're doing a spectacular job of it, you know."

"What?"

"Apologizing. Saying your father is making you apologize isn't really the same thing as actually apologizing, is it?"

He grinned and said, "What's your name?"

"I'm not sure I should tell you. I'm still waiting for that apology."

"Tell me your name and I'll give it to you."

She gave him her best stink eye. "Leigh Merrill."

He held out his hand for her to shake, and she took it, tightening her fingers around his, still determined to hate him, still keeping up her defenses. "I'm Jacob Rhodes. And I'm sorry, Leigh. Truly. Your granddad's place here is lovely, if you don't mind a talking ass saying so."

When he turned and went back to his father's truck in a nimbus of dust, his jeans sliding around his hips as he walked, Leigh remembered all her anger slipping off like a snake shedding its skin. For the first time she understood what the girls at school were always fussing about. A boy like that would be worth falling for, if he managed not to ruin everything by opening his mouth.

She went back inside to finish her homework, but it was no use; she couldn't think of anything except Jake the rest of the day.

Damn him anyway. He *would* have to be charming.

By the end of that first week they'd established something of a routine: after their chores were done, Leigh and Jake would ride out together to the hillsides and the woods, following the trails along the stream that bordered her grandfather's property, just a trickle in the heat of midsummer but a nice cool swimming creek in April and May. They would explore the caves up in the hills, full of bats and sometimes coyotes, but other times cool and abandoned and private, only the drip of water for company. They would ride in companionable silence, and before long the ice between them had melted away.

They were determined to be just friends, telling each other their stories, their secrets. Leigh told Jake about her mother, introduced him to Chloe and her friends at school, helped him find his way in the halls of Burnside High. Jake told Leigh about Amy, his girlfriend back in Kentucky, the farms he'd lived on, the horses he'd ridden, the horses he'd helped his father train, his voice swelling with pride. How he planned to go into the family business when he was old enough, train his own horses, be his father's partner. Maybe they'd even have their own place one day, he said.

"You should," she told him. "You'd be great."

"You think so?"

For Leigh, who had never had a sibling, it was like she had a brother all her own. "I do," she said.

Her grandfather, who hadn't known Ben had a son to bring with him to Wolf's Head, was less pleased. He tried to discourage Leigh from seeking Jake out in the afternoons, tried to encourage her to hang out with her friends in town after school instead of coming straight home to spend time with the boy. He didn't think teenagers of the opposite sex should be so close—to her protests he only said, "It isn't right, Leela, it just isn't"—but despite his objections Leigh and Jake would rush to the barn every afternoon, saddling up a couple of trail horses and take off, not coming home sometimes until well after supper. Her grandfather never did anything but scold her, so Leigh did exactly as she pleased.

Then came the day when they rode out to Mammoth Cave, a larger cave higher up in the hills behind her grandfather's ranch that Leigh had only seen once, from far off—her grandfather had said he'd hide her if she ever went in there alone, that it was too dangerous. She'd never understood why, but if Jake was there, her grandfather couldn't object, surely? So she and Jake took two good trail horses and spent the afternoon picking their way around the old cattle trail until they found the mouth of the cave, damp and yawning on the hillside.

Inside it was dark and smelled strongly of rotten stone and stagnant water. The entrance was littered with animal bones and petrified coyote scat, but nothing moved in the dark when they threw stones inside, so whatever used to live there must have moved on. They went inside, shining their flashlights on colonies of bats hanging from the ceiling, clambering over the slippery stones. At one point they'd encountered a stone corridor that started off wide and grew gradually thinner and lower until they were squeezing their way through, unsure of where it led or if they'd be able to find their way out again. Leigh nearly panicked, but Jake was there, saying, "Almost there, Leigh. Don't be afraid. Keep going."

Then, in near-total darkness, they'd sensed they were in a large empty space, a kind of room or hall within the cave. They shone their flashlights at the ceiling. "My God," Leigh breathed. "I've never seen anything like it."

They'd come into a large inner chamber, perhaps twenty feet high and thirty or forty feet long. The stalactites from the ceiling and stalagmites from the floor had grown together over the centuries, drip by drip, until they touched and fused, long white limestone posts like the columns in a cathedral. Glittering chips of mica flashed their lights back at them, and they stood hushed and awed at the sight.

"Listen to this," Jake said, taking a deep breath and shouting, "Echo!" His voice came back to him: *echo!*

"It's like a church," she said. "It's beautiful."

"I wouldn't know. I never went to church."

"Well, you've gone now," she said, thinking if she ever saw God in anything, it was here. "I wonder if we're the first people who ever came here."

"If anyone used to come here," said Jake, "they don't anymore."

"It'll be our secret," she said. "Like our own church. But better, because there's no one but you and me to join it."

"Except the bats," he said.

"Except the bats," she said, and then shouted out, "Echo!" Her voice reverberated through the cavern, coming back to her faintly: *echo!*

She must have startled the bats, because suddenly the air was full of them. They swarmed around the two intruders, flitting close, and Leigh yelped and covered her head with her hands, crouching down. Jake flung himself over her, covering her up with his body. Underneath him she felt cocooned, safe. "Hold still," he said. "They'll go in a minute."

After several long seconds the bats flew off again in the darkness. Jake raised his head to look around. "All clear," he said, but neither of them moved. It was as if they were afraid to break the spell, to break contact. She could feel the length of him pressing down on her, another cave within the cave.

She leaned into him, leaned into his warmth, and suddenly she was aware of how alone they were, how cool it was in the cave, the heat coming off his skin under his clothes, every millimeter of the places where their bodies touched. She was not surprised, not exactly, but pleased—she realized it was something she had been waiting for, all those months.

He pulled her toward him. His mouth was soft and surprisingly gentle, even with his teeth full of braces.

"What about Amy?" she'd asked, coming up for air.

He grinned. "We broke up when I moved away. I didn't want to tell you, because I didn't want you to think I was hitting on you."

"So you're not hitting on me?"

"Okay, yes, maybe now I'm hitting on you."

"What took you so long?"

"I can't remember," he said, leaning in for another kiss.

They kissed for a long time in the darkened cave like the last two people on earth. But that was part of his appeal, too—the secret nature of their friendship, its taste of the forbidden. Years later she would understand that more, after she'd grown up a little, that her grandfather's disapproval had lent a special glow to all those furtive kisses, all those secret afternoons. Maybe Jake wouldn't have kissed her if he'd thought he'd been allowed to; maybe she wouldn't have fallen for him if he hadn't seemed so unavailable, if she hadn't known her grandfather would hate it right from the start.

Of course her grandfather tried to put a stop to it. Of course he didn't like Jake and Leigh spending all their time together. He told her he thought Jake was a distraction, something that would get her in trouble, the way her mother did, and you don't want to end up like her, do you? You don't need to be getting serious about boys at your age, Leigh. You're too young, too smart to end up like Abby.

Leigh had tried to defend her mother. "What was so bad about Abby?" she'd asked. "She was a good mother, a good daughter. I thought you loved her."

"I did. I do. But you have a long way to go if you think she was a good daughter." Leigh had listened in shocked silence. Gene had never said a bad word about Abby to her before. "You have to understand. She disobeyed me. She quit school when she was seventeen and ran away, got in trouble, and she had only herself to blame for it. She could have done anything she wanted with her life, and she threw it away. I don't want the same for you, Leigh."

When she was older she would realize the old man was scared, that he was afraid she'd run away like Abby had done, drop out, disappear, put herself in the path of dangerous people. But at sixteen, Leigh had only thought he was being petty and small-minded, and immediately she'd been angry and wanted to punish him. "What are you saying?" she'd asked. "Are you sorry I was born, Pop?"

The old man had sighed. It was the first time she'd ever remembered him looking old—his face settling into a net of fine wrinkles, his sunburned skin softening into old age. "No, of course not. You know I love you. You know that I wouldn't trade you for a bag of gold."

"What, then? Do you think Jake's a bad person? That he's using me?"

"No, it's not that exactly," Gene had said. "But Jake's a farm boy, and he's happy being a farm boy. You have all these plans. You've been talking about moving to New York and becoming an editor since you were eight years old. Don't you want to make sure that happens?"

"What makes you think it won't happen?" she'd asked, but she'd known what he was thinking.

He didn't have anything to worry about, not yet. She and Jake hadn't slept together then, not that Leigh hadn't wanted to. It was Jake who said he wanted to wait. His girlfriend back in Kentucky—well, he'd told Leigh, the sex had just complicated everything. They'd moved too fast, and after a while he had realized she never cared about him the way he cared about her.

"This time I want everything to be perfect," he'd said. "I want us both to be ready, when it happens."

She had been surprised, but she respected him for it: he was waiting until he was sure, until she was sure. She hadn't known there were boys like that in the world. The losers Chloe always dated would have pounced as soon as they got the chance.

So when her grandfather had insinuated that she was risking her future by sleeping with Jake, Leigh had exploded at him. "You think I'm stupid enough to get pregnant? Well, I got news for you, Pop: *we aren't sleeping together.* Jake's a gentleman. He's never laid a hand on me, not the way you're thinking. You're the one with the dirty mind."

"Leigh—"

"You don't like Jake because he's the help. You think I should date boys with money, boys from rich families or with important daddies, is that it?"

"I never said—"

"I can't believe you're such an elitist. All that talk about pulling my own weight, following my ambition, it was just bullshit, wasn't it?"

Gene had blanched; she'd never dared to use profanities in front of him before.

"Here you are trying to breed me off like one of your mares, only the best bloodlines, the best pedigree. I might as well go on out to the breeding shed and let you pick my husband for me."

Gene's face had gone completely white then. "Enough, Leigh," he'd said quietly, but when she started to say something else he'd cut her off, his voice booming through the house: *"That is enough."*

She went silent. She'd gone too far now, and she knew it, but she was angry. She wanted to find a way to take back her words, but she couldn't, she wouldn't—he had no reason to think Jake was wrong for her, none but one, that Jake was the hired help. He wasn't good enough for Gene Merrill's granddaughter because he wasn't from a wealthy family, because he wasn't going to college or making any other grand plans. That was what galled her. That her grandfather, secretly, was something of a snob.

She'd been about to say something else to this effect, but her grandfather had cut her off with a sharp jab of his hand. "I want you to put an end to it. That's it. I'm finished with this discussion," he'd said. "Put an end to it, or Jake and his father are off this farm tomorrow. Don't test me on this, Leigh. I've said my piece, now I expect you to obey."

Before she could have said anything else, he was out the door, leaving Leigh behind to scream at the walls in frustration. Why wouldn't he listen? Why did he have to be so *unreasonable*? She'd started to have an understanding of what Abby had gone through with Gene all those years ago. The old man had said his piece, and that was the end of the discussion.

After that she and Jake were never allowed to be alone together. Gene must have said something to Jake's father, insisted Ben put a stop to their romance or else, because Ben made sure to load Jake up with chores every day after school, mucking stalls, working the race-horses, even letting him break a few of the yearlings. Keeping him too busy for romance.

Always, always she and Jake still managed to find each other again, after supper, late at night, a few minutes in the hayloft, where they could talk in secret, where they could kiss and cling to each other, promising their love, making plans for the day they'd get out of there, the day they'd break free. Instead of keeping them apart, Gene's orders only cemented their connection to each other.

It was only a few days after Gene issued his decree, in fact, that Leigh and Jake slept together for the first time. She'd come home after school one day and found Jake gone. His father had sent him into town for some feed and other supplies, and Leigh, disappointed yet again, had gone into the house to do her homework and sulk. Her grand-father must have seen her bedroom door closed and knocked twice, softly. "Just checking in," he said, opening the door a crack.

She could see his face, tanned from the sun, out of the corner of her eye. He looked sad, but she would not give him her forgiveness, not yet, not after what he'd said and done. "Just checking that I'm alone, you mean," she said. She was lying on her stomach with her math book open in front of her. She wouldn't look him in the eye.

"Watch your tone, Leela," he said. "I put up with a lot of sass from you, but you know I'm right about this."

"You are *not* right about this."

"Enough," he said. Then he stomped back up the hallway and down the stairs while Leigh, in frustration, flung her book at the closed door.

She stayed in her room right through dinner and would have stayed in there all night if there hadn't been a knock on her window just past eleven, when she was starting to get sleepy and hungry, when the big house seemed as silent and lonely as a tomb. Then the *tap, tap* of pebbles hitting her window. She looked out, and there was Jake standing in the bright moonlight, in a clean blue T-shirt and jeans, grinning at her like a crazy fool. She raised the sash a little and said, "Are you nuts?"

"Must be," he said. "Come on out here."

"I can't. He'll hear me."

"Climb on out the window."

"Oh sure, no one will hear that."

"The longer we argue about it, the more likely he is to hear you."

Leigh groaned. "All right. Hold on."

She turned the light off in her bedroom to make her grandfather think she'd gone to bed, then raised the sash on the window and swung herself out onto the windowsill. Jake reached up and took her around the waist. She leaned back into him, and he eased her down, then spun her around to face him. "Look at that," he said. "I was wrong about you, that first day. You aren't a horse; you're a monkey."

"And you're still a talking ass."

"Ah, but I'm *your* talking ass."

"Lucky you," she said. She kissed him.

A noise around back startled them, and they went completely silent: it was her grandfather opening the window in his bedroom.

"The barn," Leigh whispered, and they went around across the lawn toward the stables, keeping to the shadows and away from the bright glow of the moon rising orange over the hills, staying low. In a minute they heard the scrape of the window closing again.

The stables were dark for the night and smelled of dust and creosote and leather polish and horseflesh. The horses nickered softly when they heard footsteps in the aisle, but Leigh gave them a reassuring *whoa there, hey there*, and they went quiet.

They went down to the tack room and found a stack of clean wool blankets. She took one, but under the bottom blanket she could just feel the cool metal of her grandfather's .357 Magnum. She picked up the corner of the wool and showed the gun to Jake.

"One of these days," she said, "the old man is going to get brave enough to open my door and realize I'm not there. When that happens, you'd better learn to run fast."

"He won't catch me."

"It's not catching you I'm worried about, it's shooting you. He's a hell of a shot, you know. He keeps this gun here for coyotes and horse thieves and debauchers of his granddaughter."

"He won't shoot me," Jake said. "Don't you fret."

They grabbed a blanket, then climbed up the ladder to the hayloft, the one place she was sure that no one would be that time of night, the one place she knew no one would look for them. She'd spent hours reading alone there when she was younger, trying to escape her list of after-school chores, dreaming of her future in New York. The hay was stacked in bricks, smelling sweetly of the fields in summertime, and the hayloft was hot even in the evening, holding on to the warmth of the day. Leigh spread the blanket over the carpet of hay littering the floor and flopped down on it. Jake lay down next to her, stretching out his full length and leaning over her.

A beam of moonlight was coming in through the open hatch of the hayloft. Below them they could hear the sounds of the horses moving in their stalls, stamping their feet, chewing a bit of hay. A breeze blew through the building, causing a wind chime outside to tinkle. Somewhere the old peacock, Peabody, was standing on a roof and giving his mournful cry: *ah-Ah! ah-Ah!*

In the dimness Jake was just a shadow, a deeper bit of darkness. His skin was hot where Leigh touched it—the back of his neck, his shoulders, the hard muscles on the back of each arm. His hands wound around her back, and he pulled her in for a kiss, long and slow, leaning into her until they were pressed together knees to chest.

She could feel his heartbeat under his ribs picking up speed like her own. Something was different. He seemed strangely intense, his touches longer, less tentative. There was a pressure in his fingers and breath that hadn't been there before, a question he was asking with his hands and his body. She realized suddenly that he was trembling.

"What's the matter?" she breathed.

"Nothing," he said, his hands stroking her hip, moving up toward her breast, the shiver working up from his core and making his voice shake as well. "I don't think I've ever been happier."

He found her nipple under her shirt, and her breath caught. "Me, too."

"Are you scared at all?"

"No," she said, and meant it. She trusted him completely. After all, it had been his idea to wait until the time was right, and it seemed the time was most certainly now. She knew he would never abuse her trust. He was worthy not only of her trust but of her passion. The time for caution was gone.

She slid her hand up his back, under his T-shirt, his skin velvety and a little damp, following the curve of his spine, the wings of his shoulder blades, the soft place at the base of his throat. She wanted to touch all of him, every bit of him. She sat up and pulled off his T-shirt, leaning back to look at him in the moonlight. He looked like a Greek statue, or a *David*, his skin marbled and white in the silvery light. The muscles of his chest and belly were flat, taut from working out of doors with the horses. A faint touch of stubble darkened his cheeks and the spot in the middle of his chest, and she kissed him there once, and felt him shudder.

She pulled him to his feet and undid the buckle of his belt, then the buttons on his jeans, and with a thump they both slid to the floor. He stepped out of his jeans and stood still.

"What is it?" he said.

"I've always wanted to look at you."

He looked down at himself and up again, abashed. She saw his hands clench and unclench, as if he were fighting the urge to cover himself, but she reached out and ran a finger up his leg from knee to hip and smiled when she heard him gasp. "Jesus," he said, his voice ragged.

"Too much?"

"No," he said, slightly breathless but grinning.

She ran another finger across his backside, enjoying the feeling of it clenching under her touch. She'd had no idea the power she could have over him, or how intoxicating that power could be—that she could tease him, seduce him, enjoy him all she wanted.

Jake's breath was coming in little gasps, his breastbone rising and falling quickly under her hands. She leaned forward and kissed the spot over his heart, then licked one of his nipples gently. She stood on her toes to reach his neck, then his mouth, all while Jake held himself still, willing himself not to move for fear of breaking the spell.

With one hand she cupped his buttocks, and with the other, she reached down to feel him hard against her thigh. She took him in her hand and felt his whole body shudder. "I can't—" he panted. "I can't—Leigh, please, please, Leigh, it has to be now."

She let go of him and stepped back, undoing her shirt, her jeans, letting them fall to the floor. Then she stood before him naked herself.

He crossed the space between them in two steps, picking her up and wrapping her legs around his waist, lowering her to the floor. She was surprised at how strong he was. His lips moved to her ears, her neck. Her body was dissolving into his, the margins between them evaporating. He put his mouth on her nipples, and she panted. "Jake," she said. "Jake, please don't make me wait anymore."

His mouth on her neck, her breasts. His mouth on the deepest place inside her, his tongue, his wetness melting into her own. Her hands on the back of his hair, on the silk of his shoulders, and she pulled him up to kiss him again before bending over to slide the condom on. Then she lay back and arched her hips to let him ease into her. A quick burst of pain and then it was done, more smoothly than she had imagined. He moved over her, hips pushing into her softness, into the ache, her body so lit with desire she no longer had any sense of where she stopped and he began.

She grabbed him and pulled him into her, deeper, nothing but his body and hers curled around the epicenter of pleasure. He lifted her hips to pull him to her, thrusting until the world went white, and her whole body shuddered. Jake cried out once, twice, and then collapsed on top of her, his weight pleasantly heavy, his neck slick with sweat.

He stroked her hair in the moonlight, rolled off her, and lay quiet while she put her head on his shoulder. It had been surprising only in that she'd enjoyed it more than she would have thought, given what Chloe and the other girls at school always said—that it was usually fast, and painful, and awkward. But maybe it was different when you really loved someone, she thought. Maybe Jake had been right to make them both wait until they were sure what they meant to each other. But as she lay there with her head on his chest, her body still tingling with pleasure, the only thing she was sorry about was that in the morning they'd have to go back to pretending in front of their families that nothing had happened, nothing had changed, when all she wanted was to shout from the rooftops that she loved him, that she was his now and always.

When she thought she could speak, she looked over at him and said, "Think you could do that again?"

He laughed. "Give me a minute," he said. "I'm sure I could manage."

Afterward they were inseparable, insatiable, finding each other in the hayloft, at the lake, in the woods. They were careful, so careful not to get caught—Gene still swore to Leigh that he'd fire Ben at the first hint that Jake wasn't keeping his hands to himself—but there was hardly ever a day they didn't find at least five minutes to spend together, hardly ever a day when they didn't have a chance to sneak a kiss in the tack room, a quick *I love you* between chores.

They managed to keep their relationship a secret from Gene, but Jake's dad was another story. Ben Rhodes watched them all the time, always aware that his job was on the line if Jake slipped up even a little. He hated Leigh for it, too, staying close whenever she was in the barn, never letting her out of his sight, yet he never spoke to her, just followed her with his eyes wherever she went, a scowl of disgust on his face.

Jake, who was a year ahead of Leigh, graduated high school and started learning the business in earnest from his dad, who sent him on errands to the vet's, to town, even long trips to deliver horses to buyers, anything to keep him away from the farm as long as possible. Sometimes he would go to Oklahoma, Missouri, Florida, staying away for days or even weeks at a time. Ben had his training partner, the dirty-minded, foulmouthed Dale Tucker, keep Jake out in the training pens for long stretches, working the horses on the lead lines, taking them through their paces on the test track. There was so much work to do on the farm that there always seemed to be some new excuse for Ben to keep them apart. That Christmas, Ben even sent Jake away to his mother's back in Kentucky for a couple of weeks, maybe hoping he might see his old girlfriend there, that he and Amy would be tempted to pick up where they'd left off.

The night he left, Jake had come to meet her, to tell her he'd be home soon. They slipped into the hayloft after dark, where he told her where he was going and when he'd be back, kissing her long and deeply. "Don't forget about me," he said.

"Never." Two weeks was hardly long enough for her to forget him, she wanted to say, but then they'd never been apart that long before.

"Look," he said, pulling up one sleeve of his white T-shirt, "I had it done today."

On the back of one arm was the small dark shape of a bat. "It's our secret. To remind us of the day in the cave, so I can carry you with me forever."

Afterward they'd made love in the hayloft and she'd touched the tattoo gently, feeling the place where the skin was raised, the permanent reminder of the day when they'd first declared their love to each other. She'd loved it, and him, more than ever. It didn't matter where he went, she'd be with him.

Whatever their families did to keep them apart, though, Leigh and Jake weren't deterred. He called her every day he was in Kentucky, sent her letters almost by the hour. They swore their love for each other, swore they'd be together no matter what his father and her grandfather had to say about it.

All they had to do, Jake decided, was grow up. When Leigh reached the magic age of eighteen, they'd be free to do as they liked. They had to be patient, and wait, and it would turn out all right in the end. Leigh wasn't sure she could wait that long, but Jake told her to keep her grades up and her nose clean, and before long they'd be old enough to go where they wanted, live how they wanted. "It's just a few more months," he said.

"A year," she wheedled. "A whole year, Jake."

"*Just* a year," he said. "Be strong. I know you can be."

So Leigh did what he said: she kept her grades up, stayed out of any serious trouble. She didn't party every weekend like most of the kids she knew; if she wasn't at home doing homework or chores, she was with Chloe, maybe hanging out in Austin, seeing some live shows, watching Chloe audition for band after band. Sometimes Jake would sneak away and meet up with them. Leigh always called home to let her grandfather know where she was; she kept her curfew religiously, stopped talking back to the old man. She and Jake would come home in separate cars, at different times, as if they hadn't been together.

She would give Gene no reason to come down on her. She was respectful and courteous and did exactly what she liked when he wasn't looking, just the way her mother had done, and it worked: Gene relaxed, stopped arguing with her so much. As long as he didn't know the truth, it seemed, he was happy.

During her senior year Leigh was at the top of her high-school class. She'd already been admitted to Harvard—she'd hardly been able to believe it when the acceptance package arrived—but even before she held the letter in her hands, she'd known it would be impossible to live without Jake in Boston. She knew in her heart that she couldn't take classes and make new friends and talk to Jake once or twice a week, go months and months without seeing him, touching him.

After Christmas, Leigh started talking about going to the University of Texas instead, staying close to home. Jake didn't like that, said she was being shortsighted, that most people would give anything they had, everything, to get into the best college in the country. "I can't let you give up Harvard," he said. "Not on my account."

"I can't go now," Leigh said one night not long after New Year's. The hayloft was cool in midwinter, and she could almost see her breath in front of her face. Jake sat up and put her on his lap, wrapping them both in a heavy wool blanket. "Let's just say I go to UT. I can commute from home, or maybe get an apartment with Chloe in Austin. You can work with your dad until you get your own training business going. Then we can go anywhere we want, do anything we want."

"You're going to Harvard. Period."

"Now you sound like my grandfather."

"The old man's just looking out for you."

"Ugh. Now you *really* sound like him."

"We will call a lot, see each other over vacations. This is your dream, your chance to get out of Burnside."

"It won't be the same without you." Leigh shivered, though not just from the cold. "I mean it, I think I might die if I have to go months and months without seeing you. Two weeks at Christmas last year was torture."

Jake was thoughtful for a minute, quiet. In the time since he'd graduated high school he'd grown quieter in general, more serious. She knew he had a lot on his mind—it wasn't easy working for his dad and living on someone else's place, a position that was always in jeopardy because he was in love with the boss's granddaughter. For weeks she'd felt it: Jake had a lot on his mind. He was getting ready to make some kind of decision, and for weeks she had dreaded hearing what it might be. Moving away. Getting a job someplace, starting his own business. Leaving her behind.

Finally he said, "Let's get married."

For a minute Leigh wasn't sure she'd heard him right. "What?"

"You and me, kid. What do you say?"

"You aren't serious."

"As a heart attack. I've always known I was going to marry you one day. Why should we wait? We'll get married and go to Boston together."

"My grandfather will cut me off, for one thing."

"I don't care."

"I can't pay for school on my own. Pop's money is the only reason I can afford Harvard."

"We won't tell him. You can live off campus. We'll get an apartment. You tell him you got a roommate."

"You think no one's going to notice you're gone?"

"I'll tell my dad I'm going back to Kentucky to live with some friends."

"We won't be able to keep it up for long."

"Sure we will. Long enough to get settled, anyway. After that it won't matter. You think your granddad will shoot me if we're married? No way. Not when it's all legal."

Leigh imagined her grandfather doing exactly that, showing up unannounced in Boston one day, just dropping in. Wanted to see how you're doing, Leela. Making sure you're okay. And then what he would do if he found Jake there, if he saw that they were living together. She imagined police sirens and ambulances and Jake in a body bag, and she wasn't entirely sure she was exaggerating.

But maybe Jake was right—if they were already married, if they were respectably and legally wed, maybe her grandfather would manage to live with it eventually. He was old-fashioned; he believed in going to church on Sunday, in holy matrimony, in babies born in wedlock. He might not like it, but he wouldn't punish Leigh after the deed was done. Her mother had come home pregnant and unmarried—that was what had galled Gene, that she'd had a child without a father. Leigh started to think Jake was right, that marriage was their only way out of this mess. She'd have college and Jake and her grandfather's grudging approval. In time he'd learn to accept Jake. He'd have to.

Jake flung the blanket off his shoulders and got down on one knee, taking her hand in his. "I love you, Leigh Elizabeth Merrill. Will you marry me? Will you please be my wife?"

Leigh could hardly breathe, but she choked out a yes. Jake gave a yelp of joy and caught her in a tight embrace, and they made love in the darkness of the hayloft with the moon shining through the window, secure in the knowledge that they would now be together forever, that there would be no force the world could muster that would keep them apart.

It all had to be done quickly, but legally. A few days after she turned eighteen, at the end of June, they'd go on down to the courthouse and get married. That summer Jake would tell his father that a couple of his friends back in Lexington had invited him to share an apartment with them, that he'd get a job at one of the stables there, start making his own way. Then he'd pack up his old Ford truck, drive up to Boston, and meet Leigh. They'd find an apartment. Jake would find a job. Leigh had some money she'd saved up—not a lot, but enough to live on for a few months until her college fund from Gene came through. So simple.

Afterward it was all they could do to keep their plans a secret. Nearly every night Jake would come to her window, tossing his little pebbles on the glass—*tap, tap*—and she'd climb out to him, kissing him fiercely in the darkness. They'd go to their place in the hayloft, lie on the blanket in the soft straw, and make love eagerly, struggling to keep their voices down, keep from getting caught. They clung to each other in a haze of sex and sweat, Jake's mouth devouring her neck, her breasts, Jake's hands pinning her down while she writhed beneath him and came so hard she thought she might faint. Her cries were so loud that Jake often had to hold his hand over her mouth to keep her grandfather from hearing a quarter mile off.

When it was over they would talk about their plans, the kind of apartment they'd look for in Boston, the classes Leigh would take, the kind of job Jake might find. Leigh said there'd be plenty of places near the city where he could look for a stable-hand job, but Jake didn't want to, said he didn't want to trade on his father's name, or Gene's, not after they were married. It was just like him to be too proud, to try to prove himself. The Honorable Jacob Rhodes, Chloe always called him. Instead he wanted to learn a trade, maybe take some classes himself at the community college. "Maybe I'll try tending bar," he'd say. "That might be fun. Get to meet a lot of girls that way."

Leigh had swatted him on his bare ass. "Like hell. After we're married, no more girls for you, mister. Besides, you're not old enough yet to tend bar."

"They won't know that." He pulled out the fake ID, the one he'd used a bunch of times to sneak into bars in Austin. "Got me a little insurance."

"Oh good. I'm sure they won't do a background check."

"I'll just use my considerable charm."

"Or you'll sound like a talking ass."

"Won't be the first time," he said, and stopped her from replying with a kiss.

The stress on both of them, the waiting, was palpable. Leigh was impatient with her grandfather again, started talking back in ways she had never before dared. The good sense of their plan, the safety she felt now being so close to her goal, made her reckless. She called Gene a snob, an elitist, whenever Jake's name came up, said there was nothing wrong with Jake except his lack of money, and for long periods of time she and Gene would go through the house without speaking, barely acknowledging each other's presence.

Jake started arguing with his father more often, too. She'd find the two of them in the barn from time to time, coming around the corner to hear Ben's voice raised to a furious whisper. *You'll do what I tell you to do, and that's that,* he'd say, and Jake would answer, *You know it's wrong. You know, but you won't stop it.* The two of them would fall silent when they saw Leigh approaching, and she'd give Jake a poignant look, as if to say, *This will all be worth it later. It will all be worth it, I swear.*

Of course it wasn't Leigh that Jake and his father were arguing about, but she wouldn't know that until later, until the trial. When she found out what they were really fighting over, she'd felt foolish, even duped.

The truth was that Ben and his partner, Dale Tucker, had been doping her grandfather's horses for years, using injections of steroids to cover up limps caused by training injuries, to cover up their own mistakes. They'd started to pull Jake into their secret, too—all those trips he'd taken for his father, Leigh would find out later, were to pick up the drugs for them, to hide what they were up to.

Jake had argued with them that it was wrong, that it was Gene Merrill's reputation on the line as well as their own. That the horses would suffer for their mistakes. But he hadn't stopped, had he? He'd kept right on going, picking up the steroids, helping Dale and his father break the rules. He hadn't told anyone about the doping, not even Leigh, not once in all the nights they spent together. He lied to her about his trips out of state, the work he did for his father. The delivery of the horses was always a pretext, a way for Ben and Dale to keep their noses clean. Ben could have sent anyone to deliver horses, but he sent his own son to make sure that the secret stayed hidden.

It wasn't until later, at the trial, that details of the doping scheme came out. Jake pleaded guilty to the drug charges and was sentenced to four years on that count. Afterward, at the murder trial, he would take the stand and admit what he and Dale Tucker had been up to, admit his own role in the scheme, although he never mentioned his father's involvement. Jake put the whole thing on Dale. It was Dale Tucker whom he had gone to see in the barn the night of the shooting, he said. Not a lame horse, the way he and Leigh had first said.

"And why were you wanting to meet with Dale Tucker when you got back to the ranch?" asked Jake's lawyer.

"Dale was anxious to get his hands on the steroids," Jake said. "I'd just come from Florida with a shipment. He needed them for the farm's best colt, which had come up lame in practice earlier in the week. He was racing in less than a week, and if he didn't improve in a hurry he was going to miss the whole season. There was hundreds of thousands in breeding fees on the line. Millions, probably."

"So you fetched the drugs, and brought them back to give to Dale?"

"I did. I got back late and met Dale in the barn."

"Then why did you argue? If you picked up the steroids as requested, and you were planning to give them to him, why didn't you simply hand them over and walk away?"

Jake raised his head to look at Leigh, just for a moment. "I told Dale I wouldn't do it anymore, fetching the dope for him. That I was done lying. That's why he went after me, because I told him I was going to tell Leigh everything. He said he'd kill me before he'd let that happen."

Leigh would meet his eyes across the courtroom, his familiar dark blue eyes, and see the shame there, the admission of guilt, and she'd realize the truth of it all—that Jake had been helping his father illegally dope her grandfather's horses, that he'd been running drugs for Ben and Dale for months. That he'd lied to her. It had been happening under her nose all the time, and she hadn't even known.

Five

I deserve this terror. I deserve this darkness, after what I did. I deceived you, and I allowed myself to be deceived. I won't let myself be a curse on your life anymore. When I think of you safe and whole, getting ready to head off to Harvard, I know I'm doing the right thing. I can atone for both of us.

I already know I won't send this letter to you. I already know it will upset you. I don't want you to think about doing something foolish. You can't save me. Only I can do that.

I hope you can forgive me for today. For everything.

Leigh set Jake's letter down and held on to the table. The room was spinning, the sunlight streaming in through the windows making everything too bright, too hot. She could hear the echo of Jake's voice in every word, the slight Kentucky twang he'd clung to even after years in Texas: *I know that I'm doing the right thing.*

But she didn't think so, not anymore. Maybe she'd never thought it was the right thing. Maybe she'd never been able to let go of the guilt, her own culpability. A man had died by her hand, and she'd let someone else suffer for it. Someone she'd loved; someone she'd promised to marry. What kind of person did that? What kind of person sat in a courtroom for weeks and weeks and listened to the man she loved lie for her, sacrifice himself for her? The fact that she would try to put a stop to it eventually didn't change all the hours she'd sat there listening to his lies, the lies he told to protect her.

Now I think it would be wrong for me to intrude on your new life. No hard feelings, read the note he'd left on top of the bundles of letters. It made her want to scream. No hard feelings? How could he say that—how could he even think it? After everything?

The Honorable Jacob Rhodes, still torturing himself over his mistakes, still trying to make up for his father's sins. He might even have managed to convince himself he was doing the right thing, for a time. But if there was one thing Leigh was sure of now, it was that no one could outrun the mistakes they'd made.

She couldn't walk away this time without another word. She couldn't let him shut her out, not again. She had to talk to him.

She opened the door and went running out into the sunlight of the vineyard, shading her eyes to look for him on the paths, the dining pavilion, the cool groves of live oaks where groups of writers sat in little clusters talking to each other or scribbling in notebooks. Jake had to be nearby, still—he couldn't have gotten far, not if he'd delivered the bundles of letters to her room in the few minutes she'd been eating lunch. He was somewhere on the property, somewhere nearby. She had to find him.

She went full speed down the hill toward the main house and the parking lot. It was like running in a dream, except she was wide-awake. Clusters of people sat in rocking chairs on the front porch. She ran when she saw a man in a brown Stetson near the far end, talking to someone, but when she put her hand on his arm she saw he was only a gray-haired cowboy in a jacket and jeans who looked up, surprised by her attention. Not Jake.

She'd been secretly hoping he might have been waiting inside for her, but the lobby of the main house had the usual assortment of conferencegoers and staff, and nowhere did she see the white T-shirt, the tattoo of a bat in flight on the back of one triceps. But he had to be here, somewhere. He *had to be.* He'd come to her talk that morning, then delivered a bundle of letters to her cottage. He had to want to be found. Didn't he?

She went back outside into the bright Texas sun. She had no car—Chloe had driven her from Austin to the vineyard—and no way to get ahold of Jake. He'd never owned a cell phone before he went to prison, and even if he'd bought one after he got out, she didn't know the number. Chloe was away in Austin for the day. Leigh was stuck. She stood in the middle of the gravel parking lot wondering which way to go, which direction to run, turning around and around until Saundra arrived and took her firmly by the shoulders, holding her still.

"My goodness, honey," she said, "whatever has you turning in circles?"

Leigh didn't even know where to begin. The only thing she could think was that perhaps Saundra had access to a car, something she wouldn't mind lending Leigh for a few hours to run an errand in town. "It's kind of an emergency," she said. "There's someone I need to find, and fast."

"A man?"

Leigh colored. "Yes, but it's not like that."

Saundra raised her eyebrows at her as if she'd heard *that* before. But still she handed over the keys to her Prius and told Leigh with a wink she'd need it back no later than breakfast the following morning. "Any later than that," she said, "and it will turn back into a pump-kin. Understand?"

Leigh threw both arms around the older woman. "Thank you so much. You have no idea how much this means to me." Keys in hand, she took off toward the parking lot. Jake couldn't have gotten far.

She started to formulate a plan as she turned down the vineyard driveway and then west on the state highway, flooring it. She'd start in Burnside; that's where Chloe said she'd first seen Jake, eating dinner at Dot's by himself one night. She kept scanning the highway the whole drive, spying tourists with Georgia plates slowing down to take pictures, a family dressed in identical white shirts and jeans having their picture taken in a field of bluebonnets, a hitchhiker in a long beard wearing a backpack and a T-shirt that read KEEP AUSTIN WEIRD. Not much had changed in a decade. This was the Texas she remembered—beautiful, conflicted, with the wide-open skies she'd missed so much.

She went west first, then north, following the river, feeling a kind of desperation rising in her throat while she scanned the roads for any sign of Jake's red truck, not seeing it anywhere, assuming he still had it. All these years, she'd wondered what he was doing, how he was, whether they would be able to move on and forgive each other for what had happened. Ten years she'd been waiting, holding herself back, either out of guilt or maybe hoping that somehow, when Jake was finally released, they could go back to the way things had been, that it would all be the same as it had been before.

Now she knew she didn't want to go back to the way things had been. They'd been kids; they'd been young, impulsive, and foolish. It would never have worked in Boston, the two of them married and living together—how could she ever have thought otherwise?

She'd have been the only freshman at Harvard with a husband. He'd have hated living in such a big city, hated tending bar or waiting tables, and she'd have hated being eighteen and already settled down. After a while she and Jake would have grown apart, grown to resent each other. It was only desperation that had led them to promise themselves to each other in the first place. Desperation, and the thrill of the forbidden. But the forbidden wasn't enough to build a life on. She knew that now. She simply had to say it to Jake in person, so they could both move on.

She pulled into Burnside just after four, parking the car in front of the drugstore and stepping outside. She'd run after Jake without her sunglasses and sunscreen, and she could feel the hot May sun burning her nose and cheeks, but she kept going, down the dusty streets of downtown, the heat rising up from the baking concrete. Behind the shops there were glints of the river, cool and gray, the occasional boat speeding past.

She looked in every shop window, poked her head in the door of the two honky-tonks, the post office, even the library. She texted Chloe to ask for help, but Chloe had rehearsals in Austin all afternoon and didn't answer right away. Leigh paused at a newish Chinese restaurant on the corner and stuck her head inside, the hostess at the front door looking at her like she must be crazy, and Leigh glanced down at her sweat-stained clothes and started to think she really *was* crazy.

Maybe he'd left town. Maybe he wasn't living in Burnside at all anymore. He could be living in Austin, in San Marcos, even one of the other little towns like New Braunfels, Granite Shoals. He could be back home, wherever he was living now, planning to let her go on with her life without him, like he'd written in his note.

She was chasing a phantom. She must be out of her mind.

Except she couldn't walk away, not now, when she hadn't been able to walk away for ten long years. It didn't matter what she'd written him in that last letter; she'd never let him go, not really. She'd held back from Joseph, she'd held back from every man she'd ever met, because there was always the question of Jake, of what she and Jake would do when he was finally released. He might have been in a physical prison, but Leigh had lived in a prison of her own making, unwilling or unable to grant herself parole.

Now, as she caught sight of her reflection in the window of a shop on Main Street—her wild hair and clothes, her skin pink with sunburn—she realized she'd been naive to cling to the hope that they could simply pick up the pieces. Jake was a thirty-year-old ex-con whose only skill was training horses, and people in the horse-training world would distrust and despise him because he was Ben Rhodes's kid.

She couldn't picture him walking with her down Broadway to see a show on a Friday night, meeting her for drinks at an upscale restaurant in SoHo. Even if she could convince him to come with her to New York, she didn't have the faintest idea what he'd do there. Drive a cab? Be a house husband? He'd hate living in such a big city, hate how expensive it was, hate the noise and the crowds and the attitude. And Leigh sure as hell wasn't about to torpedo the publishing career she'd built so carefully to come back to Texas and do—what? Edit tractor manuals? Wait tables? Sing in bars with Chloe?

No—it wouldn't work. She had to say good-bye to the hope she'd been clinging to all these years, that when Jake got out for good, they'd be able to pick up the pieces. Before she could give Joseph an answer to his proposal, before she could even think about being his wife, she had to say good-bye to Jake once and for all.

The problem, though, was that she couldn't find him anywhere. He wasn't at Dot's. He wasn't at the Foxhead. He wasn't at Booches. By the time she gave up looking for him, she was hot and tired, and the sun was starting to go down.

Chloe texted back that she was sorry, she'd been in rehearsals all afternoon without her phone. But, she asked, if Leigh was free did she want to grab a bite? Leigh was footsore and discouraged, and texted back, SURE, LET ME GRAB A SHOWER FIRST.

Leigh was about to get in Saundra's Prius to head back to the vine-yard just as the sun was sinking behind the hills, lighting up the river in pink and gold. She loved the river—when she and Chloe and Jake were kids, they'd head to the end of the long dock after dark and sit cooling their feet in the water, sometimes joined by their friends around town, sometimes not.

Leigh walked down to the water and stood on the shore, looking out at the sun's reflection. It was dusk—in a few minutes, when the sun went down, the colonies of bats that lived in the caves up in the hills would come out for the night. It seemed strange that bats could be so lovely, but they were. The sight of them was one of the few things Leigh had looked forward to when she came home to Texas. She waited, watching the sun's reflection washing the world gold. It sank down and down, the light changing over to pink, then orange, purple shadows creeping up from the east.

The first bat swooped past, followed by another, then another. If you didn't look too closely you'd think they were birds, the small dark forms fluttering here and there, but they didn't move like birds, didn't swoop gracefully on the air. Instead they flitted and chittered like mosquitoes, following their sense of hearing, calling to each other and listening to the echoes coming off the water, the hills, the trees. The bats flew past in a great black cloud, then rising into the air, went off in the night to hunt for bugs.

Leigh remembered the day she first kissed Jake, in the darkness of Mammoth Cave after the bats had gone, and felt an ache that she knew would always be there, the ache of regret. She'd never be able to look at the bats again without thinking of him, no matter whom she married.

But she could let Jake go. She had to. If she didn't, she'd never be whole again.

"Leigh."

She didn't turn. If she didn't turn, she wouldn't have to see him, wouldn't have to say good-bye to the one hope she'd been clinging to for the last ten years of her life: that he still loved her, that he didn't blame her, that once he was released they'd be able to move forward together. If she didn't turn she wouldn't have to tell him what she'd come to tell him—that she couldn't see him again, that it was over. She was marrying Joseph and going back to New York, and that was that.

"Leigh. Leela." He put a hand on her shoulder and turned her around slowly to face him. She raised her eyes into his familiar dark blue ones, the ones she hadn't looked into once since that day in the courtroom all those years ago, when the foreman had stood in front of everyone and read that awful verdict. Guilty. Guilty of murder.

But now here he was again, taller than she remembered, tall in his cowboy boots, his eyes full of doubt, even fear. The ache she'd felt in her gut tightened, a feeling so old and familiar she'd almost forgotten about it. Here it was, the moment she'd waited more than a decade for. Jake was out. Jake was free. And he was standing in front of her, waiting for her to say . . . something.

"I've been looking for you all day. Where the hell have you *been*?" she said, and then burst into tears.

Six

The week before the shooting Jake's father had sent him to Florida, ostensibly to see another trainer about a horse her grandfather was thinking of buying, but Leigh wasn't so sure. For weeks Jake's jobs for his dad had been taking him farther and farther away, to meet with people in parking lots and under bridges, dicey prospects that had Leigh worried sick. She had begged him not to go, said she was afraid of some of the men his father sent him to see, but Jake said it would be all right, he'd be safe and home in no time.

"Anyway, you don't know the people I'm going to talk to," he said, his voice taking on a hard edge of defensiveness. She knew he didn't like it when she criticized his dad or Dale. "These men, they're hard workers. Horsemen. They know things about the business. Things that will help all of us."

"I know things about the business, too," Leigh said, her voice rising. "I've been around horses all my life. I'm in the barn the same as you. I feed, I muck the same as you."

"Not the same as me," Jake said quietly.

"I don't trust some of your dad's 'business associates,' Jake. I don't think you should either."

"I have to," he said. "You don't understand. My dad's the best trainer in the business. He knows what he's doing. If I could have half the success my father has, I'll think I've really made it." He raked his hand through his dark curly hair, making it stand up black in the summer heat. "Just trust *me,* okay? Can you do that much?"

"No."

"No?"

"Not when it comes to Ben. You have blinders on, Jake. I don't know what's happening, but I don't like it."

"You don't have to like it, but just please, don't do anything foolish."

"Like what?"

"I don't know. Just keep your distance from my dad, and Dale. Don't pick any fights. They're already jumpy. It's just for a little while longer, until we can get out of here."

Leigh had walked off in a huff. But she wasn't going to let him off that easily. "Fine," she said. "Go on to Florida. See if I care."

"Don't do that," he said. "Don't get angry. It's just something I have to do."

"Yes, well," she said, "this is just something *I* have to do." And she kept walking.

She expected him to come after her as she crossed the yard and went into the house, but he didn't try to stop her. She sat inside all afternoon, waiting, until she finally saw his truck pull out of the half-moon driveway not long before supper. She couldn't believe he hadn't come after her, that he had left anyway.

She played the scene over again and again in her mind. Maybe she should not have been so bitter about it. Maybe she should have apologized. She trusted his judgment, didn't she? But it was too late—he'd already left.

Jake was gone for nearly a week, a week with no calls, no messages. Nothing. Leigh had fretted the whole time, worried that something might happen to him on the road, that she wouldn't get a chance to talk to him, to apologize. Every moment without him left her with a physical ache of regret and worry.

It was unusually hot that May, and Leigh had been cranky and restless, unable to enjoy the graduation parties, the talk of the colleges her friends were heading to, the jobs they were taking. Whenever anyone asked her about Harvard, she froze, then did her best to sound nonchalant about the subject, bored even, like it was yesterday's news. No one—not even Chloe—knew that she and Jake planned to get married the day she turned eighteen at the end of June, that Jake was coming with her to Boston. The slightest whiff of their plans and her grandfather would fire Ben Rhodes, send him away, and God only knew where they'd go or when she'd see Jake after that.

On the day Jake had promised to be back, Leigh rushed home after school. She ran to the barn to see if he was there, but when she looked in the tack room, in the feed room, in the hayloft, she was greeted by nothing but dust and the quizzical looks of the many farmhands who worked for her grandfather.

The old man, too, was distracted—he had the vet out again, the third time in two months, to put down a young colt, one of the farm's most promising yearlings, because one of the horse's back legs had come up lame after his last practice. Nothing anyone had tried had done any good. The colt was damaged.

With two injections, the vet put him down. Her grandfather was heartbroken. "Damn," he said, stroking the horse's brown neck as his breathing slowed, then stopped. "The best one of the lot, too."

"I'm sorry, Pop," Leigh said. She knew how hard he took the loss of any one of his horses. She hesitated, folded her arms. She wanted to mourn the colt but had other things on her mind. She couldn't ask her grandfather if he'd seen Jake—the old man would take her head off for sure.

Instead she kept looking for him in the tractor garage, the practice ring. Frustrated, she made the mistake of heading into the breeding shed, where Dale Tucker was setting up for one of the mares to be covered by the stud, Blizzard, Leigh's own childhood pet, now among her grandfather's best horses.

Leigh had seen Dale standing inside, and hesitated. The two of them had never seen eye to eye about the horses; she thought he was too rough with them, ran them too hard and too often, but whenever she spoke to him about it, he only said, "Thank you, Your Highness," and went back to doing just as he pleased. Since he worked for her grandfather, not her, there wasn't much she could do to get rid of him, but she'd taken to avoiding him over the years, tried not to speak to him unless she had no other choice. She always remembered the way he looked at her that first day he'd arrived on the ranch, when she'd arrived braless and soaking wet from her afternoon swim. As if he were sizing her up for sale, or worse.

That day, as she poked her head in the big double doors of the breeding shed, she saw no one except Dale holding the mare's bridle, waiting for Ben to bring Blizzard in from his pen. Dale saw her at the same time as the mare, who whinnied a greeting. Leigh froze with one foot turned in flight, but it was too late.

Dale tugged on the mare's rope and gave Leigh an evil grin. "Hear that?" he said. "She's all ready for it. Ready for the stud to come in and give it to her. Likes it rough, too. Soon as the old boy comes in, she'll be raring to go, won't she?"

Leigh had stood very still, like a rabbit sensing a fox. Somehow Dale had thought having a secret over Leigh—knowing the truth about her and Jake—gave him the right to talk to her like that. For more than a year she'd been listening to taunts like this from him, had grown to hate and distrust the sight of him, his filthy baseball caps that read FBI: FEMALE BODY INSPECTOR, and DON'T BE SEXIST! BITCHES HATE THAT. The heavy smell of his cheap cologne. His eyes, looking her up and down. Leigh had held her head up and turned to go, but Dale came up close to her, came closer than he had any right to. The smell of his sweat and the tobacco on his breath was so overpowering she nearly gagged.

She stepped back. "Do you mind?"

Dale stepped in closer, his breath hot, his small, piglike eyes burning into her. "What's the matter? Don't like me as much as that boy of yours? He's just a kid. If you want to learn the ropes, you'll need a man."

"I'll be sure to let you know when I see one."

"Oh, you're seeing one, all right," said Dale. He leaned into her, so close their noses almost touched. Leigh refused to give an inch, to back down to this disgusting excuse for a man.

"I think you like what you see, too," Dale said, reaching down to cup his hand around her breast.

For one long moment he stood there with his filthy hand on her. Leigh looked around, but there was no one; they were completely alone. The only person who might come in was Ben, and he wouldn't side with her, not against his own partner. She knew enough about Ben to know that he hated her, hated that Jake loved her, that her grandfather had threatened his job because of her. No—she was on her own with Dale Tucker.

She pushed him back with two hands against his chest, spooking the mare.

"What's the matter?" he said. "No one's here. No one will see."

She took two steps back and said, "You keep your hands off me."

He laughed. "You think you can just walk away? If I want you, I'll take you, and there won't be a damn thing you can do to stop me."

She was trying to think, to look around for a weapon, for something. Her grandfather's gun was far away, back in the tack room of the barn. Might as well be a million miles. "I would stop you," she said, her voice trembling. "I'd kill you if I had to."

He laughed. "You couldn't hurt me. You're a good girl. You'll take it all, and it will be so sweet. You're gonna like it so much, you'll thank me afterward."

"Not in a million years."

He kept coming, closer and closer. She started to realize she might have to fight him off with her bare hands, that even as short as he was, it wouldn't take much for him to overpower her. She should never have come to the shed alone. She should never have thought she was safe.

She was backing toward the door now. It would all be okay as long as she got out, got back to the house.

But Dale couldn't resist one last gibe: "Where're you going, honey?" he asked. "Show's just about to start. I *know* you're just dying to stay around and watch." She backed up slowly. "No? Then I guess I'll be seeing you later." She took off to the sound of his harsh laughter.

She'd gone back to the house feeling shaken to her core, sitting alone in her room in tears, angry that a man like Dale Tucker had felt so free to put his hands on her, that he'd looked at her and spoken to her like she was something he owned. She couldn't go to her grandfather and tell him what had happened; Dale would surely tell Gene about Leigh and Jake. No—she'd have to deal with Dale Tucker on her own.

All afternoon and into the evening Leigh sat in the window watching the half-moon driveway, where Jake would pull up when he came home. Her room seemed to get smaller and smaller, the world outside bigger and bigger, when she thought of Jake alone out in that world, all the things that could happen to him before they had a chance to make up. A carjacking. An accident. Jake trapped in a ditch in his overturned truck for days and days. And she could admit it—she felt naked without him there, standing between herself and a man like Dale Tucker. If Jake had been there, Dale would never have touched her, not in a million years.

When he wasn't home by dinner, she was nervous; by midnight, when he still hadn't returned, she was terrified. Something had happened. *Where are you, Jake?* she wondered. *Why aren't you home?* She vowed that next day, first thing, she was buying him a cell phone no matter how much he objected.

Not long after midnight, when her room was so close and small that she felt suffocated, Leigh at last saw the lights of Jake's truck heading into the driveway and coming to rest outside the stables. She watched him climb out of the cab and open the barn door, slipping inside in darkness. The moon was up, and as she raised the sash on her window and climbed out of the house, she could see her own shadow on the grass. She crossed the yard toward the open door of the barn, dark and yawning like a mouth.

When she came close she heard an argument in progress, something angry from Jake, another voice answering. The two voices were lowered, nearly whispering, but there was no mistaking the hostility in them. She crept closer to listen. "I don't care. I don't care what you do to me anymore, I'm done. I'm finished with this, Dale, I mean it," Jake was saying, and Dale Tucker answered, "You're not done till we say you're done. You're not done, or you know what comes next."

"I don't care anymore. I'm telling Leigh everything. I'm telling her tonight."

Dale laughed. "You wouldn't dare, because you know how pissed she'll be. She'll never speak to you again."

"She will. She trusts me."

"Oh yeah, she trusts you, all right. That girl doesn't know the first thing about what's going on here. What do you think she'll do if you tell her? Think she'll thank you? Think she'll still open up her long legs for you then?"

Leigh froze. They didn't hear her. They didn't know she was there. What was really going on here? What had Jake been holding back?

Dale thought he was safe, so he kept talking. "If you want to start your own training business someday, you'll keep quiet. You spill your guts to Leigh or Gene, to anyone in this business, and no one will hire you. Your future depends on being the son of Ben Rhodes, superstar. You screw us, you're only hurting yourself."

"My future," Jake said, "is none of your goddamn business. I can make my own way from now on."

"You couldn't make your own way on a bus, Jake. If you want to train, if you want to trade on your old man's name, you're going to want that name to be a good one. Remember that."

"I don't want to train anymore," Jake hissed. "I don't want to win at all costs. You're a liar and a cheat. You *and* my father." She could hear the hurt in his voice, his wounded pride. The Honorable Jacob Rhodes. She knew how much he admired his father, how he'd always looked up to him. He always said if he could have half the accomplishments his father had, he'd think his life was a success.

That admission—that his father was a liar, that Jake didn't want to be like him anymore—must have cost him dearly. But why had he said it?

She heard a stall door open, heard the sound of something soft hitting wood—a person, maybe. Someone made a grunting noise, as if in pain. "I'm warning you," Jake said, his voice laboring now. "Keep your goddamn hands off me. I don't have your stuff. It's over."

In a minute she could see the shadow of Jake walking away, could see him trying to leave. Dale raised his voice now, seemingly not caring if anyone heard. "You little shit!" he shouted. "I'm not letting you torpedo your daddy's whole career for a worthless piece of ass."

"You can't talk about Leigh like that," Jake said, turning around.

"Why not? She can traipse around here in her wet clothes and her tight jeans like some little tramp, but no one's supposed to notice? Don't kid yourself, she wants us all to notice her. You and me *and* your dad. She's just begging for us all to pay attention. Just because she's fucking you in the hayloft doesn't mean I have to bow and scrape to that little slut. I don't care if her granddaddy owns half of Texas."

"You don't talk about her like that," Jake said. "You don't say another word against her. I'm going to marry her as soon as she turns eighteen. She's going to be my wife, and I won't let you talk about her like that. Not now, or ever again."

Leigh had held on to the stall nearest her to keep from falling over. He shouldn't have told Dale about their plans—not Dale Tucker, of all people. It was too risky; it could expose both of them.

Oh, Jake, you didn't!

Dale had laughed, actually laughed. "Whoo, boy," he said. "You are dumber than I thought. That little whore is never going to marry a country boy like you. You think her granddaddy's going to will his millions to *you*?"

"I don't care if he does or doesn't," Jake said. "It's only Leigh I want."

"Then you're definitely dumber than I thought. The only reason to marry that little bitch is her granddad's millions, Jake. She'll break your heart faster than you can spit. She'll be screwing everything that moves."

"You're just pissed I got to her first."

Dale's voice dropped an octave. "She should be glad you got to her first. If I'd gotten to her first, I'd knock some fucking sense into that head of hers. Now I mean it: hand over the stuff or I swear I will go straight to the house right now and tell Grandpa that you're fucking his baby girl. Let *him* deal with you. If you get out of it without a bullet in your ass, it won't be because I didn't try."

Leigh knew he meant it. He'd expose both of them. It would all be over. But what did Dale want that Jake had?

"I told you, I didn't bring it. I never went to the place and picked it up." Dale snorted. "Laugh all you want, but it's true. I won't be your dog anymore."

Scuffling, grunting. The sound of fists. Jake and Dale were fighting in the darkness. She couldn't see them, but she could hear the sound of them hitting each other, could hear Jake cry out.

"I'll kill you," Dale was hissing. "I will fucking kill you."

She could see them fighting. It was dark in the barn, but she could see well enough that Jake was too much for the smaller, older man, that Jake was tall and broad and powerfully built. He swung out and caught Dale under the chin, knocking the other man into the dirt.

She watched as Dale Tucker grabbed a lead line, looped it over Jake's neck, and pulled. Jake gave a strangled gasp and fell to his knees.

Leigh's heart was in her ears. Jake was in trouble. She had to help. She had to save him.

She slipped around to the outside entrance to the tack room, running now. The barn was completely black, so that the two men fighting were nothing but shadows in the darkness, a blur of movement and grunting. She turned the handle of the door to the tack room, where her grandfather kept the .357. She found the gun right where her grandfather always kept it, under the pile of horse blankets on the shelf. It was loaded. It was always loaded—Gene said an unloaded gun was no better than a baseball bat.

Holding it low at her side, she opened the tack room door into the barn. The fight had spilled out into the aisle of the barn. She could see their shapes, but could barely make out who was who. Dale Tucker was nearly a head shorter than Jake, wearing his dirty old trucker hat even in the dark, but he was muscular, strong, nearly as wide as he was tall. Jake was kneeling, and Dale had the rope tight around his throat, squeezing, his other hand pulling Jake's arms behind his back at an angle that looked so painful Leigh nearly cried out.

"Give me the stuff, you pussy-whipped little shit! I know you have it!"

"Fuck. Off." Jake's voice was nothing but a hoarse whisper, the air nearly squeezed out of him.

Leigh raised the gun to sight at Dale's head. She cocked the weapon, a loud metallic clicking, unmistakable even in the dark. Both men froze.

"Step back," Leigh said, her voice quavering in fear, or anger, or both at once. "Get your hands off him, Dale. I may be nothing but a worthless piece of ass, but you know as well as I do that my rich grand-daddy taught me how to use this gun."

Dale let go of the rope around Jake's neck and stepped away. "Well, look at this," he said, his voice dripping sour honey. "Mommy's come to break up the fight. Jake, you didn't tell me you called for your mommy."

"He didn't. I came looking for him and heard you talking garbage about me."

Jake was lying on the floor, gasping, but at least he was breathing again.

"Honestly, sweetheart, I didn't know you were here. If I had, I might have said some things different."

The gun was heavy in her hands. She'd never aimed one at a person before—she'd shot at cans along a fence line, once at a bunch of coyotes that were harassing some of the horses—but she'd never felt the adrenaline rush into her veins the way she did now, the throb of her own power.

As Leigh pointed the gun straight into Dale Tucker's eyes, words flooded her brain. Every nasty thing he'd said to her, every disgusting look, it all came into razor-sharp focus. She remembered the look on his face earlier in the day, when he'd compared her to a mare in heat, just waiting for the stud to come in and ride her. She saw the self-satisfied expression he'd worn when he'd reached out and touched her breast like it was something he owned.

Now he was sneering. She could just make out his face in the dark, could just see the curl of his lip as he looked at her. Nothing but a worthless piece of ass, he'd called her, because she didn't like him, because she'd recoiled when he touched her. She was only worthless because she wouldn't back down to someone like him.

"You tell your boyfriend about today?" Dale said. "How you took it in the breeding shed like a good little bitch?"

She watched Jake's head snap up. That had caught his attention, like Dale had wanted.

"The only thing that happened in the breeding shed today," she said, "was when I told you to keep your hands off me."

"Oh, come on, now. Tell lover boy here the truth, Leigh. You wanted it. You loved it."

"The only thing I want from you," she said slowly, "is the sight of you walking away. Let him go, and no one gets hurt."

"That's not what you said this afternoon."

"I will never," she said, "let you put your filthy hands on me again. Not ever."

"You will. You know you will, because you don't dare tell Granddaddy on me. The minute you do, lover boy here is yesterday's news. I think you'll get down on your knees and do whatever I tell you to, just to keep ol' Jakey here on the farm. Now, that's a thought. We could work out a deal, a little tit for tat. That's all it takes for me to keep my mouth shut about you and Jake. Easy as pie for a girl like you. Sound good?"

Jake was struggling to get to his feet. "If you ever . . . If you hurt her, you son of a—"

Leigh kept the gun pointed at Dale, but she could feel her hands begin to shake. She couldn't. She wouldn't even think about it. Not ever.

"Now let's talk turkey," said Dale. "What I want right now is for lover boy here to give me the stuff his daddy sent him for. If he doesn't, then he can be sure that the next time I catch you alone, I won't be so gentle."

"You smug asshole. I'm the one with the gun."

"You won't do it. You don't have the balls for killing, sweetheart. Might as well give me that gun right now. Come on, give it over."

He still didn't think she'd do it. He didn't think she was capable of actually pulling the trigger. She held the gun steady.

"Leigh." It was Jake now, coughing, pushing himself to his knees. "Don't give it to him. Don't listen to him."

Dale was moving closer, his shadow coming at her in the dark, slowly. He held out his hand to take the gun from her. He kept talking— low, soothing—like calming a balky horse. "You angry about today, honey? All I did was give you a taste. You liked it, too, didn't you? Been thinking about me all day?"

Her face burned, because she *had* been thinking about him all day. About how much she hated him, about all the ways she wanted to humiliate him, pay him back for humiliating her. And that was the point, she realized—he wanted her to hate him. He wanted her to think about him, to insinuate himself into her head, because to a man like him hatred was the most powerful aphrodisiac.

"Come on, honey," he said. Dale was only a few feet from her now, reaching out his hand. "Come on, give me that gun. You don't know the damage you could do with it, do you? You don't want that. You don't want that kind of mess in your life."

He was close, closer, sidling up to her, moving slowly, talking low. He was coming for the gun, probably thinking to take it from her. He was enjoying his game, enjoying thinking he had the upper hand.

But he didn't have the upper hand, because she still had the gun.

Maybe, if she'd given it to him, he would have simply put it away. Then again, maybe he would have turned it on her and then Jake. Afterward—for many years afterward—she would try to decide which it might have been. Both. Either.

What she did remember, what she dreamed about sometimes at night, was the feel of her own fear, the knowledge of another human being who wanted to do her harm. It didn't matter that he was outnumbered. It didn't matter that he was unarmed. It only mattered that she hated him and that she was afraid of him and that she was the one who held the gun.

In the dark she could see him coming toward her, see the broad expanse of his chest in the checkered shirt, the muscular shoulders, the curl of his lip. She'd known that afternoon in the barn that he hated her, that he wanted to hurt and humiliate her. *The next time I catch you alone, I won't be so gentle.*

Her finger tightened on the trigger. A flash.

All the noise in the world seemed to coalesce around her then. The next thing she remembered the lights were on, and she was on the floor of the barn, Jake bending over her, Jake taking the gun out of her hand. He was saying something to her, something she couldn't hear. "What?" she asked him numbly. "What, Jake?" His lips were moving, but she wasn't understanding him. It was as if he were speaking in a foreign language, something dense and impenetrable.

"Are you hurt?" Her ears were ringing, but she could just make out Jake's voice through a fog. "Are you shot?"

She sat up, felt her limbs and chest. Everything was where it should be. "I don't think so," she said.

On the ground a few feet away lay the body of Dale Tucker, a dark stain spread across the front of his shredded gray-checkered shirt.

His mouth was open, and his mean little eyes were staring up at the ceiling, at nothing. She'd caught him full in the chest with a high-caliber round at close range, and it had torn through him like a stone through wet paper. A dark puddle of blood spread out from beneath him.

Jake bent over him, still holding the gun. "He's dead."

Leigh wrapped her arms around herself, started to shake. "Oh God," she moaned. "God, God, I killed him." She could hardly see. The barn started to go white around her, and she collapsed on the floor. "I killed him. I killed him, Jake."

It was all going away—Harvard, New York, herself and Jake getting married. It was slipping through her fingers like sand. They'd take her to prison. They might even give her the chair. She felt a noise roiling in her throat, realized the keening sound she heard was her own voice.

Jake shook her. "Stop. Stop it. Look at me, Leigh. Look at my face, just my face. Breathe." She tried to do what he said, to look in his face, to breathe, but how could she? How could she? She might as well take the gun and put it to her own head. "I'm going to jail," she said. "I killed him. I killed him, Jake!"

"Listen to me. You didn't. You didn't do anything wrong."

"I did. I did it. I did it."

She was panicking, but Jake was looking around at the blood on the floor, his hands on the gun. Then he knelt next to Dale and took aim at the barn door, firing a single shot—*bam*—into the wood.

"What are you doing?" she screamed. "Why did you do that?"

"Powder burns," Jake said. He took her by the shoulders and hauled her to her feet. "Listen to me, Leigh. I did it. We tell them it was me."

"You're crazy—"

"No, listen to me. We say we came out here to check on the gelding, the one with the lame leg. We say we heard an intruder. A thief.

We went to get the gun just to warn him off. He wrestled me down to the floor and was choking me. I shot him to protect myself. We didn't know it was Dale until we turned on the lights. It will work, I swear."

"I can't," she sobbed. "It was me. It was me. They're going to arrest me, they're going to take me to prison. I might get the death penalty."

"They won't. I won't let them."

"I can't, I can't. I can't let you do that. I did it. I did it. It was me." She was still screaming, nearly hysterical now. "I killed him. Oh my God, Jake, what have I done!"

"Listen." He was bending down to look in her eyes, trying to calm her, but there was a weird energy in his voice, a sense of urgency she hadn't understood at the time. "Listen to me, Leigh. Leela, look at me."

Her eyes snapped up.

"This is what you tell the police when they come: that we came out to the barn to check on the gelding with the lame leg. We saw a man, a horse thief. We went to get your grandfather's gun. The man fought with me. He had me down on the ground. I fired twice. We didn't know it was Dale until we turned the lights on. Leigh, repeat what I just said."

"No, no, I can't let you do that."

Jake's voice boomed: *"Repeat to me what I just said, Leigh."* His fingers were so tight around her shoulders she nearly cried out.

Leigh felt like she was choking. The words were like ashes in her mouth. "We came to the barn to check on one of the horses. We heard an intruder and went to get the gun. We warned him. He lunged at you, and you fired, and then he had you down on the ground and was choking you. That's when you killed him. We didn't know it was Dale until we turned on the lights."

"That's it. That's all you ever have to say."

She was weeping now. "I can't. I can't do it. I can't lie." She didn't know where it was coming from, this determination to take the blame for something he hadn't done, but she couldn't think, she couldn't even see straight. She was thinking about Harvard, about having to tell the university she'd been arrested, about her grandfather coming to visit her in jail, about police and lawyers and judges. The electric chair sizzling her flesh. It was over; it was all over, except it hadn't even begun. "I won't let you do this."

"You will. It was self-defense," he said, lifting up her chin to look him in the eyes. "I can handle a couple of weeks in jail. What I can't handle is watching you get handcuffed and put in a squad car because I screwed up."

"Jake—"

His face twisted in pain. "Don't argue with me, Leigh. If it wasn't for me, you could have gone to your grandfather and got Dale fired a long time ago. You wouldn't even have been out here tonight if it wasn't for me."

"That's not true. I—"

Then someone was shouting, someone else was in the barn. "Jesus Christ!" said a voice.

Jake pulled her close as Ben Rhodes arrived on the scene, as her grandfather came running from the house. The arrival of other people in the barn made the situation seem very real all of a sudden.

"My God," said her grandfather. "What the hell happened here? Leigh? Leigh, are you all right?"

She held on to Jake to steady herself. "I'm okay, Pop. I'm not hurt."

Ben was kneeling down next to his friend. "Dale," he said. "Dale, hey, buddy."

"He's dead, Ben," said her grandfather. "Nothing you can do for him now." He looked from Leigh to Jake, who still had the gun in his hand. "You better put that gun down, Jake, and tell me what happened."

Jake gingerly set the gun down on the floor of the barn.

"He didn't—" Leigh started, but Jake cut her off.

"He tried to kill me. I didn't have a choice."

"Jacob," said his father, "what the hell have you done? You shot Dale? You killed him?"

Gene shook his head, trying to keep things calm. "Threatening you how?"

Jake said, "I didn't know it was Dale. We came out here to check on the gelding, the one that's favoring his front leg. We saw someone coming out of one of the stalls with a horse, didn't we, Leigh? I went to get the gun, just to warn him off, of course. He came at me. He wrestled me down to the ground, got his hands around my neck. He said he was going to kill me, so I shot. Isn't that right, Leigh?"

Leigh didn't answer. She couldn't speak.

"That doesn't make sense. What were you arguing about? Why would Dale say he was going to kill you?"

Jake looked over at Leigh. She opened her mouth to protest, but the look in his eyes stopped her. *I'm doing this,* it said. *I'm doing this whether you want me to or not.* "He was angry."

"Angry about what?"

"Jake," said his dad in a warning tone.

Jake shook his head. "He came at me. I thought he had a knife, maybe. He would have killed me if I hadn't shot him first. He said so. He said he was going to kill me, didn't he, Leigh?"

"Jake—" she said.

"I shot him. He said he was going to kill me. You heard him, Leigh. You heard what he said. Tell them what he said."

"Is this true, Leela?" her grandfather asked.

This was the moment. She could have, should have told the truth right then, but something stopped her. Jake was so certain, so calm, and she was so scared—scared of hurting her grandfather, of getting Ben fired, of going to prison. Maybe he was right. Maybe what he said would work. It was self-defense, wasn't it? Jake had the bruises on his neck to prove it. If she told the truth there would be handcuffs and confessions and jail time. She'd lose Harvard, lose her future . . .

She looked up. Her grandfather's face was so stern, forbidding. The thought of telling him what had really happened, of explaining what Dale had said in the breeding barn, the thought of explaining how he'd put his hands on her, how he'd tried to blackmail her into sex just now—it was unbearable. Gene would have to know everything; she'd have to tell him about her and Jake, about them running away together. He'd never let her see Jake again.

Later she would know all that was an excuse. She did it because she was scared, and because Jake seemed so sure it was the right thing, the only thing.

Over her grandfather's shoulder she could make out Jake giving her a pleading look. She took a breath and said, "He said he was going to kill Jake. He was strangling him."

"Why would he want to kill Jake?" Gene was getting angry now. "Someone had better tell me for real what the hell's going on here."

Jake shook his head no. Gene stood up and said, "If you don't explain it to me, Leigh, you'll have to explain it to the cops."

"Then I'll explain it to the cops."

Ben stood up and fixed his son with a stony glare. Probably he already knew what was going to happen, how it was going to go: that the police would find the steroids; that Ben would lose his job; that Jake would go to prison. "You have no idea what you've done, Jacob. You have *no fucking clue.*"

Under the harsh lights of the barn, his face ashen, Leigh could hear her grandfather talking to the sheriff on his cell phone, and the reality of what was happening hit her hard. Dale's body lay on the floor of the barn, his blood pooling on the floor of the aisle, and she'd felt sick, she'd run out into the darkness to throw up in the bushes, retching over and over until her guts were empty.

"A man's been shot," Gene Merrill was saying. "A man's dead at my place. You'd better send your people out right away."

When the sheriff's deputy arrived, Jake told the story he'd concocted about the gelding and the intruder and the two shots in the dark. Leigh had listened in a kind of stupor, her thoughts thick and slow as honey. When she thought about it later, she realized she had probably been in shock. She'd killed a man. She, Leigh Merrill, had committed a murder, and to protect her Jake had decided to tell the authorities it was him.

As he was speaking, telling the story they would both tell so many times, to police, to prosecutors, to a jury, she thought, *It's all a lie.* She was ready to blurt it out, to tell the truth, but whenever she caught Jake's eye she could see that he was determined, that he thought this way was best. That he loved her enough to sacrifice himself for her.

A couple of hours later, as Leigh watched the two officers put Jake in the back of the squad car, she thought, *That could have been me. That should be me in there right now.* And God help her, she was glad, in that moment, that it wasn't her heading off to jail.

Some detectives came, searched the barn, Ben's house, the vehicles. In the glove compartment of Jake's truck they found eight vials of illegal steroids and horse-sized syringes. The detectives showed these to Gene and Leigh, to Ben. "Here's what they were fighting over," said the detective. "Must have been doing it for years. We're going to have to call the feds. Transporting illegal drugs over state lines is a federal offense, you know. That boy's going to need a good lawyer, that's all I can say right now."

"That's not possible," Leigh said, looking at the syringes like they were snakes. She wouldn't believe it. Jake wouldn't dope her grandfather's horses. Jake wouldn't be involved in anything illegal. He couldn't be.

Could he?

Gene shook his head angrily. "I knew something was going on. I knew it." He turned on Ben. "That colt today—you've been running the animals too hard and using the steroids to cover it up."

Ben's faced closed up. "You knew. You knew the whole time. How else could we get the best from these rotten nags of yours?"

"You're off the farm," Gene said, wagging his finger at Ben. "To-night."

"Just a second, now. My boy—"

"Your boy's done enough damage for one lifetime. I want you gone by morning, Ben. Leave quietly or I get the sheriff involved."

"You think this is best, Gene? You think this will be the end of it?"

"It better be."

Ben stormed off, and the sheriff drove Jake to the station, the blue and white lights of the cruiser fading into the darkness. Her grandfather had put his arms around her, but she shrugged him off. The old man was partly to blame, too, and Leigh felt all the anger in her settle, finally, on him. If he hadn't forbidden Leigh and Jake to see each other, none of this would have happened. She made herself stand still and not embrace him in return. Her whole body felt like it was made of glass, like it would shatter if she moved.

"I told you that boy was no good. Now you're seeing why, Leigh."

"Not one more word, Pop," she said, wrapping her arms around herself, feeling like she might come completely apart if she didn't hold herself together right then. "Now's not the time for I-told-you-so's."

When they returned home she'd gone back into the house and locked herself in her room, not coming out, not speaking to anyone, even Chloe, who called and called the next day when she heard the news. She didn't answer when her grandfather knocked to ask if she wanted breakfast, if she was feeling all right. He was trying to make it up to her, but Leigh was determined to punish him.

She spoke to no one, not until the police came to the house to take her statement. To all their questions, she gave the answer that Jake had demanded of her: They'd gone to the barn to see about the injured horse. They'd heard a noise, thought there was a horse thief in the barn. She hadn't seen the man, hadn't known who it was at first. They argued. Jake got her grandfather's .357 Magnum. The man lunged, and Jake had shot once and missed. Then the man got him down on the ground, choking him. The man said he was going to kill him, kill Jake, and to stop him from choking him, Jake shot him once in the chest.

"So when did you realize that the man in the barn was Mr. Tucker?"

"When the lights went on. Until then I didn't know."

"Did he ever say Jake's name? Did he ever identify himself to you?"

"I don't think so."

The detective wrote something in his notebook. Leigh had the feeling she'd said something wrong, somehow, that she'd messed up, but she couldn't think how.

"Very well, Miss Merrill. We'll be in touch."

Afterward, standing on the front porch in her bare feet and watching the detectives pull away from the house, she thought, *It will be all right. A good lawyer can get Jake off by claiming self-defense. He'll be out soon with time served.*

That was the hope she clung to—that it would blow over, it would be written off as an accident, a simple misunderstanding.

How wrong she'd been.

That last summer—when she should have been looking forward to starting college and planning her move to Boston, her life with Jake— was nothing but a blur of noise and worry. Leigh spent long hours at the sheriff's station, the county prosecutor's office, telling the same story over and over, and each time she got the feeling she wasn't giving them the answer they wanted, that she was missing something. She saw them giving each other looks: they didn't believe her. Jake was in trouble, and the more often Leigh told the story of what happened in the barn, the more certain she was that somehow she was doing him more harm than good.

Ben Rhodes left the farm, but it wasn't an amicable parting of the ways. He came to see Gene one last time before he cleared out, asking for six months' severance pay, which Gene refused to give him. Leigh watched the whole thing from a corner of the foyer, half hidden in the shadows.

"You think this is an early retirement?" the old man had asked when Ben laid out his demand. "You're lucky I'm just firing you and not taking you to court. Get off my property before I have you thrown off."

"I think you should reconsider," said Ben. There was a threat in his voice that Leigh didn't quite understand. "I think it would be better for both of us, and our kids, if you reconsidered. Don't be stupid, Gene. Think of it as a donation to the future safety of your family."

"Like hell," said Gene. "I won't give you another dime, Ben. You or your boy. Get your ass off my property." Ben's jaw clenched. "You come after my family, and you'll have me to deal with."

Ben stormed off, spinning the tires of his truck, but for the next few weeks, Leigh sometimes still saw him stalking around the side-walks of Burnside—scowling over a beer at Dot's, glaring at her when she drove her grandfather's truck down Main Street. She kept expecting him to turn up on her grandfather's front porch once more, but he never did, and after a while she and Gene forgot his threat. They chalked it up to the actions of a desperate man, and that was all.

Leigh was supposed to head off to Harvard in September, but she decided to defer her enrollment until after the trial. Instead she spent her eighteenth year at home, helping her grandfather, who seemed to have grown very old very quickly. Gene was having more trouble getting around the farm, and often spent whole days in the house, brooding. Maybe Leigh should have asked him what was troubling him, but she had too many of her own worries to brood on, and for that year they circled each other warily, like two shipwrecked passengers sharing the same lifeboat.

With Ben and Dale and Jake all gone, they were short-handed around the farm, so Leigh's mother's brother, Gene Jr.—whom everyone called Sonny—started coming down more on the weekends, bringing his wife, Becky, and their two boys to help out around the place. They were helpful and treated Leigh with the utmost kindness, but Wolf's Head was not the same without Gene's sturdy presence in the barns and on the tracks, and the business suffered a bit. Leigh couldn't bring herself to go to the barn, the scene of her crime as well as an aching reminder of Jake's absence. She huddled in the house, spending whole days in her pajamas, not speaking to anyone. Her aunt Becky's attempts at cheering her up by taking her into town for lunch and shopping only made her wish her mother were alive so she might have someone she felt she could confide in.

Jake's case was assigned to the public defender, a harried but determined kid of twenty-nine barely out of law school. The lawyer said there was nothing to be done about the drug charge and declared that Jake should plead guilty, take his four years, and be glad it wasn't worse. But the lawyer seemed to think Jake had a good case on the murder charge and urged him to plead not guilty to the charge of murder by reason of self-defense. Let a jury hear the trial, he'd said, and determine Jake's guilt or innocence.

The trial wasn't set to begin until the following September, just after Leigh was supposed to have started her sophomore year at Harvard. They'd all had to testify at the trial—Ben, Gene, and Leigh. And Jake, of course. When he admitted the truth about the steroids. When he admitted the truth about everything except who'd been holding the gun when it went off.

He'd never written. He'd never called. He never came to the visitors' room at the Burnside County Jail when she visited. She was starting to be afraid that he blamed her, and rightly so. She had no idea what was happening to him in there, how he was suffering. Anyone would start to doubt they were doing the right thing when they were sitting in a jail cell day after day. Anyone would start to have regrets, surely.

Leigh didn't see Jake again until the day the trial started. Settled in the back of the courtroom, her eyes raw with lack of sleep, she had watched the bailiffs bring Jake in, looking very young and scared in his gray suit. He looked thinner and even more tired than she did, and at first she wasn't even certain he was aware that she was in the room—he came in with his head held high on his neck, his jaw muscles clenched, eyes forward. He sat down at the defendant's table with his hands folded in front of him. Leigh kept willing him to turn around, *turn around, Jake. Look at me, Jake. Look at me.*

His father, sitting just behind him, leaned forward to say something, and that was the moment Jake finally turned around and caught Leigh's eye. She opened her mouth to say something, but he shook his head no. What did that mean? Was he angry, did he blame her? He must blame her. She watched every twitch of his shoulders and nod of his head, but she could no longer read his body language. Could a year apart have really changed him so much?

On the way out of the courtroom on the day of his testimony, he finally gave her a small smile, his eyes holding hers for just a moment longer than necessary. It gave her a momentary hope, but when she went to the jail the next day to see him, he still wouldn't speak to her, and afterward he still wouldn't write.

Talk to me, Jake, she wrote him. *Why won't you talk to me?*

The trial dragged on for weeks. The thrust of the prosecutor's argument seemed to be that Jake had murdered Dale Tucker over the steroids—that he was trying to keep them for himself, to sell, which was just the most ridiculous thing Leigh had ever heard. There were arguments over the timing of the two shots, over the angle at which the bullet entered Dale's body, every bit of evidence seeming to point to the idea that Jake was lying, and at every moment Leigh wanted to stand up and scream, *It was me! Jake didn't do anything! It was all me!*

Her guilt and misery were so acute that most days all she did was sit in the back of the courtroom and weep, silently, her grandfather trying to comfort her by patting her hand or her arm. She could see the eyes of the prosecutor on her from time to time, catching a glimpse of her from the front of the courtroom.

By the time it was her turn on the witness stand, she knew it was no longer in her to lie. She couldn't even look Jake in the eye; he was nothing but a smudge of gray at the edge of her vision, looking, in his pressed suit and blue tie, like a kid playing dress-up with his dad's wardrobe. When she passed him on her way to the witness stand, she saw him sit up a little straighter, try to catch her eye, but she walked across the courtroom with her head down and took her seat, not looking at him. *Let him see how he likes it,* she thought.

On the witness stand she sat with her hands in her lap, wringing the fabric of her skirt. Her testimony was mostly a blur. She remembered the prosecutor only as a flash of discolored teeth and an oily voice, her own feelings somewhere between resignation and terror. She had to get through this. For Jake. For their future together.

"Now, you originally told the police you went to the barn that night to check on a lame horse, but that isn't really true, is it?" the prosecutor asked, staring through her. Jake had already admitted the truth about his involvement in doping the horses and been sentenced to four years on that charge. She couldn't hide behind a fictional intruder any longer.

"That's right. There was no lame horse."

"So what *did* happen?"

"I wanted to talk to Jake. We'd had a fight before he left, and I wanted to make up with him. I was looking to apologize." This was the first real truth that Leigh had uttered since her grandfather had arrived the night of the shooting. A rush of relief flooded her body, and she knew that soon she was going to have to tell the whole truth. She wouldn't be able to live with herself otherwise.

"What did you fight about?"

"I didn't like him running errands for his father and Dale. I said I didn't like the people they sent Jake to see. I didn't trust them."

"What didn't you trust about the people Dale Tucker sent Jake to see?"

"I thought they were shady. The meetings were always happening in bars or behind someone's truck, always at night, always hours and hours away. It didn't seem right to me."

"Tell us about that particular night in the barn. Why didn't you turn on the lights when you first came inside?"

"I knew my grandfather would be angry if he caught me out at such an hour, especially with Jake. I didn't want anyone to know I was there."

"So was this a regular occurrence, then? You and Jake sneaking around in the dark?"

Leigh blushed, heat spreading across her face as Gene looked out from the gallery.

"Yes. Jake and I often met up in the barn."

"What did you witness inside the barn?"

"I heard Jake and Dale arguing. I couldn't see them clearly."

"What were they arguing about?"

"Something Dale wanted from Jake. I didn't know what it was they were talking about, but Dale was angry. He threatened to go to my grandfather and tell him that Jake and I were still seeing each other unless he got what he wanted."

"And did Jake give him what he wanted?"

"No. So Dale choked him. He got Jake down on the ground and was choking him with a lead line."

"You said you couldn't see them clearly. How did you know who was who?"

"I could hear Jake choking. Dale was still talking."

"What did Dale say to Jake?"

"He said, 'I will fucking kill you.' "

The prosecutor stopped a moment as the courtroom burst out in whispers. "And what happened next? When did Mr. Tucker realize you were in the barn also?"

"I spoke to him. I told him to take his hands off Jake."

"And did he?"

"Yes. He let Jake go and started walking toward me."

"Did Mr. Tucker say anything as he was walking toward you?"

"He tried to blackmail me. He said if I had sex with him he would keep his mouth shut about me and Jake."

"He wasn't threatening you?"

"I just told you he was threatening me."

"I meant physically threatening."

"I took it as a physical threat, yes. From Dale any threat was physical." Leigh was angry now, remembering the feeling of Dale's hand on her breast, the way he always pushed up so close to her. Her face went hot. The courtroom was utterly silent except for the sound of the blood rushing in Leigh's ears.

"But he had no weapon? You saw no knife, no gun?"

She answered quietly, "No."

"But Jake has testified that this was the moment he went to get the gun from the tack room. If Dale didn't have a weapon, why would Jake go fetch your grandfather's gun?"

Leigh was looking down at her hands. She didn't know how much longer she could keep this up. The story Jake had already told on the stand wasn't true; Leigh was already holding the gun when Dale started walking toward her. But that was the problem, wasn't it? The gun had been in her hands. *Her* hands, and not Jake's at all.

"Miss Merrill, if Jake was no longer in any danger—if, as you say, Mr. Tucker's attention was on you at the moment—why would Jake need a gun? You could have walked away at that point. Why wouldn't you simply tell Dale Tucker you weren't going to have sex with him and let that be the end of it?"

"Dale was making terrible threats. He wouldn't shut up." She was coming very close to her breaking point now. They were circling the heart of the lie, and she was starting to think only the truth would get Jake, and herself, out of this mess.

"But now was the time you and Jake could have walked away safely, isn't that true? Mr. Tucker was unarmed. Neither of you was in any imminent physical danger any longer. Isn't that true?"

Leigh remembered the sound of the gun going off. The flash. "Yes," she whispered.

"Instead Jake executed an unarmed man. He went and got your grandfather's .357 Magnum from the tack room, and he shot Dale Tucker once in the chest. He shot him over five thousand dollars' worth of steroids."

So this was the gist of the prosecutor's argument: that Jake had lied when he said Dale's murder was self-defense. That he was covering something up. And the prosecutor was right about that much: Jake *was* covering something up. But the prosecutor was wrong about what it was.

Leigh hadn't been able to look at Jake, hadn't been able to make herself keep up the lie any longer. The real truth was like an explosion in her chest, and when it would come out, finally, it would blow her to bits.

"Isn't that what happened, Miss Merrill?"

"No," she said. "It wasn't."

"What was that?"

"Jake didn't kill Dale over the steroids."

"How can you say so? You know he's already pleaded guilty to the drugs charge, Miss Merrill."

"Jake didn't kill Dale over the steroids. Jake didn't kill anyone at all. He didn't go get the gun." She rushed forward, her mouth dry as dust. "It was me. I got the gun. I'm the one who shot Dale Tucker."

A murmur of surprise went up across the courtroom. She didn't look at her grandfather or Ben Rhodes or the prosecutor, the judge or jury. She didn't look at anyone but Jake, whose face across from her was a mask of horror, his blue eyes shocked. *No,* he mouthed at her. *Leigh, don't.*

After the murmur died down, the prosecutor recovered himself and said, "You don't really expect the court to believe that, do you?"

"Yes," she said. "You wanted the truth. It's the truth."

"Miss Merrill, may I remind you you're under oath? That perjury is a serious offense? You've already admitted to one lie today. Are you sure you want to add another?" His voice fairly dripped with condescension. "It's admirable that you'd like to protect your ex-boyfriend, but perjuring yourself is not the way to do it. You'd both go to jail, you realize, for lying under oath."

Leigh hesitated. She hadn't thought about perjury. She hadn't expected that they would not believe her. She'd only thought that the truth was something she owed Jake, that she would prove to him she was still worthy of his love and he'd forgive her. She'd thought the truth would make everything simple.

What do you do when you finally tell the truth, but people have already decided to believe the lie?

She was making another horrible mistake. She was too late. It was all useless—the truth, the lie. All of it.

Across the courtroom, Jake widened his eyes at her. *No,* he mouthed again. *Don't do this.*

She looked back down at her lap. Her fingers looked like they belonged to someone else. Her clothes felt like lead weights, pulling her down. She wanted to run, far from Texas, far from the courtroom. She closed her eyes and imagined herself standing up, walking out the door of the courtroom, and running away, running free. Running until her heart burst and her legs collapsed. Running until she found a place where no one knew her, where she could start over.

"Now, let's get back to the real story of what happened, Miss Merrill. No more fairy tales, please. Can you do that?"

It took a minute for Leigh to come back to herself, a long minute in which she could feel the impatience of the people in the courtroom, the prosecutor, even the judge. "All right," she said finally, and looked back down at her hands. "I'm sorry. I promise to tell the truth from now on." A lie. Another lie.

The prosecutor smiled. He was back in familiar territory now, thought he knew exactly where he was going, but he didn't know anything. No one did.

"Okay, then. Where were we? Yes—how Jake killed Dale over five thousand dollars' worth of illegal steroids."

He kept talking, asking Leigh questions, and she answered them, her voice robotic. She had tried to stop the machinery of justice, but it hadn't worked. That machinery was moving inexorably to convict the man she loved, and she was too weak to stop it. She was too weak, because everyone thought that she, Leigh Merrill, was incapable of cold-blooded murder. They thought it was a joke, a last-ditch Hail Mary pass meant to spare Jake from going to prison.

Everyone was wrong.

For months Leigh's own conscience had been a millstone around her neck, threatening to pull her to the bottom of the river, and as she sat on the witness stand, she knew if she didn't remove the weight, she'd never be able to breathe freely again. The person Leigh had been trying most to save that day in the courtroom had been herself.

"Thank you, Miss Merrill. No more questions, Your Honor."

OCTOBER 4, 2005
Burnside, TX

Jake,

I came to see you yesterday after I left court, but again they said you wouldn't come out of your cell. The guard, the surly woman who registers the names of visitors to the jail, didn't even look up at me when I said who I'd come to see. "He still doesn't want any visitors," she said, "but keep trying if it makes you feel better." Then she laughed, a mean little laugh with no humor in it. At least I made it outside before anyone could see I was crying.

I keep thinking it has to be some mistake, that you wouldn't really turn me away if you knew I was here. Maybe no one's told you I've come, even though they're supposed to. Maybe someone's messing with us. Maybe you've sent me letters, too, lots of letters, but the guards are taking them away after you put them in the mail. Maybe my grandfather is hiding them from me. I wouldn't put it past him. He's done plenty to keep us apart all this time.

I picture you writing me letter after letter, addressing them to me, dropping them in the prison mail, then the guards or my grandfather snatching your letters away and ripping them up, tearing them into tiny little pieces and laughing at you, and at me.

But I know that can't be right. If you wanted to see me, you would come to the visitors' room and talk to me, wouldn't you? It must be true that you don't want to see me.

Maybe there are things about you I didn't know, but I didn't think there was anything so earth-shattering that it could change everything between us. Maybe I was wrong. Maybe my grandfather was right, and you don't love me after all, not like I thought. Am I a stupid little girl for still wanting you to come back to me? For loving you, in spite of everything?

I want to give you a chance to explain. I want to understand why the drugs were in your car that night. You knew it was wrong to dope the horses. You knew it, but you helped your father and Dale, knowing it could be the end of my grandfather's business and Wolf's Head.

We could have lost everything. We still could. Several more of the horses have come up lame, and three have had to be put down. My grandfather's health has been bad since you were arrested. It's like he's lost heart. Uncle Sonny and Aunt Becky try to help, but I don't know if I can leave him like this. I don't even know if I want to go. It's all spoiled for me, Jake. I don't know how to picture the future anymore without you in it.

I hope you know I tried to do the right thing yesterday. I thought it would help, but as usual I was wrong. I've been wrong about so many things lately. I don't know why you're doing what you're doing, but I want you to know I tried to tell the truth. I tried, but they didn't believe me.

Please write to me. Please forgive me. I don't know how to go on without you.

                                                        Love,
                                                        Leigh

Dear Leigh,

They told me you came by again yesterday. I was in my cell when I heard, reading. *Anna Karenina*. For weeks now I've been reading. In prison you read, or work out, or fight. Sleep won't come easily, and when it does it's accompanied by vicious dreams. I'm back in the barn and Dale is coming at me. Sometimes you point the gun at me. Sometimes you pull the trigger. I wake up thinking I'm dead.

Sometimes I wish I were.

I was on the part where Anna leaves her husband for Vronsky. Funny that Anna's brother can have as many affairs as he likes without consequences while Anna loses everything. Maybe Tolstoy doesn't like Anna much. Maybe he's wishing bad things on her, trying to make her suffer. Maybe some woman somewhere hurt him once, and this is his revenge.

I should have told you the truth a long time ago. I could see it in your face in that courtroom, how much I hurt you. I hope you understand. Dale threatened over and over to go to your grandfather if I didn't go along with them. I knew if my dad lost his job, we'd have to leave, and I might never see you again. I couldn't stand the thought of losing you. Now I wish I'd told, no matter what might have happened. I'm in here, and you're on the other side of the wall, and there's no way in heaven or on earth for us to be together. I'm starting to think it might be a very long time before I get out of here.

It was my fault. The gun. Everything. If I'd only been able to stand up to my old man.

I want to say all this to you in person. I don't want to write it in a letter. I want to see your face when I tell you I'm sorry and ask your forgiveness. I'm so ashamed of myself. If I'd been braver, or smarter, you wouldn't have been in the barn that night. We'd be together in Boston right now.

You wouldn't have looked at me today with stones in your eyes.

I will hold those stones in my heart. I will hold them until they sink me down. When I come up for air again—if I ever come up for air again—I hope you will have let them go.

Love,

—J.

Seven

The jury deliberated only six hours before they announced Jake's fate. Leigh sat in the back of the courtroom watching the proceedings next to her grandfather, who was shaking with anger (or was it relief?) as the foreman read the verdict: guilty of murder. Leigh hadn't made a sound, just gripped the arms of her chair so tightly that they ached for days afterward. She looked at the back of Jake's head, willing him to turn around and look at her, or lash out, something. Something other than meek acceptance.

It wasn't possible. She whispered, mostly to herself, that there had to be some mistake.

"You'll be all right," the old man had said, leaning over to whisper to Leigh. "You'll go off to school and get yourself an education, and in a little while all this will be nothing but a bad memory."

But instead of arguing with him, instead of telling him he didn't know her at all if he thought she'd forget about Jake so easily, Leigh had simply sat there and watched the back of Jake's head as the verdict was read, watched the way his shoulders sagged. The jury didn't believe it was self-defense, not when Dale Tucker had been unarmed and Jake had probable cause to shoot him over the missing steroids. They'd all miscalculated, and now Jake was going away for a very long time.

The bailiff came and put the handcuffs on Jake once more. The click of the cold metal around his wrists seemed to release Leigh from the trance she was in, because suddenly she was out of her chair, pushing through the crowd, flinging herself at Jake as if she could shield him with her body.

"This isn't happening," she moaned. "There's been a mistake, a terrible mistake."

Jake had gently pried her hands from around his neck. "Don't do this, Leigh."

"I'll wait for you," she whispered in his ear as the bailiffs tried to pull her away. "It will all be like it was before, I swear."

"No, it won't," he'd told her. His voice was low, choked with so much emotion that Leigh thought her heart would break. "Move on with your life, Leigh. Forget about me. I'm no good for you."

She tried to tell him he was wrong, but the bailiffs were already pulling them apart. She saw his back as they led him out a side door of the courtroom, looking very young and scared in his gray suit. He turned and looked back at her once and gave her a shaky smile. Then he was gone.

That was the last time she'd seen him.

The man she loved had gone to prison to protect her. For ten years Leigh had tried to live with that knowledge, the knowledge that she was a horribly selfish person, because she had been afraid to tell the truth, because she had known it would cost her Harvard and her dreams of a career. The fact that it cost Jake his dreams hadn't entered into her mind until it was too late. She didn't deserve him; she didn't deserve to be happy.

She didn't know it in that moment in the courtroom, but she'd feel that way for a very, very long time. She'd spend years punishing herself for being too gutless to do the right thing sooner than she had, for not speaking up right away the night the sheriff arrived at the barn and saying, *It was me. I did it. Arrest me. Prosecute me. Send me to prison.*

It was where she'd felt she belonged, all these years. A lost decade. Harvard, then on to New York and Jenks & Hall—all of it with a heavy dose of self-loathing. The stone of guilt around her neck had become a weight so permanent it left her crippled.

Now, with Joseph, she had a chance to move on, start again. She'd met someone who didn't know her past, someone who was giving her a chance at a fresh start. Joseph Middlebury was a good and decent person, worthy of her in every way, and she'd never have to feel guilty with him, never have to spend her life looking backward, making amends. It was a lot to be thankful for.

Still, there on the boat dock with Jake in front of her—Jake in the flesh for the first time in a decade—she didn't think of Joseph, or her career, or her life back in New York. She only thought of everything she owed him, everything that had gone unsaid and undone since that night in the barn when he had taken the gun out of her hands and made her promise to keep the truth locked away inside her like a rotten little disease, since that moment in the courtroom when he had told her not to wait for him.

In the golden light of dusk, as the shadows crept down from the hills and turned the land purple, Leigh could smell the green smell of the river and trees, could hear the music from a nearby restaurant tinkling in the evening air. But all that faded around her as she took in Jake's expression. He was smiling a little, the edges of his mouth just turning up, but it didn't reach his narrow blue eyes, which looked straight at her, boring into her with a measure of sadness or apology. Or possibly anger, she thought.

His face was not as soft as it had been when they were kids—there was a hardness around his mouth and his jaw that hadn't been there before, the wide planes of his cheekbones more visible under his skin. There were little creases at the corners of his eyes and he seemed taller than she remembered, more muscular. He'd thickened up, like Chloe had said. When she'd seen him last he was still a kid, skinny and awkward, still growing. He'd been jovial and easygoing in his expressions and movements. Now he was a full-grown man—more sure of himself in some ways, more guarded in others—who'd been through things she couldn't imagine.

She took a couple of steps toward him, as if she meant to embrace him, but then stopped herself. It wouldn't be right.

"It's good to see you," he said. "I'm sorry if I scared you, just showing up like that."

"You don't have anything to be sorry for," she said. "I'm glad I found you. I wanted to see you."

"You look good. I like the clothes. Your hair's gotten so long. New York must agree with you."

"Thanks," she said. "You do, too. Look good, I mean."

"You're all pink, though. Haven't spent much time outside lately, have you?"

"No, not really. I don't get much sun in the city."

"You should get outside more. Texas always suited you. I remember how tan you used to get swimming at Wolf's Head."

She shook her head and made a little noise, half laugh and half breath, the sound of disbelief. After ten years in prison he thought *she* should get out more?

"I read the book, Leigh. The Millikin. It's great. You should be proud."

"Thanks."

"I saw the ads for the conference and thought I'd pop in, to . . . well, you know."

"I'm glad you did. I wanted to see you. I hadn't heard you were out until I got here."

"Who told you?"

"Chloe. She said she saw you in town. Are you living in Burnside, then?"

"I have a little place in town. Just a room really. One of those places to help ex-cons get back on their feet."

Leigh shifted her weight from one foot to the other. She'd been hoping neither of them would get around to mentioning Jake's prison time, but that had probably been wishful thinking. "Oh," she said. "Is it nice?"

"No," he said flatly. "You probably have a great place. A big apartment in the big city with a view of Central Park. And your boyfriend? Joseph, is that his name? Are you living with him now?"

He said this last so casually that it took a second for her to realize what he was saying. Leigh felt ill, suddenly dizzy and nauseated. Jake knew about Joseph? He'd found out, somehow, when all this time she'd imagined he was totally ignorant of who she was, what she was doing. "How—?"

"The magic of the Internet. I saw some photos of you two in the newspaper maybe a year ago, at some party or book thing. You were wearing a blue dress. You know that was always my favorite color on you."

"That's right. I'd forgotten."

"He's good-looking. Handsome. His clothes are nice. He works at the publishing company, too?"

Leigh took a deep breath. The idea that Jake had been googling her from prison had never entered her mind. "Let me explain—"

Jake stuffed his hands in his pockets and looked out over the water. "No need," he said. "I told you to live your life, didn't I? You did. No harm done."

No harm done? Really? "Jake," she said, but then she didn't know what else to say.

Still looking away, he asked, "Do you love him?"

She started to say *I do* as a matter of course, but then stopped. Were they really going to have this conversation? Jake was practically a stranger to her now. It was none of his business if she loved Joseph or not. He'd given up his claim on her the minute he refused to see her, refused to write her. If he'd wanted Leigh's love he could have had it long before now, if only he'd reached out and taken it when it was offered.

Jake shook his head. "Forget I said that. It doesn't matter if you love him or not. I don't think either answer would make me feel better." He laughed a little, as if to himself, and said, "We were over a long time ago. No hard feelings, right?"

"Right," she said, but it was all she could do to hide her disappointment, her overwhelming frustration. *No hard feelings.* The Honorable Jacob Rhodes, still clinging to his pride. Always trying to do the right thing, and hurting everyone in the process.

"Take care, Leigh. I'll leave you alone now. I promise."

At last she looked up into his eyes, the hurt so plain that she nearly wept—here was the Jake she remembered, the one who could undo her with a single glance, a single word. How had he managed to make her feel like she was eighteen again, eighteen and scared of disappointing her grandfather, scared of losing the man she loved, of losing her chance at happiness?

But then she was angry, too, angry that he'd torpedoed it all.

He was turning to go. His back was to her as she said, "You did leave me alone."

"What?" He whirled around.

She'd started, and she wasn't going to back down now. "I waited ten years to hear from you. Ten years without a word of any kind." She wasn't able to keep the hurt out of her voice any longer. "I think I was prepared to deal with you in prison, even me in prison. Almost anything except you cutting me out of your life." She choked down a breath. "I mean, what was I supposed to think? And you give me the letters now? Why bother writing them if you never meant to send them?"

He looked down at his feet, as if there were some answer there that would make everything all right between them. "I don't know," he said. "I thought about it, thought about sending them, but I thought it wouldn't be a good idea. I didn't want to scare you. Then you were gone, off to college. It just seemed easier after that to leave you alone. I mean, how could I ask you to take time off from school and your friends to come all the way to Huntsville, to a place where you didn't know anybody, to talk to a convicted murderer through a plastic wall?"

"I would have. I would have done it gladly."

"That's just it, Leigh. I didn't want you to. I wanted you very far away from that place. Why do you think I told them I did it to begin with?"

"But no letters, no calls? I wrote you every week, Jake. You must have read my letters. You must have known I was desperate to hear from you. Even after my grandfather died, I never got a single line from you. No sorry, no condolences. I mean, that was just cruel."

Jake took the four steps between them so quickly, and with so much force, that Leigh actually stepped back. He raised his voice. "I was ashamed, okay? I thought maybe you'd be happier if I left you alone."

"I wrote you all the time. I wrote you how unhappy I was. It was so hard—"

Now he was practically shouting. "It was hard for me, too! I helped my father and . . . and Dale—"

"All this time I figured you were angry with me, that you blamed me. I just . . . I don't—" She squared her shoulders, blew out another breath. If this was how he wanted it, fine. He'd made his bed and now he could lie in it. "I moved on. I felt like I had to, that if I didn't I might as well go ahead and die."

Jake looked stricken, his hands clenching and unclenching at his sides. "You can't say that, Leigh. You can't even think it."

"Why not? What did I have after my grandfather was dead and you were in prison? You don't know what it was like for me in Boston, waiting every day for four years—four *years,* Jake—to hear from you. I still considered us engaged. I never dated. I never went out with friends or went on trips for spring break like everyone else. I had school and Chloe, and that was it. All you had to do was send me one word, one letter. It would have been enough to keep me going for years, I swear it. I would have waited for you forever, just like I said that day in court."

"I'm sorry. That wasn't what I wanted for you. I wanted you to have fun, make new friends. You went away to college, like you were supposed to. You were supposed to be happy."

Leigh looked out over the water. The bats swooped over her head, and the sun on the hills and the water was dimly gold, growing dimmer, blurred by tears. She felt wrung out, utterly spent. She could hardly see.

She whispered, "How could I be? How could you think I'd ever be happy without you?"

He stepped closer to her now, blotting out the storm clouds that were building on the horizon, the lights of the town, the last of the sun. She couldn't see straight; the world beyond Jake was a blur.

"You said you were moving on. In your last letter to me, you said good-bye. I figured we were through." He was reaching out for her now, his hand following the curve of her waist, down to her hips, his fingers burning her skin. She couldn't see, couldn't breathe. "You mean to tell me we're not?"

She felt his warmth and the rhythm of his heartbeat as he bent his head to her, his mouth pressing against hers, warm and soft and *right*. This is what she had waited for, all those years—some sign that he loved her, that he still wanted her. That she didn't need to be brave anymore, that she wasn't alone.

She meant to protest, she meant to pull away, but there was no point: *this* was what she had come home for. She stayed with him in that kiss, on that dock, with the bats flying around their heads, as long as she could. The feel of his mouth on hers, soft but searching, was the answer to a question her heart had been asking for a decade. *What will we be to each other, Jake? When all this is over, what will have changed?*

From the clanging of her heart, she knew now: nothing. Nothing had changed between them.

"Leigh," he breathed into her dark hair. "My God, how long I've wanted to touch you again. It's all I thought about." He swallowed. "Tell me you thought about me, too."

He slid his hands up her back, smooth on her hot skin. She was aware of the smell of him, a peppery scent like leaves, along with soap and his own musky, leathery smell.

"I did," she said, truthfully. "I do. Every day. I hardly think about anything else."

His fingers reached up into her hair, his mouth firm and insistent, and with his other hand he pulled the small of her back until she was pressed against him knees to breasts. She was drowning in him. She was suffocating on a heady mixture of happiness and grief and longing. They'd lost ten years of their lives. They'd had, separately, to find ways of making it through those years alone. But now they were here together, and there was nothing keeping them apart any longer. They were free to pursue the path their hearts, and their bodies, chose for them.

She could feel his heart thudding against his ribs, his breath deep. His desire, hard and urgent against her belly. "I still want you, Leigh," he breathed. "Like nothing else I've ever wanted. I can't—I don't know if I can wait. Ten years is a very long time."

She pressed herself more firmly against him, as if by desire alone they could cross what little distance there was left between them. "It is," she whispered. "Too long."

"Where—?" he started, but suddenly they were aware they were drawing a crowd—on the street, people had stopped to watch them. Maybe the middle of town wasn't the best place to complete their long-awaited reunion.

"Not here. Come on."

They hurried up the dock hand in hand, not speaking, back to Saundra's Prius parked on Main Street. A storm was coming up, distant lightning and thunder coming closer, and Leigh fumbled with the keys nervously, succeeding in setting off the panic alarm before she got the doors unlocked. Finally they were able to get inside, laughing all the while.

Before Leigh could put the keys in the ignition, Jake was leaning over toward her, taking her face in his hands, and kissing her again. In a moment, Leigh thought, they would simply end up tumbling into the backseat and making love in front of the entire town.

"I just can't believe I'm kissing you," he murmured. "It's like you're not real, and this is some kind of dream, and in a few minutes I'm going to wake up back in my bunk in Huntsville."

Leigh wrapped her arms around his neck and said, "I'm real. I promise, I'm real if you are."

Halfway back to the vineyard the sky opened up, and by the time they made it to the parking lot, it was a small lake. The air shuddered with lightning, and the wind picked up, sighing through the oaks and the grapevines, the bluebonnets dotting the hillside. The conference guests were running for cover, up the hill and into their cottages. Leigh and Jake made a mad dash to Leigh's cottage hand in hand, the rain pelting their backs and faces, and by the time they got to the porch, they were both drenched to the bone and laughing like crazy people.

On the porch they took stock of the damage. Leigh's T-shirt was soaked through, her breasts clearly visible underneath, her whole body shivering with the sudden cold. Jake was equally soaked, water dripping off the brim of his Stetson and down his back, soaking the waistband of his jeans, his boots splattered with mud.

Before she could get the key in the lock, Jake spun her around and kissed her hard, their mouths pressed together fiercely, his tongue firm and insistent in her mouth. He had a light layer of stubble around his jaw, and it rasped her cheeks and her mouth. He pulled her toward him again, like he had at the dock, and she felt every inch of him underneath his wet clothes—the hard, flat muscles of his chest and belly, the length of his long legs encased in wet jeans. Between them, the growing weight of ten years of lust and longing, the swell of want. Leigh reached down and touched him through the fabric of his jeans, and felt him recoil.

"Don't," he said, his voice low and ragged. "Let me take it slow, or this will be over in under a minute. I've waited ten years to touch you again, and I have no intention of rushing things."

It was cold and damp in the cottage. Leigh wrapped her arms around herself and said, "I'm freezing."

Jake bent over the fireplace and in a minute had a soft little blaze going. Leigh stood back and watched him, pretending to warm herself, but instead watching his face lit by the firelight, the angle of his jaw, the golden light on the stubble there, the yellow flicker reflected in his dark blue eyes. If it was possible, he was even more handsome than he'd been as a kid, now more comfortable in his own skin maybe, less garrulous than he'd been when they were young, less jokey, more serious. Prison had taught him to say as little as possible, maybe, though at the moment there was nothing much to say, nothing to do except to bask in the presence of each other at last.

He stood. Slowly he turned her around and stripped off her wet T-shirt, her sodden bra. He bent over her neck, her ears, his mouth tasting her skin, his hands reaching up for her wet and goosefleshed breasts. A shivering that had only a little to do with the cold rattled her teeth and limbs.

"You're so cold," he said. "Come closer to the fire."

He stripped off his shirt and boots, leaving on his jeans. Then he wrapped both of them in the down comforter from the bed, his arms around her back, Leigh resting her head in the middle of his chest and looking into the fire, the shivering in her belly lessening. In the cottage on the hillside with the rain pouring down, they were completely alone for the first time, learning to be comfortable with each other again, with the idea of the other as a real and solid and physical presence. There was no grandfather to catch them, no father or job or jail cell to stand in their way. For the first time since the night Jake had left for Florida, there was only the bliss of the two of them, completely alone, completely free to take their time and do whatever they wished.

When Leigh's shivering lessened, she felt Jake's fingers stroking her arm, gently at first, then more purposefully. He bent to tilt her mouth toward his. His mouth on her was electric—the scratch of his light beard, the pull of his lips on her skin, the low burning that started in her belly and spread all through her, feet to head, until she was glowing like the fire itself.

Over their years apart she'd started to think it was all in her imagination, the way her body responded to Jake's hands and mouth, but here it was again, both familiar and entirely, pleasurably new.

He slid his hands down into the waistband of her jeans and pushed them off her hips. There was a kind of feverish desperation in his movements as he pressed her onto her back in front of the fire, as he pulled off her panties and left her naked in the white comforter, sitting back to look at her.

"Leigh," he said hoarsely, and the firelight was shining in his eyes. "My Leigh."

Her eyes were blurring as she reached up to pull him down to her. "So you didn't forget about me after all?"

"No," he murmured. "I never could. I wanted to. I tried to forget about you, and I tried to make you forget about me. I thought it would be easier for both of us."

"You were wrong."

"Seems I was."

Then he was hovering over her, pinning her arms over her head while he pulled off his jeans with the other hand, his knee pushing her thighs apart.

"Don't make me wait anymore," she said, and when Jake raised his hips to enter her, she grabbed him and pulled him into her with both hands, and he gave a long, low moan like a man who'd thought he was dead suddenly come back to life.

They lay still, joined together, for several long seconds, Jake's breath heavy in her ear. But then she twined her arms around his neck and bent his mouth first to her own, then to her breasts, as he began to move—gently, at first, like he was afraid of his own good luck, then more forcefully, the pressure between them building. She raised her hips higher to admit him, and grabbed his buttocks and pulled him into her, deep, deeper. She pulled him in until she thought her ribs would crack and her body would collapse with wanting.

At last they both cried out and shattered against each other, first Jake, then Leigh a second later. They fell back in a wet and tangled heap of limbs and discarded clothing, Jake shivering against her, Leigh running her hands through his hair. Jake. Her Jake, at long last.

"God, how I missed you, Jacob Rhodes," she said.

Jake looked over at her, grinned, and said, "So does this mean we aren't through after all?"

"Oh, babe," said Leigh, pulling him toward her again, "not by a long shot."

Dear Jake,

I arrived on campus today. My grandfather put me on the plane in Austin and made me promise to call as soon as I got in, but I couldn't. I think I cried the whole way. When I touched down, I could see the Atlantic, cold and gray under a low gray sky, and the city was gray and frozen solid. I cried the whole way to Cambridge, too, so that the taxi driver kept asking me if I was okay, if I needed to go to the hospital. No, I told him. Just homesickness. But it definitely made him nervous. He kept watching me in the rearview mirror as if he expected me to grab the car-door handle and jump out in the middle of the highway.

I think you would have liked it here. Harvard looks pretty much like I expected, all red brick and ivy, but I don't think I was quite ready for how cold it is in the winter. The coat I bought doesn't even begin to cut the chill, and my shoes are all wrong—I think my feet have been frozen from the moment I stepped off the plane. My roommate has promised to take me shopping soon to get some better winter clothes. I don't even know what stores are here and where to find them, much less what to buy. The snow is pretty, though. I wish you could see how beautiful the commons are when the snow is fresh and clean and white. It's like a clean white page. The beginning of something new. I feel like I need that right now.

Somehow the girls in my suite all know the story of why I'm starting school a year and a half late, and they've decided they feel sorry for me, I guess. The proctor came to see if I was getting settled in, and I could see her exchanging looks with some of the girls. At least I don't have to explain the trial to them. They've been nice, but I'm such an outsider here, having to catch up on everything the other girls learned the first week of fall. They already have certain bars they like to go to and certain routines for studying and eating. I don't like to intrude, so I tell them I can't come, I have homework to do.

My accent draws attention, too. The first day, one of the girls in the opposite suite asked me a completely innocent question about my major, and when I answered, she started to develop this strange little smile on her face, and before I was done I had to stop and ask her what was so funny. And she said, "Your accent. It's so cute." Cute, she said, like she was talking to an eight-year-old.

So now I'm self-conscious. I find myself sometimes trying to tone down the accent. I feel like an intruder in their midst, an impostor, putting on the costume of an East Coast prep-school girl and pretending to be one of them. What would they do, I wonder, if they knew the real truth about me?

I wish you'd write me, Jake. I keep hoping these letters are finding you, that they mean as much to you as they do to me. Right now they're the only thing keeping me sane. I hope that now that I'm not living at home, your letters will find me.

Please write me, Jake. Without seeing you, hearing from you, it's like you've died. I don't care anymore about the drugs or why you didn't tell me the truth. I just want to hear from you, how you're getting through the days. Whether you still think of me at all. I need to believe you're still thinking of me, that you still love me. That someday, when you're out, we can be together again.

Love,
Leigh

Dear Leigh,

I keep thinking about the snow. I was there, too, getting with you into the cab. Riding with you from the airport, my feet sloshing through the cold and wet. The flakes in your eyelashes, falling.

How beautiful, to think of you there. Safe.

I finally finished *Anna Karenina* yesterday. I kept putting it down, feeling sorry for myself for a few weeks, then coming back to it later. I can see why you love it. I was there with poor Anna when she threw herself under the train, just as I was with you on your way to Boston. Don't know if I've ever read anything sadder. I keep thinking about it, in that good way you do with books that mean something to you.

I want to do better. I want to improve myself, my station. It's all I have. Maybe my reading here in prison will be like college is for you. A university for convicts. I like to imagine you reading Tolstoy near the cold, gray Atlantic. Talking about novels in stuffy classrooms that smell like chalk, with intelligent people, well-read people like you.

Tomorrow I'll be getting on a corrections bus for Huntsville prison. I heard a couple of the guards laughing about it—apparently they wanted me to hear them laughing about it. Making rape jokes. I don't understand why people think prison rape is such a laugh. They knew I was scared.

They wanted me to be scared. They must think I deserve it.

I do deserve it. I do. But that doesn't mean I'm not scared.

The way people look at you when you're in prison isn't like the way they look at you anywhere else. Their eyes turn toward you, their face is turned toward your face, but there's something vacant in the eyes. Their attention isn't on you. Noticed this first with the guards, but it happened, too, with the judge, with the prosecutor. Even, as the trial went on, with the jury. That's how I knew when I was in trouble: I looked at the faces of the people on the jury. I could tell they weren't looking at me anymore, they couldn't see me. They could only see what I'd done. I wasn't a person anymore but the crime I'd committed. An unsettling feeling, being there and being invisible at the same time.

I'm getting ready for the trip to Huntsville, steeling myself for whatever I encounter there. I'll serve my time, get out in one piece. Going to keep my head down and my nose clean. If I'm lucky and someone takes pity on me, maybe I can get out early. Hear there may even be a program that will let me study for my degree. Might as well use the time. I can't train horses anymore when I get out, that's for sure.

You're angry that I don't send these letters to you, and I don't blame you, but I refuse to torture you with my thoughts, my fears. I'm no good for you, Leigh. I've already done enough damage to you for one lifetime. It will be better for both of us if I stay away. It will be better for you if you do think I'm dead.

If you remember me at all, I hope it will be the way I was when we first met. Cocky, hopeful. I like to think that someone in the world still remembers me that way.

One day, when I get out of here, I might be able to go back to being that person. I hope.

Love,

—J.

Eight

When Leigh woke the next morning in the soft white bed of her cottage at the vineyard nestled in Jake's arms, she had a moment in which she wasn't sure if she was awake or still dreaming. She'd had an image of herself standing at the top of a very tall building, screaming something into the wind at someone who could not hear her, someone just out of reach at the top of another building shrouded by mist and fog. There was something she had to say, something important, but she couldn't hear the sound of her own voice, couldn't make out the words. They were being torn away by the wind, tattered and shredded until all she was left with was a vague feeling of unease, like she'd forgotten something important she needed to do, a matter of life and death.

The sun was in her eyes. She covered her face with her hands and turned away, looking instead at Jake asleep in the bed next to her. He was naked still, his mouth open slightly in a light snore, stubble on his chin dark in the morning light. She leaned over and kissed him softly, and he shifted, reaching for her with his eyes still closed. "Mmmmm," he said. "I had the most wonderful dream that I made love to the one and only Leigh Merrill last night."

She leaned on one elbow to look down at him. "You did," she said. "Three times, I think it was."

"That can't be right. Leigh Merrill isn't speaking to me. She still hasn't forgiven me."

"Yes, she has," Leigh said, and leaned down to kiss him again with the greatest tenderness, blotting out all thoughts but the feel of her mouth on his mouth, like she was far away on some half-deserted island, where no one knew her and there were no consequences to her actions. Whatever happened yesterday didn't matter; whatever happened tomorrow didn't matter. There was only now, and the feel of his flesh beneath her hands, his breath in her lungs. She never wanted to leave this room, this man, this moment.

They sank further into the kiss, Leigh's hands running up the length of Jake's body, this new body that was so strange and yet so familiar. The broad, flat muscles of his chest, the tufts of dark hair on his belly—could this really be the same man, the same boy she'd loved so long ago? Did it matter that she didn't remember him like this, that in her mind's eye she could still see him as a kid of eighteen, seventeen, skinny and sunburned with a mouth full of braces? She kissed the hollow of his throat, the soft place behind his ear, which tasted of sweat and her perfume.

"Hmm," he said. "That's nice."

"Nice?" Leigh said, and pinched his nipple. "That's all you have to say?"

"I meant tremendous, exquisite," he said, squirming away from her. "Ow! Okay, I give up! The best I ever had! When did you get so rough?"

"That was tame, buddy. You haven't seen rough yet," she said, reaching down to smack his bare ass once, twice, leaving a red hand-print.

"Ow."

He jumped up and flipped her over onto her belly. "How would you like it if I did that to you?" he said, and gave her rump a playful smack.

"I might like it very much," she said, and stretched out to her full length. "Care to try that again?"

Jake gave a low whistle of appreciation. "I would, but I think I need a shower first. Care to join me?"

"I like the way you think."

He ran the water hot and stood under the spray. Leigh climbed in behind him, soaping him up, running her hands over his arms, his hips. Already she felt like she was beginning to remember the rhythms of his desire, the tempo of passion and rest and more passion, the hunger in him less boyish but more powerful than it had been when they were kids. They'd always had a natural compatibility, a chemistry that was both emotional and physical, and she felt it click back into place as she licked his neck, his nipples, feeling something inside her catch and flare once more.

She was surprised at her own desire, how powerful it was, that even after a night of almost unbearable passion she was still ready for more.

The running water of the shower offered a new and different kind of pleasure, one they'd never dared when they were kids and living at home under Gene's watchful eye. Jake turned to kiss her, his body slick with water and soap, his hands and mouth gliding over the silkiness of her breasts, between her legs. There was no friction but only the pressure of desire.

Leigh closed her eyes and felt the water spraying them both, a wetness on top of wetness, Jake's tongue flicking over the center of desire gently at first, then more and more insistent, until she felt a gentle pop and the world was warm around her.

Jake stood up and ran a hand over his hair to get it out of his eyes. "Had enough?" he asked.

She reached out and pulled him to her. "Not quite," she said.

Later, when they collapsed on the bottom of the shower stall with their arms around each other, Jake stroked her hair, the water spraying them both.

"I missed you so much," he said. "I dreamed about you. For years. Every night in my dreams you'd come to me, and we'd talk and make love over and over. I'd wake up, and for a moment I'd have forgotten where I was. It was torture. But man, those dreams—they were something."

She reached over and turned off the water, wiping the hair out of her face. "I dreamed of you all the time, too. My roommate freshman year, she asked about you. She said I called out for someone named Jake in my sleep. Said it sounded like I was enjoying it."

"Oh yeah? Was I as good in your dreams as in real life?"

"Better," she said.

"Damn! And here I was hoping fantasy Jake was a dud."

"It's all right," she said, pushing her wet hair out of her face. "Fantasy Jake never could make me really happy. Not like this." She kissed his jaw, his neck.

In the bedroom the phone was ringing. She wrapped a towel around herself and ran to answer it, but the sight of the bedside clock made her gasp: 9:10 A.M. She was late. She'd been so absorbed with Jake that she'd completely forgotten her day was already filled up with pitch meetings from aspiring authors—and the conference was the whole reason she'd come to Texas in the first place.

She picked up the phone; it was Saundra. "Are you up yet, dear?" asked the conference director. "Your first appointment is all ready and waiting for you."

"I know. I'm sorry, I overslept," Leigh said, feeling a momentary wave of panic wash over her. Out of the corner of her eye she saw Jake pulling his jeans over his narrow hips, the smooth expanse of his back. "I'll be down in ten minutes."

She hung up the phone and gave Jake a wan smile. "I'm so sorry. I'm supposed to be at work already," she said.

He sat up. "I'll go."

"No, please stay," she said, her mouth already foaming with toothpaste. "Read a book, watch some TV. I have a break at lunchtime. I'll pick up some lunch for us."

He wrapped his arms around her naked waist and buried his mouth in her neck, murmuring, "I know what I want for lunch."

She rinsed her mouth and turned around to kiss him. In the full light, half naked, he was even more beautiful than she remembered. She pulled on a skirt and blouse and brushed her hair up into a quick chignon. "Promise you'll be here when I get back."

"Will you be wanting a nooner?" he said, and grabbed her one more time for a kiss.

"No, I mean I think we should talk."

"That's it?"

"Maybe more, but only if you're good." She planted a quick kiss on his lips. "I'll see you in a couple of hours," she said. Then she grabbed her bag and hurried out the door.

Outside it was cooler, less confusing. She stopped and took a deep breath and let it out again, slowly. Whatever she and Jake were or weren't going to be to each other, she wasn't going to be able to decide with the feel of his hands still on her body.

When she felt the door click shut behind her, she took another deep breath and hurried down the hill.

In the lobby of the main house Leigh checked her phone for the time: 9:20. *Damn.* And her phone kept beeping angrily at her: there were six calls from Joseph, some of them dating from the previous morning, and several texts from both him and Chloe—the gist of them was *where the hell are you?*—and at least two voice mails she didn't have time to listen to at the moment. She'd spent a stolen night with Jake, but her life was still rushing forward without her, and now she had to deal with the consequences.

As she ran toward the conference room, muttering under her breath, she was seized with a sudden need to see Chloe, talk to her, tell her everything, and beg her advice. As the only person who knew both Leigh and Jake and everything—or nearly everything—they'd been through, Chloe was the one person who could offer a truly sympathetic ear. Leigh's night with Jake had been passionate, intense— better than she ever, in her wildest fantasies, had imagined—but now it seemed it was going to come at a price.

What did she think she was doing, sleeping with Jake, inviting him to stay in her room and her bed, when just two days ago she'd made up her mind to tell Joseph she'd marry him? Had she lost her mind? That moment on the porch with Jake, with the rain coming down—had it been just an impulse, a momentary physical urge? She didn't regret it, or at least she didn't regret it entirely. But she didn't know yet if it was a new beginning or a final period on a sentence that ended long ago.

She was no longer sure who she was, what she wanted. Had she only been kidding herself in thinking she could marry a man like Joseph, be happy with Joseph, when her heart—and her body—still wanted Jake so badly? She thought of him back in her room, lying in her bed, and she nearly turned straight around to pack her bags and tell him to come with her, run away with her. Let's go now, Jake. Let's run away, far away.

She shook off the thought. Running away wouldn't solve anything—it hadn't fixed anything the last time. She didn't have to decide what to do today, and after all, there was still a day's worth of work to get through before she could think clearly about Jake and Joseph, Texas and New York, the past and the future.

Time to get back to work.

Down at the main house there was a line around the door of aspiring writers and conferencegoers clutching sample pages of their books to their chests, smiling hopefully at Leigh as she hurried inside. She apologized profusely to Saundra and her first author of the morning, a retired teacher who'd grown up on a farm in Oklahoma who wanted to pitch Leigh a novel about a retired teacher who'd grown up on a farm in Oklahoma. It was an old story, and the author didn't seem to have anything new to say that would make it fresh.

While Saundra went to get her a cup of strong coffee, Leigh listened to the pitch politely, asking a few gentle questions about the direction of the book, knowing in the first five minutes that the novel would never fly at Jenks & Hall, that Joseph would think it was too dull, that it had no hook. She could practically hear him making his *hmmm* of impatience, see his lips pressing together in a straight line. No—the book might be good enough for another publisher, but not for Jenks & Hall. Leigh took the manuscript politely anyway, wished the author luck, and then collapsed back into her chair, pressing her fingers into her temples.

Joseph. The thought of him, even in a professional capacity, was so painful that she felt her eyes blurring.

She let herself imagine the look on his face now if she told him it was over, they were through—that she was going back to Jake, quitting her job, moving back to Texas, giving up on the two of them and the future they'd imagined. She felt ill, and pushed the image from her mind. *Not now, Leigh. You don't have time for that now. Think about him later.* Scarlett O'Hara would think about that all tomorrow.

When the door opened again, revealing her second appointment of the morning, she saw a familiar gentleman with salt-and-pepper hair and a very formal bearing. Leigh recognized him as the man who'd spoken to her after her opening remarks the day before, the one who apparently enjoyed a little light flirting with a potential editor. Had it really only been the day before? So much had happened between then and now that it felt like a different life.

"Hello!" she said warmly, holding out her hand for him to shake. "I remember you from yesterday. Jim Stephens, is that right?"

"You have a terrific memory," said the man, clearly flattered. He took Leigh's hand in his own. Instead of shaking it, though, he pulled her in for a brief but pleasant hug. Normally she would have been irritated, but for some reason she felt a genuine smile spread across her face, and she hugged him back. There was something about him that spoke to her, some quality he possessed that she didn't quite understand, something that made her normal cool reserve with strangers slide into warmth. She didn't quite understand what it was, but she felt immediately comfortable with him, as if she'd known him all her life.

"So lovely to see you this morning," said Jim. "Looks like you had a good night's sleep. You're glowing." Leigh blushed—there was no way he could have known about the kind of night she'd had. "There," he said. "You're doing it again. Putting all the other ladies to shame."

"Well, thank you," she said. "Nice to see you, too. I was so happy when I remembered you were coming this morning."

"Awfully nice of you to say," he said, setting his manuscript down on the table between them. He had a shock of thick dark hair cut short, graying at the temples, and a very broad, very white smile, putting Leigh in mind of a country Cary Grant. "I've been looking forward to it myself. Not every day I get to talk to a pretty young lady about books."

Leigh laughed. "You're a bit of a flirt, aren't you? I'll have to keep an eye on you."

"Promise?"

Leigh laughed again—he was a *huge* flirt. "Are you local? Or just in town for the conference?"

"I'm in Houston these days. I worked for the oil companies after I retired from the Marines, and my kids are there, so . . ."

So she'd been right about his military background. "How many do you have?"

"Two girls. Thirty-two and thirty-five. And three grandkids. They keep me on my toes."

"And your wife? What does she do?"

"Ex-wife. She divorced me during my second tour."

"I'm so sorry to hear that," said Leigh.

"I guess it's a lot to ask, keeping the home fires alive while your spouse does long tours of duty in dangerous parts of the world. I don't really blame her. I'm not interested in holding grudges, I guess."

"I like that. Maybe we should all be more like you. More forgiving."

"That's the spirit! Anyway, she lives in Dallas with her new husband." He laughed. "I say new, but they've been married thirty years now. I still don't quite know how I got to be so old."

Leigh broke out in a grin. "I'd hardly call you *old*," she said. "Maybe *well seasoned*."

"Ah, you're flattering me. You should hear my girls. They talk like I'm at death's door. Like I'm prepared for the old folks' home. They inspect all the women I date, like I'm the kid and they're the father."

"They're looking out for you."

"They are. They're good girls."

Leigh laughed. It was the kind of thing her grandfather might have said, if he were still alive. "So I want to hear about your project," she said. "It's a novel?"

"It's a memoir about a field officer who gets roped into running illegal missions in Laos during the war."

"Nonfiction?" Leigh was a little taken aback. "You know you could get into serious trouble admitting your personal involvement. You sure you want to take that kind of risk?"

"I know. I don't care anymore—I think it's time I told what I saw, what I did. If it means that these kinds of secret wars won't happen again, then I'll consider it time well spent."

"You're willing to risk a lot to tell the truth."

"I am. I'm starting to get old, and at a certain point I realized that truth is the only thing that matters."

Leigh shifted in her seat uncomfortably. "As long as you understand the risks."

"I do. Took me years to write this book, but I think I've finally got it where I want it. I know you've worked with really top-notch authors, especially Millikin, but I was hoping you might be willing to take a chance on an unknown guy. This book means everything to me. I don't want it to go just anywhere. It really needs an editor who will do right by it, believe in it as much as I do, stand behind it."

He said this with such sincerity that Leigh was moved.

"I figured if I was going to do it, I wasn't going in halfway," he said. "Your speech yesterday really spoke to me, about writing from your passion. Made me think I was right to come today."

"I like to hear that. It makes me think you'd be just as passionate about getting it out there, selling it."

"If you ask me to do something, I'll do it."

"I can't say anything for sure until I've read it, since the success is always in the execution, but I promise I'll do my best to see the potential in it. If it seems like something that will have an audience, then we'll talk some more. Does that sound okay?"

His face broke into a broad smile. "Thank you. That's all I ask." He paused and said, "If you're not too busy, maybe I could buy you a cup of coffee tomorrow and we could talk some more? If that's not too much."

She hesitated, thinking about Jake and Chloe. She wanted to find time for them before the conference ended, but she was sure she had time for a cup of coffee, right? Leigh thought through her schedule. She had another day of pitch meetings tomorrow with an hour lunch break . . .

Jim, seeing her face, said, "It's too much, isn't it? It's too much. Sorry, forget I asked. I'm sure you have plans." He raked his hand through his hair, as if trying to put himself back together.

"No, no," she said. "I was just trying to remember everything I have to do tomorrow. I think I could manage, if that's still okay?" She felt comfortable with him, as if they were old friends. Comfort and friendship were something she desperately needed just then. "What do you say you meet me in the dining pavilion tomorrow at four?"

"I will. Thank you."

She took the manuscript from him and shook his hand. He pressed her one hand between his two. What *was* it about him that spoke to her so intimately, that made her let down her guard with him? She couldn't quite wrap her head around it. "Take care," she said as he went out the door.

The rest of her morning went pretty much as planned—meeting after meeting, some promising, some not—and it was creeping toward noon, when she could go back to her cottage, to Jake, and to the avalanche of texts and phone messages that kept showing up on her cell from Joseph and Chloe. Leigh looked at her schedule—one more appointment this morning. If she hurried she could still make it up the hill to see Jake for lunch.

She was writing a note in her notebook to remind herself about her meeting with Jim the next day when the door opened and her next appointment came inside. "Knock, knock," said a voice.

"Come in," she said, still writing, slightly annoyed that she couldn't have two seconds to jot down a note when she looked up to see the man she'd met at the bar two nights before, the one with the long gray ponytail who'd offered to buy her a drink at the last show of the night before Chloe whisked her away. He'd known her name, said he'd known all about her. Her memory was a bit fuzzy, but she seemed to recall that she'd gotten a creepy vibe from him. What had he said to her? *I know all about you, Leigh Merrill.*

The man sat down now at the table across from her, leaning forward and knocking his knuckles on the table, twice, as if he were about to make some kind of request or demand. Leigh was immediately on her guard. "It's you," she said.

"It's me," he said. "I wasn't sure you'd remember me. You were pretty sloshed the other night."

"You said you knew who I was . . . now I understand it a little better."

"You didn't understand it at the time?"

"Not really, no. I try not to engage with people who hit on me in bars."

"You thought I was hitting on you?" he said. He looked around at the conference room— the windows, the lights, the tables and chairs, the whiteboard, even Leigh's bag on the chair next to her—with a proprietary air. "You must be so used to men hitting on you that you always think that's what they're after. How cute."

"What can I do for you?" she asked, trying to turn the conversation back to business, trying not to show how annoyed she was.

He produced a thin white envelope from under the table and set it between the two of them, thumping it twice more with his knuckles for good measure. "I have a bit of a thriller on my hands, you might say. A bit of a fast read. A murder mystery, you might call it. I think it will interest you."

She seriously doubted that—she didn't publish thrillers; didn't this guy do his homework?—but she put on her most polite expression and asked, "Really? Looks a bit thin for a thriller."

"More of a book proposal, say."

Leigh was prepared to say no already—a book proposal? really?—but she humored the creep. "Okay. Why don't you tell me more about it?"

"It's about a pretty young editor from New York City with a dark and mysterious past, you might say. She's got a dirty little secret she's been hiding from everyone, including the man she loves."

Leigh swallowed. An uncomfortable coincidence—nothing more.

"It seems this young editor—let's call her Laura—once shot a man in cold blood and let her boyfriend at the time take the fall for it. She does a pretty good job of hiding it, too. For a little while, anyway. She becomes a big shot in the publishing world, meets a rich jerk who wants to marry her, but it all falls apart when her ex-boyfriend gets out of prison and the truth about the murder comes out. She loses everything—the ex-boyfriend, the job, the rich jerk. She loses everything because she isn't smart enough to play the game right."

The room had gone very small and very dark. The only thing Leigh could see was a dim tunnel connecting her and the man with the gray ponytail. Somehow he knew her secret, the thing that no one, not even Chloe, had ever known. He was threatening to expose her—to Joseph, to the world.

It had to be some kind of mistake. A misunderstanding. *Please, let it be a misunderstanding.* "It sounds pretty awful," she said.

"It's based on a true story, if that helps at all."

"It couldn't be."

"You don't think so? You think I made it up?"

"I don't know what you're talking about."

His voice dropped an octave, all the false charm flying out of it, replaced by menace, even hatred. "Oh, I'll bet you do. I'll bet you know *exactly* what I'm talking about."

Leigh's mouth went completely dry. This wasn't happening. "Who are you?" she whispered.

"We have a mutual acquaintance, you might say." He grinned at her, showing teeth that seemed very small and sharp, like a rodent's. "A common friend."

Leigh's terror was replaced by anger. She folded her arms across her chest and leveled her gaze at the man. "Don't be coy. You're dying to tell me, so go ahead."

"I spent some time up in Huntsville. I saw . . . a lot of mail, you might say. Letters, postcards, catalogs from correspondence schools. You learn the most *interesting* things about people through the mail."

"You were at my talk yesterday. You must know I don't get much mail."

"No, but you *wrote* a lot of mail. All those letters in green pen, on the nice stationery. No one got letters like Jake did. They stood out. For example . . ." And here he took a slip of paper out of the envelope and started to read. "'*I'm serving a sentence, too. Maybe it's the wrong kind of sentence—maybe you don't think it's fair, and it's not—but I can't change that now. I can't change the fact that you weren't the one who really killed Dale Tucker, and I can't change the fact that you decided to tell everyone you were, and that the jury decided to believe you. We both have to live with the decisions we've made.'*"

Leigh felt her breath stop in her lungs. Those were her words, all right. How could she forget? She'd been so upset that day. She'd been angry, and she'd let her guard down, admitted the thing she'd been too scared, until then, to admit. And now it seemed she was going to pay for it.

The only person who'd been in the barn besides Dale and Jake was Leigh herself. Everyone knew that. It was still possible for her to go to jail for Dale's murder even though Jake had already served time. A new prosecutor receiving new evidence, like a letter, might mean a new trial.

"Who are you?" she asked. "Were you a guard? An inmate?"

"I think the less you know about me, the better."

"What do you want?" she asked, her voice husky with fear.

"What does anyone want, Miss Merrill?" he said. "What makes the world go round?"

She swallowed. "I wish you would stop being so cryptic. Tell me what you're after."

"Money, and lots of it."

"I don't have any. I work in publishing, you know. My salary wouldn't make your car payment."

"Now, you don't think I'm that stupid, do you? I'm talking about your grandfather's money. I know ol' Gene left you a nice chunk. I'm sure you could get your hands on some of it for me, now."

He was after her trust fund? The money her grandfather had left her? No—absolutely not. The trust was the only thing she had left from her family. Her grandfather had left the horse-breeding business to Leigh's uncle Sonny, which was only fair since Sonny was the horseman in the family and Leigh was hell-bent on moving to Manhattan and working in publishing.

Still, Gene hadn't left her out of his will: he'd set aside almost a million dollars in a trust for Leigh, along with enough cash to pay for Harvard. He'd wanted her to be able to get a start in life without relying on anyone. She'd hardly touched it—she'd never really been able to bring herself to think of it as hers—but it was always there if she needed it. It had offered her a measure of comfort and independence, even if it was only psychological.

Now this creep wanted her to just hand it over? Out of the question. It was her grandfather's money, the result of her grandfather's hard work and determination, and this man didn't deserve a dime of it.

"No," she whispered hoarsely. "I don't care what you think you have on me. I won't do it."

The man knocked again on the table, as if this was the answer he'd been expecting. He grinned at her almost with pleasure, almost as if he were looking forward to the damage he could do now that he had his answer. "You sure about that?" he asked. "Wouldn't you prefer to stay out of jail?"

"They won't put me in jail."

"Oh, sure they will. When they see your confession in your own handwriting? You better believe it. And just think what a good time a beautiful girl like you will have in prison."

"You don't have my letters. I have them. I have all of them."

"Now, you don't think Huntsville prison had a copy machine? I could plaster the state highway with copies of you confessing to Dale's murder if I wanted to. You think the county prosecutor won't notice something like that?"

Leigh couldn't speak.

"And there's your nice rich boyfriend to think about. You think he'll still want you after you've done time? Your boss, that fancy British dude? You think they'll still respect you when they find out what you did? You won't have much of a career to worry about then, little lady."

"I can't even get the money," she lied. "It's all been spent."

"No, it hasn't. You rent your apartment. You don't own a car. Your boyfriend pays whenever you travel, so I know you're not blowing anything on that. Let's see. Did I leave anything out?"

No, he hadn't left anything out.

"If you won't pay up, I'm willing to bet there are plenty of other editors in New York who would. Tabloid editors. Gossip columnists. You think I'm wrong?" Silence. "No? I'm right, then? Well, I'm glad to know I haven't wasted my time with this project. Guess I'll jump on a plane to Manhattan and start making some connections. See you in the funny pages, Miss Merrill."

"Wait . . ." Leigh said, weakly, but he was already on his way out the door with the envelope—her future, her past—in his hands.

Dear God, she thought. *What am I going to do now?*

Nine

She climbed the hill of the vineyard to her cottage once more, staring up at the line of live oaks lining the hillside, the blue-bonnets waving in the breeze. The stone path felt like jelly under her feet, like the world was no longer solid. On her back she could feel several long red scratch marks from Jake's fingernails. Had that only been the night before?

She felt like collapsing to the ground, crying out—anything. The smug look on the face of the man with the ponytail when she'd told him no, she wouldn't give him her grandfather's money, when he'd said that he'd turn her in to the police, humiliate her in front of her colleagues and friends. How arrogant he'd been, how gleeful, as if he relished ruining her reputation. He'd said he could plaster the state highway with copies of her letter if he wanted to, and she had no doubt, really, that he wanted to.

There was absolutely no way she could pay him off. It would leave her with nothing, and who's to say he wouldn't make her letter public anyway, just to spite her?

He'd never told her his name. She couldn't look him up on the Internet, couldn't see what she was up against. He'd known everything about her, including how much money she spent and on what, and she didn't even know something as simple as his name.

Leigh's phone was ringing when she reached the door of the cottage, but she didn't answer it. It had to be Joseph or Chloe, and neither of them could help her out when the problem was blackmail. She pressed ignore on her phone, trying to resist the impulse to look behind her. If the man with the ponytail knew about what had happened in the barn with Dale Tucker, what else did he know about? He said he'd been at Huntsville with Jake, but what did that mean exactly? How did he know Jake, really?

She opened the door to the cottage and dropped her bag inside, near the closet, feeling an immense weariness come over her, her limbs heavy, even her head. She didn't want to talk about the past anymore, with anyone, but it wouldn't leave her alone. The prospect of chewing over ancient history with Jake, now, also was unappealing to her. She still didn't know, in the end, what she truly wanted.

Jake was asleep on the bed, his head thrown back, snoring softly. She lay down beside him as quietly as possible, trying not to move the bed, but he shifted and stirred; waking, he pulled her to him. "Mmm," he said. "If I keep waking up in your bed like this, you'll never get me out of here."

She sighed and leaned down to kiss him. "I missed you."

"Already?" he said, undoing the buttons on her blouse one by one, kissing lower and lower with each new button.

"Please." Leigh closed her eyes, feeling the tears squeezing out of them. She felt completely exhausted, wrung out. She didn't want to think anymore, didn't want to make decisions or plans or anything. Right now the only thing that made sense was herself and Jake in this room. "Please, can you hold me a minute? I just need a minute. I can't—"

His arms went around her immediately, cradling her against his long, lean body. "Of course," he said. He brushed her hair from her face. "Are you okay, Leigh? What's wrong?"

Her heartbeat slowed, her breathing calmed. Nestled in Jake's arms, she was thinking of the man with the ponytail, of Huntsville prison, of what Jake had written in his letter to her all those years ago, that the guards had made jokes about prisoners being raped there. She shuddered, not wanting to imagine such things happening to Jake, to the boy he'd been back then. "You were gone such a long time," she said. "I don't know how you managed. It must have been awful."

He looked up at the ceiling. "Some of it. Most of it was manageable, at least. Lonely, but manageable."

She touched his face and said, "What about the parts that weren't manageable?" She brushed a finger over his cheek, his neck, but he was as still as a deer that's scented a wolf.

"You don't really want to talk about that."

"Maybe I do," she said. "Maybe I'm wondering what happened to you there. The people you met."

He stood up suddenly, dislodging Leigh. His skin flushed with anger and embarrassment, Jake stalked to the bathroom. Leigh got up and followed him, watching him turn the shower on, hot. "I don't want to talk about that," he said. "It was bad, okay? You don't want the ugly details."

The bathroom was filling with steam. Jake got in the shower and let the hot water run over his head. Leigh leaned against the counter, folding her arms across her chest. "It was just a question. We don't have to talk about it until you're ready."

"Maybe I'll never be ready, did you think about that? What's the point?"

She was staring at the shower curtain. Jake was just a shape behind it, moving. "You did ten years. That's a lot of your life I don't know anything about."

"And what about you? I haven't heard a word from *you* in six years. You have anything you're dying to tell me about yourself? About what you did in all that time?"

She looked down at her hands. "I'll tell you whatever you want to know."

Jake turned the water off, then grabbed a towel, wrapping it around his waist. When he came out his skin was so red it looked like it had been scalded. "Okay." He took a breath and then said, "Tell me about what's-his-name."

Leigh felt her face burn. She did not want to talk about what's-his-name, especially not now, and not with Jake, of all people. "What do you want to know?"

"Start with when you decided to sleep with him."

She went back into the other room. She'd known they were going to have this talk eventually, but she would have preferred that Jake wasn't so bitter, and that she wasn't so scared.

"That's what matters to you? That I slept with him? I slept with other people before him, Jake. It's not like he's been the only one."

"Anyone serious?"

"No. I didn't want them to be."

"Okay, then. How did this one get serious?"

She sat on the edge of the bed. "You have to understand, I was young, I didn't know anyone in the city. When I first got to the company, I was trying to prove myself. He took an interest in me."

"I'll bet he did."

"It was never like that. He was helping me with my career."

"You know, strangely enough, listening to you defend him doesn't make me feel any better."

"After I got my promotion, I don't know. Maybe he thought it wouldn't be a problem if he asked me to coffee. I said no, the first couple of times. But waiting around for you started to feel so . . . futile. I hadn't seen or heard from you since that day in court. It started to seem like a kind of insanity, all that waiting. The next time Joseph asked me to coffee, I didn't see any reason to keep saying no."

"He seems pretty uptight, if you ask me. I can't believe you'd pick him, of all people."

She felt anger explode inside her—Jake didn't have the right to criticize Joseph, not after so many years of conspicuous silence.

"You don't know anything about him," Leigh snapped. "Anyway, we work together, we have a lot of the same friends, the same interests. It made sense to me then. It still does."

"Does it? Does that mean you're still going to go back to him?"

Leigh hugged her arms more tightly around herself, as if doing so was something strong enough to repel the emotions that suddenly threatened to overwhelm her. "I don't know," she choked. "I haven't had a chance to think clearly yet. I didn't plan any of this."

"And you think I did?"

She made a dry laughing sound, but there was no mirth in it. "Some of it. You planned to show up at the conference with those letters, at least. You must have known that it would throw me for a loop. You wanted a reaction, or you wouldn't have shown up here."

"A *reaction*?"

She couldn't believe they were having this argument again. She could see where this conversation was going already, devolving into a litany of recriminations and old resentments, and yet she couldn't stop herself from pushing him a little more, just a little more.

"Give me a break, will you? You had no intention of staying out of my life, no matter what you wrote in your note. If you had, you'd never have showed up here in the first place. You wanted to see what I would do, Jake. Admit it."

"Hell yes, I admit it. I wanted to see if there was still something between us. I haven't thought of much else in a decade! And I was right. We still belong together, Leigh. Why can't you admit it?"

"I never told you that sleeping with you meant I was leaving Joseph. I—"

"—want to have your cake and eat it, too. I get it, Leigh. Boy, do I. You want to keep both your ex-con boyfriend and the rich respectable guy from Manhattan who's promoting your career. Who goes by *Joseph,* too."

Leigh felt her anger boiling up again, the same anger she'd felt the day she wrote Jake and told him she was through waiting, that four years without a word was long enough. Why did he have to be so damn *stubborn*?

"Lots of people don't like nicknames."

"Yes, rich East Coast pricks with a country-club membership and a big, fat bank account."

He was being impossible. He was picking a fight—for what? To force Leigh to make a decision right here, right now? Was that the idea? Well, he was in for more than he bargained for if that was the case. She was an adult now, with connections and responsibilities he didn't know about and couldn't understand. If he wanted to punish her, she could punish him right back.

Jake came up close and grabbed her by the shoulders, hard. "If you think I'm going to wait around for months while you go back and forth between us—"

"That's not going to happen," she said, taking a step back. "Joseph's not just some rich boyfriend from Manhattan, Jake. He's my fiancé."

The color seemed to drain from Jake's face. He sat down hard on the bed, his voice very small, very young. If Leigh hadn't been so angry, she would have gone to him immediately.

"You're *marrying* him? Really?"

"He proposed right before I came home. Had a ring and everything."

He looked at her hand, ringless, before she had a chance to hide it behind her back. His eyes narrowed. "You didn't say yes."

She was still angry, still determined to punish him for picking a fight with her. "I will, though. I already decided, before you dropped off all those letters, that I would. I'm telling him as soon as I get home."

Jake stood. The towel around his waist fell to the floor, and he stood before her completely naked, his body flushed, strong—a mountain she couldn't or wouldn't climb. She wasn't sure where to look: at him, his body? His face? She stared straight ahead; she wouldn't give him the satisfaction of letting him see how the sight of him charged her.

"And now?" His voice dropped an octave; his eyes were a hot, sizzling blue. "Nothing has changed? After last night, this morning?"

"I don't—I mean, I haven't had a chance—"

"Right," he said, reaching for her. "Let me tell you how much I think you're going to marry that guy."

He kissed her, his mouth soft, searching, but insistent. Leigh dropped her hands; she wouldn't reach up and embrace him, not now. She was still too angry. "Don't," she whispered. "Stop it."

"I don't think you want me to stop," he said.

"I do," she said. "Please. Please." She put her hands up to push him away, took a step back.

He took a step toward her. "I don't want to stop," he said. "Not with you. Not after so long. You're what I want, Leigh. You're everything. I hate that guy. I hate that you'd even think of marrying him."

She couldn't see past his shoulder—Jake was everywhere, blotting out the sun. He was so much bigger than she was, so much bigger than he'd been back in the days when they loved each other, when they used to be happy, and she was suddenly realizing how little she knew about him. Everything she had been feeling was based on some old picture of Jake that may or may not match with present reality.

Leigh's mind was swirling; she couldn't see, couldn't think. She took another step back. "I have to go back to work," she whispered.

"Work can wait." He pulled her toward him again and kissed her, hard.

"It can't. I have appointments I have to keep."

"They can wait. I did."

"Jake. I—I need . . ." she said, turning, as if there were any way for her to get away from him. "I need . . ."

"You need *me*," he said, kissing her neck.

But right now she didn't need more lovemaking, she needed a little comfort and safety. She pushed away from him and crossed the room. There, on the dresser, were the letters Jake had delivered to her the day before. Several of them were open, lying in plain sight. Only now they weren't just a remnant of a long-ago past, they were a threat, a noose around her neck. Someone had read them besides Jake. Someone knew her most intimate secrets.

Not just someone—the man with the gray ponytail. How smug he'd seemed, how sure of himself. He could even now be faxing the Burnside County prosecutor about Leigh Merrill's dark secret. She looked at the stack of letters—the yellowed paper, the green ink in her handwriting. How had the ponytailed man gotten his hands on them?

Had Jake *given* her letters to him?

She remembered what Dale said so many years before, that the only reason to marry Leigh was her grandfather's money. Maybe Jake had decided that her trust fund was payment for ten years in Huntsville.

"Jake," she said, her voice going flinty. "Did anyone else ever see my letters while you were in prison?"

He blinked. "What?"

"My letters. Did anyone else ever read them?"

"Why would you ask that?"

It was now or never. Could Leigh really trust this man—a man she barely knew after so many years locked away?

"Something strange happened today. One of the writers who made an appointment with me said he knew all about what happened with Dale Tucker. He said he'd been at Huntsville prison with you. He was hinting that he'd read something in one of my letters that made it pretty clear who was the one who'd pulled the trigger."

Jake was shaking his head. He looked alarmed. "That's not possible," he said. "I never showed anyone those letters."

"Where did you keep them?"

He raked his hand through his dark hair, as if he were trying to remember. "In my mattress, in a slit on the underside of it. The guards never found them, even, and they tossed our cells nearly every week. No one could have seen those letters, Leigh."

"He was very specific. He knew all the details, apparently. He wanted my trust fund in exchange for keeping his mouth shut. Said that if I didn't pay him off, he'd make my letter public."

"Jesus."

"What I want to know is what you know about it, Jake."

His jaw clenched. "What do you mean? I don't know anything about it."

"He knew I was involved. He said he knew I had shot a man and let someone else take the fall for it. I sure as hell didn't tell anyone."

"You think I did?"

Leigh folded her arms over her breasts. Her voice was close to cracking as she said, "I don't know. You could have decided to come after me for the money. It's pretty strange that you and he both showed up at the same time, don't you think?"

Jake came up close and grabbed her by the arms. When he spoke, his voice hissed through teeth so clenched she thought they might crack. "How can you ask that? How can you even think it? After everything I did for you, you think I'd sell you out for your grandfather's money?"

She felt her chin start to tremble and willed it to be still. "I don't know. I don't know who I can believe anymore."

"You can believe in me," he said. "Of all the people in the world, Leigh, you know you can trust me."

"I want to. I don't know how."

"I need to prove it to you? Again?"

"For all I know, the two of you are in this together."

Jake walked away with his fists clenched, then took a breath and turned around. "What was his name? This person who came to see you?" A harder edge had crept into his voice.

Leigh stood very still, like a trapped animal. "I don't know his name. He didn't say, and I didn't think to ask. I'm guessing I'll find out sooner or later."

"What did he look like?" His voice was ringing with fury now.

"He was maybe fifty. Thin, scraggly, with a long gray ponytail." She breathed in and out, slowly. "And I'll never forget this: he kept rapping his knuckles on things when he talked, like he was calling me to order."

"Oh my God," Jake whispered. "It's Russ."

"What?"

"That's got to be Russell Benoit. He served at Huntsville, four years for fraud. He was my cellmate, for a year or so. The knuckle thing, that was something he always did. Used to drive me nuts."

"Your cellmate." So Jake did know him. So Leigh had been right to be worried.

"He was a con artist. His specialty was ripping off rich old ladies by posing as a housepainter and then rifling through their papers for their dead husband's Social Security numbers. Used to work in the laundry with me. I always hated that prick." Jake was pacing the room now, back and forth, back and forth. "God, I can't believe you met him today. I thought I was done with all that. I thought *you* were done with all that. I thought that when I finally got out, I'd never have to see or hear from anyone I knew on the inside."

At least now she had a name to go with her disquiet. Russell Benoit. "Do you think he's serious? Will he really expose me if I don't pay him off?"

"I don't know. He's dirty enough for anything."

"I could pay him off. I mean, I do have money, I could give it to him, if you think it would really keep him quiet."

"But that's the problem, isn't it? It might keep him quiet for a little while, but then what will he want next?" She could see his jaw working, his eyes narrow. He was figuring something out—and it was scaring Leigh.

"What are you going to do?"

"I don't know. Something. Did he say he was going to get in touch with you again?"

"No, he said he was getting on a plane to New York to try to sell the story to someone else."

"That's not how he works. He'll try again before he follows through on any kind of threat."

"So you think he's bluffing? The New York tabloids would pay for a story like that. I know they would. "

"He might be. Then again, Russ is ruthless when money is involved. He'd sell out his own mother for less than he'd get for our story. But I still can't figure out how he'd know about the letters. I was always so careful to keep them put away."

"He knew, though. He said he saw my letters, the green pen and everything. He read me part of one."

Leigh sat on the bed. Her body was so heavy, so filled with dread, she couldn't even keep her head up. She stared at the floor, at a stray pair of panties she'd thrown off the night before, still lying where she'd left them. Already last night seemed like a long time ago.

Jake sat next to her, not looking at her. "I thought I was so careful," he said. He took Leigh's hand. "Maybe I shouldn't have come to find you. Maybe you were right, what you wrote to me all those years ago. Maybe it would have been better if we'd never met."

"Don't say that."

"Why not? It's true, isn't it? I've messed up your life. All I seem to do is find ways of getting you in trouble."

Her phone buzzed. She didn't even look at it. "I have to go back to work," she said, standing up and hefting her bag on her shoulder. "Promise me you'll be here when I get back."

Jake reached for his belt and threaded it through the loops of his jeans, pulled his T-shirt over his head, and slipped on his boots. "No," he said. "I won't be."

"Jake, wait—"

"I have to find Russell and figure out what his game is. Don't do anything until I get back. Don't give him anything. Don't even talk to him."

"What are you going to do?"

"I'm going to find Russell."

Then he was gone, out the door and into the Texas sun.

All afternoon, while she finished her meetings for the day, Leigh was distracted by thoughts of Russell. How far was he willing to go for the money? Did he really mean to get her locked up in prison for murder? She knew that at the very least she could be labeled an accomplice and given her own sentence should the letter be made public.

Maybe it was only fair. Maybe it was what she deserved—after all, she *was* the one who'd pulled the trigger.

It wasn't fair to the authors she was meeting with, but Leigh wasn't hearing them the way she should have been, not really. Her mind was elsewhere—in Huntsville prison, in Manhattan, in her grandfather's barn the night she'd killed Dale Tucker. She wished for the millionth time that she'd never left her room that night, that she'd stayed in the house like her grandfather had wanted.

Maybe she should just pay off Russell Benoit. Maybe that would be the safe thing, the smart thing. But she kept hearing her grandfather's voice in her ear, saying, *Don't you dare, Leela. Don't you dare give your money to that worthless crook. It's yours. I gave it to you—to you, and no one else.*

After her last pitch meeting of the day, weighed down with worry, lack of sleep, and a massive stack of unread manuscripts, Leigh dragged herself up the hill to her cottage, looking forward to nothing more than a long, hot bath and a quiet dinner in her room.

She opened the door to the sound of the TV. Jake was back already, watching some twenty-four-hour cable news show in which a bunch of talking heads shouted nonsense at each other. It was the last thing she wanted to hear right then.

"I'm back," she said, the words coming out in a weary huff of breath. No response. "Hey, you want to turn that thing off? I have *such* a terrible headache."

The TV switched off. Leigh leaned down to peel off her uncomfortable shoes. "You want to get dinner, maybe order in? I think we should talk—"

She came around the corner, but it was Joseph, not Jake, who was sitting on her freshly made bed, the TV remote in his hand. Leigh felt her knees going out from under her and sat down hard on the nearest chair.

He tossed the remote on the bed. "I'd love to. But how did you know I was here?" he asked, standing up to embrace her. "Hey, you," he said, and brushed her hair away from her eyes. "I was starting to get worried."

"Hi," she said.

Wait. Wait, what's happening here? Where's Jake?

One quick scan of the room told her Jake wasn't there. For the moment, at least, the two parts of her life were still completely separate.

"I—I heard the TV. I figured it must be you. I mean, who else would it be?"

He gave her a quick kiss and then said, "You look terrible. Where were you all night?"

"What?"

"I called and called, and you didn't answer. I figured you must have been out with Chloe, but I called her this morning and she said she hadn't seen you either. Did you go out with people from the conference? You look like you've been up for days."

Leigh's hand went to her hair, which had been a mess all day because it was still wet from her shower with Jake when she had to leave for her appointments. She hadn't bothered with makeup either in her hurry to get out the door. "Oh," she said, "you know I don't sleep well on the road. Lumpy beds. Unfamiliar rooms. I feel as bad as I must look."

She was looking around the room, searching for any evidence Jake had been there—an incriminating boot, a sock, anything—but the room was free of traces of him except for the stack of his letters on the dresser, sitting in the same place where she'd dropped them yesterday. Jake himself seemed to have disappeared.

"So why are you here?" she asked.

"Thanks for the warm welcome! And after I flew halfway across the country to see you."

She gave a half smile and put her arms around his neck, gave him a quick kiss. "You know I don't mean it like that. I mean why did you decide to come?"

"You weren't answering your phone. I started to get worried," he said. "It's not like you to be out of touch for two whole days. I started to think you'd been kidnapped by cultists and carried off into the night."

"I'm so sorry. It was thoughtless of me. I should have called you back a long time ago, I know. I wasn't trying to dodge you or anything like that."

"So what happened? Cell reception here doesn't seem too bad."

Leigh gave a little laugh and tried to act like everything was normal between them. "Oh, you know, I was busy. The conference. Chloe. We had a lot of catching up to do. Think I've had maybe a little too much fun on this trip. I'm still a bit hungover—you know how Chloe is."

"I know. Why do you think I was so worried?"

Joseph came close and wrapped his arms around her waist. Up close to him, she felt completely confused, both grateful to see him and irritated that he felt the need to be constantly checking up on her, to keep her on such a short lease. She'd never had a dad and didn't need one now.

"I guess I couldn't wait to see you again. Not after our last phone conversation. You seemed so . . . upbeat, about us. I was hoping, I guess, to get that answer from you in person. I just didn't want to wait anymore."

Not now. Oh, hell, Joseph, your timing is terrible.

"That's so romantic," she said. "So unexpected. You've never done anything like that before."

"Maybe it's time I started," he said, stroking her hair. His hands felt so good, so familiar—part of her wanted that familiarity right now, after the day she'd just had. She sighed and put her cheek against his shoulder, knowing she had no right to do so, that she wasn't being fair to him, or to Jake, but she needed so badly to feel the world solid under her feet. She had bigger problems than Joseph's marriage proposal, Jake's pride. There was a con artist out in the world who was trying to undo her entire life. She had to decide what to do, and soon.

I can't think straight like this. I just can't.

Joseph stepped back and sat on the bed where Jake and Leigh had made love. She blushed, but Joseph didn't notice. "Leigh, I've been thinking. About the other night . . . maybe I was too hard on you, when we were—you know."

She stifled a laugh. He wouldn't say the word "sex." It embarrassed him.

"Well, you were trying to tell me something, something about what you want, and I wasn't listening," he said. "I thought maybe we should try again. This time I promise to be more open-minded."

"What?"

He gave another embarrassed half smile. "In the bedroom. You know, when you tried to tie me up. I was thinking . . . I was thinking I shouldn't be so much of a prude. That maybe I should give it a try. The bondage thing. That is, if you still want to."

Did he mean sex? *Right now?* She'd slept with Jake four times in the last twenty-four hours—she was drained, and worse, saddlesore. She was thinking about Russell Benoit and blackmail, not bondage. She couldn't, she absolutely could not muster enough arousal for one more encounter, not today.

"I can't. I mean, I've had appointments all afternoon, I haven't eaten, I haven't had any coffee—"

"There you go again, rushing around to take care of everyone but yourself. You need me around, Leigh. Someone has to take care of you."

She felt her annoyance flare again, a quick burst of anger. But she didn't want to start arguing with him right then. "I overslept," she said. "I barely made it to my first appointment this morning. Hungover, like I said."

He was leaning with his back against the stack of letters, threatening to topple them. *Please don't notice them. Please don't see who they're addressed to.* "Did you get any good manuscripts?" he asked.

"I don't know. Maybe one. I haven't had a chance to really read it yet. A war memoir, a tell-all about a soldier's personal involvement in secret missions during Vietnam."

"That's risky."

"You'd like him. I'm having coffee with him tomorrow to talk about the book."

"Coffee, huh?" Joseph said, coming close and putting his arms around her. "You know, our first date was coffee, too. Should I be jealous?"

"That's right," she said. "I almost forgot." He looked crestfallen. "Oh, don't be so dramatic. When I think about our first date, I think about that picnic you made me in the park, that's all."

"Dramatic? Me?" He pouted. "And that was our second date."

"It was romantic," she said. "The most romantic date of my life. That's all I'm saying."

That was a lie, another lie in a long line of lies Leigh had told, and couldn't stop telling. The most romantic date of her life had been in Mammoth Cave, when Jake had kissed her for the first time, but she couldn't very well tell Joseph that. Sometimes she felt like her whole life was built on one long string of lies, beginning with the first and worst of all lies. One more to make Joseph feel better wasn't going to tip the scales any further.

Facing Joseph in person didn't seem to help clarify her feelings. She still didn't know what she was going to do. Yesterday she'd been so sure about marrying him, but sleeping with Jake again had called everything into doubt. Both men were good and decent and honorable. How was she going to move forward with one, if it meant hurting the other?

And where was Jake? He'd disappeared to find Russ, and this time she didn't have the faintest idea of where to start looking for him. She turned around the room, and then turned again, as if looking for something in the cottage that would give her all the answers.

"You okay?" Joseph asked. "What are you looking for?"

She stopped spinning, wrinkled up her nose in embarrassment, and laughed. "I can't remember," she said.

Joseph was staring at her like she was insane, but all she could think of was that she had to get him out of this room now, immediately, before Jake came back. He had gone to find Russell Benoit, and God only knew how long that would take. He didn't own a cell phone. He'd never had one before he went to prison, and in prison they weren't allowed. She didn't know where he was living now. She had no way of getting in touch with him to tell him not to come to the hotel, and he had no way of telling her if he'd found out anything about the con artist. He could show up anytime and ruin everything before Leigh even had time to figure out for herself what exactly it was that she wanted.

"Let me take you out for dinner," said Joseph. "Your favorite Austin meal. There are some things I think we should talk about."

She resisted the urge to cringe. She knew he wanted to hear that she wanted to marry him, that she'd been wrong not to accept his proposal the first time, but she hadn't been able to find even three minutes since she'd left Jake to think through what she was going to do, what she wanted, what was the smart decision, the right decision. If she was going to decide what to do with the rest of her life, she wished Joseph would give her a little more space in which to think it through.

She almost laughed. Joseph never gave her enough space, and Jake always gave her too much. But she didn't have it in her to ask Joseph to leave, not now.

Okay. Okay, breathe. You can do this. Just pretend everything is normal. Just pretend you're back in Manhattan, on your way to work. He doesn't know anything. If you don't want him to know, he never has to.

While Joseph's back was turned, Leigh opened a drawer and tipped Jake's letters inside. She'd have to think of a way, later, to move them without Joseph seeing. And she didn't even want to *think* what would happen if Jake came back to the hotel room and found Joseph there.

"Where should we eat?" Joseph was asking as they went out the door and into the evening air. "I want to go someplace really authentic, really Texas. What would you be doing right now if I wasn't here?"

If you weren't here right now, I'd probably be looking for Jake. They went down the hill in the pink sunset hand in hand, just another handsome, well-dressed tourist couple ready to enjoy a romantic night together. The trees were strung with white fairy lights; the wind sighed and rustled the leaves. "Let's get burritos at Guero's," she said. "That was always my favorite place when I was a kid."

"It's good?"

"The best."

Joseph put his arm around her waist and led her down the hill, through the field of bluebonnets.

Jake, she thought—but she wouldn't, she absolutely *would not* cry—*where the hell have you gone this time?*

Dear Leigh,

They call this place the Walls. That was the first thing I saw when we drove up, these heavy red-brick walls topped with coils of razor wire, like the gateway to hell. There were guard towers at the corners. The men with machine guns watched us as we pulled up in the corrections bus. We got off the bus and they looked us over. First thing, The Look came over their faces, the one where the eyes focus about six inches behind your head. Even though they were looking right at us, they didn't see us. We weren't there.

Get moving, they said. Don't bother crying, ladies, it won't help you now.

I'm a ghost, disappearing little by little, and when I go inside the Walls, I won't exist anymore.

It didn't get much better inside. Last night I went into a room with three other inmates, two guys in their thirties or forties, one old veteran of maybe sixty or so who was totally hairless from chemo. They pointed me toward the empty bottom bunk, which smelled like vomit and cigarettes. One of the two guys introduced himself. "I'm Russ," he said. "And that's Dwayne."

I said, "Nice to meet you." They laughed. Apparently polite intros are no use in here.

They nicknamed me "Bones." A steady diet of prison food has left me thin and light-headed. What are you in for, Bonesy? they said, and when I said murder, they whistled and stepped back. Gave each other looks. The Walls might be the only place on earth where murder gets you respect.

"We'll have to tell the boys to watch out for young Bonesy here," Dwayne said. "He's a killer." Not afraid of me. Amused.

The older guy, whose name is Harold, told them to leave me alone. They went out again, laughing to each other and winking at me. I thanked him. After they were gone he frowned and said, "I don't give a shit if the three of you kill each other, as long as you're quiet while you do it."

I'll have access to the library in a few days, after my paperwork is processed. Then I can take out some new books. I was thinking *Crime and Punishment* might be a good next choice. The Russians, they know things about prison.

It's lights-out time. The guards come and make sure we're in our beds.

I'm writing these words to you in the dark. I will always be writing to you, Leigh. In my head, in my heart. Everywhere. I don't need the lights to see your face in front of me, to feel your body under my hands. You're the air in my lungs, the blood in my veins. You're everywhere, even in the Walls.

Love,

—J.

Ten

After a series of increasingly frantic text messages asking where Leigh had been for the last twenty-four hours—was she dead, kidnapped, or had she lost her phone?—Chloe agreed to meet her at Guero's for dinner.

WHAT HAPPENED LAST NIGHT? DID YOU EVER MEET UP WITH JAKE? Chloe had texted.

Leigh had written her back: NO TIME TO TALK. JOSEPH FLEW IN TO SURPRISE ME.

WHOA! DID HE CATCH YOU IN THE ACT?

I NEED YOU ASAP, Leigh wrote. NO JAKE TALK, OKAY? WILL TELL YOU EVERY-THING WHEN I CAN.

JUICY? Chloe asked.

YOU HAVE NO IDEA.

Chloe answered back, HONEY, YOUR LIFE IS THE WORLD'S SEXIEST DISASTER MOVIE. But she said she'd be there as soon as she could.

Meanwhile Joseph spent half an hour perusing the menu, tryin ,
to figure out the ingredients in the soy chorizo and asking about
the difference between an enchilada and a burrito. Leigh gulped
her margarita and was just beginning to feel the alcohol hitting her
system—the wave of pleasant blurriness, the relaxing of her clenched
jaw—when Joseph peeled the drink from her hand, then leaned in for
a kiss.

"So," he said, "ever since we talked last time, I've been dying to see
you. We have so much to think about."

"I know," she said, looking down at their hands entwined on the
tabletop, the clean white crescents of Joseph's fingernails, her own
hands red-brown from walking outside all afternoon looking for
Jake. Had that been just yesterday? And now Joseph was here, and
he'd want to talk about the proposal, about the future. What was it
she'd said to him the last time they'd talked, two days ago? *I'll make it
up to you when I get home, I promise. I think I was just scared. Maybe I just
needed to let go of some old ghosts.*

She hadn't exactly let go of those ghosts, had she? No—she'd slept
with them instead.

"The first thing we need to think about," Joseph said, "is when
we're going to make the announcement."

Leigh felt a wave of exhaustion overtake her. He couldn't be
serious—she hadn't said a definite yes to his proposal, not yet. "Announcement?" she asked.

"That I'm moving up to publisher," he said. "And about Leigh Merrill
Books. Randall and Marty want to do it soon, maybe by next Monday."

Her imprint. She'd nearly forgotten. "Isn't that a little soon?"

"Yes, but it's all been approved, so there's really no point in waiting, is there? Randall and Marty signed off on it yesterday. We can get
started as soon as we get back."

"It's so much responsibility," she said. "I worry that maybe I'm not

more experienced editors at the press, Joseph. Don't
ight feel a little overlooked?"

e Millikin book. It's your reward. And mine, too,
to be honest—Randall and Marty said I had to be commended
for supporting the career of—what did they call you?—'the next
Gordon Lish.' "

"Oh no, no, not me," she said. "I just got lucky. Millikin was ready
to start publishing again. I just gave him a push."

"It was more than luck, it was damned hard work, and it's all paying
off now. You should be proud."

"You should be, too," she said. The least she could do—the very
least—was be supportive of Joseph's career, especially now. "I'm so
happy for you, Joseph, really. Everyone at the company will be thrilled.
You've done so much for everyone there. The writers, the editors. They
have complete faith in you and your vision for the company, and now
your name will be on the spine of every book."

"And you?" he asked. "Do I have your complete trust, too?"

She put her hand over their entwined ones. "I know you'd never
hurt me. I know you love me."

"You love me, too," he said. "I know it."

"I do. You're a good man—"

The next word out of her mouth was going to be "but." She pressed
her lips together, sat up straighter, as if only good posture stood between herself and the worst mistake of her life. She would not say
"but" to Joseph Middlebury, the man who had given her a career and
life in New York. She *would not*.

He blushed and looked down at the table, fumbling around in his
pocket for something. "I was thinking . . . I mean, I was hoping—"

Just then, like an answer to a prayer, Chloe entered the restaurant
in a rush, pink hair and red boots flying. "Well, hello, stranger," she
said to Joseph, who stood to greet her with his customary kiss on both

cheeks. "I didn't know you were coming in today. What brings you to the Lone Star State at the last minute?"

"Nice to see you, too, Chloe," he said. "I didn't know myself. But I had to come check on Leigh and make sure she was still alive. I called her for two straight days with no answer. Two days! I finally decided she must have been snagged by some rough-and-tumble Texas cowboy, and I was going to have to lasso her cowboy style and drag her back to New York kicking and screaming."

"Is that so?" Chloe said, her voice dripping sarcasm. "Can't leave her alone for five minutes without worrying about her running off, eh?"

"Really, Joseph, I was just busy with work," Leigh murmured.

"Well," he said, taking Leigh's hand across the table, "I couldn't wait until you came back home to see you. We have a lot to talk about, don't we?"

Leigh was grateful, for the millionth time, for his easy personality, his unruffled calm. "We do," she said, and squeezed his hand. *As soon as I figure out what I'm going to say, that is.*

As he sat back down Chloe rolled her eyes at Leigh, who gave her friend the most imperceptible of head shakes. "Well," said Chloe, "you're here now. Is this your first trip to Texas?"

"It is. You'll have to show me the ropes. Help me blend in with the locals." He picked up his menu again.

"First thing you'll have to ditch is that pole up your ass," Chloe said, and winked at Leigh.

Joseph looked up from the menu. "What was that?"

"Ignore her," Leigh said. "Who wants another margarita?" She flagged the waitress.

"Could I have a glass of Pinot Noir?" Joseph asked the waitress.

Chloe groaned, "This isn't the Ritz, Joseph. Unclench, okay?"

"Chloe," said Leigh.

"What? A little ribbing between friends isn't allowed? He's practically family, aren't you, Joseph?"

"It's okay, Leigh, I know she's kidding," he said.

She felt like a mom refereeing between two irritable kids in the backseat after soccer practice, but Leigh could hardly keep her attention on her boyfriend and her best friend bickering when all she could think about was Jake coming back to the cottage to look for her, Jake knocking on the door of her room and wondering where she was. He didn't have a key to the room or Leigh's cell-phone number, but maybe he would wait outside the door of her cottage until she came back, not realizing she now had Joseph in tow. Maybe he would sit on top of the hill to watch for her, and see her coming back arm in arm after dinner with Joseph. The scene that would follow would be awful for everyone involved, to say the least.

Or—and this was the thought that really scared her, that made her really want to weep—maybe he wouldn't come back at all.

The neon lights blurred; the music playing in the background suddenly seemed too loud. She couldn't quite focus on what Joseph was saying to her at the moment, the looks that Chloe was shooting in her direction. She kept picturing Jake showing up at the darkened cottage, Jake leaving her a note under the door. There was no way she could get up and head back to the vineyard alone so she could talk to him, ask him for a way to get in touch with him later, but Joseph would surely notice if she was in the bathroom for an hour.

No—she was stuck. Only Chloe would be able to leave without attracting suspicion. She had to get Chloe alone to ask her to go back to the cottage, to run interference with Jake. She was just about to excuse herself to the bathroom when the waitress came with their drinks and took their food orders.

"You okay?" Joseph asked when the waitress had gone. "You're so quiet."

"Just tired," she said. "It's been a long couple of days."

"We'll eat and go back to your room. Then you can rest."

Chloe looked at her and mouthed the word *rest? That's hot!* But Leigh shook her head, *not now*. Chloe rubbed her hand over her hair, the telltale sign that she was doing her best to hold her tongue.

"You okay?" Joseph asked Leigh. "You look flushed."

She stood up, waving for Chloe to come with her. "I just need to use the ladies' room. Chloe, come with me?" Chloe gave her a look, but stood up. "Be right back," Leigh said, and squeezed Joseph's hand.

In the bathroom Chloe looked like she was going to burst from the hundred questions she'd been holding back. "All right," she said. "Talk."

"You're never going to believe this," said Leigh, and told her friend about the letters Jake had left in her cottage, about searching for him all over Burnside, about how, when she'd just about given up, she'd finally found him waiting for her at the end of the boat dock jutting out into the river. "There he was, as if he knew that's where I'd be," Leigh said. "I couldn't believe it. He looked so different—he's grown up, like you said."

"And?" asked Chloe. "What happened next? Don't tell me you shook hands and said good night."

Leigh's face burned. "Not exactly."

"Dirty details, please. The man's been in jail ten years; he had to be all pent up. I hope you made it a nice homecoming for him."

"I did. I mean, we did. *Very* nice."

"How many times?"

Leigh had to think. "Three. No—four, including this morning. After that we had a big argument, and he took off."

"This *morning*? And then Joseph shows up out of the blue, and now—"

Leigh started waving her hands around. "I know, it's all a complete mess. But, Chloe, seriously, I need you right now. I don't have any way of getting ahold of Jake, and if he comes back to the cottage looking for me, and Joseph's there—"

"What on earth did you have to argue about? It should have been all sex and cuddling."

Leigh didn't want to explain about Russell Benoit and the black-mail, not yet, so she said, "I know, I know. He asked me if I was still going to marry Joseph, and I told him I needed time to think about it."

"You sure know how to make a guy feel welcome."

"He was making me angry. He just assumed I was going back to him, didn't even ask whether that was what I wanted. I don't like having other people make up my mind for me," Leigh said, her eyes flashing. "But that doesn't matter now. I need you to go back to the vineyard and find Jake. Take my key. If he's there waiting for me, get his number and address and tell him to go home and that I'll come see him tomorrow morning at eight. Then text me to let me know when he's gone so I'll know it's safe to come back."

"What if he's not there? What if he won't leave?"

Leigh sighed. She wished she hadn't had so much to drink. "Then text me that, too," she said. "At least then I'll know what I'm up against."

"What are you going to tell Joseph?"

"I don't know. I still haven't figured anything out. If I leave Joseph I will be basically torpedoing my whole career. But with Jake . . ." She groaned and leaned against the wall, rubbing her temples. "The only thing I'm sure of is that I'm not ready for the two of them to bump into each other in my room. My plan is to keep them apart until I can figure out what to do."

"That's a *great* plan, by the way."

"Here's my key. I'll wait for your text."

Chloe took the key out of Leigh's hand and looked at it like it might bite. "I hope you know what you're doing."

"Of course I don't, but that's never stopped me before, has it?"

When Leigh came back from the bathroom and sat down, Joseph looked up from his phone and asked, "Now where did Chloe run off to?"

"Oh, you know Chloe. Got a message from some guy she's been seeing about meeting up. She said she'd text me later." *And now I will burn in hell,* thought Leigh, *for once again lying to the man who loves me.*

But that was just the problem, wasn't it? There were two men who loved her. And she loved both of them, she was realizing now as she sipped her margarita—loved them in completely and totally different ways, for the completely and totally different men they were, and the completely and totally different women she was when she was with them. With Joseph she was calm and competent and smart and successful. With Jake she was young again—unbridled, innocent, passionate. *Very* passionate.

Saying good-bye to one of them would mean saying good-bye to part of herself. But which part?

It was an impossible decision. Jake was her past. Joseph was her present. And the future could include either one, or neither. Or both.

Dear God, she thought, putting her head in her hands, *I don't even know what I want. I don't know what's right anymore.*

Joseph took one of her hands in his own. "Let me see your face," he said. "I love to look at you. You're so beautiful."

"No, Joseph. I wish you wouldn't say that."

"Why not? It's the truth." He coughed and looked at his lap. "What were we talking about? Before Chloe came. There was something I wanted to talk with you about."

"My imprint. Your promotion," she said wearily.

"No, that wasn't it. It was something else. Something about us promising to love each other the rest of our lives."

Joseph was rummaging around in his pockets for something,

finding it in the inner pocket of his coat. In the light of the restaurant she saw him pull the ring out once again, watched mutely as he knelt beside the table, took her hand (*oh God, everyone's watching!*), and said the words again that he'd said in that restaurant in Manhattan, what seemed a lifetime ago. "Everybody said I shouldn't do it, that you'd come to me when you were ready, but I can't wait that long."

Joseph Middlebury, you have the worst timing of any man I've ever known.

"Leigh Merrill," he asked again, "will you marry me?"

He didn't wait for her to answer but slid the ring on her finger to a sudden eruption of applause around them, all the people at Guero's thinking they were witnessing the happiest of occasions. The waitress was there, popping the cork on a complimentary bottle of champagne, and Leigh felt the weight of the ring on her hand, the weight of her future crashing down around her. She had not said yes—she had only hinted on the phone, two days before, that she was thinking of doing so—and Joseph had taken that for agreement, Joseph whom no sane woman would ever reject.

Leigh felt sucked under by an enormous wave of exhaustion. She didn't have to say yes or no. She didn't have to say anything at all, and twenty or thirty years could go by while she sat at the table with her burrito going cold in front of her, accepting the congratulations of a hundred perfect strangers.

It was in that moment that she looked up and saw, in the light of the red and yellow neon, the man with the gray ponytail. Russell Benoit— that was the name Jake had given him. He was sitting at the bar with a beer in his hand, his eyes narrow and mean, staring at her. When he noticed her noticing him, he waved a smug little wave, mouthing the words *talk to you soon,* and turned to the bartender to order another beer. Leigh looked away quickly. She couldn't let Joseph see her watching him, couldn't explain who he was and what he was doing there.

What is he doing here?

The elderly couple at the next table were beaming at Leigh, offering both her and Joseph their best wishes. "I proposed to my wife in a restaurant, too," the old gentleman was saying, and the wife said, "He hid the ring in a glass of champagne, and I swallowed it by accident."

Leigh gave the couple her best smile. She would ignore Russell Benoit, forget he existed. "Is that so?" she said. "What happened next?"

The old couple chuckled. "We spent the night in the hospital!" said the man. "I was getting that ring back come hell or high water."

The four of them were still laughing when someone else joined their conversation. "Wonderful, wonderful," said a man's voice, and Leigh felt her hand being pumped vigorously up and down as she looked up into Russell's face. "You two are just the cutest couple," he was saying. "Congratulations. Let me buy the happy couple a drink."

He pulled out the chair that Chloe had been sitting in and plopped down in it. Leigh froze. What was he doing? What did he think he was going to accomplish, ambushing her like this?

Leigh found her voice, nodding at the bottle of champagne the waitress had just cracked, and said, "We're all set, thanks. Bye, now."

Joseph said, "Don't be rude, Leigh. He's just offering his congratulations."

"I'm not being rude, I would just like to celebrate alone with you. I don't see why everyone else has to get involved."

Russell sat back in his chair, a wide Cheshire-cat grin on his face as he said, "Oh, I'll let you two alone in just a second, but you have to let an old bachelor like me bask in your glow for a minute. It's a lucky man who lands a beautiful woman like you, Miss . . . ?"

Leigh didn't speak. He knew damn well what her name was—she wouldn't play his game.

Russell turned instead to Joseph. "Where you two from?" he asked.

"New York," Joseph said. "Just visiting."

"You don't say? I was just talking to some people from New York earlier today," he said. "Newspaper people. Lots of great newspapers and magazines in New York. Publishing capital of the world."

"I guess you could say that," said Joseph. Leigh stayed very still, like an animal that had been scented by a predator.

"I was thinking about taking a trip up there. Where do you think I should stay when I get to town? What should I do there?"

Joseph looked somewhere between amused and irritated that the guy was still talking. "There are a lot of great museums to visit, shows to see. I'm particularly fond of the Guggenheim."

"Oh, you are, are you?" said Russell, affecting a mocking touch of Joseph's East Coast accent. "What about real estate? I was thinking of investing in some nice condos. Maybe something on West Sixty-fifth."

Joseph gave a slight frown. "That's where we—" he started, but Leigh cut him off.

"The *Times* real-estate section is the best place to start looking, if you're seriously looking. Will you excuse us, please?"

"Oh, I'm always seriously looking," Russell said, glancing from Joseph to Leigh and back. She could see him making mental calculations, trying to decide if now was his moment or if he should wait. She felt like a hostage strapped to the train tracks, hearing the whistle of the oncoming locomotive. *Go ahead and say it,* she was thinking. *See if I care.*

But she did care. She cared too much—that was the whole problem.

Finally he picked up his beer and said, "Well, then. Good luck to you two kids. Hope your life together is just perfect!" He raised his glass to them and walked away, his gray ponytail flicking across his back. Leigh watched him go, but the relief she felt was, she knew, entirely temporary.

"Hmm," said Joseph, taking a drink of his Pinot Noir and watching Russell leave, "I always feel sorry for weird old guys like that. How lonely their lives must be. No wife, no kids. He's in here drinking alone on a Wednesday night."

"I don't feel sorry for him," Leigh said. "Not at all. We didn't ask for his company. I wish he'd just leave us alone."

"Don't be such a grouch. He just wanted to congratulate us. No harm done."

No harm done. Well, Joseph didn't know what was really going on, and Leigh didn't bother correcting him. She watched Russell until he went out the front door, back into the Austin night, but she knew she wasn't seeing the last of him. She was sure he'd show up again and again, until she gave him what he wanted. But would it be enough?

Leigh's phone was buzzing. JAKE'S NOT HERE, Chloe wrote. SHOULD I WAIT?

NO. LEAVE THE KEY UNDER THE DOORMAT, Leigh wrote. I JUST HOPE JAKE DOESN'T COME BACK TONIGHT.

YOU OWE ME ONE DINNER AT GUERO'S, Chloe wrote. AFTER THE CONFERENCE IS OVER.

DEAL, Leigh wrote. LOVE YOU. THANKS.

LOVE YOU, TOO, HUSSY, Chloe wrote. CALL ME TOMORROW. I STILL WANT DIRTY DETAILS.

At least there was one thing in her life Leigh could still count on. Chloe was family, always there when she needed her, no questions asked. The thought of leaving her behind again in a few days—of having to face the wreckage of her life without Chloe—gave her an actual physical pain.

You can go home again, Leigh thought, *but no one said it would be easy.*

Arriving back at the conference, Leigh felt hyperaware of every person she saw, every man and woman she and Joseph passed on their way up to the cottage. She was conscious of the weight of the diamond on her third finger and kept fiddling with it, twisting it around and around and catching the twinkling fairy lights strung in all the oak trees glittering in it.

Jake still wasn't anywhere to be found, but Leigh worried, every moment, that he might pop out from behind a tree or come around a corner of the path. Even at the cottage, when she unlocked the door to her room and peeked inside, she worried that Chloe might have missed him in the half hour it took Leigh and Joseph to get back to the vineyard from the city.

She flipped on the light and looked around the room: no sign of Jake, nothing but her own mess, and Joseph's carry-on propped up on the luggage rack.

She took a breath, but she didn't get any relief. Jake could still come back at any time.

As soon as the door shut Joseph was catching her in his arms, kissing her deeply. After the events of the day Leigh was utterly exhausted, spent physically and emotionally, and she was realizing she had nothing left, not right now.

"Wait," she said. "I don't think I can. I'm completely worn out."

Joseph frowned. "But I thought—"

"I know. I'm so sorry, but I barely slept last night, and I worked all day, and—"

"If this is about the other night," he said, stepping closer to her, "about me stopping you—well, I told you I wanted to try again. I promise to be a little more open-minded this time."

"It's not that, really. I'm just really, really tired. These conferences take so much out of me."

He slid his hands down to her hips, kissed her neck, pushed her ever so gently back toward the bed, more aggressive than Leigh had ever known him to be. "Are you sure I can't tempt you?" he murmured, pinning her hands behind her back. "I promise to be very convincing."

"Joseph, I—"

His mouth was on her neck. He bit her, gently, on one earlobe. "You taste so good," he said.

"Stop. I don't—" She twisted from side to side, trying to get away from him.

He made a noise of frustration and let her go suddenly. "Don't *what*, Leigh? I don't understand you. I thought this was what you wanted. I thought you wanted me to be a little more aggressive, a little more passionate."

"It was," she said. "Last weekend it was what I wanted. Tonight I said I was tired."

"I flew all the way here to see you . . . I thought that's what you wanted, too. On the phone, you said you wanted to marry me."

I didn't, she thought, *I only said I was sorry and that I would make it up to you.* But it didn't matter what she'd actually said, what Joseph had heard was *I've totally reconsidered, and when I come home I'll tell you I want to marry you.* He'd taken that for a yes, when all she'd meant was maybe.

The look in his eyes was so wounded, so fragile. There was something in his expression that reminded her of pictures of him as a boy, pictures his sister and mother had shown her of the young, awkward, bookish Joseph Middlebury, and she hated herself for rejecting his advances.

She wanted to say yes this time and mean it. It was the right thing, the smart thing. It made complete sense. She would make him so happy. She would make herself so happy.

So why in God's name couldn't she do it?

"I don't want to fight," she said finally. "Sweetheart, I'm so glad you came today. I'm so glad to see you. But all I've wanted to do all day today is lie down and read some manuscripts and go to bed."

"Read some manuscripts instead of sleeping with your fiancé," he said. "How sexy." He had no instinct for sarcasm; Chloe must have been rubbing off on him.

"I have meetings tomorrow with authors. I haven't had a chance to look at anything today. Just let me skim this one, and then I can get a good night's sleep."

"All right," he said, but he couldn't quite hide the disappointment in his voice. "Maybe a little wake-up call instead?"

"It's a date," she said, and kissed him.

In a minute she was in her nightgown, teeth brushed, and the two of them climbed into bed side by side. Joseph read a magazine for a few minutes and then rolled over to sleep, shutting off his bedside lamp, but Leigh stayed awake with Jim Stephens's memoir open on her knees. She hadn't lied to Joseph about that much, but after a long and passionate night with Jake, she wasn't up for any more lovemaking that day, not even with the man who'd just proposed marriage to her for the second time in a week.

I saw the man I'd been sent to kill. I saw him, and he saw me. We locked eyes across the river, looked at each other. I raised my rifle to my shoulders, touched my finger to the trigger. I could feel the heavy thump thump of my heart beating in my chest, the wet heat of the jungle in my lungs, the cold, greasy metal of the gun in my hand. I could still taste the cold corned-beef hash straight from the can.

I was here to kill. I was here to kill another human being, a man who quite possibly had a family, children, a wife. I had those things back home, and even though I was the one with the gun, I didn't think I'd ever been so afraid in my life.

Then he waved to me. He put two fingers to his forehead in a salute, his eyes never leaving mine. I had him in my sights, but he was completely unafraid.

For a long moment we stood and looked at each other, and before I knew it I had put my gun down, stood up, and saluted him back. He looked at me for one long moment, then turned and disappeared.

That was my last mission. Two days later I was on a plane for home, in chains. I was being court-martialed, and I'd never been so happy in my life.

Leigh put the last pages down. It was two in the morning, and she hadn't been able to stop reading. Jim Stephens was every bit as good a writer as she'd hoped he be—better, even. The story was gripping as well as brutally honest, carefully researched, and well crafted. The man who'd gone to war as a sniper had found his conscience and refused to fight. He'd been court-martialed and then spent three years in the hellhole of Fort Leavenworth prison. His wife hadn't left him while he was in the war, like he'd said—she'd divorced him when he'd gone to prison, ashamed of the dishonor he'd brought on himself and the family by laying down his arms and refusing to fight. *But how could I blame her for thinking so,* Jim had written, *when the same thoughts went through my own mind every day? Who was I, if I refused to do the one job I'd been sent to do, if I refused to kill?*

She'd found the first title for Leigh Merrill Books, Leigh thought, gathering the pages together. If that was still something that was going to happen.

She looked over at Joseph, asleep next to her, his mouth open slightly in a snore, his eyelids moving slightly in a dream. She did love him, she really did. She loved his charm and his calm; she loved that he was in love with her. There was something intoxicating about being wanted so very much, being loved. But was that all there was to it, really?

She caught sight of the ring on her left hand, a large clear diamond surrounded by a circle of smaller ones, in a heavy setting of platinum. It was a little big—it kept sliding around her finger—but she could always get it resized. A little fix and her life would go on as it had before, more or less. It wasn't settling, like Chloe had said. It was the choice of a certain kind of future, a certain kind of life.

She thought of her apartment back in the city, the old lady who lived across the hall with her little dog, her doorman, the friends she'd made in the office, the little silver cart in front of the office where she bought her bagel and coffee every morning. She thought of it all with a pang of longing, remembering Sunday mornings with the light streaming in the high-floor windows of her apartment, autumn in Central Park, the air growing cool, leaves crunching underfoot as she walked to the museum. It was a good life, a happy life. An easy life.

It could continue being easy, too. The only thing she had to do to keep it was give up her grandfather's money, pay off Russell Benoit, and go on back home like nothing had changed, go on back to her apartment in Manhattan, her job, Joseph. There was nothing wrong with that. In many ways it made perfect sense to her.

And what was the alternative, after all? She couldn't stay in Texas, that was clear. Nothing had gone right since the minute she stepped off the plane. Since the minute Joseph had proposed to her, actually, in front of all their friends and coworkers. But that was her fault, mostly—for always holding back from Joseph, for not recognizing a good thing when it was standing right in front of her. She'd never really given him all of herself, not the way he'd deserved.

She had an image of herself at forty, fifty, sixty, sleeping next to this man, raising kids with him, publishing books with him. They'd have a great apartment in the city, beautiful children, interesting friendships, extensive travels, every luxury imaginable. They'd be the envy of their friends and neighbors, the kind of couple that never fought, the one invited to every dinner party. They'd be the Middleburys, bastions of the society pages, going to charity balls, hosting salons and literary galas. It would be—could be—very satisfying, that kind of life.

How she wished all that were still enough for her, that nothing, in the past few days, had changed. A sudden feeling of grief squeezed her, took her breath away, and then was gone, replaced by determination.

She reached over and turned out the light. *Everything's changed. Everything.*

Starlight Motel

Huntsville, TX

Dear Jake,

My grandfather had a stroke, a little blood clot in his brain that's rendered him about as helpless as a nine-month-old baby. He's been in the hospital for two days, and the doctor says it's very likely he'll die, and I guess hating him forever doesn't extend to the grave. I couldn't let him go without coming to say good-bye, without forgiving him. It wasn't easy, but it was the right thing to do, and I'm glad I did it. He barely knew me—he kept calling me Abby—but I think some part of him knew I was there. He seemed more peaceful. My uncle thought he was waiting for me to come home so he could die. I'm hoping rather than believing that's not true.

I'm afraid even now that the phone will ring and Sonny will tell me he's dead.

It was hard to lose my mom, but she was always this kind of dreamy, silent figure in my life, and when she died, it was like she just drifted into another room, like she'd come back at any moment. This is different. This feels like I'm dying along with him, and if I go, I might never come back.

My aunt and uncle are decent people, but I can't impose on them. They have their own kids to worry about. Without my grandfather, and you in prison and not answering my letters, I won't have anyone but Chloe.

Since I was in Texas anyway, I thought I'd drive up to Huntsville and see if you'd changed your mind at all about seeing me. Maybe a few months have given you a different perspective on things, I thought. Clearly I was wrong. I never asked you to take on this burden alone, Jake. I never expected you to go so far for me. I would never have asked it of you. I would never have let you do it, if I thought it would be the end of us.

I know now that you aren't writing to me. You don't want to see me. Maybe you're angry, and you deserve to be. But don't make me go on without you. It's the one thing I can't bear.

Love,

Leigh

Dear Leigh,

During the day I walk in circles. I walk the track, I talk to no one. I work in the laundry, cleaning other men's clothes. The clothes are stained with shit and urine and semen. They don't come clean, not really.

At night I don't sleep. I'm always afraid. When I close my eyes I see you with the gun in your hand. I see you point it at me. I see you cry. I can't sleep, knowing I'm the one who's hurt you. I can never take it back.

For months now I've been keeping my head down and my nose out of other people's business. The other inmates leave me alone, for the most part. I keep thinking about time off for good behavior. That and the image of you in your blue dress like a meteor shower, your long hair in my face. Drowning me.

Yesterday I was in my bunk reading a magazine. One of the jokes made me laugh out loud. The old man, Harold, looked up and asked what I thought was so funny. I told him. A judge asks the defendant: "Do you have anything to offer the court before sentencing?" and the defendant answers, "No, sir, my lawyer took my last dollar."

It was then that Russ walked in. A little guy, not even five-foot-five. He has the outsized attitude of little guys everywhere, always starting trouble to prove that he's a badass. His arms are so big he can barely put them down at his sides. He's covered with tattoos, including one of his girlfriend's face on his belly, bent over like she's giving him head. He has small brown teeth.

He heard us laughing but not what we were laughing about.

What's so goddamned funny? he said, and got up in my face, pushing me. I tried telling him. He kept saying he must be a joke to me, was that it? Did I think he was funny? He didn't care what we were really laughing about. Sometimes guys need to blow off steam. He got right up in my face, pushing his nose into my chest, shoving my shoulders with both hands, trying to get me to hit him back. Snorting like a bull.

It would have gotten worse if one of the guards hadn't heard. He threatened to send us both to solitary if the argument continued. Just try me, he said. He tapped his baton on my bars. They rang like a xylophone.

Russ shut up after that. He was fuming like Yosemite Sam. The guards can't be around all the time. You think you're so smart, don't you, pretty boy? he said. You think you have all the answers. You sit alone on your bunk and pretend you're better than the rest of us. But you're not. You're not.

The trouble is, I know he's right.

My dad wrote the other day. He found a new job, some little outfit where they train Arabian horses. It was all he could find. He comes sometimes to visit. I hate seeing him. He's always angry, always bitching about the people who've done him wrong. I don't think I have to tell you who's on that list. I don't bother telling him it was all his own fault to begin with. He doesn't want to hear it. It's easier for him to blame you, or your grandfather. Or me. Me most of all.

He told me your grandfather was sick. Something about a stroke. It's hard for me to forgive him, even if he's your family and he loves you. He was trying to protect you from me, to keep you safe. Maybe he was right. If I had left you alone to begin with, none of this would have happened. I'd be free and you'd be happy.

This morning the guards told me I had a visitor, and I knew

it had to be you. Maybe you came home to visit your grandfather, decided to come to Huntsville to see me, try to talk to me. I told them I wouldn't come out. They kept asking if I was sure, didn't I want to see who had come? A gorgeous thing like her could keep a man going in here a long, long time. They said you kept insisting you wanted to see me. I couldn't. I told them to tell you to go away, and they did, shaking their heads like I was crazy.

Maybe I am crazy.

I'm not myself here, Leigh. I'm bitter. I'm angry at my father for caring more about himself than me, angry at myself for allowing my father to abuse our relationship. I'm angry at your grandfather for trying to keep us apart. I'm angry at my lawyer for telling me he thought I could get off on a self-defense plea. I'm mad at Russ for picking a fight. I'm angry at myself most of all, for being so gullible. For loving you so much.

I'm not angry at you. I hate to think of you lonely and scared. It isn't like you. It's not what you were made for. You should be happy. If it weren't for me, you would be happy. That's why I can't send these letters. If you go on without me, you'll be happy again.

If I die in here, I've told Harold about the place where I hide my letters, in a slit in my mattress where the stuffing is loose. He promised to mail them to you. He didn't seem too happy about it, but he promised. I want you to know I was still thinking of you. I want you to understand the decisions I've made and why. I hope you can forgive me my ugly feelings. It's only fear that makes me think this way.

I hope you know what you mean to me, what you'll always mean to me. I'd die for you, Leigh. I always said so.

Every night I pray I will be strong enough to let you go.

Love,

—J.

Eleven

In the morning Leigh opened her eyes even before her alarm went off, exhausted from having stayed up so late two nights in a row. She hadn't slept, not really, just drifted into a quasi-conscious state at some point during the night. Her dreams were all exhausting, violent: Leigh in the jungle with a rifle in her hand, raising it to her shoulder, sighting down its length at a target that started out as Dale Tucker, then turned into Jake, then turned into herself.

She was looking back at someone aiming a semiautomatic rifle at her, someone whose eyes were hidden by the brim of his hat. She raised two fingers, like the man in Jim's story, and gave a salute to the enemy on the other side of the clearing, but instead of turning around and going, the man pulled the trigger.

The gun went off three times—*pow pow pow*—and she felt the bullet pass through her body, fast and sharp as a red-hot poker. Her chest burned. She had only one thought—*he shot me!*—and then her eyes snapped open.

She pressed her hands to her chest, in the place where she'd felt the bullet enter her body, and it was several long moments before she was sure she was safe and whole, alive. But for several seconds, while consciousness returned, she remembered the feeling of the bullet passing through her, the heat, the sudden weakness in her limbs. Maybe Dale Tucker had felt the same thing the night she shot him. Maybe he had that same final thought, the shock of realization—*she shot me!*—before he slipped away.

The sun was coming in through a crack in the curtains and Joseph was snoring beside her. The cottage, decorated in roughhewn wood and river stones and clean white linens, looked the same as it had the night before. Her suitcase open, clothes strewn everywhere. Jim's manuscript lying on the floor beside the bed. Everything was perfectly undisturbed except for Leigh herself.

Then she heard it, *knock knock knock*, three times fast, like in her dream. Someone was knocking on the door to her cottage.

Jake.

Beside her Joseph was stirring in his sleep. She jumped out of bed and ran to the door, unlocked it and swung it open, but instead of Jake, what she saw there was the face of a maid, blinking apologetically in the morning light. "Housekeeping," she said, and then, seeing Leigh in her nightgown, asked, "Should I come back later?"

Leigh's hands were shaking. She steadied them on the door and said, "Yes, just give me an hour, thanks."

Behind her she could hear Joseph sitting up, starting to wake. "Who is it?" he asked in a voice still thick from sleep.

"The maid. She said she'll come back," Leigh said.

She was both disappointed and relieved. No Jake meant no explanations, no confrontations. And yet some part of her had wanted him to be there behind the door, waiting. To get all her secrets out in the open the way Jim Stephens had done in his book, consequences be damned. What a relief it would be—to be finally rid of her secrets, and her shame, once and for all.

She went to shut the door, her thoughts turning to her morning cup of coffee and all the meetings she had lined up that day, all the work she had to do, but as the maid pushed her cart on down the path Leigh saw someone else sitting there, someone with his back against the wall of the stone cottage, a brown Stetson with a rattlesnake band in his lap. There were shadows under both eyes, and he had three days' worth of stubble on his chin, but he stood up when he saw her and crossed to her door in one long step.

"Wait," Jake said, putting his hand on the door. "I need to talk to you."

"Not now," she hissed in a low voice. "Let me get dressed, and I'll meet you down the hill."

She started to close the door, but he put his hand out to stop her. "I found out something about Russell."

Leigh felt her breath catch. "Did you see him? Is he going to leave me alone?"

"I couldn't find out where he was living, but I talked to someone who might know where to find him."

"Who?"

"My dad."

"Your dad?" Leigh realized she hadn't had enough caffeine for this conversation, not yet. She wasn't following him exactly. "Wait. What does Ben have to do with Russell Benoit? How do they even know each other?"

From his place in the bed, Joseph called out in a sleepy voice, "Leigh, who's there?"

Leigh instinctively narrowed the door to a crack, but it was too late—Jake had heard.

"Still the maid," she answered. "Hold on." She went out onto the stoop, shutting the door noiselessly behind her. So much for getting everything in the open.

Jake's eyes narrowed to stormy slits. "I take it that's him," he said. "Where do you find the energy?"

"Don't," she said.

A sound from inside the room—the rattle of glasses on a nightstand, the sound of someone picking up, and putting down, a cell phone.

Jake started to say something else, but Leigh said, "Wait. Not here."

There was nowhere private at the top of the hill, and she couldn't very well let Jake into her room at that moment, so she led him toward a small supply shed on the other side of the cottage. Inside there were brooms and toilet paper, a soda machine and an ice machine, which whirred and hummed in the background. She flipped on the light. It was cool inside, but too bright, too fluorescent for the morning hours. Already Leigh felt a headache coming on.

"You do like your little secrets, don't you?" Jake said. "I take it you never told him about me. But now he's here, and I'm here. How cozy. Any second now it could turn into a sitcom."

"Listen, him coming here wasn't my idea. He just showed up yesterday. What should I do, tell him to turn around and go home?"

Jake crossed the distance between them. He stood so close she could barely see over his shoulder. If he was trying to intimidate her, it wouldn't work.

"Shouldn't you?" he asked. "After yesterday, the day before?" His hands slid down her shoulders.

Leigh was getting angry now, fear and frustration boiling over into fury. She pushed both hands into his chest, made him step back and drop his hands. "You disappear yesterday, and I don't know where you are or even if you intend to come back. I have no way of getting hold of you. I don't even know where you live, and I'm supposed to make a decision about the rest of my life based on one night?"

"You don't want him. I know you, Leigh. You don't love him."

"You don't know me, not anymore. We're different people now, Jake. I'm not saying I can't be with you, I just need some time to figure things out. Because of my job, and Joseph . . . it's just not as simple as snapping my fingers."

Jake went quiet. "I thought—well, it doesn't matter what I thought."

He was softening, starting to back off, and she lowered her voice again, her anger easing. She touched his arm. She needed a little space to clear her head, just a little. "I'm winging it here. I have no idea what the right thing is under these circumstances. Can you be patient, just a little patient with me? A few days is all I ask."

"Okay," he said. "I can do that." He was looking down at the floor, chastened, but something else must have caught his eye: the shine of the diamond on her left hand. She tried to turn her hand away, but it was too late.

"I see," Jake said, grabbing her wrist, his fingers tightening as he waved the ring around between them. "This is the part where *I'm* supposed to be patient?"

"I didn't—" she started.

But Jake wasn't listening anymore. His body was tensed with fury, and suddenly he filled the whole shed, he was everywhere. "You agreed to marry him on the same day you slept with me?"

"Jake, I—"

"I can't believe you. Why would you agree to marry him? Because of a fancy ring, a nice apartment, a job? What are you really selling yourself for?"

Leigh stiffened. "You don't know anything about it. I owe him a lot."

Jake gave a single *ha*, a sound flat and hard as stone. "That's a funny thing to say to a man who went to prison for you."

"He needs me," she said, but it sounded feeble even to her own ears.

She knew what Jake wanted from her, but after the last few days, she wasn't sure she could give it. He was too erratic—pulling her toward him one minute, pushing her away the next.

"If you dumped him today, you think his life would change at all? He'd find someone else, you know it."

"I don't know that."

"He would. He'd be a little sad for a while, but he'd move on," Jake said. "I've tried—God knows, I tried—but I can't move on. Not without you. I need you, Leigh. I need you so badly I can't breathe."

He crossed what little distance remained between them, coming close now, and then his hands were on her, his manner intense but not hurried. He pulled up the hem of her nightgown gently with his fingertips, touching her as if it were the most natural thing in the world, as if there had never been a time when they were apart. His hands were sliding up the back of her thighs, cupping her buttocks. He pulled her close, slowly, until they were just millimeters apart, his mouth nearly brushing hers. The heat of him crept over every inch of her skin. He was so close she could feel him everywhere, even deep in her lungs.

"*I* need you," he said, breathing the words into her mouth. "Don't you know that by now? That there's no place in the world that's home for me, except you?"

Her body yearned toward him, her skin crackling with the electricity between them. If he so much as kissed her now, she would forget Joseph, her career, everything. She would give up all of it to be with him.

He was coming close to her, pressing her back against the wall next to the ice machine, parting her thighs with his knee. "I know you want me. I know it. I can feel it." Something was vibrating, either the ice machine or the air between herself and Jake. "I felt it yesterday. I feel it now."

She didn't answer. She could feel the heat coming off him, the smell of his skin making her dizzy, the space between them taut with sorrow and longing and a want that was so palpable it nearly had a shape and a voice. She couldn't see anything but his dark blue eyes pushing their way into her, leaving her naked. If he touched her then, she would dissolve completely.

With one hand he opened the lid of the ice machine and took a piece of ice. With the other he slid the strap of her nightgown off her shoulder, revealing her breast. He touched the ice to her nipple, and she shivered. She couldn't move. She was pinned there by his body, his hands, her own pulsing desire.

"I tried to forget about you in prison," he said. "I tried to hate you, tried to get you to hate me. I thought you'd be safer that way."

"Safer from what?" she choked out.

"From me."

The ice tightened something deep inside her. His lips were just an inch away. All she had to do was tilt up her mouth to kiss him, and the decision would be made. There would be nothing else to keep them apart, ever.

Jake kept pushing, coming closer. He rubbed the ice up her neck, watching it dissolve on her skin. She shivered.

"Tell me you love him. Tell me you want to marry him." When the ice was gone his hands slid downward, his fingers still cold and wet and slick. "If you tell me to go, I'll go. Tell me you want me to leave right now, so I can leave you behind once and for all."

His hands slipped beneath her panties, felt the wetness at the center of her. Leigh's body arched toward him, and she felt her throat close up. She couldn't speak, not even the word "wait." She would never tell him to go away, never. Not when she wanted him as much as this.

"You think he'd ever touch you like this? You think he could ever know your body the way I do? Your heart?"

Through the window, they were in full view of the hillside path, where people could walk by at any moment, where Joseph could find them at any moment. It didn't matter. Nothing mattered but his hands and the searing look in his eyes, and the flutter of greed in her belly that said *more*.

"Tell me to go. I'll go."

She realized, dimly, that if she told him to stop he would leave immediately, and she would never see him again. The thought made her belly clench with fear.

"Jake."

"What?"

His hands. The electricity in them. *Please. Please, don't stop.* She closed her eyes, her breath coming fast and hot, not caring that Joseph would come outside at any moment looking for her. He'd wonder what was taking her so long and come looking. Then he'd see. It would be awful, the repercussions, but she didn't care, she didn't care at all. In that moment the only thing that mattered was Jake, his hands, his mouth. Her body, alive with wanting.

Just then the maid came in with her cart, flinging the door wide and making them jump apart. "Sorry," she said, looking down at her feet, her face turning scarlet. "I didn't know anyone was in here."

"No, no," Leigh said, pulling her nightgown down again, her body still charged with Jake's touches, clumsily coming back to herself. "We're sorry."

"I'll go," the maid said, moving to close the door, but Leigh, trying to stop her, bumped into the cart and knocked over a dozen rolls of toilet paper.

"Oh no, I'm so sorry," Leigh said, bending down to help the maid pick up the supplies and put them back on the cart. "I'm so embarrassed! We shouldn't have been in here."

She finished picking up the mess and pulled Jake away. It no longer mattered that anyone at the conference might see them, Saundra, Joseph. Everything would be out in the open, as it should be.

Except that Jake was standing over her, his face closing up, his body stiffening with anger. He laughed, a stony, bitter laugh.

"God," he said. "I'm such an idiot."

"What are you talking about?"

"You can't do it, can you? You can't choose because you don't want to."

"What?"

"You want to fuck me and marry him. That's it, isn't it?"

She hugged her arms around herself. "That's not it. I—"

"You're scared to be with me. Maybe you're right to be scared. I've done things I'm not proud of."

"So have I," she whispered.

"You don't owe that guy anything, not your career, not your hard work and intelligence. No one gave those things to you. It's not loyalty to him that's stopping you. Real loyalty is right here in front of you."

He looked at her with such contempt that she took a step back. "Jake, stop—"

"So I have to assume it's something else. Your money, your rich Manhattan lifestyle. I don't have anything to offer you. I don't have anything except myself, and that scares you, doesn't it?"

Leigh stood mute. The anger in Jake's voice was painful for her to hear, but not as painful as the substance behind the words. He was right—he'd found out the truth about her, the real truth. She was afraid of what would happen if she chose Jake. She was afraid of who she'd be, how she'd live. How would they manage? What would they do? Without her life in New York, her precious and longed-for publishing career, who was Leigh Merrill, anyway?

He took another step back, and another, retreating from her as he would from a poisonous snake. "I should have known it was too late for us, but I guess I'm a slow learner. I don't see the truth until it agrees to marry someone else," he said, and in his anger, he wheeled around and gave a tremendous punch to the door of the ice machine, leaving a deep dent behind. His knuckles were bleeding, but apparently he didn't notice.

She flinched. "Jake—"

But he was already backing toward the parking lot, toward his red truck. "Go on back to New York and your friends and your job. Marry that guy. Pay off Russell. What's a million dollars to Leigh Merrill anyway? Maybe he'll even leave you alone afterward."

"Please . . ." she started, but then she wasn't sure what was supposed to come next. *You're wrong? I'm sorry?* Nothing she could think of would make things right between them. She'd been a coward—she'd tried to have it all without thinking of the consequences—and now it was too late.

"You were right the last time you wrote me, Leigh," he said. "All those years ago. You were right when you said maybe it would have been better for both of us if we'd never met at all."

"No," she started. "Jake, I was wrong—"

"Don't worry," he said. "I won't bother you anymore. Good luck, Leigh. Have a nice life." Then he went down the hill. She watched him get into his truck, spinning away in a hail of gravel.

She slumped to the floor of the porch, feeling cold and blank and empty. She'd wanted something to happen that would push the decision to the breaking point, some sign from the universe that she was doing the right thing; she'd wanted something to come along that would take the decision out of her hands.

Now that it had been, she knew it was the wrong decision.

She watched him go, knowing she didn't deserve Jake, but she wanted him, wanted him in ways that she hadn't been able to admit, even to herself. She'd loved him her whole life, since that first day in Mammoth Cave when the bats had swooped around them, when he had first kissed her in the dark space of the cavern like the inside of a church. She had pledged herself to him then in spirit if nothing else, and there had never been anyone else but him in all the years since, not really. She had been selfish and she had been scared—she had made some terrible, awful decisions that even now she didn't know how to atone for—but the only person she ever wanted was Jake, and everything else was just a stopgap, a placeholder in her heart. It was Jake, or no one.

Only moments before she'd been ready to give him everything he wanted, but now she was back to where she'd started—with Jake gone, clinging to whatever was left. And what was left didn't seem like enough anymore.

It wasn't until the maid came by again with her cart, giving her a strange look, that Leigh stood up and wiped her face. She had work to do today, after all. She had pitches to hear, authors to meet, decisions to make. The machinery of life still ground on, even when you felt like you couldn't face it another minute.

Her meetings. Her authors. Russell Benoit. She would see her blackmailer again today, she was sure of it. She just wasn't sure what she was going to tell him. What was right and what was fair no longer made sense to her.

She'd also never gotten a real answer from Jake about his dad, about why he'd gone to talk to him about Russell. What did Ben Rhodes and Russell Benoit have to do with each other? How had they even met? She still didn't know. Maybe now she'd never know. There was no way to find Jake to ask, and he'd seemed resolute in his decision to leave her alone. No—she was going to have to deal with Russell on her own.

When she opened the door to her cottage, she could see that Joseph had fallen back asleep probably as soon as she had gone out the door. He was lying on the pillow—head thrown back, mouth open in a light snore, his thin, handsome face still and untroubled. As far as he knew, everything was fine.

She felt a sudden weariness overtake her and wished she could climb in bed beside him, wished he would wrap his arms around her and tell her it would be all right. She wanted to be angry with him for not comforting her, but that wasn't fair—it wasn't his fault he didn't understand the enormity of the situation, because she had never told him the truth about herself. Not once. The only one who deserved her scorn was Leigh herself.

Hearing her come in, Joseph sat up sleepily and looked around as if trying to reorient himself in the world. "Is that you, babe?" he asked. "Want to get some breakfast?"

She went into the bathroom and stood in front of the sink, staring angrily at her own reflection. She looked ghastly—red and puffy, her skin and hair greasy, like she'd been up all night drinking—but she felt worse than she'd felt in years, sick to her stomach, sick at heart. She didn't deserve Jake. She didn't deserve Joseph. She didn't deserve to be happy.

All she could do was go on pretending. She had to. After all, what other choice was there?

Joseph was still sitting up in bed, waiting for her. Waiting for an answer.

"I'd love some breakfast," she said, doing her best to keep her voice neutral and even. "Just give me a minute, will you?"

Twelve

She headed for work that day in a fog, her mind clouded with regret. In the dining pavilion she grabbed some coffee, the ring on her finger sparkling every time she lifted her hand.

Even Saundra noticed and congratulated her. "Good morning," said the woman, leaning over to pour some raw sugar into her morning cup of tea. Today she was wearing long gray gaucho pants and a red crocheted vest that made her look like a hippie cowgirl. Her long gray hair was braided and lay straight down her back like a horse's tail. "I saw you coming home last night after supper, you and the man in the suit. You looked so good together, I thought for sure you'd have the most beautiful babies. That was him?"

Leigh nodded. She could hardly speak. She felt a sudden pang of longing for her mother, a stab of resentment that she'd had to figure out her life without her mother's help. Surely if anyone would have understood what Leigh was going through, it would have been Abby Merrill, the woman who'd run off to New York and defied her own formidable father with all the calm of a Buddha.

"Oh, honey," said Saundra, "I didn't mean to make you cry."

"It's all right. I'm all right," Leigh said, though she was anything but.

"You want to talk about it? I realize it's none of my business."

She shook her head no. "I'm sorry to be so unprofessional."

Saundra gave her a warm hug. Her hair smelled like cinnamon toast, and Leigh nearly broke down. Some small, deep-down part of her was wailing *I want my mother!*

"My door is always open," Saundra was saying in a sweet voice. "You know where to find me."

Leigh gave a weak smile. She wanted so much to confide in someone, anyone. Chloe wasn't here, and there was literally no one else.

"I'm not sure I love him," she blurted out. "Not the way he deserves."

"Oh, honey," Saundra said, "it's not about what he deserves. It's about making a partnership with someone who makes you happy. *Deserve* has nothing to do with it."

"He surprised me by showing up last night. He asked me to marry him before I left New York, and he was so crushed when I said I needed some time to think. When he asked me again last night I just couldn't refuse him again. It was too painful. But I don't think I can marry him, and I don't think I can break up with him."

"Why ever not?"

"He's the publisher at my firm. He's my boss, basically. I'd lose my job. He wouldn't fire me, but it would be impossible to work with him. I'd have to quit."

"That shouldn't matter," said Saundra, patting her hand. "You'd find another job."

"I could, but I've worked so hard to get where I am at the company. It would be like starting over."

"No—"

"It would. I can't do it, I can't."

"I'm an old lady," said Saundra, stirring the sugar in her tea, "but we're not that different, you and me. I used to be young once, too, you know."

Leigh smiled. She could picture a younger version of Saundra Craig, with long hair down her back, wearing crocheted vests and bell-bottoms.

Saundra went on: "My mother was a very controlling woman. She had very strict rules about how late I could stay out, who with, everything. Eventually I married a man I barely knew because I wanted so desperately to get out from under my mother's thumb." She smiled. "It was the sixties, and there weren't a lot of options for women in those days. It was fine at first. I got to have my own house and a little independence, and I loved having those things, but only for a little while. Because we didn't love each other, not really. When he started sleeping around I was grateful, because it gave me a reason to get out."

"I'm so sorry," Leigh said.

"Don't be. It was best for all of us. Because then I was free to meet someone I really did care about, and now I've been married to him for thirty-five years."

"Really?" Leigh asked. "Why do you think the second marriage worked?"

Saundra looked around and lowered her voice to a conspiratorial whisper. "To be honest, the sex was—*is*—fabulous," she said, and Leigh had to stifle a sudden laugh. The thought of Saundra and her husband . . . well, it was not what she was expecting. "Don't underestimate the power of chemistry. It will get you through a lot of tough times, believe me."

But Leigh couldn't see how that helped her at all. "Don't you think there should be more to it than that, though? I mean, sex is just a little part of your day. What do you do the rest of the time?"

"Chemistry isn't just about sex. It's everything—a shared sense of humor, common interests, common history. My second husband was a boy I knew from high school. We'd grown up together, came from the same hometown. After my divorce I ran into him again, and it was like nothing had changed in all those years. He knew me when I was a kid. He knew who I was and where I came from, because he came from the same place, the same kind of people. That matters. It matters a lot, believe me."

All of a sudden Leigh felt a sense of rising panic. Maybe she should have tried harder to get Jake to stay. Maybe she was putting her heart at risk for the sake of her career and her wounded pride. But he'd been so intent on going, so sure they would be better off apart. Who knows—maybe he was right. Because she couldn't see how the two of them could ever get past the hurt they'd inflicted on each other, intentionally or otherwise.

"Your career and the rest of it don't matter," said Saundra. "The best way to be fair to him is to be honest about your own feelings. Your fiancé's a big boy. He'll manage his own disappointment if you don't marry him. What you shouldn't do is pretend your feelings are something they're not. That isn't fair to you, or to him." Then, giving Leigh one last pat, she walked off toward the barn, her gaucho pants kicking up dust.

Leigh wiped her face with both hands, feeling the weight of the ring on her finger. She looked at it—it *was* beautiful, but maybe Saundra was right: she should stop pretending the ring meant more than it did. She slipped it off her finger and into the pocket of her blue cotton skirt. At least she wouldn't have to answer any more questions about it, at least not right at that moment. And she had to talk to Joseph. She just didn't know right then what she was going to say.

The rest of the morning Leigh worked on autopilot, politely listening to authors and their pitches, asking dutiful questions and nodding along with their responses. It wasn't until lunchtime, when she grabbed a quick salad in the dining hall, that she even remembered she'd promised to meet Jim Stephens for coffee at the end of the day to discuss his book.

Leigh felt a pang of regret. Jim's wonderful book—it was one thing she *did* have a good feeling about, the same way she'd felt about Millikin. She still wanted to publish it. It was raw and it was rough, but she thought she knew how she could help him polish it up. She had no idea how he'd feel about editorial comments from anyone, most especially from a woman thirty-five years his junior who'd never spent a day in a war zone. But that didn't mean she couldn't try. No one had thought she'd talk Richard Millikin into publishing again, but she had.

The first title from Leigh Merrill Books. She still liked the sound of that—she was still grateful to Joseph for believing in her, for making the dream a possibility—but there was still too much that was unsettled, uncertain. Leigh and Joseph. Leigh and Jake. New York, Texas. Her career, her future.

She was only sure of one thing: she couldn't agree to buy Jim's book. Not under these circumstances.

For once in her life she was determined to do the right thing, to put other people's feelings before her own. And if that meant she couldn't publish Jim's book, then so be it. But it was a hard thing to do, to tell a man whose work she admired so much that she couldn't take it, not because it wasn't wonderful, but because she was afraid she was going to be out of a job soon. She couldn't very well keep working for Jenks, Hall & Middlebury if she and Middlebury weren't going to be on speaking terms anymore.

So when four o'clock rolled around, and her last meeting for the day wrapped up, it was with dread that she walked to the dining pavilion, where she'd promised Jim she'd meet him. His manuscript was tucked into her bag, the white pages poking out like a flag of surrender. She'd make it up to him somehow. She just wasn't sure right now how she was going to do that.

The hot, bright May sun was in her eyes, so that it took a few seconds for her to see him clearly, but then she glimpsed Jim at the picnic table nursing a glass of iced tea, waving her over. He wore a dark blue baseball cap with the insignia of the Marines on it, his pale gray eyes twinkling under the brim. "Welcome!" he said, standing up when she came close, a gesture that made Leigh grin—it had been a long while since a man had stood up when she arrived at a table. It was pleasantly old-fashioned and entirely lovely of him. "Thank you," she said, and sat down.

"What can I get you?"

"Oh, no, I'll get it," she said, standing up again, but Jim waved her down. "I can fetch you a coffee. It's the least I can do. What kind?"

"Vanilla latte," she said. "Thank you."

While he was at the coffee station she took the manuscript out of her bag and put it on the table. She'd always liked the look and feel of manuscripts, the white expanse of unbound pages, the thrill of opening one up and finding new people, new voices, the undiscovered countries that, until they were written down, existed only in the minds of their authors. New books were new hopes, with the promise of buried treasure.

She flipped to the first page and read the opening line once more. *My first day in-country,* Jim had written, *a stranger saved my life.* It was a great book that deserved an editor who would love it, and see it through to success. Leigh just wished it could have been her.

Jim came back and set the coffee in front of her and another iced tea for himself. He was watching her face, reading it for signs of encouragement. "That good, huh?" he said. "Oh well. Guess it's back to the drawing board for me, eh?" He was smiling, trying to maintain his good humor, but Leigh could see how disappointed he was.

She took a gulp of her coffee as much to be polite as to swallow the lump in her throat. "Oh, it's not that," she said. "The book is wonderful, Jim, absolutely terrific. I couldn't stop reading it. I wanted to publish it right away."

"Wow." He sat back, smiling broadly. "That's incredible. It's better even than I was hoping for. I thought, maybe . . . Thank you. Thank you so much, Miss Merrill."

"Please, call me Leigh. I think we know each other better than that by now."

"Leigh, of course."

"It's a bit rough in spots, but I think with the right editor you could really have something spectacular on your hands."

A note of caution crept into his voice, and he looked puzzled. "Wait. Wouldn't you be the editor?"

"I loved the book. Absolutely loved it without reservations, that's the truth . . ."

"I feel a 'but' coming on here."

"But."

"Uh-oh."

"I think my circumstances might be changing. I'm not sure I could take it on right now. My situation at Jenks and Hall . . . well, let's just say I'm no longer certain of my place at the company."

"That sounds bad," Jim said, leaning toward her across the table. "Can you talk about it?"

She was afraid if she kept talking she'd burst into tears. How unprofessional would that be? Here was a talented writer who'd offered her his book. He didn't want to hear about her problems with the company, with her love life. Just as she'd done with Saundra, she was losing it, she was falling apart.

"I'm sorry," she said. "I didn't want you to see me like this."

"Miss Merrill. Leigh. Oh, damn, don't cry now," he said, and then he was grabbing a napkin to hand across to her. Of course—Jim was the one who'd just gotten the bad news, but it was *he* who was comforting *her*.

"Thank you," she said. "God, I feel so stupid. I'm sorry about this. It's got nothing to do with your book, which, truly, I think is spectacular. My personal life is a huge mess, a total disaster."

"I'm so sorry," he said. "Maybe we should have done this another time." He put a hand on her arm. She took several deep breaths and stopped crying.

"You're such a good person," she said. "Here I should be apologizing to *you*. I never do this. I never cry, and this is the second time today. It's so unprofessional."

"I don't care about all that," he said. "We can talk to each other like human beings, can't we? Isn't that more important?"

"Yes, you're right." She wiped her face with the napkin. "I've always been so careful to keep people at arm's length. Keeping things inside. Keeping my problems to myself." She laughed, crumpling the wet napkin in her fist. "Guess it just spilled over."

"It's not always good, keeping things inside. Take it from someone who knows."

"No, you're right. I don't know why I have to be so guarded. Maybe it's because I always feel so alone. I don't have much in the way of family or friends."

"I'd like to be your friend, if you'd let me."

"I could use that right about now."

"Do you think you could trust me enough to tell me what's upsetting you?"

"I can try." She took a deep breath and said, "My boyfriend proposed to me yesterday."

He smiled. "That's it? I thought that was a good thing."

"It should be, but I don't think I can go through with it. And he's being named publisher of my company next week, so there's that, too. If I break up with him, I'll probably have to look for another job. I can't in good conscience sign your memoir to Jenks and Hall under these circumstances. I hope you understand—the book would be orphaned if I left the company."

"Never mind that right now," he said, taking her hand in both of his. "My trust is in you, not the company. If you want to wait until you find a job someplace else, then I'll wait, too."

"You'd do that? Really?"

"Really." He handed her another tissue. "Now tell me what happened between you and your boyfriend."

"I don't know if anything happened. I think it's me. Maybe I mistook friendship for love. I've been alone so long, I suppose that's only natural."

"Are you afraid of being alone?"

"I don't know. Maybe. Yes. I lost my mother when I was so young, and I never had a father, or siblings. Her life seemed so sad to me. She never had anyone. Whoever my father was, he was out of the picture before I was born. She was alone. Sure, she had me and my grandfather, but she died alone, without finding real love. I don't want that for myself."

"There's nothing wrong with being alone. I've been alone most of my life, but it doesn't mean I will always be. Every day that I wake up and get myself out of bed brings another chance to meet the person who will change my life. Fear is a powerful force, Leigh—it keeps you from hearing your own heart."

"So—what? You're just okay getting your heart broken over and over again?"

"Sure," Jim said, meeting Leigh's eyes. "Better than not having one. I'd rather take a risk and end up alone than never love anybody."

Jim's hands were warm, pressing Leigh's between them like a flower between the pages of a good book. "If there's one thing I figured out from the war, it's that you don't waste your chances. When something or someone comes along I think is worthwhile, I go for it. The fear that the other person might not feel the same way doesn't mean I regret taking that chance."

What a strange, lovely man Jim Stephens was. Maybe he was right—maybe it was better to take a chance on love than to freeze yourself solid, hold yourself back from happiness.

She thought of what Jake had said, that if she broke up with Joseph today, he'd find someone else tomorrow. He was right, of course—a man like Joseph wouldn't be single for long, not in New York. He'd meet someone new, maybe someone who loved him the way he deserved.

She was in tears again. "What is *wrong* with me? Joseph's educated and cultured and successful, and kind. He loves me. I should love him. I do love him, just maybe not the way you're supposed to love your fiancé."

"There's no *should* when it comes to love. The heart wants what it wants."

"I think mine must be broken," she said, her voice catching.

"No," Jim said. "You're stronger than you think. You deserve to be happy. You only have to figure out where that happiness is."

"You're such a good person, Jim Stephens. I'm glad I met you." He touched the back of her hand with his fingertip, briefly, a suddenly intimate gesture—fatherly, or rather grandfatherly. It reminded her of being home again, on the farm at Wolf's Head. It reminded her of afternoons spent swimming in the springs, of her room at home, of being safe and whole and young. It reminded her suddenly and completely of Gene Merrill, and her eyes filled with tears.

"Are you okay?" he asked. "Is there anything I can do?"

"I'm all right, really," she said. "It's . . . good to have a friend right now. I haven't had enough friends in my life, I'm starting to think."

"I'll be at the conference until tomorrow," Jim said. "If you want to talk, or grab another cup of coffee . . . Well, you know where to find me, okay?"

Leigh felt back in her pocket for the ring Joseph had given her. It was still there, waiting for her to put it on. It was her choice now. A future with Joseph wasn't one she could slide into out of fear.

"Whatever else happens, you deserve to be happy, Leigh Merrill," he said. "Don't forget it."

"I won't," she said. "And thanks."

Leigh was halfway to the cottage, thinking what she would say when she saw Joseph again, when she realized she wasn't alone: a man stepped from underneath a tree to walk beside her. "Miss me?" asked an oily voice. She turned around to find Russell Benoit walking at her side.

"Not really, no."

"Oh, sure you have. You just didn't realize it. I see you're still keeping yourself busy," he said, looking back at the picnic table where she'd just been sitting with Jim. "Another Leigh Merrill groupie. Where do you find these guys?"

"I have to get back. Excuse me."

"I think you have time for me. You know what I can do to your life if you don't."

Leigh stopped walking. His cockiness, his attitude—she hated it, she hated him. She was sick of being afraid of him, of worrying about finding him behind every corner or under every tree. She whirled on him. "I don't know what you think you found in those letters, but you can't blackmail me. I wasn't convicted of anything. I'm not scared of you."

"I think you are," Russell said. "You know you can still go to jail for a crime someone else has been convicted of. You still have an awful lot to lose up there in New York. Your fiancé, for instance. Your job. Your nice cushy life."

Leigh felt cold.

"But you can keep it all, too. All you have to do is give me the money your grandfather left. It's so close, so easy to get. It's in the First Austin Bank, just downtown. A few minutes of your time. I'll even wait here for you to come back with it. The whole lot—the full million— and you'll never hear from me again. One easy transaction."

Leigh froze, considering her options. She could give it to him. She'd still have Joseph, her life in New York, her reputation as an editor. It wouldn't be easy, but it was possible. Other people did it all the time, managing to live without family money propping them up. It might be good for her, even.

Maybe it would be payment, finally, for what she'd done—killing a man and letting someone else take the fall for it.

But giving this man—*this* man, Russell Benoit, the con artist—her grandfather's money? The thought galled her. He'd done nothing to earn it, nothing other than get lucky finding a couple of letters. *Stick it where the sun don't shine,* Gene Merrill would have told him, and Leigh was sorely tempted to say the same. If she was losing the job and Joseph, she'd need that money. She might have to live on it for some time.

She tried to think fast. "I can't take out that much without alerting the IRS. They'll come around to find out what I'm doing with all that money. They'll suspect something."

"Not my problem. Make something up."

"I can't get it today anyway," she said finally. "It takes at least twenty-four hours for a large cash withdrawal."

"That sounds like bullshit to me," he said. He was cleaning his fingernails, not looking at her, as if Leigh Merrill and everything about her bored him. She wished she knew something more about him, something that she might be able to use against him. *Dammit, Jake, why didn't you finish telling me what you'd found out about the connection between your father and Russell?*

But it was too late now. Jake was gone. Russell was here—and she might need to pay him off to get him out of her life. It might be worth the money to her, she was realizing, to get him to leave her alone.

"It's not bullshit. It's the truth. Large withdrawals in cash need twenty-four hours' notice. Call the bank if you like and check. You think you can just waltz in on a whim and clean out the safe? Not likely. "

He looked up and for the first time smiled at her. He had terrible small brown teeth that looked like baked beans. "Well, then," he said, "I suppose, since you're being so agreeable, I can give you a day to get the money together."

"Good," she said, relieved. "Just one thing, though. How do I know you'll really leave me alone? How do I know you won't be coming back around in two years or twenty? A million dollars doesn't go as far as it used to."

"Cash gets you the photocopy of the letter."

"How do I know there isn't another copy someplace?"

"You'll have to trust me."

"You're kidding, right?"

"There are no guarantees," he said, shrugging. "Maybe you'll just have to get used to looking over your shoulder." And he slipped away, past a copse of oak trees and down the hill, out of sight.

He was right: there was no guarantee he wouldn't show up again somewhere down the line, and what would he want then? Five million? Ten? Where would she get the money then to pay off this worthless piece of crap, especially if she broke up with Joseph now and struck out on her own?

Maybe you'll just have to get used to looking over your shoulder. Jesus.

The future was uncertain. Maybe he'd leave her alone, and maybe he wouldn't. There was only one thing she knew for sure: if she didn't pay him off now, she'd probably be in jail by the end of the week, not to mention on "Page Six" of the *Post*. Her reputation, her career, would be ruined. And right now her career was the only thing in her life that was going well.

Maybe she should pay him off. Maybe it would be simpler. It would be the easiest thing in the world to go back to her old life like nothing had changed. Put the ring on. Go home. For a moment she wanted nothing more in the world than to be lying in her bed in her apartment on Central Park West, doing the *New York Times* crossword with Joseph in the morning light. She could still have that life.

She took out her cell and called the bank.

Thirteen

Chloe's car—a rusted-out orange Karmann Ghia older than she was—came flying down the gravel road to the vineyard in a rattle of loose parts and bitter exhaust, screeching to a stop in the parking lot in front of the main house. Chloe sprinted up the path to Leigh's front porch, where Leigh sat waiting for her in a rocking chair, nervously rocking back and forth, back and forth. It had felt like forever waiting for Chloe to get to the winery from Austin, and she needed her friend now, desperately—she couldn't keep crying to people at the conference.

But first there was something important she had to do, something she'd been putting off for way too long: she had to tell Chloe the truth.

Chloe pulled up short in front of the cottage and fixed Leigh with an expression that was half puzzlement, half irritation. "This is your big emergency?" she asked, raking her hands through her pink hair. "Sitting on the porch in a rocker like an old lady?"

The next few minutes would determine how brave Leigh felt about the other unpleasant choices she had to face. Her pulse throbbed in her ears; she gripped the arms of the rocking chair to keep from shaking.

"Chloe," she said, "I have a favor I need to ask of you. Something important. You better sit." She indicated another rocking chair on the porch.

"Sounds serious," she said.

"It is."

Chloe took her seat and looked around. "Where's Mr. Wonderful?"

"I sent him into town for supplies."

"Supplies?"

"Lunch. I wanted us to be able to talk in private."

"Won't he be back any minute?"

"I'm not worried. It takes Joseph a year to pick out something he likes."

Chloe grimaced. "Okay, then. Shoot."

"I need to ask for your help with something."

"You know you've got it. Why so serious?"

"I need you to find Jake for me. I'm not sure where he's living, and I need to talk to him. He has some information I need."

She chortled. "Information? That's a funny way to put it."

"I'm serious, Chloe. He started to tell me something yesterday, something important, and then we got into another argument and he took off again. I don't know how to find him. I don't have a car, Jake doesn't have a phone. You still know a lot of people in Burnside. Your mom. Your friends. I need you to ask around town and see if you can find out where he's living and ask him to come find me. The sooner the better."

Chloe's expression had gone from puzzled to bemused. "I don't know if the two of you should get back together. All you seem to do is fight. At least tell me there's decent makeup sex."

"Chloe, it's urgent. I need this. Please, please do this for me."

"You are serious." Chloe's expression darkened. "This isn't about a booty call. Something else is going on here."

There was only one way for Chloe to understand the urgency of the situation. Leigh took a deep breath, blew it out slowly, and said, "Someone here is blackmailing me. He's not a conference guest; I checked. It's someone else, someone dangerous. He wants my trust fund, the money my grandfather left me." She was talking fast now, her words thrumming. If Chloe wouldn't understand, no one would. "Apparently this person, Russell Benoit, knows Jake's dad. I need to talk to Jake about how Russell knows Ben. I need to know what Jake knows. I need to know before I can decide whether or not I should pay Russell off."

"Back up," said Chloe. "There's something I don't understand. Why would this Russell want to blackmail *you*?"

"He says he knows something about the day Dale Tucker died. He says he'll make it public if I don't pay him off. He'll get me sent to prison, Chloe. For real."

Chloe was giving her the side-eye. "Send *you* to prison?" she asked. "What are you saying?"

Just days ago she'd promised to tell Chloe the truth. Now that moment had come, and she found she didn't want to do it, didn't want to admit the thing that she'd been holding in so long. What if Chloe turned her back on Leigh? What if the truth was something neither of them would ever be able to get past?

But that wasn't fair. Not Chloe. Not Chloe, of all people.

She swallowed and said, "It was me. I killed Dale Tucker. Jake went to jail to protect me."

For once, Chloe didn't make a joke or underplay the seriousness of what Leigh said. "You couldn't have. You're not a murderer."

Her heartbeat slowed. Her breathing evened out. She felt a little light-headed, but the chunk of concrete that had been settling in her gut for a decade suddenly seemed to dissolve, to wash away like a burst dam. Funny—once the words came out, they lost all their power to make her afraid.

Leigh was starting to realize that secrets were the thing that destroyed you, not the truth—even when the truth was unthinkable.

She took another breath and continued: "It is true. I was telling the truth that day in court when I tried to confess. I know you didn't believe me back then—no one did. But it was all me. I was the one who went and got my grandfather's gun. I heard them arguing, and I saw Dale trying to choke Jake. At first I thought I was just going to protect Jake, get Dale off him, but then Dale turned on me. I always knew Dale hated me. He hated me because I was in love with Jake and not him. You remember the stuff he used to say . . ."

Chloe nodded. She'd been the target of Dale's unwanted attention once or twice herself.

"I was scared, though that's no excuse. When he got too close to me, I pulled the trigger. Maybe I thought I was just warning him off, but . . . It doesn't matter now what I thought I was doing. He's dead."

Chloe was still confused. "But Jake was convicted. Jake went to prison."

"He did it to protect me. He thought he'd get off on a self-defense plea. When they found the drugs, they thought they had a motive for Jake to shoot Dale."

Chloe looked at her shoes and then up at Leigh. "Well, that worked out for the best, didn't it?"

"Don't make jokes, Chloe. Why do you think I didn't want to come home all this time? I was so ashamed of myself. I should have told the truth much sooner than I did. I should have insisted, or something. Jake said no one could know. My grandfather never knew either. Jake felt responsible for what happened because he was helping his father dope the horses. You know how he is. He told the sheriff it was him before I could even open my mouth." She looked up. Chloe looked shocked: pale, shaken. "It was a mistake, Chloe. It was a huge mistake, and I can never take it back. I can't give Jake back ten years of his life."

"Jesus, Leigh. Je-sus. No wonder you guys had a fight."

"I promised you the truth, but now I need you, Chloe. I need you to do me a very big favor."

Chloe breathed in and out, in and out, looking out at the horizon, away from Leigh, and for the first time Leigh felt the full weight of what she'd done, how many mistakes she'd made. She should have gone straight to the police and told them the truth that night in the barn, consequences be damned. Anything would be better than living with the awful guilt of knowing the man she'd loved had suffered for her sake, of knowing that she'd lied to everyone else in her life for so long that she hardly knew what was real and what was fiction anymore.

"Chloe . . ." she said, her voice trembling. "Chloe, I need to know what you think. What are you going to do?"

Chloe took a deep breath and looked up. "I'm going to do what I always do," she said. "I'm going to help my friend Leigh. Because no matter what mistakes you've made, you're my best friend, and I love you."

Leigh felt more tears stinging her vision. She'd never cried so much in her life as she had over the past two days. "Thank you," she whispered. "Thank you so much. You don't know what it means to me to hear you say that right now."

They embraced, then Chloe stood back and said, "All right, enough mushy stuff. I'll find Jake even if I have to drag him here kicking and screaming."

Leigh blew out a long, frustrated breath. "That's exactly what it might take."

She waited nearly an hour for Joseph to come back to the cottage with wine and something small for dinner. He'd borrowed Saundra's car and taken his time, as Leigh had predicted, lingering over the local offerings of cheese and fruit and wine and fresh bread until he'd arranged the perfect stay-in dinner for the two of them. He'd chosen something small and intimate, the way he always did at home in New York, and though the local supermarket was not Zabar's, he still spread out his offerings on the table in the corner with such evident pleasure that Leigh felt her heart break a little.

"This will be nice," he said when he was finished, his posture ramrod straight, his dark hair soft and perfectly combed even in the heat. "Just the two of us. We'll celebrate properly this time."

He stood behind the chair where she sat with her stack of manuscripts beside her and touched her shoulders, kneading gently. She'd been reading the same page for twenty minutes, trying to think of what she was going to say to him when he came back. Now here he was, and it all flew out of her head again, replaced by determination. She'd already told the truth, the whole truth, once today. She could do it again now.

"Hey," he said, picking up a manuscript. "See anything good in this pile?"

"A bit. Maybe one or two," she said, her eyes never leaving the page. "A war memoir. Had coffee with the author today," she said.

"What's he like?"

She remembered how much he reminded her of her grandfather and felt a flush of warmth toward Jim. "He's nice."

Joseph chortled. "Nice? That's it?"

Leigh blushed. "I mean, I liked him. He's very talented. I think I'd like working with him on the book."

"More than Millikin?"

She gave a small smile. "I'm sure he'd be easier to work with than Millikin."

"So would anybody," Joseph said. He put the manuscript down again. "You going to sign him up?"

Again she went through all the reasons why she couldn't, just yet. But standing in the doorway looking at Joseph, she couldn't say so, not until she was sure what she was going to do. "I'm thinking about it."

He went back to his reading, pulling another page off the top. "Well, don't wait too long," he said. "If we don't snap this one up, someone else will."

It was the same thing he'd once said about her. *If I don't snap you up now, someone else will.* Fear of competition was a good motivator in business, but it didn't seem like such a good reason to get married. Leigh wasn't a business venture, something that needed to be launched before the competition moved in. She was a very flawed and confused woman who was afraid to do the thing that needed to be done.

"Hungry?" he asked, leaning down to nibble on her neck.

Leigh shrank away from him. "Now?"

"There's no time like the present."

She couldn't imagine sex right then. She still felt awful after running into Russell—dirty, like her soul had been soiled. "I can't. I need a shower."

"Go ahead, then. I'll wait."

She ran the water hot, as hot as she could stand it, letting the spray sting her skin nearly raw and hide her tears even from herself. She scrubbed off the feel of Russell Benoit, the greasy sound of his voice, his cigarette smell. If Russell were dangerous, as Jake seemed to think he was, she might be risking more than jail to refuse him the money. He knew so much about her. Who was to say what he might do out of anger, or revenge?

Then again, if she stayed with Joseph, she wouldn't need her trust fund. Joseph had his own family money; they'd never want for anything. But she couldn't marry a man she didn't love just to keep from being broke. She thought of Saundra marrying to get out of her mother's house. Marrying Joseph would be a little different, maybe, but not much.

She pulled back the curtain and toweled off, wiping the mirror so she could see her face in the steam. *You brought this on yourself,* she thought, meeting her own sad and desperate eyes. *No one is to blame but you, and no one should pay but you. It's time to stop pretending otherwise.* Maybe then, finally, she could put the past behind her and move on.

The bank had told her they'd have the cash ready to go in the morning. All she had to do was drive into town to pick it up. She wasn't sure if it was the right thing, the smart thing. At the moment it felt like the only thing.

Outside the bathroom she could hear Joseph rustling some pages, pulling the cork on the bottle of Pinot Noir he'd bought to let the wine breathe. She felt seized by a sudden determination. Telling Chloe the truth had been such a relief. Maybe it was time to do the same with Joseph. He deserved that from her, after all.

She went into the bedroom and stood in the doorway, watching him. His thin, handsome face was frowning now, looking at the pages of Jim's manuscript, turning the pages quickly, engrossed in his reading. Clearly he was loving it as much as she had. It was one of the things that had first attracted her to him, the fact that they shared such similar tastes in books, that they both looked at books the same way—as a passion, not just a profession.

But that attraction had never, in the years they'd been together, deepened into the something more that made it possible for her to go from fantasizing a life with him to actually wanting that life. It was a beautiful picture—but she knew, now, that she could not enter that picture. It wasn't for her, the parties in the Hamptons and the glamorous fund-raisers, the social stratosphere of New York's elite. She was still a farm girl from Burnside, Texas, and after she paid off Russell she wouldn't be a wealthy one anymore either. She'd be just like everyone else, doing the best she could to get by with her bank account and her dignity intact.

She'd be alone, but she'd be free. There was that, at least.

Joseph flipped another page. "I don't know what you're still mulling over," he said. "You should definitely be signing this guy up. It would make a great debut for Leigh Merrill Books."

"It would."

He looked up and frowned. "Okay, then. So what are you waiting for?"

It was time for Leigh Merrill to face up: to the reality of what she'd done, to whatever consequences there were left to bear. She'd just have to do it without the help, or support, of Joseph Middlebury from now on.

She dug the ring out of the pocket of her jeans, which were lying on the floor. Then she set it down on the nightstand next to the bed. The heavy platinum made an audible *click* when she set it down. "We need to talk," she said.

Joseph looked up, the expression in his eyes going from surprise to dismay to grim acceptance. He rubbed a hand over his face and looked at the ring on the nightstand. "I'm not going to like this, am I?" he asked.

"No," she said. "I don't think you will."

Fourteen

eigh lay in bed most of the night, watching the lightning of a summer thunderstorm illuminate the inside of the cottage and then go dark again. Then the thunder would boom, the cracks closer together, the lightning coming thick and furious. It was hot inside the cottage, the ceiling fan doing little to move the air around; it clung to Leigh like a wet blanket. Her mind couldn't rest; her thoughts were jumbled together, knocking into each other like stones in a raging river. Soon she would have to make one more decision that would affect the rest of her life. She only hoped she was making the right moves in what was starting to seem like an impossibly difficult and dangerous game of chess.

She was exhausted but too nervous to sleep. Joseph had gone hours before, called a taxi to take him to the airport so he could fly home to New York. He'd been heartbroken, as Leigh had feared, but he'd also been indignant.

"I don't think you know what you're saying," he'd said at first, in that way that seemed to indicate that he knew better for her than she knew for herself. Then something came over him, some darkness, and he asked, "Is there someone else? Someone you'd rather be with?"

Leigh had hesitated and said, "No. Does it even matter? No." It was true enough, since Jake had made it clear he planned never to come near her again. Whatever they'd had—it was gone now. For good, this time.

"You don't seem so sure."

"There could be someone else eventually. Maybe I even wanted there to be someone else. But it doesn't matter—this is about you and me."

"Someone at the conference?"

"You're not listening," she said. "There's something between us that's missing. It might be fine now, but down the road . . . I'm just afraid we'd end up hating each other."

Joseph had looked shocked for a moment, and asked, "Whatever it is, I can work on it. I don't want to give up on us so easily. Tell me what you want, Leigh. I can give it to you. I can give you the whole world if that's what you want. If you need more time . . ."

"That's just it. I don't want more time."

Leigh thought carefully. She wanted to say what she had to say with the minimal amount of damage. She remembered what Saundra had said, about how the physical parts of a relationship could carry people through even the roughest patches. With Joseph, it was clear now, the physical part of the equation was missing, or at least not powerful enough to carry them through every crisis.

"It's nothing we can work on," she said. "There's just a level of chemistry we don't have. It's no one's fault, Joseph."

His eyes darkened again. "Chemistry? Is that what this is about? You'd torpedo our whole lives over sex. What about everything else we have? Our friendship? Our work?"

"And those things are important to me, too. But it's not enough." She couldn't help remembering Jake in the storage shed, the way her body seemed to turn itself inside out at his touch. "I'm not just talking about sex. It's intimacy, it's complete trust. I've never been totally honest with you, maybe ever. Not just in the bedroom. You don't know anything about my past, about my life. You don't know who I am, not really." His face registered no small amount of shock. "I'm starting to realize how much of a problem that is."

"What aren't you telling me?" he hissed. "Did you sleep with someone while you were here?"

Leigh's face was burning. He'd asked her point-blank the one question she'd wanted to avoid. But he deserved the truth, the whole truth, from her. If she was going to quit lying, if she was going to start being honest, truly honest, with the people in her life, she was going to have to bear the hurt she'd caused others, even if it cost her their respect and friendship. Even if, in the end, it cost her everything.

"Yes," she said at last. "I did."

Instead of howling in rage and punching the wall, like Jake would have done, Joseph stood very still, his voice going very small and cold. For a moment, he looked and sounded exactly like his aristocratic mother. "Who is he? Tell me his name."

Leigh met his eyes. She'd caused this mess; she wouldn't back down now. "Does it matter? I felt this way before I came here, Joseph, you know that. It's why I couldn't say yes when you proposed at the launch party. The only thing that's changed in the last few days is that I understand more now what's been holding me back all this time."

"I can't force you to love me. I know that." He looked up sharply. "Is this about the imprint? Did someone else offer you a job?"

"No, no," she said. "Nothing like that. I don't have any other job offers." She took a breath and blew it out, screwing up her courage. "But since we're on the subject, I don't think I should stay at the company, do you? You think you're upset now, but imagine how you're going to feel in a month or two. I don't think it's a good idea for us to keep working together under these circumstances. Maybe it would be best if I looked for another place."

"Maybe it would be best," he said. His voice was still so cold that Leigh nearly shivered. "I don't know if I can keep working with you like this. I don't think I can even look at you." He sat down heavily on the nearby chair. "No Leigh Merrill Books, then."

"No."

"I can't believe you slept with someone, Leigh. My God."

"I know. You didn't deserve that from anyone, least of all from me. I know 'sorry' isn't enough."

"Where will you go?"

"I don't know. I haven't figured that out yet," she said. "But I did figure out it was time I was honest with you about my feelings. I value our friendship and our work relationship, but I don't think in the end that it's more than that for me. I wished I'd figured that out years ago, but I didn't. I'm so sorry."

"Did you ever love me? You said you did. You said it for months. Was that another lie?"

Leigh felt tears starting again—*why* was she incapable of stoicism when she needed it most?—but she choked them back and said, "I do love you. But . . . it's not the kind of love a wife has for a husband. It's admiration. Respect. But admiration and respect aren't enough to build a marriage on," she said. "I want you to be happy. I want you to find someone who deserves your love. That person isn't me. But I know you'll find someone else, and I know you'll move on and be glad, in the long run, that you didn't marry me. Truly, Joseph, I am *not* the woman for you."

"I can't even think about looking for someone else, Leigh. I feel like my whole life has been upended."

"You will, someday. Any woman would be lucky to have you. I wish it had been me. Believe me, if I could have spared both of us this conversation, I would have."

Joseph left after that. He said there was no point in staying, and she agreed.

So that night Leigh lay in bed watching the storm, watching the light go from black to gray as the sun rose. She got up and went to the window, looking out at the hills and the vineyard below, the light changing from dull gray to pink, then gold. A quick trip home to Texas had gone from pleasurable to preposterous in less than a week, but it was a new day, a new chance to make things right.

She'd lost her fiancé and her job. She was about to lose her money, which meant losing her apartment and possibly her mind, but she still had her work reputation, if not her personal one. Maybe that would be enough to start her life over. It had to be.

The only question was *how*?

In the morning she borrowed Saundra's car and made the drive into Austin to the bank, her hands gripping the wheel, white-knuckling it all the way into town. The Hill Country was a blur passing by the windows, the little ranches and the farms, the long, snaking arm of the Colorado glinting gray and sinister in the hot morning sun. Every once in a while she got the feeling she was being followed and looked behind her, but the succession of trucks and cars always seemed to be changing—a blue pickup here, a brown Chevy there, a shiny black Honda. She was being paranoid, convinced of trouble even when there wasn't any. Convinced she was being watched at all times. The familiar landscape of her childhood started to take on the hard, ugly cast of a war zone.

The bank manager met her personally, escorting her to a private office away from the lobby. He gave her several forms to sign, checking her ID and then checking it again. When he was satisfied that Leigh was who she said she was, he went to a back room and returned with a large cloth bag, setting it down on the desk in front of her.

One million in crisp hundreds. Every cent she had left from her grandfather.

She shifted the money into the duffel she'd brought for the occasion and turned to the bank manager, who looked a little wan. "We're sorry to be losing your business," he said. "If you change your mind, just know we'd welcome the chance to serve you again."

Leigh gave him a grim smile. "Thank you. I will keep that in mind." *If I come by another grandfather who leaves me a trust fund, I'll be sure to look you up,* she thought. She was starting to sound like Chloe.

Leigh picked up the duffel and strode out of the bank, pausing only once to look behind her. The daily life of the city ground on—tourists stopping to take pictures on the Congress Avenue Bridge, a hipster on a unicycle playing the bagpipes for tips, cowboys in Stetsons and giant silver belt buckles rattling up to the bank in enormous pickup trucks, kids on day trips with their parents to the capitol, eyeing everything with wonder. She'd missed Texas. She'd miss it all over again when she went back to New York to try to pick up the pieces.

She was starting to realize that places, like people, get under your skin and become a part of you. That you could leave them, but they changed you somehow, and you could never quite go back to being who you were before. That the dirt of a place under your fingernails was as powerful, as transformative, as any kiss.

She startled: there was someone else on the street, watching her. She could just barely make out the hunched form of Russell Benoit sitting behind the wheel of a dull brown Chevy. He'd followed her. He'd followed her to make sure she was getting the money. Then he'd make his next move, Leigh knew. He'd come for the money. He wasn't taking any chances.

She'd be waiting.

She made the drive back to the winery looking in her rearview mirror the whole way. Russell was following her, but not too closely—he'd hang back from time to time, let other cars get between them for a couple of miles, then move up closer again. There was no need for him to be anxious. She'd done what he'd asked—picked up the cash—and it was clear she was headed back to the vineyard to meet with him. He was probably relaxed now, thinking of all the things he was going to buy with her grandfather's money. Money he didn't deserve.

Leigh's search for him on the Internet had turned up next to nothing, a few searches hit on white-pages websites, a single notice about Benoit's trial and sentencing in 2004, but no word about his crime. If only she had remembered to ask Jake what he knew before he left that last morning, she might have a better idea of what to do now. But aside from a quick text from Chloe late last night—SIT TIGHT, GOT A COUPLE OF LEADS—there was still no sign of Jake.

Hurry up, Chloe, please.

Back at the winery Leigh turned down the long driveway toward the main house, watching in her rearview to see what Russell was going to do. While she parked Saundra's car in front of the conference center, Russell drove his brown Chevy down the road past the entrance to the winery and kept going, playing nonchalant, as if she hadn't known that he'd been following her all along. Whatever he was going to do, he wasn't going to do it right away. He was going to let her squirm a little bit first.

She ran into the office to give Saundra her keys and was heading up the hill, back to her own cottage, when she saw a man coming down toward her: Jim Stephens, his gray eyes crinkling in the sun. "Hey there!" he said. "I was just looking for you. I thought I'd see if you wanted a ride to the airport." He looked at the duffel in her hand, the one filled with a million in hundreds. "Is that all the luggage you brought?"

The airport—the conference was nearly over. She'd nearly forgotten. Leigh knew she'd have to go back home soon, but she couldn't think about that yet. She had one unpleasant task left to perform.

"I'm staying a little while yet," she said. "But I appreciate the offer."

He looked at the duffel in her hand, then up at her face. "You need help?"

Instinctively, Leigh clutched the duffel to her chest. "No—it's okay. It's not heavy."

"I didn't mean the duffel."

"I—I know," she stammered. "I'm not sure you can help me. I'm not sure anyone can."

She kept going up the path toward the door of her little stone cottage on the hillside, Jim a few steps behind. The wind was sighing through the trees, lifting the hair on the back of her neck, the valley below carpeted with bluebonnets, tingeing the air purple, but at that moment Leigh felt she couldn't enjoy it, couldn't look at it and feel calm, content. And for that, as much as anything, she hated Russell Benoit.

At her cottage she turned the handle and opened the door, standing in the doorway, looking inside as if she expected Russell to jump out at any moment. But no one was there. No Russell. No Joseph. No Jake. Just Leigh and the mess she'd made. She stood in the doorway as if uncertain how even to begin to tackle the things that needed to get done.

Then Jim was behind her on the porch, watching her. She felt him there but didn't turn around. "You okay?" he asked.

"Not really."

"I take it you talked to him. Your fiancé."

Leigh gave an apologetic smile. "I did. Late last night." She went inside the room and set the duffel behind the door, where she knew it would be safe, but still she felt vulnerable, exposed, with all her money in cash just sitting there for anyone to take. Like she'd been caught swimming naked.

She whirled on Jim. "Wait a minute. How did you know I talked to him?"

"Because I spoke to him myself about an hour ago. He asked if he could publish my book."

"He did *what*?" She took two steps back and bumped into the bed. She sat down hard.

Whatever Leigh had been expecting from Joseph, it was certainly *not* that he would try to poach one of her projects just hours—minutes, maybe—after she had dumped him. So much for breaking his heart.

"What did he say?"

"He said he loved it and wanted to publish it. That he'd give me a nice advance and a big marketing push. That he could send the contracts this week."

"And what did you say?"

"I told him to stick it where the sun don't shine," Jim said, and grinned at her. "I already told you, darlin', I won't trust this book to just anyone. I'm giving it to you, and no one else."

Jim was standing in the doorway, watching her. He was being proper; he wouldn't come inside a woman's room unless Leigh invited him, which she did with a wave of her hand. She couldn't believe Joseph had taken Jim's manuscript with him. She couldn't believe Jim had turned down the offer. He'd probably just made the biggest mistake of his life.

"Oh, Jim," she said. "I don't even know where I'll land, or how long it will take. It might be months before I can start signing projects again. Was it a big advance?"

"More zeros than I've seen at one time ever in my life," he said, coming in but leaving the door open. "But I didn't write this book for the money. So you two are over?"

Leigh invited him to sit down, then closed the door behind him. "We are," she said. "It's for the best, really. I told him I'm quitting the company. He was pretty angry, and he deserved to be."

"He'll get over it," Jim said. "What about you? Are you doing all right?"

Leigh collapsed in the chair opposite him. "Not as well as I'd like. It had to be done, but it was a lot to give up. I'm going to have to rethink a lot of things I used to take for granted."

"Only natural," he said. "I'm sorry you had to lose your job over it, though."

"So am I. I loved that job. But it wouldn't be unheard of for me to get another one. I just scored the biggest publishing triumph of the year. There are probably other places I could work."

"Just 'probably'?"

"The thing is," she was saying, "I'm not sure I want to go back. Part of me wants to stay right here. If I could come home, somehow . . . But that's stupid. There are no publishing companies in Texas, not the kind that do what I do, anyway."

"There should be," Jim said. "All those writers at the conference, they'd be thrilled to have someplace local publish their work."

"I agree, but all the biggest firms are in New York." She sighed. "I guess I just don't want to face the mess I've made. Maybe I think it would be easier if I don't go back."

She was looking over her shoulder at the door. Any minute now, Russell would come knocking, she was sure of it. He knew she had the money. Probably he was waiting for Jim to leave, but he wouldn't wait much longer than that, she was certain. He'd want to collect his duffel and get the hell out of town, get on with the business of spending money that wasn't his. All she had to do was hand it over and she'd be rid of him, rid of the threat of jail. She only hoped a million would be enough to keep Russell out of her life forever.

Jim was watching her closely. "Everything all right?" he asked. "You keep looking at the door like you're waiting for someone."

"Do I? I'm sorry. It's been a trying couple of days."

He reached across the table and patted her hand, and she let him. For a minute it was as if Gene Merrill were still there, trying to ease her mind. "If you need me," he said, "I'm here."

"Thank you," she said. "You remind me of my grandfather. I miss him a lot."

"I don't think I'm quite old enough to be your grandfather."

"Not in age, but physically the resemblance is remarkable. Look," she said, pulling out her wallet and taking out the picture of her grandfather she kept there. In it, the old man was leaning on a white fence post, his thumb hitched through the loop of his jeans, his skin deeply tanned and his pale eyes twinkling. He was smiling directly into the camera with the same kind of casual confidence Jim had, the same careful expression of pleasure deeply masked. "He died when I was in college. We were very close. My mother died when I was ten, and he nearly raised me. It wasn't until just now that I realized how strong the resemblance is."

"I'm flattered."

"You are?"

"Of course. He obviously meant a lot to you. He must have been a good man, to earn your love and respect. I'd like to do the same."

"I'd like that," she said. "When I get back to New York and get settled, expect a call from me."

"You sure?"

"Absolutely. You're the first person on my list." She meant what she said—she would do what she could to help him, in whatever capacity she could, whether or not it was her name on the spine of his book. That's what good editors did: they brought good work into the world.

"All right. I'll look forward to it." Then he was gone.

Leigh closed the door behind him with a little bit of reluctance. Gene Merrill had been her last and practically only family; it was natural for her to feel a deep affection for a man who looked so much like him. But watching him leave was a little like losing Gene all over again.

She laughed to herself, thinking about what Chloe would say when Leigh told her about it. *Welcome to* Issues *with Leigh Merrill, where we discuss the strange inner workings of the subconscious female mind!* Chloe would say.

She wished Chloe were here now. While she was wishing for things, she wished Jake were here now, too.

Then, a knock. Someone was at the door.

She opened it up to find a man in a scruffy-looking business suit and a baseball cap standing there, lifting his chin at her arrogantly.

"Hello, beautiful," said Russell Benoit.

Fifteen

eigh's first instinct was to block the door and bar Russell Benoit from entering. This disgusting man was the last person she wanted inside her cottage at the moment, but she realized quickly that any attention she drew to the situation was going to be bad for her—calling the cops was not an option. She would just have to let him inside and get it over with. All she could do was hope for Chloe to show up with Jake in time to put a stop to Russell's ridiculous scheme.

"Well?" he asked. "You gonna invite me in or not?"

She couldn't choke out a proper invitation, so instead she stepped aside to let him pass. "Thanks, sugar," he said, and gave a long, low whistle as he looked around the room. "These are some nice digs, let me tell you. I might have to get me a little place like this, a nice little business with some property."

"Thanks," she said sourly. "But I don't think you'll be able to afford it even with my money."

"We'll see. Where's Pretty Boy?"

"Excuse me?"

"The guy with the expensive haircut you were with the other night. Where'd he run off to?"

Leigh went cold. "He went home."

"Without you? What happened? Did he find out you're a murderer?"

"I'm not. It was an accident."

"Tell it to the judge, sugar."

Russell moved slowly through the discarded clothes and piles of paper, picking up a vase from a table and setting it back down again, fingering the curtains like he owned the place. She didn't know if he was appreciating the cottage or planning to raid it.

"Lost your boyfriend and your money," he said. "Oh dear, oh dear. Whatever will you do?"

"I'm doing just fine. Thanks for your concern."

Somewhere in the mess her phone dinged: someone had sent her a text message. It had to be from Chloe; no one else ever texted her. But Leigh didn't see where the phone was, and she didn't want to turn her back on Russell for even a minute.

Russell flopped in the chair where just last night Joseph had sat while she'd broken his heart. But unlike the day before, Leigh felt no pang of sorrow, just a cold rage, a towering hostility. It was no use getting angry—there was nothing to do but pay him off and get it over with. She only had to get through this one last distasteful chore, this final task, and then she'd be free to move on with the rest of her life.

Russell put his feet up on the coffee table, dislodging a stack of manuscript pages and sending them tumbling in a heap to the floor. "Sorry about that," he said as Leigh bent over to pick up the pages, though she could tell he wasn't really sorry, not at all. "You ain't much of a housekeeper, are you?"

"Not really," Leigh said through gritted teeth.

"You ought to be. Good for a woman to keep a nice house," he said. "Maybe after you're broke you'll learn how to do for yourself for a change. Won't be able to afford a maid to do it for you anymore." He cackled at the thought.

"I never had a maid," Leigh said.

"Well, maybe you needed one." Russell continued to eye her with amusement while she crouched on the floor cleaning up his mess. "I do like to see a woman on her hands and knees. Makes me remember the natural order."

Leigh looked up. "Don't get too used to it," she said. "It won't happen again."

"If you say so, little lady."

He was grinning at her with evident pleasure, his baked-bean teeth glistening in the pale light of the room. She wished she could call the cops on him right now, get him thrown out of her room and back in jail. While she was wishing for things, she wished she'd called the cops on Dale Tucker all those years ago instead of getting her grandfather's gun. How different her life might have been if she'd been smart enough never to go into the tack room for the .357 in the first place. Jake wouldn't have gone to jail, for one thing, and Russell Benoit wouldn't be in her room right now. Her grandfather might still be alive, even.

There was no point in wishful thinking. She'd pulled the trigger, and that action had consequences. It was time for her to pay up, finally. The only problem was that she was paying the wrong person.

Underneath a stack of pages, she felt something buzz insistently: her phone. She picked it up and unlocked it to find the text from Chloe. She opened the message and read. DON'T GIVE HIM THE MONEY, it said. WE'RE ON OUR WAY RIGHT NOW.

She'd found Jake! *Oh, Chloe,* she thought, *I love you.*

But how to stall Russell until the two of them got to the ranch? He knew she had the money—he'd seen her drive into town, go into the bank—but he didn't know where it was now, hidden behind the door of the cottage, half buried beneath the mess in Leigh's room. He could search the room, take the duffel and run, but that wasn't his style, was it? Russell Benoit was enjoying himself too much, enjoying getting the best of her, the rich girl from Wolf's Head who'd never struggled a day in her life. He wanted her to offer the bag to him. He wanted to take it straight out of her hands before he could enjoy spending it.

Russell was eyeing her. He said, "So. You gonna make me wait all day, or what, sweetheart?"

Leigh stood with a stack of pages pressed to her chest, then set them down, sliding her phone back into her pocket. All she had to do was stall a little.

She stood up straight, and said, "Not much longer. I'll be glad to have you on your way, but there's something I want to know first. Some answers I want, in exchange for my money."

He crossed one foot in front of the other, but he looked skeptical. Maybe he'd tell her what she wanted to know, and maybe not. "Shoot," he said.

"So I was wondering about something. Jake told me you knew his dad, Ben. You'd known Ben Rhodes from a long way back, he said. What I want to know is how you know him."

For the first time Russell looked surprised by something she'd said. "Ben? Oh, old Ben and I go way back."

"Way back to what?"

"I don't think you really want to know that. Still in love with his son and all. Still pining for your first love."

Leigh's stomach flopped. "I don't know what you're talking about."

"Sure. Your tearful reunion was some kind of act, let me tell you."

"What?"

"You think the boat dock is a private place for a reunion? Please. Get a room. Oh, I forgot—you did."

Had Russell been following Leigh and Jake all this time? He could have been behind her the minute she stepped off the plane. She felt cold all over, picturing him lurking behind every corner and every curtain. How had he even known she was coming back to Texas?

Maybe he'd been following Jake, not her. Maybe he and Ben Rhodes had worked out this blackmail scheme together. Maybe Jake had been in on it the whole time. She accused him of being in on it once, and he'd denied it, vehemently, but maybe that was all an act, too.

"Maybe it would have been better if we'd never met." Was this what you meant, Jake? That you knew Russell Benoit was coming to find me? Maybe even that you were involved?

Leigh chose her words carefully and said, "A million dollars isn't really going to be enough for you and Ben to live on forever. It'll go fast. Cars, houses, travel. A bunch of money like that, it makes people crazy, makes them do stupid things. What makes you think Ben won't take it for himself? Screw you over?"

Russell looked at her sideways, a slow grin spreading over his face like honey. "What makes you think your money is all we've got?"

He'd practically admitted that he and Ben were in this together. Leigh's mind whirled. "There are others?"

"Of course."

"Other people who don't want to go to jail for murder?" she said. "You meet a lot of those types?"

Russell smiled as if Leigh had told a joke. "Other people who want to keep their reputations intact, let's say. I believe in diversifying my portfolio. Looking for new opportunities. I'm a businessman, like."

Leigh thought a minute. Who else in Ben's world would be worried about their reputations?

The Thoroughbred breeders.

It made sense. Ben must have been doping the horses and bribing the owners into keeping their mouths shut because their breeding businesses would suffer if everyone knew their horses weren't healthy. A horse with an injury wasn't worth the paper its pedigree was printed on. There were millions of dollars on the line. Hundreds of millions, probably. Ben knew every Thoroughbred breeder between Kentucky and the Colorado. He'd worked for dozens of farms before coming to Wolf's Head.

But if he'd made so much, why was he after Leigh and her trust fund? And what was Russell's role in the operation? "Ben wouldn't need a partner. He wouldn't need you."

"Sure he would. He needs a bagman, and I'm the best."

"A bagman?"

"He doesn't want to pick up the money himself, does he? That just looks bad. Might be too obvious." Russell tilted his head to get a better look at her. He was not only relishing the fact that he'd caught a fish, he wanted the fish to know just how it had been outsmarted. His repulsiveness was matched only by his ego.

"When I got out of Huntsville, I knew enough about Ben from Jake's letters that I was sure he was dirty. I looked him up, found out where he was working. He gave me a chance, got me in on the ground floor. He needed a new partner after you killed his old one."

Come on, Chloe, where are you? "How much has Ben made over the years, do you think?" Leigh asked.

"Oh, I don't keep track."

"You must have some idea."

"Lots. Millions, probably. Tens of millions. Your grandfather was supposed to be his biggest prize, but then the old boy up and croaked before he could pay. Ben thought Gene was going to be the one who got away. Was he ever happy when I showed up with photocopies of the letters you wrote to Jake in prison! You should have seen Ben's face. He knew he was finally getting what your grandfather promised him all those years ago."

"My grandfather was paying him off?" Leigh asked. It couldn't be—her grandfather would never have tolerated such behavior on his place. Would he?

Still, there were signs that, in retrospect, started to make more sense. The brand-new shiny red pickup truck Ben had driven to the farm that first day. The expensive saddles and boots, the riding clothes, the trips to Vegas—it had all been stolen money, extorted from other horse owners.

Now it sounded like Leigh's own grandfather had been a victim of Ben's schemes, too. No wonder he'd been so anxious to keep Leigh away from Jake—he must have known even then that Ben Rhodes was a crook, and that he was trying to get his son involved in the family business. *That boy's no good, Leigh,* he'd told her. *I want you to stay away from him.*

It wasn't snobbery that was making Gene so cautious. He'd known something Leigh hadn't. He'd been trying to protect her.

Oh, Pop, I'm so sorry. I didn't understand.

There was one thing she still didn't know: whether or not Jake had been in on that part of the operation. Had he known all along his dad was blackmailing Leigh's family? Leigh felt sick. Their tearful reunion, their lovemaking—was it all a lie?

"What about Jake? What's his involvement?"

Russell gave a wolfish grin. "Sweetheart," he said, "how do you think I found you in the first place?"

Leigh felt the blood drain to her feet. *No. Oh, no.*

She struggled to regain her composure. Russell had told her a lot— too much, probably.

"I could go to the police, you know. Tell them everything you told me."

Russell looked pleased she'd said this, as if he'd been waiting for her to come around to that conclusion. "You know you don't want to do that," he said. "If I even smell the cops behind me, it's off to jail with you, sugar. A nice fat anonymous packet of letters in your own handwriting will arrive at the district attorney's office. And don't think Ben Rhodes won't enjoy doing it, too, seeing as how you got his only son wrongly convicted and Ben fired from his job and all. He's practically salivating at the thought of you doing some serious time."

Leigh felt cold. The money would not be enough to get Russell and Ben off her back—she was now complicit in their crimes, and to save her own skin, she was going to have to keep silent. Even Jake's arrival wouldn't be enough to put him off now, because Jake was in on all of it.

They had her, they owned her completely; they could keep extorting money from owners all over the country, and Leigh would have to keep her mouth shut, just like everyone else.

She felt dirty, like she needed a shower.

"So, that about it, Sherlock?" he said, rapping his knuckles on the arm of the chair with relish and standing up. "Can I have my money now?"

Leigh kept her eyes on him, only on him. She wouldn't think about Jake on his way here. She wouldn't answer.

"Oh come on," Russell said, his temper flaring. "I saw you come out of the bank. I saw you come back with a duffel bag. I know it's here. Just hand it over, and you can go on back to your nice little life."

There was no point in stalling for more time: Jake and Chloe weren't going to be able to fix this mess. It was time to pay up.

Finally Leigh went to the door of the cottage and pulled the duffel out from underneath a pile of clothes. She shoved it at him. "Here," she said. "And I never want to see you again in my life."

Russell looked at the bag greedily. He set it down on the bed and unzipped it, picking up a couple of bundles of cash and flipping through them quickly. "You may see me again, you may not," he said. "Depends on whether you're a good girl or a bad girl from now on. I suggest you be a good girl, Leigh Merrill."

She flung open the door of the cottage. Outside, a couple of conference attendees packing up to go home were startled by the noise and looked up to see what the commotion was about. "Get out," she said.

Satisfied, Russell put the money back in the bag and zipped it. "Gladly," he said. He paused at the door and put his clammy hands on her waist, pulling her close to him and laying a long, wet, disgusting kiss directly on her mouth. Then he pulled away and took a long, lingering look at her.

"I don't blame Jake," he said. "I'd have gone to jail for you, too." Then he turned and went out the door.

Leigh flopped down on the bed of the cottage, exhausted, heartsick, and now completely broke to boot. Every cent she had left. She'd managed to live frugally her whole adult life, but that had always been easy when she knew she had a safety net in the bank, something to land on if everything else went wrong. Now she was going to have to reconsider all her financial decisions. She'd need to go back to Manhattan and look for a new job, and the sooner the better. She'd probably have to move out of her apartment, not to mention look for a roommate, and she really didn't want to have to deal with *that* right now.

If only she hadn't been forced to pay off the nastiest, foulest, lowest form of life on earth, she could have lived with herself. If only she'd done something useful with that money, something positive. She should have given it all to charity a long time ago. She should have given it all to Jake the minute she saw him again at the end of the dock. She should have given it to him to leave her the hell alone.

She sat on the floor and looked into the cold ashes of the fireplace.

She hadn't felt so lost since Jake went to jail and her grandfather died. She'd brought all this on herself, after all. Being careless. Being selfish. Being so young and scared in those few seconds before the sheriff arrived, that night long ago. She'd sold her soul. She'd given it all up for her freedom, and her trust fund was simply the price that had to be paid.

She was about to start packing up the cottage when she heard Chloe's orange Karmann Ghia pulling up to the winery once more, the muffler rattling, tires skidding to a halt in a hail of gravel, the car doors slamming. Chloe seemed to be drawing as much attention to herself as was humanly possible.

"Jesus, Chloe," Leigh said, coming down the hill in her bare feet, "take it easy! I already gave it to him. He just left."

"You didn't!" Chloe said. "I told you not to! Don't you read your own damn text messages?"

"What's the point?" Leigh groaned. "He's got me, Chloe. I didn't have a choice—"

Then Jake was flinging open the passenger door, a frown contorting his features. Leigh's stomach tightened. She didn't want to see him, didn't want him here. From what Russell had told her, Jake was in on the scheme as much as Russell and Ben; more so, since he'd seduced her and then told the other two where she was. The sight of him there, at that moment, just reminded her of how foolish she'd really been.

"Where did he go?" Jake demanded.

"What do you care?"

Jake gave her a strange look. "Chloe told you not to pay him, Leigh. He's a dirtball. But don't worry, I think we can get the money back from him."

"Sure," Leigh said, barely containing her anger. "That part of the plan, too? Pretending you don't know what he's up to? Seducing me and then dumping me again so you could scam me for my trust fund?"

Jake crossed the distance between them in three long strides, grabbing Leigh hard by the shoulders. "What the hell are you talking about?"

"Russell told me everything."

Jake's fingers tightened on her shoulders. "*What* did he tell you?"

"That you're in business with him and your dad. That you're the one who led them to me. And I let you. I even slept with you. Jesus, I'm so stupid. I can't believe I didn't see it sooner."

Chloe said, "Leigh, hold on—"

"Stay out of this, Chloe," she said. "You only know part of it."

Jake was breathing like a bronc in a rodeo pen, his skin rippling with anger. "You think that's why I'm here? To help Russell and my dad rip you off?"

Leigh was exquisitely angry, filled with a fury towering into a thunderhead; she wouldn't back down now. "That's what Russell told me."

"And you believed him? I told you he's a con artist, Leigh! He'd say anything to make you feel like you were out of options."

Leigh, didn't know who or what to believe, she only knew that she'd lost everything, that she'd never felt so alone. Russell had said Jake was involved, and it had sounded like sense to Leigh, who had been bewildered by Jake's erratic behavior ever since he turned up at the conference, telling her he loved her, he wanted her, then disappearing again in a fit of anger.

"It sure is a coincidence that he turned up the same time as you," she said.

"It sure is a coincidence that he turned up the first time you came back to Texas. You ever think of that?" Jake said. "It's not like you were in the witness protection program, Leigh! Your face was in every newspaper and magazine for five hundred miles. The governor probably knew you were coming, for God's sake."

"Maybe I want to believe him," she said, lifting her chin. "Maybe

Russell makes more sense than you do, showing up here, telling me you still love me, and then running away again."

"I can't believe you'd think so little of me, after everything."

Leigh's anger, which just a moment ago had burned white-hot, started to collapse on itself. If she was wrong . . .

"I don't know what I think," she said at last. "I only know you left. You could have stayed, but you left me, Jake. You told me it was over, said I should have a nice life. What was I supposed to think?"

"Hey, Romeo and Juliet, can we talk about this later?" Chloe asked, shifting impatiently from one foot to the other like a junkie waiting for a fix. "Which way did Russell go?"

Leigh was still looking at Jake, whose eyes were sparking anger. "He took off down the road about five minutes ago," she said. "Just before you got here."

"Which *way*?" Jake demanded.

"I don't know! Left!" Leigh shouted. "What the hell difference does it make?"

"Get in, Leigh," Jake said.

"Why? I—"

"Leigh, get *in*," Chloe said. "We have to catch him."

"Will someone please tell me what's going on?" Leigh demanded.

"Leigh," Jake said, "we got the letters. The copies Russell made of your letters. We found them. We took them."

"What?"

"Look." Jake held up a fat manila envelope. Leigh opened it to see a stack of photocopies, four years' worth of letters written in her own hand. "Where did you find these?"

"Ben's truck," said Chloe.

"He's been leaving it parked behind Dot's Diner lately, since he's been sleeping with Dot," Jake said. "When you first told me what Russell was up to, I started looking through my dad's apartment, his office, but I never found any of the letters, nothing but his phone bill with a bunch of calls to Russell's cell. I knew he wouldn't let Russell keep the only copies of the letters. He never trusts other people with something this important. When Chloe found my place and told me Russell was coming back for the money this morning, I remembered to look in the truck. He had them in the glove box, same place he stashed the drugs."

"The man's consistent," Chloe said. "You have to give him that."

Jake never took his eyes off the envelope in Leigh's hands. "You're safe," he said. "My dad and Russell, they can't touch you, not anymore. It would be your word against theirs." He raised his chin, giving her a grim look. "Unless you think I'm still part of my father's scam to get my hands on your trust fund."

Leigh was completely, thoroughly rattled. She wanted to believe him. She wanted it more than anything, but the sands had shifted under her feet so many times the past few days that she always felt like she was about to fall. Wrung out, on the brink of tears, she asked, "Is this the truth, Jake?"

He crossed the distance between them and kissed her, deeply and firmly, so there could be no doubt any longer of his heart. "I couldn't hurt you," he said. "I never would. I swore to protect you my whole life, Leigh. That hasn't changed."

She felt like weeping, but she wouldn't—she was spent. She looked at the spot in the middle of his chest, the place where she always used to rest her head. She wanted to do so again now, but she wouldn't, she wouldn't, she absolutely would not.

She said, "I don't know who I can trust anymore."

"You can trust me," he said. "You know me. You know it's never been about the money for me, Leigh. I just wanted you. That's all."

Leigh felt like she could hardly breathe. After everything she and Jake had been through—after everything they had put each other through—he had still helped Chloe find the letters and bring them to Leigh. He had still rushed right out to find out where Russell was and what he was up to. That had to count for something, especially against the word of a con artist. If Jake were in it with Russell and Ben, he wouldn't even be standing in front of her now, would he? He'd be off spending her money, celebrating with them. There was no reason for him to be here anymore, none but one—that he still loved her.

She took a deep breath and blew it out again, slowly. "Okay," she said. "I believe you. You're not involved with Russell. I believe you, Jake." It felt good to trust him again. She took a step toward him. "You might be the most stubborn man who ever lived, but I know you'd never deliberately try to hurt me."

"Thank you," he said. His voice was low and husky with emotion. "That means a lot to me. I know my dad hasn't made it easy for you to believe in me, but I hope I can prove to you that I'm not a part of his schemes. That I never will be, not again."

"Aw, ain't that sweet?" Chloe said, stepping between them before they could embrace. "But can we get going before Russell gets away? This is the most fun I've had in years, and I am *not* letting you two spoil it for me."

They were less than a mile outside the town limits of Burnside when they spotted the taillights of Russell's brown Chevy up ahead, braking as he turned off the highway and into the dirt driveway of an abandoned homestead. As they pulled up, they saw the drive lead through an overgrown green pasture to a small wooden house faded to a peeling salmon pink. Out back an old dairy barn had collapsed like a diseased lung, and a series of small outbuildings with broken windows showed spaces filled with rusted-out farm equipment, old oil-company signs, a creaking windmill leaning at an impossible angle. An old hardware-store sign staked next to the drive read NO TRESPASSING in bright orange letters.

Chloe drove past the driveway a little ways, then pulled up and stopped along the grassy ditch, pulling to the side away from traffic. She left the engine running.

The whole thing made Leigh nervous—the situation, the scene. It was Russell's place, Russell's advantage. They had no idea what the inside of the house looked like, but if the outside was any indication, it would be a hoarder's paradise, probably covered in boxes and crammed with old newspapers and overrun with mice. Even now Russell was probably stashing the money someplace deep inside the house. It was possible they could tear the house apart and never find it. Not a good situation in the best of circumstances. In these circumstances, well . . .

"What do we think, kids?" Chloe asked. "Do we go in or not?"

But Jake already had his hand on the handle of the door. "I'm going," he said. "You two stay here."

"No way," said Leigh. "I'm not staying in the car." She was thinking of all the ways this situation could go wrong, not to mention that she was terrified of what might happen to Jake in that house, with that man. What would Russell do when he realized his back was up against a wall?

But Jake was having none of it. "He might have a gun, Leigh. In fact, I'd be shocked if he didn't. I don't want you risking yourself again over my father's stupid schemes."

"Russell won't shoot me," said Leigh. "He's having too much fun ripping me off. You should have seen him gloat this morning."

Jake crossed his arms over his chest. "What happens when he stops having fun?" he asked. "You think of that?"

"You said he was in prison for fraud," said Leigh. "You really think he'd risk a murder charge?"

"He might," said Jake, "for a million dollars. A lot of people would."

"Then he'll have to shoot all three of us at once," said Chloe. "Come on. We can't let him get away with it. At least not without trying. Let him see he's outnumbered."

Jake groaned, but Leigh was already halfway down the driveway. Chloe got out and slammed the car door. "Quietly," Jake said. "We don't want to make him more nervous than he is already. And let me go first, at least. Give me the letters, Leigh."

"Why?"

"I think I have an idea how I might get him to talk to me."

She handed over the envelope. They went silently through the tall grass, the grasshoppers leaping whenever they came near, the buzz of cicadas rising and falling in the heat. The grass and the numerous outbuildings hid their approach from the road, but they kept their eyes on the front door the whole time.

The house looked like it had sat abandoned for some time until Russell decided to make it his place. Leigh wondered briefly if the place was in fact his or if he'd just started squatting there after he got out of Huntsville. Out front, the porch was covered with lawn chairs and empty paint buckets and maybe two or three years' worth of dust. The screen door was open in the heat, and a scrawny cat scratched at it forlornly, begging to come inside. In the corner of the eaves, an enormous yellow spiderweb flickered in the breeze. The smell of old motor oil and creosote clung to everything.

"Adorable," said Chloe. "It looks like a serial killer's hideout."

"Quiet," hissed Jake.

Behind the screen door someone was whistling. Russell's car was the only one parked outside. The three of them, Leigh and Chloe and Jake, stood behind a cluster of sumac bushes and an old bur oak, half hidden from the front of the house.

Then they heard Russell talking to someone. "Hey," he said. "I got it. You coming over?" Silence. Then, "Well, don't keep me hanging, buddy. You want your share, you better come get it." Then more silence. "All right. See you in a bit."

"You think that was Ben on the phone?" Leigh whispered.

"Yeah," Jake said. "He'll probably be here any minute."

"When he gets here, it will be two against three," said Leigh. "I like our chances better now."

"Then let's go," Chloe said.

Leigh started toward the house, but Jake held her arm. "Wait," he said. "Let me go first."

"No way."

"You and Chloe wait here. Let me talk to him. I have an idea how I might find out where the money is. If things go wrong, though, I want you two to get the hell out of here."

"No," she said. "I won't leave you."

"You will, and you won't tell anyone you were here, Leigh. Promise me."

"If he hurts you . . ."

"I can protect myself, but I can't protect all three of us. Promise me you will *not* go in that house."

She would promise no such thing. "You don't have to do this, Jake."

He gave her a grim look. "Yes, I do." Then he stood and went up the drive toward the house, his white T-shirt shining in the sun like a flag of surrender.

Leigh watched him go with a measure of trepidation and not a little breathlessness. What did Jake think he was going to do, going in there alone? It was unlikely Russell would tell him where he'd hidden the money, but maybe Jake knew something that would trick Russell into admitting it. Jake had known Russell for years; they'd been cellmates, and probably Jake had more insight into Russell's way of thinking than just about anybody, including Ben. If anyone could talk him into revealing where he'd hidden the money, it might just be Jake.

She and Chloe held back and waited, bracing themselves when they heard Jake knock on the screen door three times fast.

"Hey, Russell," he said. "Russell. It's me, Jake."

Russell's dusty form appeared behind the screen door. From where she stood behind the sumac, Leigh couldn't see his face, but she could hear a certain amount of hesitation in his voice as he said, "Jake. Hey, buddy. Long time no see." His body language, even through the screen door, looked tense, almost hostile, belying the politeness of his tone. "What're you doing here?"

Their voices carried easily across the slight distance to the place where Leigh and Chloe were hiding. Leigh was immediately afraid. *Be careful, Jake. Please, be careful.*

"My dad sent me. Said I was supposed to talk to you about a bit of business you got going on."

"Did he now." Russell's tone was flat. "Did he tell you what business?"

"Nope. Just that I was supposed to come on over here."

Russell still looked suspicious. "How'd you get here so fast?"

"I was in the neighborhood."

He must have seen the envelope in Jake's hand, because he said, "What're you doing with that?"

"Old man said to bring it with me."

"He did, huh?" Russell held the screen door open for Jake. "You better come in, then."

Jake disappeared inside the house. Leigh and Chloe could still hear the two of them talking, more faintly now. Murmurs from inside. Some sounds of shuffling, then a door opening. Leigh's heart hammered at her ribs.

"Want a beer?" Russell asked.

"Isn't it a little early?" asked Jake.

The sound of a can hissing open. "Never too early."

They were moving around from room to room inside the house, so that their voices sometimes came a little more clearly, sometimes a little less. Now there was a murmur Leigh couldn't quite make out, followed by Jake saying, "That's right."

Ben was going to be there at any moment. Jake had to find out where the money was before he got there, before the odds turned against them.

Leigh turned to Chloe and whispered, "I'm going to go closer. It's safe."

"It's only safe because he thinks Jake's on his side."

"Stay here, then," Leigh answered. "I'll go."

"The hell you will."

"Seriously, Chloe. Stay hidden. If there's trouble, call the police right away."

"You sure about that?"

Getting the police involved in this situation would be a big problem for Leigh, but that didn't matter anymore. They had to be safe about it. "Absolutely," she said. "I don't care what happens to me, no one else dies. If things start to go bad, you call right away. Got it?"

"All right," Chloe said, pulling out her cell phone. "Though I can't say I'm happy about it."

Leigh stepped behind the sumac and walked slowly up to the front door, her vision narrowing to the screen, the shapes of Jake and Russell moving around in the shade inside, their voices coming to her in a murmur, her steps thick and slow and difficult. The front door of the house gaped like the mouth of a tomb. It took everything in her not to turn around and run.

But if Jake was right—if the copies of the letters in his possession were the only ones—she could destroy them, she could burn them up and never have to worry again about Russell Benoit or Ben Rhodes coming after her. She'd be free. If they weren't the only copies, it wouldn't matter if she burned them. She had to be certain—she couldn't face the rest of her life wondering if Russell and Ben were going to be behind every corner, under every rock. She had to know exactly what they had to keep her in line.

Then, of course, there was the matter of her trust fund. It was somewhere in this house. If there was any chance of getting it back, she had to do it. Not for herself, she was realizing—she would give it to Jake. All of it.

She went slowly through the tall grass to the front door of the sagging pink house. Inside the big window of what must have been the living room, she could just make out the shape of Russell sitting on the arm of an old chair with its stuffing poking out. He was eyeing Jake warily, the envelope of Leigh's letters in his hand, and drinking his beer with a long, deep swig.

"Surprised your dad gave you those," Russell said, nodding at the envelope. "Figured he'd keep them someplace safe."

"He wants me to get your copies, along with the money. Said it would be better if we kept them together in one spot, now that the job's over. Just so we're all on the same page and all."

"He did, huh?" said Russ, taking a long drink of his beer. "You think the job's over?"

Leigh started to hear warning bells going off. *He's not buying it, Jake. He doesn't believe you.*

"Isn't it?"

"I'm starting to think it's not," Russ said, "since your dad specifically told me to keep my set of your girlfriend's letters hidden away here. Just in case something happened to the first set. And your dad would know that, wouldn't he, since he was the one who said so in the first place?"

Damn. The game was up. And not only that, Russell had admitted he had another set of letters hidden somewhere in the house. Just as Leigh had feared—she'd never be rid of him. Never. They'd been too careful, too clever.

But Jake wasn't giving up so fast. His voice was smooth and unperturbed. "Why don't you give those letters to me, Russ?" he said. "It'll just be easier if you do. Give them to me and we'll call it a day."

"Why?" Russ said, laughing harshly. "So you can give them back to that girl of yours? You think I'm as stupid as you are? They're worth a fortune. You're an idiot if you give those back to her." He nodded at the envelope still in Jake's hand. "You should hang on to them, Jake. She owes you. She owes you big-time."

"They're worthless now. She gave you all her money. So what's the difference if she gets them back or not?"

"You think a tasty little bitch like her is going to go hungry for long? Naw, she's going to be a meal ticket for a long time to come, Jake. She's going to marry that rich jerk, and he's worth a lot more than she is. Millions. I think I'll keep my copies, Jake. Just in case." Russell finished his beer and set the bottle down. "You should think about doing the same."

"No," Jake said quietly. "I won't."

Through the screen door Leigh could make out the shape of him, a shadow in the middle of the room, and the manila envelope that held her letters, a young girl's pleas to the love of her life, and an accidental confession of her crime. His shoulders were set in a straight line, his carriage very stiff. Jake held up the envelope, his mouth set, and then something in his other hand flared, orange and yellow.

A flame—Jake was holding up his lighter to the envelope.

"I won't keep them, and I won't let you keep them either."

"What are you—?" said Russ, but the envelope caught, the flame spreading quickly, eating up the paper, turning the pages to ash. The copies of her letters—her confession of everything she'd done wrong—was going up in flames.

Russell lunged at Jake, trying to take the letters. They fought, but Jake was at least a head taller than Russell, with maybe forty pounds on him; he knocked Russell back with one swipe of his right arm while with the left he held the burning paper aloft.

But Russell wasn't going to be so easily put off. He launched himself at Jake's knees and knocked him to the floor. The burning envelope fell out of Jake's hands and skittered across the floor while Russell sat on his chest, landing several hard blows on Jake's jaw, the side of his head. "You pussy-whipped son of a bitch! I'll kill you!"

While they struggled the envelope landed on the floor next to the overstuffed chair. The paper was still half on fire, the yellow flames licking at the manila envelope, the white photocopies within. A single long flame reached out, caught the stuffing coming out from the underside of the old and rotten chair, and lit the chair on fire.

The upholstery was so dry that in just seconds the whole chair was alight, licking across the faded floral fabric, charring the pattern of roses and baby's breath until they were black. Flames and smoke shot toward the ceiling, toward the peeling wallpaper, a pattern of ducks in flight, which curled and blackened and gave off wisps of white smoke. The old photographs hanging at crazy angles on the walls burned in their frames, the glass cracking.

Seeing the flames, Russell jumped off Jake and stomped on the envelope, trying to put out the flames. Too late—the envelope was nothing but ash.

Next to the chair the old drapes caught on fire, the flames licking up the fabric toward the ceiling. Jake stood and ripped the curtains down, beating them against the floor to put out the flames, but a pile of magazines next to the drapes caught and flared, and then the old tweedy beige sofa, covered with dust bunnies and bits of lint.

Russell saw the sofa burst into flames and spat an epithet. While Jake beat at it with the charred curtains, he ran into the kitchen, coming back a few seconds later with a large bowl filled with water.

He threw it at the sofa, but it barely made a dent in the fire that was growing rapidly larger and fiercer with every passing second.

While Jake pulled down the rest of the curtains and beat at the flames as hard as he could, Russell ran back to the kitchen with his bowl. He came back a minute later with an old fire extinguisher, red paint peeling, but when he pulled the pin, nothing came out.

Everything was so dry and cluttered, so haphazard and disorganized, that it lit up almost immediately. Papers, magazines, old furniture, wallpaper, cobwebs—in less than thirty seconds the whole front room of the house was fully engulfed.

Jake, sensing the battle was lost, stumbled toward the front door, covering his nose with the collar of his T-shirt. "Russell!" he said. "Get out of there! It's too late, the whole house is going."

Leigh was moving back now, jumping down from the porch, but she could still see Russell rushing back to the kitchen for more water and towels. The fire was spreading fast now. He came back, clutching wet towels to his chest. "The money!" he said to Jake, drenching one end of the sofa with the bowl of water. The other was still alight, though, so he dropped the bowl and beat at the sofa with his wet towels like his life depended on it.

"Where?" Jake said.

"In the sofa. The cushions," he said.

Through the window Leigh could see the form of Russell Benoit dark against the blaze, plunging his hands into the fiery sofa cushions and pulling them apart. The money hidden inside the cushions burned fast and hot, like kindling, but Russell grabbed at the bundles, clutching at them even as they disintegrated in his hands. Leigh could see the stacks of hundreds curling at the edges as they burned, the fire scorching the skin on Russell's hands, but it was like he felt no pain, or else he was so consumed with greed that he didn't care.

The whole house was going up in smoke. Black clouds billowed from the chimney and the edges of the roof. Feeling the heat coming from the front room, Leigh ran back to where Chloe was already on the phone with the fire department. "Come quick!" she was saying. "The whole place is on fire!"

Then a scream. Leigh dashed toward the door once more, fearing for Jake, but before she got there the screen door opened and Russell Benoit stumbled out.

He was on fire. His shirt had caught, and the flames were spreading up to his shoulders and into his hair. Jake flung himself at him, half dragging him out the door and onto the porch, and flung himself on top of the smaller man, rolling him over and over and smashing at the flames with his hands. All the while Russell was sobbing, "My money! My money!"

He was looking back toward the house, and Leigh realized the man didn't know he was hurt. He didn't feel anything yet—he was only thinking of the million dollars he'd had stashed in the sofa cushions. And before Jake could stop him, he jumped up and ran back into the house.

"Wait!" Jake was screaming. "Russ, don't go back in there! It's too late!"

But Russell Benoit had gone back into the house. Now the second story was on fire, too, smoke billowing from the windows as the roof caught on fire. From outside the house, they could hear him screaming. Leigh caught a glimpse of him running back into the kitchen with his hair on fire, his mouth wide open, stretched nearly to breaking, his eyes flickering with the light of the flames. She caught a glimpse of him falling, and something from the ceiling, a burning beam maybe, falling down on top of him.

And then it was gone. The house. The money. Russell. It was all too late.

Jake stumbled off the porch and stood in the yard clutching his own burned hands to his chest. The heat from the fire was so intense that Jake, Leigh, and Chloe kept moving back toward the road, silently watching the unbelievable scene unfolding in front of them. The smoke rose overhead like thunderheads, building over the wide blue Texas sky.

Ben Rhodes's truck broke the trance as it pulled into the driveway. He slammed the door of his truck and dashed toward the house, getting only as far as the front steps before the heat and the flames drove him out again. "Russ!" he called. "Russ, buddy, where are you?"

"He's dead," said Jake quietly.

Seeing his son there, not to mention Leigh and Chloe, Ben started to get a sense of what had happened. He grabbed Jake by the collar. "What did you do, boy?"

"I took your letters," Jake said. "The copies of Leigh's letters you got from Russ. I found them in your truck. I lit them on fire."

"You did this? You killed Russ?"

"He made it out alive. He made the choice to go back in. He was screaming about the money. Said it was hidden in the couch cushions."

Ben advanced on his son with his fists clenched. "Then it's all gone! The money, the letters, Russ—everything's gone. It was all in the house. Jacob, what the hell have you done?"

Despite her nausea, despite her fear, Leigh felt a surge of hope. If the other copies of her letters had been hidden in the house, along with her money, then they were gone, too. The originals would be the only copies left. If Ben and Russell had each had a set, then all the copies were burning up as they stood there. She'd be free.

"I knew I couldn't trust you," Ben snarled at Jake. "You worthless son of a bitch. You've ruined everything over that stupid little whore."

Jake got to his feet slowly, his face both sad and angry at once, and clenched his fists. "You're not allowed to call her that. In fact, you're not allowed to speak about her ever again, *Dad*. Do you understand me? Not ever."

Even in his late sixties, Ben Rhodes was a formidable man, wiry and tough from decades of training the fastest horses in the world. He stalked toward Jake like he meant to kill him, his jaw clenching and unclenching. "I understand I'm going to knock you on your ass, boy. Don't think I can't do it still, if I want to."

Jake straightened up to his full height. He had a good fifty pounds on his dad, all of it muscle, and maybe half a foot of height. Ben was overmatched, and as Leigh watched, she could see him realize it, see the dawning of recognition on the father's face, the determination on the son's: Jake Rhodes was not afraid of his father, not anymore. Every doubt she'd ever had about his divided sense of loyalty dissolved: he was not his father's son.

"Get the hell out of here, Ben," Jake said quietly. "Get out before the cops show up. If you go now, you might be able to avoid going to prison yourself. It's not a pretty place, prison. You wouldn't last a month."

"I'd last longer than you, you little son of a bitch."

"It should have been you, all those years ago. You were the one who was doping the horses and bribing the owners. You were the one sending me to pick up your drugs. I'm still trying to dig myself out of the mess you made. You were the one who should have gone to jail, not me."

"I'm the only family you've got, Jacob. You better watch how you speak to me."

"Why? There's nothing you have that I want. Not even your love." Jake shook his head sadly. "I always wanted to be like you, you know. You used to be larger than life. But you took my love and respect, and you used it to hurt the people I cared about. What kind of a father does that?"

Jake looked over at Leigh and then down at his burned hands. Leigh had to resist the urge to reach out and comfort him. That time would be coming, but it wasn't now. She could see the emotions working over Jake's face—anger and sadness, shame and regret and determination. He wouldn't back down anymore.

"I'll never forgive you, boy," said Ben. "Never. You've ruined everything."

"I don't want your forgiveness, not anymore." Jake turned his back on his father at last, turning instead to face Leigh, whose eyes were blurry with tears of relief and sadness.

Jake didn't look at his father as he said, "From a man like you, forgiveness is nothing but a crime."

They left before the fire department arrived, driving Jake to the clinic in Burnside to have his burned hands treated. While Jake was in with the doctor, Chloe and Leigh sat in the waiting room, streaked with smoke and leaning against each other in exhaustion. "So that's it, then," Chloe said at one point.

Leigh, who'd been half asleep, roused herself to say, "What is?"

"Your trust fund is all gone."

"I know."

"And you dumped Joseph and quit your job."

"True. But at least the letters have been destroyed. I won't have Ben or Russell on my back anymore. I can start my life over. Not quite from the beginning, but close enough."

"They'll find Russ's body in the fire. They'll have questions. Everyone from the fire department saw us there. You going to tell the police the truth?"

"Yes. I'll tell them Russ was a damn fool who went back inside the house after we all got out safely, which is just the truth." Leigh swallowed hard and said, "There's no point lying anymore, Chloe. It never did me any good anyway."

"Ben will tell them what he knows about the letters. They could still arrest you for Dale's murder."

"I've been thinking about that, and I don't think so."

"No?"

"He'd be in even worse trouble than I would at this point. Extortion is a crime, too. No, I figure Ben will tell them it was an accident and they'll leave it at that." She took a breath. "Even if he doesn't, without the letters, the district attorney probably wouldn't bother prosecuting me over Dale."

"That's a lot to risk on 'probably.' "

Leigh sighed. "I know. But really, I don't care anymore, Chloe. If the police want to come after me, I'm not going to stop them. I'm done trying to run away from my mistakes."

Then Jake came out, his hands bandaged, his face black with soot and pinched with the pain of his burns. He looked at the two women sitting in the waiting room. Leigh jumped up and went to him, but he shrugged and said, "It could have been worse."

When Leigh offered to drop him at his apartment in town, he said no, thanks, that he would walk, it wasn't far. His expression was neutral, and he wouldn't look at her. Leigh got the sense that maybe he didn't want her seeing where he lived, that he was ashamed of his place and thought that if Leigh didn't see it, she wouldn't know.

"Better I go now," he said. "You have to get back, Leigh."

Despite herself, Leigh clutched at his arm. "You're leaving? You're leaving me again?"

He stood in the middle of the clinic waiting room looking at his feet. "I think I have to. I can't tell you how sorry I am for everything," he said. "I'm sorry you lost your job and your fiancé. I'm sorry you've lost the money your grandfather left you. I can't tell you how sorry

I am. But from now on, I promise you won't have to deal with Ben Rhodes anymore. He'll never come after you again, I'll make sure of it."

"Jake, please. Please let me help you. You don't have to start over on your own. I thought . . . I thought maybe we were going to give it a try again. For real, this time."

He shook his head. "I can't be a burden to you, Leigh. Because of me you've lost all your money. I've been trouble for you from the get-go."

"You haven't."

"I have, and I know it now. It just wouldn't work, Leigh. There's too much water under this bridge. Dale, and prison, and now Russell's death. I can hardly look at you for the shame I feel," he said, and in fact he wasn't looking her in the eye, but past her, at the wall behind her shoulder. "Go on back to New York. Be happy."

She didn't want to do any of those things. She wanted to tell him she wasn't going back to New York, she was going to stay, that they'd find a way to push through their past and find each other again, make it work somehow. But how? She had next to nothing to her name anymore, nothing except her skill as a book editor. And if she was going to use that skill, she'd have to go back to New York. She'd have to leave him again sooner or later. Maybe sooner was best.

She said, "What will you do?"

He gave her a rueful smile. "Start over. Find some kind of work. Prove everybody wrong."

Her voice nearly cracking, she said, "You have nothing to prove."

"I do, if only to myself," he said. "If I can find something with a future, it will be a start."

She realized they were saying good-bye. That these might be the last moments they ever spent together. Her breath caught. She stifled back tears and said, "I should have given you the money, Jake. It would have been better than watching it burn up. You deserved it, after everything."

For a moment Jake looked like the boy he'd once been. Young, vulnerable, stubborn. She was seized by the urge to cradle his head in her lap and brush the hair out of his eyes, but she made herself stay where she was, to let him be. They were both going to have to learn to live without each other from now on.

"I wouldn't have taken it," he said. "I never wanted it, no matter what anybody said. It was just you, Leigh. You were all that mattered."

"Well," she said, "that was a long time ago, wasn't it?"

"It was. A very long time."

Now that the last ties they'd had were severed, Leigh could see that there was nothing left for the two of them. After ten years apart, they were virtually strangers, after all. If Jake thought it was a mistake to pretend otherwise, she'd have to abide by his decision.

"Leigh."

"What?"

"Take care of yourself."

He clutched his bandaged hands to his chest, then turned and went out the door. Leigh and Chloe stood in the cold waiting room and watched him go, his brown Stetson shading his shoulders against the afternoon sun.

It was all gone—the money, the job, Joseph, and Jake. Strangely, though, Leigh wasn't afraid anymore. It was as if the fire had burned away all her fear, and all that was left was pure, clean. Leigh Merrill was standing on her own two feet for the first time in her life.

She sighed once, put her hand on the door, and stepped out into the bright sunlight.

Back at the cottage—still strewn with papers and discarded clothes, as if a bomb had gone off—Leigh was struck by a sudden urge to take a match to it, too. To light it all on fire and dance around the flames.

It sounded so much easier than going inside to clean up and go home.

"You okay?" asked Chloe, behind her.

The light coming in the windows was milky white, the sky hazy and hot, and though she should have been frantically packing up to go—her flight was in just a few hours, after all—what Leigh really wanted to do at that moment was dive into the cool springs at Wolf's Head, to bathe naked under the midday sun until she turned brown. She wanted to slip under the water and open her eyes to the green light, watching the little fish that swam there, watching for the coyotes and deer that came to drink. To be baptized, to start anew.

"I guess," Leigh said. "It's hard to know, exactly."

"You're shell-shocked, that's what," said Chloe.

"I don't think so. More like relieved. I know it sounds strange, but I never felt like that trust fund was mine, not really. Maybe that's why I never spent it. Pop left it to me so I could live a better life, but it would have been a life built on a lie. Now that the truth's out, I guess part of me is glad it's gone."

Chloe snorted. "If you were so anxious to get rid of all your money, you could have given it to me, you know."

Leigh put her arm around Chloe's waist. "I know. I'm sorry."

"Ah, it's all right. I probably would have spent it on stupid stuff like rent and food anyway."

"I know," she said. "I love you, Chloe."

"I love you, too, hussy," Chloe said. "I wish you didn't have to go."

"Me too," she said. "It's weird, but for so long I dreaded coming home. I couldn't imagine anything worse than having to come back and live in Texas. But now that I'm here, it's like I never want to leave. Does that sound crazy to you?"

"Do you really want me to answer that question?"

Leigh laughed. "No. I guess not."

"Come on. We'd better get you to your plane."

So Leigh started packing, beginning with the manuscripts, packing them in her suitcase, weighing it down like stones. Then the toiletries stacked on the back of the toilet, the clothes strewn around the floor. In less than twenty minutes the mess was cleared up and repacked and she was ready to catch her flight. She checked under the bed for stray earrings, opened all the drawers to make sure nothing was left behind.

That's where she found them: Jake's letters.

They were lying in the top drawer of the dresser where she'd left them three days before, her own faded letters and Jake's unsent ones. The originals. The only copies that remained.

"Are those . . . ?" Chloe asked.

Leigh nodded.

She picked them up and turned them over in her hands, the two bundles. She should burn them, too, get rid of them once and for all so that no one could ever again use them against her. They were nothing but the words of a child, a scared, lonely kid. They were angry, desperate. She was ashamed to think of what they said, the record of her selfishness and foolishness, her awful, awful mistakes. She should burn them up, burn the world clean of them, and then maybe she really could give herself, and Jake, a fresh start.

Clutching the bundles of her letters to her chest, Leigh went to the fireplace and crouched down in front of it, taking out the final letter and setting it in the ashes.

"Can I have your lighter, Chloe?" she asked.

Chloe handed it to her. Leigh flicked on the flame, then set it against the corner of the last letter, the one in which she had meant to say good-bye to Jake forever and inadvertently ended up confessing to a murder. *I don't think I can keep doing this, writing and writing every week without a word from you. Any word would do. Even "good-bye."*

If you won't say it, then I will. Good-bye, Jake. I'm finally moving on, like you said I should.

The flame caught and spread. In a minute the letter—that foolish and impulsive and dangerous thing—was gone forever.

Leigh held out the rest of the bundle in front of her, turning it over and over in her hands. She had burned one letter, why not burn the rest? Start fresh, as if the old Leigh Merrill had never existed. There was something seductive in the idea of putting a torch to everything in her past once and for all, erasing her past self as if it had never been.

And yet—she couldn't do it. She couldn't bring herself to destroy something that was so raw and vulnerable—her words to Jake, Jake's words to her. For many years the letters had been her only link to him, and to the rest of the world. They'd kept her alive, in a way, during the long cold months in Boston after her grandfather died, during those lonely years when she was afraid to make friends, to date other men, to let people into her heart. They were a part of her past—they told a story of love and loneliness—and she couldn't run away from that. She'd tried that once already.

There were Jake's letters, too. Jake wrote so honestly, with such rawness, more than Leigh could have imagined. Reading the letters was like getting to know a little piece of his soul, a little patch of sun amid the clouds of the past decade. He'd spent so much time and love on those letters—he'd given her everything, held back nothing. It was a shame he'd never sent them to her back when they would have mattered, back when she'd needed them the most. How much happier might the two of them have been if only Jake hadn't been so damn proud, so stubborn, so unwilling to let her read what was in his heart until it was too late?

Really it was a shame the whole world couldn't read them, couldn't see the power of Jake's words and thoughts. He was a gorgeous writer, and a gorgeous writer deserved a rapt and attentive audience.

Leigh clutched the letters to her chest, an idea forming in her head. It was all so obvious. Why hadn't she thought of it before?

"Chloe," she said, her breath rushing from her lungs. "I need you one more time. Can you take me to Jake?"

"Why?"

"Because I think I've figured out a way to save us both."

Sixteen

Jake wasn't at his apartment over the hardware store. He wasn't at Dot's Diner. He wasn't at Booches or the Foxhead having a drink, or the library, or the grocer's, or the saddle shop. He wasn't at the end of the dock by the river. Chloe drove her from place to place looking for him, but he wasn't anywhere you might find a grown man in broad daylight.

Where the hell are you, Jake? Why have you disappeared again? Like a bat avoiding the sun, he'd swooped out of sight once more.

Maybe that was it—maybe he was hiding from the daylight. And if he was, she had a good idea where she might find him.

Chloe went slowly down Main Street, the Karmann Ghia rattling beneath them both. "Chloe," she said, "can we go one more place?"

"Sure. Where to?"

"Home."

When the two women pulled up the drive to Wolf's Head, under the row of live oaks, something caught in Leigh's throat. It was like no time at all had passed. The big house still peeked white between the trees, the ancient live oak still stood in the middle of the circular drive, its branches still holding up the tire swing she'd played on as a kid. The horses grazed in the pasture, some of them still the horses her grandfather had bred before he died. She saw her white stallion, Blizzard—sire of maybe a third of the foals her grandfather had produced—in his green paddock, his many offspring dotting the hillside behind the barn. He looked up toward the sound of Chloe's car rattling down the drive, but it wasn't until Leigh got out of the car and whistled to him that his ears pricked up. He whinnied and came running to the fence.

"Hey, boy," said Leigh, coming close now, not quite believing that Blizzard was still alive. He nickered and nuzzled her hand. "Sorry, boy. I didn't bring you any carrots today. Next time, I promise."

Leigh hadn't been back to Wolf's Head once in the years after her grandfather's death. There was no point—her grandfather had left the farm and the business to her uncle Sonny, who had moved his own family and his horses onto the ranch immediately after Gene died, taking over where his father had left off. Sonny had learned the business from Gene—he was a talented breeder in his own right—and since Leigh had always made it known she planned to move to the East Coast for college as soon as she turned eighteen, it made sense that Gene left the farm to his son.

Sonny had Gene's magic touch with the breeding, so the farm had flourished in Leigh's absence. There were still the barns, the breeding shed, the big house and the outbuildings, the trees, the pastures, the springs, all of it as lovely and familiar as a memory. Leigh knew she would have been welcome home at any time—her uncle was a jovial fellow, her aunt kind—but she'd felt ashamed every time she so much as looked at the barn, the scene of her crime. At the cottage under the trees where Jake had once lived with his father. It was all spoiled for her, all tainted with her mistakes. So she'd stayed away, trying to forget, even when her aunt and uncle begged her yearly to come home again.

So when she heard the sound of a screen door creaking open, Leigh looked up to see Uncle Sonny, her mother's older brother, standing on the porch and shading his eyes to see who had come to the farm. When he saw her, he waved. "Leigh!" he said, and then opened the door to yell inside. "Becky! Leela's home."

Her aunt, a slender blonde of about fifty who looked years younger, peeked her head out, smoothing down her neat blue jeans and patting her soft hair while Sonny bounded down the stairs to embrace Leigh. "My God, you're really here. Let me take a look at you. I'd almost forgotten what you look like."

"Uncle Sonny, I'm sorry to just show up like this—"

Aunt Becky came and hugged Leigh, too. "Who'd have thought it possible? You're prettier than ever."

Leigh gave an embarrassed grin. "Thanks. You know, good genes."

"True. You're the spitting image of your mother."

"You both remember Chloe?"

"How could we forget?" said Uncle Sonny. "Give us a hug, darlin'."

Chloe leaned in for a squeeze. "Nice to see you, too," she said, looking sheepish. Chloe's own family was too sarcastic for public displays of affection, but Leigh knew she secretly liked it.

"How are the boys?" Leigh asked. Her two cousins, five and eight years younger than Leigh, were good kids, with the Merrill stubborn streak.

"Oh, you know. Making us worry all the time. David has one more year left at UT, but his grades are better at least. Jim just finished his last stint in Afghanistan. He'll be on his way home in a couple of months."

"You must be relieved."

"They're good boys," said her uncle. "But we've missed you, honey. I wish you'd have come home sooner."

Leigh shifted from one foot to the other. "I'm so sorry to just show up like this, out of the blue. You must be wondering—"

"Not at all," said Aunt Becky, giving her a knowing smile. "Your young man's already here."

Leigh was confused. "What?"

"Jake. He got here maybe an hour ago. Said he wanted to take a look around the farm, and did we mind if he meandered a bit."

Leigh was shocked. "You *didn't* mind?"

"Of course not," said Sonny. "He served his sentence, and now it's time for the rest of us to give him the chance to move on." He looked serious a moment. "He was just a kid when all that happened, Leigh. I don't believe in holding grudges forever. The farm was his home, too."

Leigh was speechless. "Thank you, Uncle Sonny. That's really decent of you."

He shrugged. "It's not like I'm throwing him a parade or anything. Besides, I knew you'd be along eventually."

"You did?"

"Sure," said Aunt Becky. "You and Jake just fit together, honey. Like tea and sugar."

Leigh sputtered, "How can you think so? After everything that happened?"

"Oh, Leela," said Aunt Becky, wrapping her arm around Leigh's shoulders, "it's a shame your mother isn't here to talk some sense into you. That boy will never love anybody else. He's yours, body and soul.

It's all really simple: if you want him, all you have to do is go get him."

Beside her, Uncle Sonny was grinning like an imp. "Go on, sweetheart. Put the poor thing out of his misery already."

Leigh turned toward the barn, the hills. Jake . . .

Chloe gave her a conspiratorial look. "And if you come back too soon, I will be *very* disappointed in you."

Leigh jumped down from the porch and headed for the pastures, turning to look behind her at the place where her uncle stood, waving her off. "Go on, get!" he said.

"Now, Chloe," said Aunt Becky, putting her arm around Leigh's friend, "why don't I get you some sweet tea and you tell me all about what you two have been up to. And how did you ever get your hair that gorgeous color?"

One by one Leigh searched the barns and pastures of Wolf's Head, expecting to see Jake around every corner. She went past the cottage he'd once shared with his father, the paddock where the foals lived in the spring, even the breeding shed where she'd suffered Dale's indignities.

After the shooting, she'd avoided any place on the farm that had an association with Dale—the shed, the barn. It had all been too painful, too raw. Now she stood in the center of the breeding floor and felt her shame wash over her, thinking of the night she killed him, how his breath had gurgled in his throat as he died. She wasn't afraid of the memory any longer—it was part of her, like the color of her eyes or the way she walked. Something she would have to live with for the rest of her life.

The shed was empty. She called out, "Jake?" in a soft voice, but he didn't answer. He wasn't there. No one was.

She was avoiding the barn, the scene of her crime, until it was clear she couldn't do so any longer. She crossed the barnyard, watching the weather vane of the running horse twist in the afternoon breeze. The big doors were shut against the heat of the day, but she slid them open now, memories thick as cobwebs before her eyes.

Inside, the barn was dark and cool. The cement floor had been swept clean, and though she was afraid there might still be a blood-stain on the floor, she saw nothing but bits of sawdust and droplets of water. Inside it still smelled of hay and creosote, reminding her of the days when she was very small and would run out to the barn to hide and read books in the loft, and the memory made her happier than she'd felt in months. Years, maybe.

One by one the horses poked their noses out of their stalls to see who was there. Some of them she recognized: her grandfather's favorite broodmare, Belle; a gelding named Trotter; the twin foals, Olly and Lily, now grown. "Hey guys," she said. "It's me." They made small noises of recognition. She was home.

Here and there were new horses, too, including a beautiful tall bay mare that seemed particularly eager for company. The mare reached her nose through the bars for Leigh to touch her, which she did. "Hello," Leigh said. "Aren't you a beauty?" The mare nickered and bobbed her head as if in answer. Leigh scratched her under her mane and moved on.

She opened the door to the tack room, where her grandfather stored the bridles and saddles, blankets and bits. Pieces of leather and nylon hung from the walls, along with rows of saddles, lead lines, all the tools and implements of horse training kept clean and polished.

She touched the pile of blankets on one shelf, slid her hands underneath. Her grandfather's gun wasn't there. She knew it wouldn't be—it had been confiscated long ago for evidence in Jake's trial—but the feel of the scratchy wool blankets made her recoil as if she'd been burned.

It was hard to be there, but Leigh made herself stand still inside the dark little room, made herself feel her own fear and shame once more, remembering the night Dale had attacked her, the terrible things he'd said, the threats he'd made against her, against her grandfather, the way his hands had tightened the strap around Jake's neck. She'd been right to be afraid, right to defend herself: if he'd been able to wrestle the gun away, he would have hurt her, maybe killed her. It was only in all the mess that came after that she had done wrong. If she'd told the police right away what had happened, she could probably have claimed self-defense, and they would have believed her. At the very least, she wouldn't have had to live with the shame of lying for so long.

Maybe, just maybe, she could still make amends for that, or start to. She took several deep breaths, let them out again, and decided, *Enough. I can't change what I've done,* she thought, *but I can change what I will do. And what I will do from now on is think of others before myself. I will be generous; I will be kind. I will be a good friend, a good person. I will love without reservation. And I will not run from my mistakes, not anymore.*

Leigh opened her eyes and looked up. Above her, the trapdoor to the hayloft lay open.

Aunt Becky had said that Jake still loved her, that no matter what he said, he belonged to her, and all she had to do to get him back was to find him and tell him she wanted him still. If he were in the hayloft, Leigh decided, she would believe it; she would know they were meant to be.

She put her hands on the rungs of the ladder and went up.

The hayloft was stuffy in the heat, the warmth of the horses and the May weather making the space feel close, and dim, distorting the familiar scene into something almost sinister. What looked like a pile of black snakes in one corner turned out to be nothing more than a tangle of bridles and lead lines someone had tossed there and forgotten. Bricks of straw sat piled to the ceiling like a wall. She turned and turned, but no one was there. No Jake. Leigh was completely alone.

The smell of the hay and the old wood of the barn were so strong, and so filled with lovely associations, that for a moment Leigh's eyes started to fill with tears. How many happy days had she spent in this hayloft, dreaming of the future! And now here she was, in many ways the adult self she'd always imagined, except for the happiness she'd always expected to be part of that life. It wasn't anywhere to be found, and hadn't been, not for a long time.

She flung herself down on a pile of hay, exhausted, heartsick, ready to weep. *Jake.*

"You were supposed to be on a plane by now."

Jake sat half hidden behind a bundle of hay. He was so still she hadn't seen him at first, lost as she was in her memories. But now here he was in the hayloft over the barn, their special hiding place, where they'd always known they could find each other when they felt lost.

"I told you to go home, Leigh. It's better if you stay away," he said.

"Better for who?"

He closed his eyes as if the sound of her voice pained him. "Don't you know it's time to let each other go? Don't you think I've done enough damage to your life?"

She knelt on the floor next to him. His hands, which he'd burned that morning trying to get back her trust fund, were still covered with white bandages. She touched them once, carefully. "Don't you think I've done enough to yours?" she said.

"A million dollars. I'll never forgive my dad this time."

"I'll get over it."

"I can't even look at you. All of this is Ben's fault. If we'd never come here, if I'd never fallen for you—"

Leigh wouldn't let him punish himself anymore. "We've hurt each other. All right, neither of us can change that. What I want to know is, what do you want to do now? How do we move forward from here?"

Jake looked down at the place where Leigh's hand rested on his arm, but he didn't move. "I don't know. I feel . . . trapped. Like there's no way to get around the things that have happened to us. Like every decision we've made has put up more and more walls between us."

She slid her hand up his arm, to his shoulder, then his neck. "You know, I think I felt the same way for a long time. Now I know that's bullshit, Jake. You're mine, and I'm yours, just like we used to say. We tried to run away from that promise, but we can't. Because no matter where I go or what I do, I can't live without you."

"Leigh—"

"And don't give me that I'm-bad-for-you line. Don't you dare keep pretending you don't love me. I won't let you get rid of me."

Jake kept his hands in his lap. He couldn't touch her with the bandages on, or maybe he was afraid to. "What about Mr. Wonderful?" he asked. "You going to tell me he means nothing to you? That you don't love him, you won't marry him? That you're giving him up and coming home to be with me?"

In all the confusion and chaos over Russell and Ben, Leigh hadn't told him that she and Joseph had split, that she'd given him back the ring. Now she put her hands on either side of his face and looked him squarely in the eyes. She wouldn't let him flinch this time.

"That's right. I told him I don't love him, that I never loved him. I told him I won't marry him. Jake, he left. He's gone for good."

For a moment it seemed like he was nearly ready to believe her, then he shook his head and looked down at his bandaged hands again. "You can't be serious," he said. "You should be with him. You work together, you live in the same city. He's rich, he can give you everything. What can I give you? Nothing. I have nothing at all. Now my hands are useless, too. I'm fit for absolutely nothing." He slammed his elbow into the wall, a quick burst of frustration and anger. "You'd have to be crazy to love me. I can't give you anything."

Leigh wouldn't be shook off. "None of that matters to me."

He gave a bitter laugh. "It should. It will. Now that your money's gone, especially."

"Believe it," she said, waving her left hand in front of his eyes. "I gave him back the ring, and I quit my job. I told him I slept with you."

He looked horrified, but she rushed on, certain for once that she was doing the right thing. "You were right, Jake. Real loyalty is here. My life is here with you and Chloe and my family, my aunt and uncle. You all are my life. I don't know why it took me so long to figure that out." Suddenly she laughed. She felt giddy, happiness like a spring inside her, bubbling up. "Well, maybe I do know why. But it doesn't matter now. I'm coming home. I'm going to start over. I want to be with you. All you have to do is say that's what you want, too."

"I can't ask you to do that."

"You're not asking it, I'm doing it. I've already done it."

"Go back to New York, Leigh. Please go. I can't, I just can't look at you for how ashamed I am."

She traced her fingers over his jawline, across the two days' of stubble there, then brushed his lips. They were dry, soft. He kissed the tips of her fingers, then her palms, with a moan of regret and fear. She cupped his face and brought it, trembling, toward her, and kissed him deeply.

Under her hands he was stiff, still. He was scared, she realized—scared of loving her again. All that baloney about him being bad for her, of how ashamed he was, was his way of protecting himself, convincing himself that he was better off without her as she was without him.

The only problem was that it wasn't true. Neither of them had been better off alone, had they?

"I won't leave you again," she said firmly. "I'm staying right here, I swear it, Jake. You can pretend all you want, but you're not getting rid of me."

"Leigh . . ." He breathed her own name into her mouth.

She caught the word and kissed him, brushing his lips with her own, softly. Her hands were on his shoulders, and she twined them around his back and pulled him closer, her body moving into his. He was holding back still, afraid to let himself go, but she would not take no for an answer. She would not be sent away to live in a prison of regret, always wondering what might have happened if she had been a little braver, a little less frightened. She said, "I swear I will stand by you until the end. I mean it, Jake."

He held his hands out in front of him, his damaged hands swathed in white bandages. "I can't even touch you," he said. "I'm a wreck. I'm the iceberg smashing a hole in your life, Leigh. Steer clear of me."

She clutched his damaged hands to her breast and said, "You're the man I love, the man I want. I choose you. I choose you, and only you, Jacob Rhodes. You're the one I want, now and always. Tell me you want the same."

Jake was still shaking his head. "Go home, Leigh. Don't do this."

Leigh threw a leg over him, so that she was straddling him now, sitting on his thighs. "Look at me," she said, tipping his chin so he was looking directly into her eyes. She would have to find a way to break down his wall of protection, to move him past his fear and into the understanding that she clutched now close to her heart. "Don't you understand, after all this time? I *am* home. You are my home, and I am never leaving you again."

She kissed him, fiercely now, but he still would not give in—the shard of ice in his heart would not melt. He held himself still, stiff, refusing to touch her, refusing to love or be loved. But after ten years—after losing everything else in her life—she wasn't giving up on him so easily.

"You don't have to be afraid anymore," she said. "You can trust this. You can trust me, I swear it."

She reached down and tugged at the tail of his white T-shirt.

"No, Leigh. Please."

"You want me to stop?" she said, a hint of anger rising in her voice. "Then stop me. Go ahead."

He didn't speak, so she pulled the shirt gently over his head, careful of his burned hands, her touches soft, all caress. He did nothing to help her, holding his eyes closed, keeping himself remote from her, as if by sheer force of will he could make her go away and leave him alone with his burning shame, his overwhelming male pride.

The hell with pride, she thought. *I am not letting you off that easily, Jake. You can stop me if you want, but I'm not letting you torpedo everything out of stubbornness!*

She knelt in front of him, her fingers tracing the flat muscles of his belly, his hips. She bent down and kissed the hollow of his throat, the place over his heart. She pulled off his boots one after the other, then she unbuttoned his jeans and laid him back in the hay to slide them off. He let her.

Naked, he looked both stronger and more vulnerable than she'd ever seen him, his skin golden in the dim light, the hairs on his belly darkening as they grew downward. His eyes were closed, but his obvious arousal drew her attention. She knelt beside him, touched him, brushing her fingers over him gently.

He shuddered and said, "Don't."

"You really want me to stop?" she said coyly.

He said nothing. The only sound was his breath, ragged with desire.

"Leigh—" He started to sit up, leaning on his elbows.

She stood and towered over him, tugging her shirt over her head, unsnapping her bra, but slowly, without anger. She'd gone past the place of fear and uncertainty and had come back to the moment with a clear sense of purpose: she was *not* leaving here until Jake stopped acting like a stubborn fool. If he didn't want her anymore, that was fine, she'd go. But after everything they'd been through, she knew that she could not stop fighting for him now.

"You want to leave?" she said. "Go ahead, get up and go. There's the door. I won't stop you."

She stood over him and slid off her jeans, then her thong, until she was naked, proud, defiant. Below her, Jake's body yearned toward her, straight and hard as an arrow. He wanted her; he couldn't hide it.

She smiled. "I don't think you really want me to stop."

"Dear God," he said, the words coming out with an animal moan. "I've never—I never wanted anything in my life as much as you, Leigh. It's killing me to say it, but I don't deserve you. I don't deserve to be happy, after everything I put you through."

"I'll be the judge of what you deserve." She reached down and brushed her hand once again over him, lightly.

Jake groaned and closed his eyes, his bandaged hands waving in front of his face. "I'm helpless. I can't even touch you. How can I make love to you like this, Leigh? I'm broken."

She straddled his legs, leaning forward. "You're not broken," she said, smiling. "You're . . . mildly sprained. Let me please you, Jake. Let me show you I mean it when I tell you you're everything to me."

Jake gasped and arched his back to meet her as she leaned into him. He reached up his bandaged hands to touch her, but he couldn't, and she enjoyed his relative helplessness, the sense of her own power over him growing. That she could do to him the very things he'd always done to her.

Leigh pulled back and looked down at him, at his eyes hooded with desire, his back arched toward her, all of him pulling toward her. "My love," she said. "My Jake. You don't know how long I've waited to say that to you again."

"I do," he said. "Ten years, four months, and five days, give or take a couple of hours."

"Then I think it's been quite long enough."

At last she reached down and slid him into her, enjoying his gasp of pleasure, her own at the feel of him filling her up. Ever since he'd touched her with his ice-slicked fingers that day at the cottage, she'd been waiting for this moment—the press of their bodies together, their mutual desire. She rocked over him back and forth, back and forth, the pressure between them building toward release.

She felt her own power surge over him, his breath fast and hot on her neck, on her breasts, as he lay helpless beneath her, pressing his hips upward into hers. She would never stop wanting him, never—and at last he cried out and she took her last stroke of pleasure only moments before he, too, exploded into her.

Afterward they lay together in the hayloft, Leigh's arms around his neck, Jake's bandaged hand stroking the side of her face, clumsily brushing the hair back out of her eyes. "Well," said Jake. He was still breathing hard, his face red, but the expression on his face was dreamy.

Leigh sat up on one elbow to look at him. "Well, what?"

Jake nodded. "I had no idea you could be so . . . persuasive."

"You'd better get used to it," she said, "because I'm never letting you get rid of me again."

Jake was quiet for a minute. Then he pushed himself up on one elbow to look at her. "How can you be so sure?"

Leigh sighed and touched the small thatch of hair in the middle of his chest. "Because I couldn't forget you. Because I tried to, and it didn't do me any good. I just can't live without you, Jake. We might as well both accept that now."

"Leigh—" He smiled, but it was fleeting, a momentary glimpse before he went back to the subject on his mind. "I want to talk seriously for a minute."

"Okay."

"You've worked so hard to get where you're at. There aren't any big publishing companies in Austin. I don't have a job. I don't even know if I can get hired anywhere. Your trust fund's gone."

He recited this litany of facts one by one, and Leigh wondered what he was getting at by restating the obvious. "So?" she asked.

"So how will we live? Where will we live? I can't take care of myself, much less a wife or, God help us, kids. I can't ask you to move into my sad little apartment. There's barely enough room in it for me."

"Wife?" Leigh felt her heart lift.

"Yes, wife. You think I don't want to marry you still?"

"I wasn't sure. You never mentioned it."

"That's because I can't marry you! Haven't you been listening? We're both completely broke. Neither of us has a job. We have no place to live and nothing to call our own, Leigh. It would never work."

Leigh smiled; this was the brilliant part of her plan, the thing that Jake didn't yet know. "That's what you think," she said. "I'm going to start my own publishing company, Jake. I'm going to do it right here in Austin."

Jake looked confused. "How?"

"I'll get a small-business loan. That's what other people do when they start a business, isn't it? Austin is the perfect location for an independent press. I have experience at one of the biggest names in publishing. I've got an excellent reputation with authors, agents, and booksellers. And I've got my first two books already lined up."

Jake looked incredulous. "You do?"

"There's a war memoir by one of the writers I met here at the conference. It's outstanding; it should sell. And an exciting debut by my new favorite author, someone with a gorgeous new voice. Something no one's ever seen before."

"Who's that?" he asked.

"You, Jake."

For several long moments, Jake was stunned into silence. It was as if Leigh had said she was planning on a trip to Jupiter, and did he want to come along for the ride? She watched the play of emotions over his face, a fleeting pleasure at the compliment suddenly replaced by confusion. "Me?"

"Your letters. I can't even tell you how they touched me. I've never read anything quite like them. I don't think anyone else has either."

Now a certain hard determination replaced the confusion in his face. He was not going to let her have the final say. He said, "You can't do that. I'm not a writer, Leigh."

She was nearly giddy now that the beauty of the plan wasn't just a thing in her mind but something they were talking about out loud, something they would do together. "Maybe no one's ever told you that before, but you are a writer. I have an eye for this kind of thing, Jake. It's the one thing I know how to do, and do well. Your letters, what you wrote—they're as good as anything I ever read. I want to publish your story and show the world how good you are."

"You're nuts, Leigh. My letters are not a book. It's just my life, and a pretty messed-up one at that."

"Your life *is* the story. All it will take is a little bravery on your part. You want to reinvent yourself, you want to start over? Here's your chance."

This was the answer she'd come up with. This was how she'd be able to move home, give them both a fresh start. She'd start her own company, and Jake would reinvent himself as a writer. The thrill at being able to speak about it—to watch it coalesce in the distance and start to take shape—bubbled up inside her like a spring.

"Let me help you, Jake. We can help each other. I can help you turn your letters into a book, a real book, with your name on the cover and everything."

He sat up, staring at her like she was insane. His body language was all incredulity. "Do you really think so?" he said. "I don't have any experience as a writer. I never went to school. Isn't it maybe a little, I don't know, personal?"

She stood and helped him get his jeans back on, then his shirt. "We fictionalize it. Changes details, change facts, so it's not *exactly* like your life. No one ever wrote something I loved more than your letters. This is a way for us to help each other, Jake. I know it's a risk, but that's what writers do. They put themselves out there. They take chances. Like you and me. We bet on each other."

"What happens," he said quietly, "if the bet doesn't pay off? Then you're out once again, out of a job and money and your career. Because of me. No, Leigh, I don't think I could live with that. I can't take you down with me again."

She pulled on her clothes and stood up to look him full in the face. "Seriously, you're going to have to stop taking everything that goes wrong in my life as your personal responsibility," she said. "I'm here because I want to be, because I love you, Jacob Rhodes. If the publishing company goes wrong, I'm sure Uncle Sonny will hire both of us to help him here. God knows there's plenty of farmwork to go around." She pulled on her boots and stood in front of him with her hands on her hips. "There. Does that make you feel any better, you stubborn Texas ass?"

She was red in the face from arguing with him, her lips pursed in a thin line. The Honorable Jacob Rhodes, taking the whole weight of the world on his shoulders. Didn't he know that Abby Merrill's only daughter could outstubborn him any day of the week?

Something about this last speech must have tickled him, though, because in a moment his face broke out into a wide smile. He drew her to him, laughing all the while. "It does, Leigh. God. You have no idea how much it does."

She threw her arms around his neck and embraced him. "Really? Are we really going to do this?"

He threw up his hands, giving in to the power of her vision at last—he wouldn't fight her anymore, wouldn't struggle with his own damnable pride. "Why the hell not?" he said. "Turn me into a writer, O great and talented editor of editors. Make me over. Give me a chance to show the world what I can do. I promise to be humble. I promise to trust your judgment. I promise I'll never be a stubborn ass again."

"I don't know that you can make that last promise, Jake," she said. "I mean, being a stubborn ass is something you're really, really good at."

"Then I promise to be an *apologetic* stubborn ass." He laughed and held out his arms. "And while we're at it, say you'll marry me, Leigh. Say you'll be mine. For good, this time."

"I'm yours," she said, clasping her hands around his neck, leaning up to kiss him one more time. "But you really cut it close, buddy. If you didn't say yes, I was going to have to catch my plane in less than three hours."

"Just think what a great story it will make for our kids," he said. They stood and climbed down the ladder, out of the hayloft.

"You going to write that one, too?" she asked, taking his hand and heading back out into the Texas sunshine.

"Probably. Now that I'm going to be a famous writer and all."

"One thing at a time, mister," she said. "Let's go home."

"Where will that be, do you think? Home, I mean?"

In the distance, she could just make out the figures of Uncle Sonny and Aunt Becky and Chloe on the porch of the brick house where Leigh had grown up. When they saw her and Jake emerge from the darkness of the barn hand in hand, Aunt Becky reached up and waved them over. *Come on back,* the gesture said. *Come home.*

Leigh waved back. For the first time in a long time, she was sure she was doing the right thing, for herself and the people she loved. For the first time she was sure that the past couldn't hurt her, that she was free.

She looked up at Jake and said, "Anywhere we want, babe. That's the fun part."

Acknowledgments

Thirteen years ago I had a meeting with a man who had a simple, yet complex show idea centered on the one subject that everybody can relate to: love. Without my good friend Mike Fleiss, and my entire *Bachelor* family (both in front of the camera and behind it), this book and this life would've never been possible.

Just a few years ago, I had the opportunity to have an amazing conversation with the man I consider to be the godfather of the fictional romance genre, Nicholas Sparks. What seemed like a casual conversation gave me the inspiration to take a chance, put pen to paper and write this book. Thank you, Nicholas.

Nobody in this business makes it alone. I have an amazing team behind me every step of the way. Thank you to Becky, Brittany, and Richard, and everyone at WME, 3 Arts, and HarperCollins for believing in me.

Last, but certainly not least, I have to say thank you to Bachelor Nation. You are the most devoted, passionate, and loyal fan base of any show on television. All of you were in my heart and mind as I wrote this love story. And now I will take a moment and say my good-byes!

Chris Harrison has been the host of ABC's hit romance reality series *The Bachelor* since the series began in 2002. He's gone on to host *The Bachelorette* and *Bachelor in Paradise*, as well as the live coverage of *The Miss America Pageant*. Chris lives in Southern California with his two children and this is his first novel.